WHEN THE CROWN BLEEDS
BOOK ONE

BATTLE OF VERDANTS

FK MENZZ

Library of Congress Control Number: 2025913059

Paperback ISBN: 978-1-966283-77-5
Hardcover ISBN: 978-1-966283-78-2

1. Main category—Science Fiction & Fantasy › Fantasy › Dark Fantasy
2. Other category—Science Fiction & Fantasy › Fantasy › Sword & Sorcery
3. Other category—Science Fiction & Fantasy › Fantasy › Epic

Published by: AR PRESS
Roger L. Brooks, Publisher
roger@americanrealpublishing.com
americanrealpublishing.com

To my beloved wife,

whose unwavering strength steadied me,

whose encouragement ignited my courage,

and whose love gave breath to every word on these pages.

You are my quiet anchor in the storm,

my counsel in the chaos,

and my ever-burning light in the darkest chapters.

When the Crown Bleeds would never have been written without you.

This story, like my heart, carries your mark.

With all my love,

FK Menzz

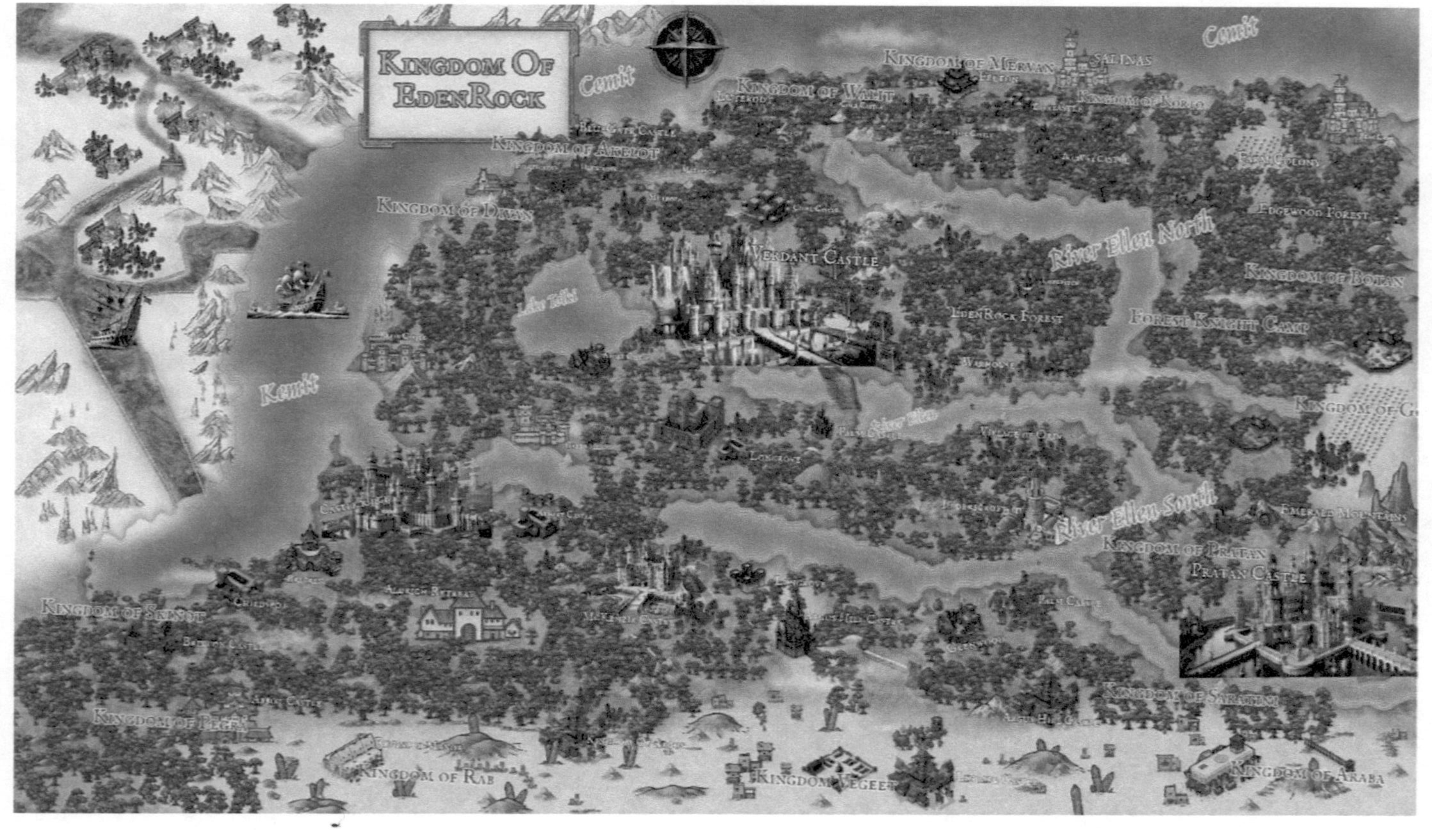

Kingdom Of EdenRock
Cemit
Cemit
Kemit
Kingdom of Mervan
Salinas
Kingdom of Walit
Kingdom of Nobis
Kingdom of Avelot
Kingdom of Divas
Verdant Castle
River Ellen North
Edgewood Forest
Kingdom of Botan
EdenRock Forest
Forest Knight Camp
Kingdom of G
River Ellen
River Ellen South
Kingdom of Pratan
Pratan Castle
Emerald Mountains
Kingdom of Skknot
Kingdom of Saragesi
Kingdom of Pega
Kingdom of Rab
Kingdom of Egeet
Kingdom of Araba

PROLOGUE

First-Year Dream

THE YOUNG MOTHER GENTLY LAID her son in the cradle while her husband stood beside her, watching. She smiled tenderly at their baby, then looked back at her husband before leaning close to whisper to the child, "One day, my love, you will be king of the realm."

Hearing his wife's words, he smiled warmly at her, and together, they turned their gaze back to the baby, their hearts filled with joy. The baby, as if understanding the affection from his parents, smiled back at them.

But the peaceful moment was shattered without warning. A sudden gust of wind tore through the room, and the flames of the torches on the wall flickered wildly before being snuffed out, leaving only one behind the parents.

The mother gasped, clutching her husband's arm as panic surged through them both. The father instinctively stepped closer to the cradle, his protective instincts kicking in, while the mother frantically searched the room with wide eyes. The baby, sensing the shift in the atmosphere, let out a terrified scream, his wail cutting through the eerie silence that followed the wind.

Before either parent could react, something shifted in the corner. A dark, hulking form began to materialize from the shadows, its presence undeniable and monstrous. A deep, resonant growl echoed through the room, making the walls tremble.

The mother squeezed her husband's arm tighter. "What is that?" she whispered, her voice barely audible over the roaring sound.

He stood frozen, his breath catching in his throat. His eyes darted toward the shadow hovering ominously over the cradle. "I don't know," he replied, his voice tense with fear. "Stay back."

As they watched in horror, the beast loomed larger, its form barely distinguishable but menacing. The creature let out a deafening roar, shaking the entire room. The baby's cries grew more frantic, piercing through the chaos. And just as suddenly as it had appeared, the beast vanished, leaving only silence and the terrified echoes of the parents' breathing and the baby's dwindling cries.

FIFTH-YEAR DREAM

It was the night of the child's fifth birthday, and his mother gently laid him down for the night. She tucked him in snugly, planting a soft kiss on his forehead before whispering, "Sweet dreams, my love." And she snuck out of his room to retire to her chamber.

The child's eyelids grew heavy as the door clicked shut, and he soon drifted into a deep slumber. His dreams carried him far from his bed into the lush garden of Bear Cave Castle.

As he wandered among the tall, swaying trees and vibrant flowers, a strange movement caught his eye—a figure standing partially obscured behind a weeping willow. As he approached, he saw the outline of what appeared to be a horse. Intrigued, he stepped closer, his tiny hand reaching out. With innocent curiosity, he tapped the creature on its back.

When the animal turned to face him, the child recoiled in terror. The horse had no ordinary face. Instead, its monstrous visage was part lion, part dragon. Its eyes gleamed with an unnatural light, and its sharp teeth curled into a menacing snarl.

The child's scream pierced the air, a shrill, terrified sound that seemed to reverberate through the garden and beyond. He felt icy fear creep over him, paralyzing him, as the creature's haunting image seared into his mind.

The maids resting in the room next to the sleeping boy heard his scream. Startled, they exchanged anxious glances before rushing to his side. They found him sitting upright in bed, his tiny body trembling, his wide eyes fixated on the door.

One of the maids, Naomi, knelt beside him. She placed a calming hand on his shoulder. "Young master, what's wrong?" she asked, her voice soft and soothing, one hand stroking his disheveled hair.

The child, still shaking, pointed toward the door, his hand trembling as he tried to find his voice. "There…there was something there," he stammered, his eyes still wide with fear. "It had the face of a lion…and a dragon. It was right there!"

The other maids hurried to check the room, peering into every shadowed corner and examining the door. But there was nothing there—no creature, no trace of anything unusual.

Naomi pulled the boy closer, wrapping an arm around him. "It was only a dream, young master," she murmured reassuringly. "You're safe now. We're all here with you."

The child, tears in his eyes, looked up at her, his young mind grappling with the vividness of the nightmare. "But it felt so real," he whispered, his voice barely audible. "I saw it—I know I did."

Naomi smiled kindly, brushing a lock of hair away from his face. "Dreams often feel that way, but I promise you, nothing can harm you here. You're safe in Bear Cave Castle." She stayed by his side, softly humming a lullaby until his tense body relaxed, his eyes growing heavy again.

As the child drifted back to sleep, Naomi remained close, watching over him. Though the room was calm once more, the faint echo of his scream still lingered in the castle halls.

THIRTEENTH-BIRTHDAY DREAM

After his thirteenth birthday, the boy lay in his bed, slipping into a deep sleep. His mind wandered into a dream in which he found himself playing in the woods with his cousin, Prince Halsten, along with their friends Albert, Leo, and Arthur, sons of prominent houses in the kingdom. Palace guards were stationed throughout the forest, ensuring their safety as they played freely.

The young boys eagerly prepared their horses for a race, marking an imaginary finish line between two towering trees. Excitement buzzed in the air as they mounted their steeds, their playful competitiveness taking over.

With a shout, the race began. Mefford surged ahead, his heart pounding with adrenaline as the wind whipped through his hair. He felt the thrill of victory within his grasp for a brief moment, but it was fleeting. With his determined spirit, Prince Halsten caught up and, to the boy's frustration, bypassed him. The young prince raced across the finish line first, victorious.

Their friends gathered around Halsten, congratulating him with cheerful laughter and pats on the back. Halsten beamed, his face flushed with the glow of success.

The boy, however, stood apart, his fists clenched at his sides. His chest heaved with a mixture of exhaustion and anger. Losing, especially to someone younger than him, gnawed at his pride. His eyes narrowed as he watched the others celebrate his cousin. Jealousy and resentment surged within him, twisting his stomach into knots.

As they all moved to retrieve their horses, the boy's emotions reached a boiling point. His hand instinctively went to the small knife he kept hidden at his side. His fingers wrapped around the hilt, and his entire body trembled with barely contained rage. Without fully realizing what he was doing, he started toward Halsten, his footsteps heavy, his face dark with anger.

His voice was low and dangerous as he muttered under his breath, "How dare he? He always wins." His grip on the blade tightened as he neared his cousin, his mind clouded with thoughts of vengeance.

Just as the boy was about to raise the knife in a threatening gesture, a vision, vivid and horrifying, appeared before him, freezing him in place. Two beasts—one with the face of a lion and the other with the face of a dragon—manifested before his eyes. They loomed large, their fiery, glowing eyes staring straight into him as if peering into the darkest corners of his soul.

Beside the beasts stood two tall men cloaked in black robes. They were warriors, armed to the teeth, with bows slung over their backs and swords hanging from their belts. Daggers gleamed at their sides. They stood silently, their expressions calm yet unnerving, their presence ominous.

The boy's heart pounded in his chest as a cold sweat broke out across his forehead. His hand, still gripping his weapon, began to shake uncontrollably. The beasts' fiery eyes burned into him, filled with something otherworldly and terrifying.

The robed men made no move, yet their presence was enough to send a wave of dread washing over the boy. His breath quickened, and his vision blurred. He wanted to scream, to run, but his body refused to obey. His legs felt like lead, and his mouth was dry with fear.

Just as quickly as the vision had appeared, it vanished, leaving only the echo of his own rapid breathing and the coldness in his veins. The boy woke abruptly, panting heavily. Beads of sweat trickled down his face as he lay frozen in his bed, eyes wide with terror. His mind raced, replaying the haunting images over and over. The beasts…the men…it all felt so real, so tangible, as if he'd truly been in the forest with them.

For what felt like hours, the boy remained still, unable to move or scream, his body paralyzed. The dark room around him offered no comfort. Only after several minutes did he slowly begin to breathe more evenly, though the fear in his heart remained.

FIFTEENTH-BIRTHDAY DREAM

On the night of his fifteenth birthday, the boy lay in bed, exhausted from a day of celebrations. As sleep claimed him, he drifted into a strange dream that began with familiarity but soon turned sinister. He found himself again in the woods. This time he was older and more aware of the changes in his body and his growing power. The playful innocence of his earlier dreams had faded.

He was standing alone in a clearing, the trees around him casting long, dark shadows. The usual chatter of birds and rustling of leaves were absent, replaced by an eerie silence that sent a shiver down his spine. The forest, once a place of adventure, now felt oppressive, as though it were watching him. The air was thick, making it hard to breathe, and an unsettling sense of dread settled in the pit of his stomach.

He scanned the forest for any sign of his cousin, Prince Halsten, or his other companions, but they were nowhere to be found. His horse, too, was missing, leaving him stranded in the middle of the foreboding landscape. The silence weighed heavily on him, and his instinct told him to leave, to run, but his feet remained rooted to the ground as if the earth itself refused to let him go.

His heart pounded wildly in his chest as he turned, his breath coming in shallow gasps. From the darkness emerged two terrifying creatures—beasts. Their hulking forms moved with a primal grace, their bodies covered in sleek, shimmering scales. Their features were like lions with dragon wings and tails, with piercing eyes that burned like fire, yet long, serpentine tails whipped behind them, coiling and uncoiling with the menace of a dragon.

Their massive paws crushed the earth beneath them as they moved closer, their teeth bared. Smoke curled from their nostrils, and their fiery eyes locked on to him, not with curiosity, but with hunger—a dark, primal hunger that seemed to pierce through his soul.

The boy's body trembled with fear, his mind racing. He instinctively reached for his knife, the familiar weight of the blade in his hand. The beasts moved closer, and he felt their power radiating off them in waves, pressing down on him, making it difficult even to stand.

The boy tried to move, to run, but his legs refused to obey. He felt trapped, as though invisible chains held him in place. His heart raced, a cold sweat breaking out across his skin as panic seized him. The beasts growled louder, and the air around him grew impossibly thick, making it difficult to breathe.

The creatures let out a deafening roar simultaneously, their breath igniting the trees around them in an inferno of orange and red. Flames licked the sky, casting grotesque shadows on the forest floor. The air seemed to burn as the lion-dragon hybrids advanced, their eyes locked on him with deadly intent.

In a final desperate attempt to escape, the boy screamed—louder than he ever had in his life. But no sound came out. His throat constricted, his lungs burned, and his world spun in a dizzying blur. The flames from the beasts' mouths swirled together in a terrifying vortex.

With a jolt, the boy woke up, drenched in sweat, his heart pounding violently in his chest. His sheets were tangled around him, and his room was cloaked in shadow, eerily quiet. His breath came in ragged gasps as he tried to steady himself, but the vision of the beasts lingered in his mind, as vividly as if they had been standing before him.

The terror refused to release its hold. The creatures in the dream were not just figments of his imagination. They felt like an omen, a dark warning of what lay ahead.

TWENTIETH-YEAR DREAM

On the night of his twentieth birthday, the boy—now a young man—lay in his bed, exhausted from a day of riding and celebrations. Sleep soon claimed him, but this time, it pulled him into a nightmare more vivid and more terrifying than any he had experienced before.

He found himself standing at the edge of a vast battlefield. The sky above him was painted an angry red, as though the heavens themselves had caught fire. The wind carried the scent of blood and ash, and the ground beneath his feet was littered with the broken bodies of soldiers, their lifeless eyes staring up at the crimson sky.

In the distance, the young man could see a massive, imposing fortress—the stronghold of his enemies. But something was wrong. The fortress was in flames, and from its highest tower, a banner, bearing the insignia of a dragon and a lion, waved ominously in the air.

His heart pounded in his chest as he began to move forward, though his feet felt heavy, as though they were sinking into the blood-soaked ground. Each step was harder than the last, but he couldn't stop. He was drawn toward the castle by an invisible force, something that called to him from deep within.

Flames shot up, and the ground split open with a violent crack right in front of him. From the chasm rose the two beasts he had seen in his dream five years before. But this time, they were closer, their blazing eyes glowing with an intensity that burned through the night.

One of the beast's massive paws crushed the earth beneath it as it moved toward the young man. Its teeth bared in a menacing snarl, and it slithered, glinting like molten metal, smoke curling from its nostrils.

Before he could react, the two cloaked men appeared again, just as they had in his earlier dream. But this time, they were not distant, passive observers. They stood directly in front of him, their expressions dark and foreboding. The man closest to him pulled back his hood, revealing a face weathered by battle, his eyes cold and devoid of mercy. He was holding a jagged, gleaming sword, which he raised slowly, pointing directly at the young man's chest.

He lay on the ground, paralyzed by the fear that gripped him. His body trembled, and he could still feel the heat of the flames, smell the smoke, and hear the growl of the lion and the hiss of the dragon. The cold, emotionless gaze of the cloaked man haunted him, echoing in his thoughts.

He was awake, but the dream's terror refused to release its hold. The beasts, the men, and the fire were not just figments of his imagination. They felt like an omen, a dark warning of what lay ahead.

CHAPTER 1

EdenRock was legendary among the surrounding kingdoms. It was a realm where prosperity seemed woven into the very fabric of the soil. Tales spoke of a land so bountiful that poverty was an unfamiliar concept. Its blessings were numerous and unique, drawing envy and admiration in equal measure. The sheep of EdenRock were famed for their fleece, which could insulate even the frailest man against the unforgiving winters. Lake Tolki, a sprawling body of shimmering water, was home to giant tawny geese, whose eggs were so enormous that one could feed three robust plowmen. Their sturdy shells also made them highly sought after, facilitating trade that extended far beyond the borders of EdenRock.

The kingdom was divided into several prominent cities, each named after the ruling family whose castle served as their domain's administrative and cultural heart. These cities stood as monuments to the kingdom's power and wealth, and their prosperity was evident in every stone and structure.

The castles of EdenRock were marvels of architecture, built with the finest materials. The local quarries provided granite and marble of unparalleled quality, their surfaces polished to perfection. Quartzite, embedded with smoky hues that seemed to dance in the light, was harvested from the volcanic heart of the land. In addition, Mongol traders brought marble that gleamed like a mirror, which was used for the opulent castle floors. Sandstone, formed from EdenRock's coastal sands and baked to unmatched strength, ensured the castles were impervious to even the fiercest sieges.

These formidable castles bore towers that reached toward the heavens, as if attempting to touch the gods themselves. Their flags fluttered proudly in the wind, each bearing the emblem of the ruling house. Among them, the flag of Aldrich City stood out, a majestic depiction of a Ligon, a mythical beast that was both lion and dragon. The deep forest-green background was bordered with gold, symbolizing the union of nature's strength with the ruling house's noble lineage and profound wisdom. This emblem of the House of Verdant spoke of Aldrich's legacy. The lion's courage and the dragon's foresight were reminders of the balance required to lead with honor and integrity.

The interiors of the castles were a testament to the kingdom's wealth and history. Vast halls echoed with stories of triumphs and trials. Tapestries hung from the walls, their gold and silver threads depicting the legendary exploits of kings and queens past. These intricate works of art served as both decoration and historical record, reminding all who passed them of the lineage they served.

Crystal chandeliers adorned the ceilings, their soft, warm light casting a golden hue over the banquets that defined noble life. These grand feasts were not merely celebrations, but pivotal moments where alliances were forged, strategies were planned, and decisions were made—decisions that shaped the future of EdenRock.

During these gatherings, the vast dining halls were filled with the finest fare the land could provide. Tables groaned under the weight of roasted game, exotic fruits, and rich desserts. Wine from the vineyards of Glenwood flowed freely, its complex flavor a testament to the fertile lands and skilled hands of EdenRock's people.

The castles were more than stone and mortar—they were symbols of the enduring strength of EdenRock and its rulers. Each detail, from the polished floors to the fluttering banners, emphasized the responsibility borne by the ruling families. They were not merely protectors of their cities but stewards of a legacy that stretched back through the ages.

EdenRock's wealth was not limited to its natural resources or majestic architecture. Its true strength lay in the unity and resilience of its people, guided by leaders who understood the weight of their heritage. The kingdom's story was one of triumph, adaptation, and enduring hope—a land where legends were not only told but lived, and where the future remained as bright as the illustrious past.

However, an invisible crack ran through the history of the royal family, a fissure that, while hidden from the eyes of the kingdom, threatened the very foundations of the monarchy and the throne upon which the king ruled. It was rooted in buried grievances, betrayal, and unspoken truths.

By Alaric Verdant's reign, this underlying tension had evolved into a hidden threat to the throne. Darius, his older brother, had been exiled to Bear Cave Castle by their father, King Edward, as a punishment and a strategy to contain his anger and ambition, but this had not quelled his ambitions. Instead, it had hardened his resolve. From the cold lands of the North, he began to build his power base, gathering allies extending to the king's council. While Alaric ruled with justice and compassion, Darius seethed with a sense of entitlement, believing the throne was his by birthright. To him, Alaric's reign was a continuation of the injustice first dealt to him.

The kingdom's stability teetered upon this hidden fracture. Though Alaric and Isadora were beloved by their people, they ruled unaware of the storm brewing in the shadows—a storm that would one day erupt with devastating consequences.

To the citizens of EdenRock, the monarchy appeared unshakable. The kingdom's wealth, strong armies, and the unity of its people seemed to ensure its future. But the secret resentment harbored by Darius and his allies spread like a slow poison, infiltrating even the most loyal ranks of EdenRock's nobility.

CHAPTER 2

FROM A VERY YOUNG AGE, Alaric showed a grit beyond his years. His father, King Edward, often went to war, and would leave Alaric in charge of the castle. The people of EdenRock frequently saw the young prince sitting on his father's chair with a wooden sword by his side. Although he was the youngest of three sons, Alaric exhibited a bravery unmatched by his brothers. He never allowed anyone else to fight his battles for him and often stood up to bullies, regardless of their age or size. He was known throughout the kingdom for his bravery and combat skills. Unlike other children his age, he preferred training with the kingdom's soldiers to playing with his peers. His sparring partners never gave him any special treatment, and he never backed down from a challenge.

The training grounds of EdenRock trembled with the furious clash of steel. Alaric locked blades with Omelic, an older boy whom their instructors had praised for his skill. The match was fierce, with the clashing of swords echoing through the training grounds. Omelic, confident in his abilities, struck hard, expecting Alaric to falter. However, Alaric's determination and skill led him to outmaneuver his opponent, delivering a decisive blow that humiliated him. Omelic, ashamed of being bested by someone younger, abandoned his military training and turned to his father's trade as the royal physician of EdenRock.

Yet, through the years, their friendship endured. Pride may have fractured, but loyalty remained. Omelic, though no longer a warrior, stood at Alaric's side in another way—proving that defeat does not sever all bonds.

Alaric's reputation for bravery and determination grew, and it was these very qualities that won him the heart of Isadora Elferidge, daughter of Lord Elferidge, the Lord of Abbot Gate. Their story began during Alaric's first participation in the EdenRock annual war games. The games, held in the local coliseum, were a grand event, drawing nobles and commoners alike to witness displays of strength. The combat roared to life around Alaric, the air thick with the clash of steel. His heart pounded loudly in his ears as the chaos of battle swirled around him.

From above, the battlefield stretched endlessly, a raging sea of clashing swords, galloping horses, and warriors locked in fierce combat. The sheer scale of the fighting became clear, dust and smoke billowing into the sky, obscuring the horizon.

Eager to prove himself, Alaric drove his horse forward, cutting through enemy ranks with determination blazing in his eyes. The gleam of swords flashed dangerously close, and adrenaline surged through him. Suddenly, an opponent's blow struck true, knocking Alaric violently from his saddle.

He hit the ground with a painful impact, breath knocked from his lungs.

Dust and dirt filled his vision as the earth trembled beneath the hooves of the approaching horse. His mind raced, his survival instincts surging. With no time to lose, Alaric swiftly rolled aside, narrowly escaping the trampling hooves.

Amidst the carnage, he lay momentarily stunned, seeing the battlefield in its grim entirety—the cries of the wounded echoing sharply, the relentless press of combatants around him, a stark reminder of the battle's brutal reality.

Before he could reach for his weapon, which had fallen from his hand, his attention was caught by Isadora, whom he had adored for a while. Her long black hair and graceful demeanor momentarily distracted him. Regaining his focus, Alaric jumped up, grabbed his opponent's leg, and pulled him down from his horse, subduing him and forcing him to surrender. The crowd erupted in cheers as Alaric was declared the victor.

After receiving his winning crown, he climbed into the stands, his eyes fixed on Isadora. With boldness, he placed it on her head, causing her to blush. "My lady," he declared, his voice strong and confident. "Let's make our love public."

The young woman, taken aback by his directness, covered her mouth with her hand to conceal her laughter, unsure of how to respond. Her friends giggled while her guards looked on, bemused.

Still blushing, she replied. Isadora Elferidge placed her hand in his hand.

Alaric scooped her up in his arms, laughing, a sound that was both hearty and genuine, and climbed down to the arena. He looked around at the spectators and asked loudly, "Do you think Isadora Elferidge should say yes to being my wife?"

The crowd, delighted by the young prince's boldness, erupted in cheers, chanting, "Marry him! Marry him! Marry him!"

Isadora, still blushing, said yes, and the whole place erupted with cheers as the two lovebirds embraced and kissed in the center of the coliseum.

That evening, at the post-game royal dinner at Verdant Castle, Alaric sought out Isadora. The two spent the evening talking, dancing, and enjoying each other's company. It was a night filled with laughter and budding affection.

After Alaric succeeded his father as king, he continued to build upon the foundation laid by King Edward. He brought even more growth and wealth to EdenRock, strengthening the kingdom's trade and defense and turning it into a significant power on the world stage. He formed friendly alliances with other kingdoms, including the Botan Kingdom and the Ishinos Kingdom. Trade from EdenRock extended as far as the Ibian Lands, located southward beyond the Ibian Sea. Within the kingdom, Alaric upheld the alliances his father, King Edward, had established with other noble families. Among them was his close bond with his trusted friend Lord Ethan, whom he consulted on almost every major decision. Lord Ethan, his wife Elara, and children Albert and Freja became close friends with the king's family. Albert and Halsten, King Alaric's children, Halsten, Eleanor, and Vivienne, were also close friends with Albert and Freja.

While Alaric was busy securing the kingdom's wealth and honor, Isadora dedicated herself to empowering the women of EdenRock. She encouraged them to learn valuable craft-making, carpet-weaving, and jewelry-manufacturing skills. Her efforts led to the creation of a home for orphans, where they could be nurtured and raised as good citizens of the realm.

The king and queen's greatest joy was their three children: Prince Halsten Verdant, Princess Eleanor Verdant, and Princess Vivienne Verdant. They were the heart and soul of the royal family, loved dearly by their parents and by the people of EdenRock.

The king surrounded himself with trusted people, including High Priest Edward Tovar of Aldrich City; Lord Cameron, a trusted council member; commanders Sir Magnus, Sir Axel, Sir Jakob, Sir Anders, and Sir Gunner; and the head of the palace guard, Sir Egron.

CHAPTER 3

The garden of EdenRock basked in the amber glow of the fall evening, its trees swaying gently in the crisp breeze. Alaric was walking among the vibrant foliage with his son, Halsten. As they strolled through the serene pathways, Alaric pointed to two chairs beneath a grand oak tree and gestured for the prince to join him.

"Halsten," the king began, his tone a blend of warmth and solemnity, "I know you've heard many tales about how EdenRock was established."

The boy sat down, curious. "Yes, Father, I've heard stories of Aldrich the Conqueror and his battle against Lord Vendigore. But is there more?"

The king nodded, a faint smile crossing his face. "There is much more. The scroll in the castle library is a summary of the account. The main scroll containing the entire story is located in the depths of Castle Ridge. And now, as you come of age, prepare for marriage, and soon take your place as lord of your own castle, it is time for you to know."

"Tell me, father," Halsten asked, leaning forward, curiosity etched on his face.

"Let me tell you what my father, King Edward, told me about our ancestor Aldrich the Conqueror and the true origins of EdenRock."

Halsten adjusted himself in his chair and focused his attention on his father.

"In a time long past," Alaric began, his voice steady and reflective, "when the world was a tapestry of warring clans, lords vying for dominion, and kingdoms being carved from the wilds, there arose a figure unlike any other—Aldrich the Conqueror. His strength, ambition, and unwavering determination set him apart from all others. But before he became the legend we know, his beginnings were humble and mysterious.

"Aldrich never knew his parents. He was raised by a hunter named Ronald Long and his wife, Margot. They were simple folk who took him in as a baby after his mother, Millie Verdant, passed away."

The king paused, looked up into Halsten's eyes, and said, "Aaron Verdant was a fearless hunter who lived in a small village near Botan's vast, uncharted forests. One fateful day, while on a hunting expedition, he discovered something extraordinary in a secluded cave—two creatures that defied imagination. These beasts, though small at the time, bore the features of both lions and dragons. Their fur shimmered with golden and green hues, their wings were vast and gilded, and their tails were long and scaly."

Halsten's eyes widened. "Dragons? Are you saying Aldrich's father found dragons?"

"Not just dragons," Alaric said. " They were Ligons, beasts unlike anything Aaron—or anyone else—had ever seen. He was fascinated, but he kept their existence a secret, even from Millie. He would venture into the forest daily to feed and observe them, gradually earning their trust. Over time, they grew large and powerful, their features becoming more distinct and majestic."

The king leaned forward, his voice lowering as if sharing a sacred secret. "One night, something extraordinary happened as Aaron stood with the beasts. They flapped their wings, ascending above the treetops with grace and power. One of them descended again while the other one circled above the trees, its immense form landing before Aaron. It crouched and emitted soft, almost inviting sounds. At first, he hesitated, unsure of the creature's intent. But as it nodded and gestured, he realized it wanted him to climb on."

Halsten leaned in closer. "What did he do?"

"With trepidation, Aaron mounted it," Alaric said, his voice tinged with awe. "And in that moment, his world changed forever. The beast soared into the night sky, carrying him high above the forest. He experienced a freedom and power that he could never have imagined. From that night on, he became one with the creatures, bonding with them as their rider and protector."

Alaric leaned back, gazing at the distant horizon as he recounted the tale. Halsten kept his eyes fixed on his father.

"Aaron's bond with the Ligons," Alaric continued, "was extraordinary and a well-guarded secret. The majestic and fearsome creatures trusted him as deeply as he trusted them. One fateful day, a group of ruthless warriors known as the Gols descended upon Aaron's village. When Aaron heard the commotion, he and his wife escaped on their horses through the back of their home toward the forest. These attackers spared no one, killing indiscriminately and leaving destruction in their wake. The attackers' shouts echoed behind them. Aaron pushed forward through the forest, guiding Millie to safety. They reached the cave where the Ligons lived, a place he knew would offer them protection. Sensing Aaron's distress, the beasts stood guard at the entrance, their golden scales shimmering in the dim light.

"Millie gave birth to two sons within the safety of that cave. Aaron was overcome with joy and gratitude. He took two golden medallions he had crafted—depicting the magnificent Ligons—and fashioned them into necklaces, which he placed around the necks of his newborn sons. He named them Aldrich and Uldrich."

Halsten asked, "Father, those medallions—are they the ones in the royal treasury?"

Alaric nodded. "Yes, my son. They are symbols of the courage and unity that defined our family from the beginning.

"After several days in the cave," he continued, "Aaron decided it was time to move his family to safety. The Ligons accompanied them as they ventured through the forest, protecting them from predators and any remaining attackers. Their journey brought them to the banks of River Ellyn, a wide and treacherous body of water.

"As Aaron and Millie prepared to cross, disaster struck. The Gols had tracked them to the river. The Ligons fought them valiantly, tearing through the enemy ranks with their powerful claws and fiery breath. Amid the chaos, Aaron lifted Uldrich and began making his way over the log bridge that spanned the stream, urging Millie to follow with Aldrich.

"But just as Aaron reached the bridge's midpoint, an arrow struck him in the back. He cried out in pain, his body collapsing into the rushing water below. Uldrich, still in his arms, was swept away with him."

Halsten's face tightened. "And Millie? What did she do?"

"She screamed in anguish," Alaric said, his voice heavy with sorrow. "But there was no time to mourn. She clutched Aldrich tightly and pressed forward into the forest, her strength dwindling with every step. Eventually, exhaustion overcame her, and she collapsed to the ground, unconscious, holding her son.

"It was fate, perhaps, that led Ronald Long, a kind-hearted woodsman, to stumble upon them." The king repositioned himself. "When he discovered Millie, he checked to see if she was alive. Relieved to find her breathing, he carried her and the infant to his home where he lived his wife.

"Millie, though grateful, was grief-stricken. She recounted what had happened to Aaron and, Uldrich, her voice filled with pain as she spoke of her loss. Despite their care, her body and spirit could not recover from the ordeal. Three weeks later, she passed away, leaving Aldrich in the care of the Longs."

Halsten asked softly, "So Ronald and Margot became Aldrich's parents?"

"Yes," Alaric replied. "They raised Aldrich as their own, teaching him the values of kindness, bravery, and hard work. Ronald, a skilled hunter, taught Aldrich the ways of the forest, while Margot nurtured his intellect and heart. They never let him forget his true lineage, ensuring he knew he was destined for greatness."

"And what of the Ligons?"

"They were believed to have flown away, never to be seen again. There have been tales of sightings, but the stories have never been verified until now. Aldrich," the king continued, his voice now laced with pride, "grew into a man of extraordinary strength and wisdom, shaped by the challenges he'd faced in his youth."

Halsten was eager for more. "What did he do, Father? How did he become Aldrich the Conqueror?"

Alaric's lips curled into a faint smile. "Margot died after some period of illness when Aldrich was twenty-six. Two years later, at the age of twenty-eight, Ronald died in his sleep. Aldrich led the people of the village to defend themselves from invaders and wild animals and was seen as a leader by the people who lived in the village. He had an innate ability to unite people, to inspire them, and to instill a sense of purpose. By the time he reached thirty-one years, the small village where he'd been raised had begun to grow under his leadership.

"As more people heard of the safety and prosperity of the settlement, they began to migrate there. Farmers, artisans, and tradespeople sought refuge from the chaos plaguing other lands. Aldrich, recognizing the importance of organization, was set on building a structured community. He encouraged cooperation among the villagers, ensuring that everyone contributed to the common good."

Halsten's eyes gleamed with admiration.

Alaric continued. "He earned their respect through his actions. Aldrich would work alongside the farmers in the fields, help craftsmen repair tools, and even defend the village against threats. He did not seek power for its own sake—his leadership was born of necessity and trust."

Halsten furrowed his brow. "There were threats to the village?"

"Many," Alaric said solemnly. "The land was still wild and dangerous. Raiders and rival groups often sought to plunder what others had built. As the village's protector, Aldrich led his people to wars and easily conquered his enemies, so they named him Aldrich the Conqueror."

"How did the village become this big kingdom?"

"Under Aldrich's leadership, the village evolved to a thriving city. Aldrich established trade routes, forming alliances with nearby settlements and tribes. His vision extended beyond mere survival—he wanted a land where people could thrive, free from the constant threat of war and oppression. Over time, those who followed him elected Aldrich as their formal leader. He served his people with great humility and gained the admiration of the citizens and other settlements near his town."

Halsten's expression was one of awe. "He built EdenRock, didn't he?"

His father nodded. "He did. Aldrich saw the potential in these lands. He chose a high plateau overlooking fertile valleys and sparkling rivers to establish the heart of his kingdom. Rich in resources, it became a beacon of hope for those seeking a better life. He named it EdenRock—a haven where the weary could find rest and the bold could build their dreams.

"But Aldrich's path was not without challenges," Alaric said, his tone darkening. "His success attracted not only followers but also enemies. Several rival warlords and jealous leaders sought to claim and enlarge their settlements by attacking EdenRock. Each battle was more difficult than the last. Yet, he never wavered. With the loyalty of his people, he defended his kingdom with unmatched bravery."

Halsten asked, "Was that when he fought Igor Vendigore?"

"Yes," Alaric said grimly. "Igor's betrayal was one of Aldrich's greatest trials. But he prevailed, driving Igor and his forces into exile beyond the seas. That victory solidified Aldrich's reputation as a leader who would not tolerate treachery.

"In the years that followed, Aldrich focused on building a kingdom that would outlast him," Alaric continued. "He created laws to ensure justice, schools to educate the young, and markets that fostered trade. He encouraged diversity and unity, bringing people from different cultures together under the banner of EdenRock."

Halsten's voice was reverent. "He truly was a great king."

"He was," Alaric said with pride. "And his legacy lives on in every stone of this kingdom, in every story passed down through our family. Aldrich built EdenRock not with greed or cruelty, but with courage, wisdom, and a vision for a better future."

He turned to Halsten, placing a firm hand on his shoulder. "Remember this, my son, a king is not defined by the crown he wears or the power he holds but by the people he serves and the legacy he leaves behind. You are a descendant of Aldrich, and you carry his blood in your veins. One day, you will lead. When that time comes, lead with the same strength and integrity that made Aldrich the Conqueror a legend."

Halsten nodded, his heart swelling with determination. "I will, Father. I promise to honor his legacy and protect this kingdom."

Alaric smiled, his pride evident. "I know you will, my son. You are a Verdant, and greatness runs in your blood."

CHAPTER 4

AFTER ALARIC ASCENDED THE THRONE of EdenRock, a string of gruesome murders and disappearances plagued the kingdom. Victims—some linked to noble houses and members of the king's council—were found in the forest and other remote areas. The killings stoked fury among the people, and whispers of incompetence or worse swirled around the crown.

For months, the royal guard scoured the land, interrogating suspects and tracking leads, but the culprit remained elusive. Justice slipped further from grasp with each failed investigation. Darius, the king's brother, took advantage of the citizens' displeasure to build his coalition, using Lord Warhouse, a member of the king's council whom he had bribed with gold and promised wealth and a prominent position. Lord Warhouse began meeting secretly with other council members to foster support of Darius's plan.

Lord Warhouse invited some of his colleagues, including Lord Ian Bluevine, Lord Jed Bracken, Lord Abe Luterodt, and Lord Lingard Kraft, to his home for a meeting.

His guests, each accompanied by their personal guards, arrived as the night took hold of the skies. Lady Lou Warhouse and the head maid had organized a delicious meal and drinks for the guests. Lord Warhouse's trusted commander, Molart Drone, hosted the guards while their masters joined their host in his sprawling mansion.

As they sat at the table, Lord Warhouse stood up, lifted his wine glass, and said, "To EdenRock."

His guests followed suit, and echoed, "To EdenRock, to the realm of Aldrich," before sitting back down.

Lord Warhouse addressed his guests, "My lords, I have invited you here this evening to discuss the recent events that have occurred in our kingdom. The recent killings and disappearances of some of our loved ones are unfortunate and must be dealt with before they become a bigger issue. I know some of you have been affected by these tragic events. Not forgetting the loss of the lives of your men from recent attacks, and this matter cannot wait."

The guests exchanged looks before Lord Luterodt stood up. "My lords," he began, "I agree with our benevolent host. People in my city come to me inquiring about what will be done, but I have no answers to give."

The other lords nodded in agreement.

He continued, "If nothing is done soon, our people will think we are weak."

Lord Brackin rose to his feet. "My lords, I hear what you are saying, but the king is doing his best for the kingdom."

Lord Kraft quickly rose, rage in his eyes. "The king is weak. He has not done enough. I am tired of all the lame excuses for not finding the culprits. Something needs to be done, and it needs to be done quickly."

Lord Bluevine, with his glass in hand, asked, "So what can we do about this?"

Lord Warhouse spoke, "I have someone who wants to speak with us. He has a plan to help, but his identity has to be kept secret. I want to know if you will be willing to meet with this person?" Lord Warhouse asked. The men looked around the room, nodding to each other before turning their attention to Lord Warhouse.

Lord Luterodt spoke, "We are ready to meet this person."

Lord Warhouse smiled and spoke, "I need you to swear an oath of secrecy with your blood. Decide now before I arrange the meeting."

The men whispered among themselves for a few moments before Lord Luterodt spoke again, saying, "I am ready."

Lord Bluevine said, "I will do it as well," followed by Lord Kraft.

Lord Brackin looked around momentarily and said, "If this will restore trust in our people, then I am for it."

Lord Warhouse smiled, took a silver cup, and placed it on the table. He then took a sharp knife and warmed it on the flame of a torch on the wall. Opening his left palm, he made a cut, and squeezed the blood into the waiting vessel. He passed the blade to Lord Luterodt, who did the same, then passed it to the rest of the lords.

Lord Warhouse took out a scroll, wrote each person's name on it, lit it on fire, and tossed it into the cup. "Till death," he said.

"Till death," the rest of the lords echoed.

After the paper was fully burned, Lord Warhouse said, "The person I spoke about is Darius."

"The king's brother?" Lord Kraft asked.

"Yes, he has been worried about the recent events and is willing to step in and help," Lord Warhouse said.

Lord Kraft looked around the room for a while and sat down.

Lord Luterodt stood up, "All I want is some kind of leadership, and I don't care who provides it."

The other men nodded.

"I will arrange the meeting and let you know." Lord Warhouse said.

Everyone nodded. Lord Luterodt smiled and said, "Tell Darius he has our support."

The rest of the evening was spent eating, drinking, and laughing. Lord Warhouse saw his companions off one after the other, with Lord Luterodt being the last to leave. As he headed toward the gate, a maid came in to clear the table. Lord Luterodt turned to look at her, making the young woman cringe.

Lord Warhouse, following his gaze, said, "I don't want you to get in trouble with Lady Zoe."

Lord Luterodt grinned and responded, "What is a lord without concubines?" The two men laughed as they walked out to Lord Luterodt's horse. His guard untied the harness, helped his master mount, then mounted his own horse, and the two rode out of Green Hill Castle gates.

Lord Warhouse scribbled something on a piece of paper, tied it to a pigeon, and released the pigeon to fly.

Mefford, son of Darius and Xinovia, nursed the same bitter resentment as his father. The royal family had denied Darius his birthright, bypassing him for the throne, and though Mefford bore no noble title, he still commanded influence as heir to Bear Cave Castle. His authority, however hollow, was his weapon—and he wielded it with quiet fury. To escape the toxic atmosphere of his family life, Mefford often sought refuge in Ghost Valley, a notorious part of town near Edgewood Forest, known for its slums, where the downtrodden and the criminally insane gathered. It was a place where society's outcasts could lose themselves in a haze of drugs, alcohol, and violence. Here, Mefford found a twisted sense of camaraderie with others who, like him, harbored deep-seated anger and resentment toward the world.

Mefford became a regular fixture in Ghost Valley's most unsavory establishments. The air in these places was thick with the foul stench of smoke and alcohol, and the atmosphere was one of constant tension. Nights would pass in a blur of intoxication as Mefford drowned his wrath and confusion in drink after drink in the company of his companions.

One evening, while seated at a corner table in the Dragon's Cup Inn—his favorite haunt—Mefford's attention was caught by a heated argument at the bar. The inn was filled with the usual crowd, the dim light barely piercing through the thick haze of smoke that hung in the air. The men were discussing a bold, almost suicidal plan—raiding the king's supply caravans. The idea was ambitious, promising substantial reward, but it was also fraught with danger.

Mefford, already several drinks deep, felt his curiosity piqued by the conversation. He leaned in slightly, straining to catch every word over the din of the tavern.

"Don't you understand?" one of the men shouted, slamming his cup against the bar, causing a splash of ale to spill over the sides. "There are too many guards watching the caravan. We'd be slaughtered before we even got close!"

His words were met with a mix of nods and grumbles from the other men, their faces etched with worry. But Mefford, emboldened by the alcohol coursing through his veins and his burning rage toward King Alaric, saw an opportunity in their hesitation.

He pushed back his chair and stood up, his tall frame cutting a menacing figure in the gloom. "You're all cowards," he declared, his voice carrying across the room. The men turned to face him, surprised by the interruption. "Do you think the king's men are invincible? They're just as human as you are, and they can bleed just like any of us."

Jason, one of the men, a brute, scowled as he spoke. "We can catch them off guard and charge them for it. In any case, the return merits the risk. Some say the wagon carries wealth beyond imagination."

Unsteadily, Mefford stood and approached the men, his voice slurred but resolute. "I want in," he declared, his eyes narrowing with determination.

Major, the other man, examined him closely, his gaze suspicious. "And who the hell are you?" he demanded. "Why do you think you can pull this off?"

"I am more resourceful than you think," Mefford said. "Let me make you an offer. I will provide all the weapons you need."

"And what is it that *you* need?" one of the men asked.

"Only the thrill of the attack and the booty," Mefford said.

Jason introduced his friend, pointing to Major, a tall and well-built man with a gold tooth in the lower front of his mouth.

Major stepped forward and shook Mefford's hand as well, then crossed his arms, his skepticism still evident. "And how exactly can you be of service?" he asked, his tone sharp.

Mefford's eyes blazed with a mix of anger and resolve. "I have all the resources you need and am ready to support your effort," he replied, staring down the man.

The men exchanged glances before sitting down at a table. Mefford, now more composed, summoned a waitress with a simple hand gesture. "Give my friends whatever they want to drink," he ordered.

One of the men leaned forward, his gaze piercing and suspicious. "What's your interest in this attack?"

Mefford's anger simmered up again. "Let's just say I have a score to settle with someone. Tell me what I need to do."

"Do you know how to hold a sword?" Major asked.

"I can supply swords and men for this adventure."

The two men looked at each other and laughed. "You can provide swords?"

"Tell me where you are meeting, and I will be there with what you need," Mefford said.

Jason turned to Major, a silent agreement passing between them. "All right," Jason said finally. "We'll meet tomorrow night at the old mill outside the city. We'll finalize the plan there."

Mefford walked away, followed by one of his guards, Merlon, leaving the men at the tavern to ponder the conversation.

The next night, Mefford, followed by Merlon, met Jason and his band of robbers in the dim confines of a secluded woodland clearing. The moonlight filtered through the trees, and a sliver of silver light cut through the dense canopy, illuminating the faces of the conspirators as they crouched in the underbrush. The air smelled of damp earth and pine resin. Their whispers were barely louder than the rustling leaves.

"The eastern route is vulnerable after sundown," Jason murmured, his fingers tracing a rough map in the dirt. *"Guards are lax, and the merchants grow careless."*

Major leaned forward, the moonlight glinting off the dagger at his belt. *"We strike at the crossroads, where the trees choke the path. No witnesses."*

The forest swallowed their silhouettes as they melted into the darkness, their plans taking root like poison ivy. Along the kingdom's trade routes, wagons began to vanish. A broken axle here, a bloodstained cloak there—all dismissed as misfortunes of the road.

Their strategy was simple but effective—strike swiftly, take everything, and vanish before the guards could respond.

Within weeks, the attacks had become a scourge across the realm. The traders they robbed of their revenue and goods were left financially ruined and deeply shaken. Word of the attacks spread quickly, creating an atmosphere of fear and insecurity. Citizens began to hire guards to protect them on the trade routes, while anger simmered among the nobles, whose own interests were tied to the prosperity of the kingdom's trade.

One evening, Mefford returned to Bear Cave Castle after another successful raid, his clothes dusty from the journey and his satchel heavy with spoils. As he crept toward his chambers, the sound of a voice stopped him in his tracks.

"Mefford," Darius called from the shadows of the corridor, his tone low but sharp.

Mefford stiffened before turning slowly to face him. "Yes, Father?"

Darius stepped into the light, his piercing gaze fixed on his son. "Don't play coy with me. Where have you been?" he demanded.

"I—" Mefford hesitated, searching for an excuse, but Darius cut him off.

"Spare me your lies," he said coldly. "I know what you've been doing."

Mefford's face hardened, and he realized the futility of denial. "Then why ask?" he shot back, his voice edged with defiance.

Darius's eyes narrowed. "Because I want to hear it from you. Tell me everything—now."

Reluctantly, Mefford related the details of his escapades, from the ambushes to the growing network of informants aiding their operations. He spoke of Jason and the crew's efficiency and their methods of evading capture. By the time he'd finished, his father was silent, his expression unreadable.

After a long pause, Darius finally spoke. "You're reckless but effective," he said, his tone surprisingly calm. "What you're doing can be turned into an advantage—if managed correctly."

Mefford frowned. "What do you mean?"

Darius's lips curled into a sly smile. "I mean this: with the right information, you can strike where it matters most. But you'll need help— my help."

"What kind of help?" Mefford asked cautiously.

Darius stepped closer, his voice dropping to a conspiratorial whisper. "I can provide you with real-time intelligence. I'll buy the loyalty of heads of the patrols for the traders, but instead of stopping you, those patrols will serve to guide you. The guards I buy will report directly to me, ensuring you and your crew stay one step ahead."

Mefford's skepticism began to fade, replaced by intrigue. "And what do you get out of this, Father?"

Darius's smile widened. "A share of the spoils, of course. That gold will finance my castle and ensure the loyalty of key nobles on the king's council. With their support, we can shape the future of this kingdom as we see fit."

Mefford let the weight of his father's words sink in. "And Jason and the others?"

"They don't need to know," Darius said dismissively. "Keep them focused on the raids. Leave the strategy to me."

After a moment of consideration, Mefford nodded. "Very well. We'll do it your way."

With Darius's support, the robberies became increasingly sophisticated. Using information from the patrols, Mefford's crew executed them precisely, evading capture at every turn. The stolen goods and revenue were divided, with a significant portion being funneled back to Darius, who used the wealth to strengthen his political influence. Nobles who had once been loyal to the king found themselves swayed by Darius's generosity and their losses from the robbers. Their allegiances shifted quietly but surely.

Meanwhile, the kingdom's coffers began to dwindle. The continuous loss of trade revenue weakened the economy, and his court grew restless. The citizens, too, grew bolder in their dissent, filling the streets with protests and demands for action. Whispers of corruption spread, further undermining faith in the crown.

Darius reveled in his growing power in the halls of Bear Cave Castle. Yet even as he fortified his position, the shadow of his ambition loomed large over the kingdom, threatening to ruin it.

CHAPTER 5

T HE KING'S DECREE TO SEARCH the kingdom for those responsible for the recent attacks was widely praised across the realm. Soldiers began their investigation in the north, meticulously working their way south. Their journey eventually led them to Bear Cave Castle, a formidable fortress in the dense forest.

The clang of armor and the rhythmic beat of hooves echoed through the valley as the army approached the castle. At the main gate, Darius's guards stood firm, their hands on their swords as they barred them entry.

One of the commanders, Sir Magnus, rode forward. His sharp gaze swept over the guards as he raised a scroll bearing the royal seal. "By the king's decree, open the gates and allow us entry!" he declared, his voice resolute.

The guards hesitated momentarily but recognized Sir Magnus. They realized that resistance would be futile. Reluctantly, they stepped aside, pulling the heavy iron gates open. The soldiers poured into the compound like a relentless tide, their discipline evident as they spread out to begin their search.

Darius, dressed in a dark velvet tunic with silver embroidery, emerged from the castle. Mefford followed close behind, his expression carefully neutral, while his mother, Xinovia, appeared poised yet unreadable at his side, her piercing eyes scanning the king's men. The trio descended the stone steps to confront them.

"What is the meaning of this?" Darius demanded, his tone cold and sharp.

Sir Magnus approached, his armored boots striking the ground with authority. He held the scroll aloft. "By order of King Alaric, every castle and estate in the realm is to be searched for those connected to the recent attacks. This decree leaves no exception." He handed the scroll to Darius.

Darius unrolled the parchment and read its contents, his jaw tightening. He turned to his guards, his expression unreadable but his tone firm. "Stand down. Allow them to proceed with their search."

The guards exchanged uneasy glances before stepping aside. The soldiers wasted no time, fanning out across the compound to comb every corner of Bear Cave Castle. They entered chambers, storerooms, and barracks, overturning furniture and scrutinizing every object. Their search led them to the dungeon, a place as cold and foreboding as the man who ruled it.

They opened every cell, their torches casting flickering shadows on the damp stone walls. They examined the prisoners, their shackles, and the dark corners where secrets might hide. Moving deeper still, they entered the storeroom, where sacks of grain and crates of fruit were stacked high. The soldiers began unloading the crates, scrutinizing their contents.

In one, they discovered fruits, including apples, peaches, and oranges, but noticed something unusual about their weight. They had begun removing the fruit to investigate further when Sir Magnus entered the room.

"There is nothing here," he said, his voice firm. "Do not waste time in this place. Move on."

The men obeyed without question, quickly vacating the storeroom and continuing their search elsewhere.

Unbeknownst to them, a hidden chamber lay behind the storeroom's stone wall. There, concealed in darkness, a man sat silently. He pressed his ear to the wall, straining to catch every word spoken on the other side. His heart pounded as he listened to the soldiers' movements, each muffled step a reminder of how close he was to discovery.

When the sound of retreating footsteps grew faint, he exhaled slowly, his tension easing. Still, he did not move, knowing that any noise might betray his presence. The hidden chamber was a lifeline, a secret known only to Darius and Mefford, who had taken great care to ensure its existence remained undiscovered.

⁂

As the soldiers regrouped in the courtyard, Darius stood at the top of the stairs, his arms crossed.

Sir Magnus approached him, his face less intense. "Our search has concluded here," he stated, his tone formal. "Bear Cave Castle yields no evidence of wrongdoing."

Darius inclined his head slightly, his voice calm but firm. "I trust you will convey your findings accurately to the king."

Sir Magnus nodded, signaling to his soldiers. They mounted their horses, their departure as disciplined as their arrival. The gates of Bear Cave Castle closed behind them with a resounding thud.

Once the army was gone, Mefford wasted no time. He descended to the hidden chamber behind the storeroom wall, his footsteps echoing faintly in the narrow passage. Reaching the door, he pulled it open and entered.

He inspected all the gold in the boxes and the sacks with a smirk on his face, walked to the door, opened it, and left humming a tune with a smile on his face.

CHAPTER 6

L ATE ONE MORNING IN THE summer, when the robberies of the preceding winter had subsided, King Alaric, Isadora, their children, and many nobles gathered in the main dining room of Verdant Castle for brunch. Sunlight was streaming through the tall arched windows, casting a warm glow on the elaborately set table. The aroma of freshly baked pastries and fragrant teas mingled with the hum of polite conversation and the gentle clinking of silverware against porcelain.

As the meal progressed, Alaric rose from his chair. The sound of the wooden legs scraping against the stone floor commanded attention, and voices hushed. The king cleared his throat, his imposing yet approachable presence filling the room. "I have an announcement to share with you all," he began. Curious gazes turned toward him as the room grew still. "After much consideration, Lord Ethan and Albert have graciously given their consent to the union of our son, Prince Halsten, and his beloved Freja."

Gasps of surprise rippled through the gathering, swiftly replaced by murmurs of approval and joy. Isadora stood gracefully and moved to her husband's side, her presence radiating warmth. "In light of this wonderful development," she said, her melodic voice tinged with pride, "we have decided to dedicate the next two months to preparing for the wedding. These festivities will culminate in a grand series of Gladiator Games to celebrate this joyous union."

The room erupted into applause, and several guests rose to offer their congratulations. Goblets clinked as toasts were raised, and smiles spread across every face.

Freja, her cheeks flushed with happiness, rose from her seat. Her movements were poised yet filled with emotion as she approached her father. Wrapping her arms around him, she said softly, "Thank you, Papa. Your blessing means everything to me."

Lord Ethan's eyes glistened with pride as he gently placed his hands on her shoulders. "This is a day of joy for us all," he said. "You have my blessing and my love, my daughter."

Turning, Freja walked toward Albert, her older brother and lifelong protector. She embraced him tightly. "Thank you for always standing by me, brother," she said. "Your support means more than words can express."

Albert returned the embrace with a reassuring nod. "You deserve every happiness, Freja. And Halsten is a good man. He'll take care of you as you deserve."

With a composed smile, Freja made her way to Alaric and Isadora. She bowed slightly, her respect evident, before speaking. "Thank you, Your Majesties, for welcoming me so warmly into your family."

Alaric extended a hand, gently resting it on her shoulder. "You've always been a part of this family, Freja," he said. "This marriage simply makes it official."

Isadora stepped forward, her expression kind and maternal. "You have brought so much happiness to Halsten," she said softly. "For that, we are deeply grateful. You are truly one of us now."

Freja returned to her seat beside her betrothed, her cheeks glowing. Halsten reached beneath the table and took her hand, his fingers curling around hers. Their eyes met in a silent exchange of affection, their bond unmistakable to those around them.

As the celebratory mood deepened, Lady Paulina leaned closer to Isadora. "What a beautiful announcement," she said, with admiration. "The entire kingdom will rejoice at this union."

Isadora nodded gracefully toward her aunt. "It is indeed a day to remember," she replied. "This is not just a union of hearts but a strengthening of our realm."

Lord Cameron raised his goblet high. "To Prince Halsten and Lady Freja!" he declared, his voice booming with enthusiasm. "May their union bring strength, happiness, and prosperity to the realm!"

The room echoed with cheers as goblets clinked. Amid the lively atmosphere, Princess Eleanor leaned closer to her sister Vivienne. "I hope these Gladiator Games are as thrilling as the last ones," she whispered with a playful smile.

Vivienne chuckled, a glimmer of mischief in her eyes. "If Father has anything to say about it, they will surpass all expectations."

"Hopefully, you will find a man worthy of your high-maintenance demands," Vivienne teased.

Alaric waved at Sir Egron, his guard, to come closer and whispered something into his ear. Egron left the room and returned with another guard, who was holding a tray with scrolls on it.

The king picked one of the scrolls and gave it to Egron, "Make sure to send these invitations by pigeons to all the noble houses of the realm and send the announcement to the whole kingdom to invite the citizens to the Gladiator Games and the wedding."

Once Egron exited the room, the king turned to Lord Cameron and Lady Emma and told them, "The queen and I would like to appoint you as members of Halsten's first council."

Lady Emma looked at her husband's face and nodded with a smile.

"Your Grace, we are honored by this appointment," Lord Cameron said.

"We want to ensure they receive the best preparation and support when the time comes for the prince to ascend the throne," Alaric said.

By the end of the day, the announcement had begun spreading like wildfire through the entire kingdom.

The celebration carried on, the air buzzing with excitement. Guests speculated about the grandeur of the wedding and the spectacle of the games, weaving stories of what was to come.

When Darius heard about the prince's upcoming wedding, his fury consumed him. He began pacing the grand hall of his castle, his footsteps echoing off the stone walls. His face twisted with rage as he muttered under his breath.

"Now you will never sit on the throne, unless you act swiftly," the voice hissed. "The prince will replace his father, and your chance will vanish, even if your brother falls."

Darius growled in frustration, his voice reverberating through the empty hall. "Leave me alone!" he screamed. In a fit of anger, he grabbed the nearest goblet and hurled it against the wall. The metallic clang echoed as it hit the floor.

His anger only intensified. Without hesitation, he bellowed, "Tapas! Caine! Come here at once."

The men rushed into the hall, their footsteps brisk. Darius turned sharply toward them. "Tapas, summon Lord Warhouse immediately."

"Yes, my lord," Tapas replied, bowing before departing.

Darius then fixed his glare on Caine. "Send someone to keep an eye on Verdant Castle," he commanded. "I want every move reported back to me."

Caine nodded, his tone calm despite the urgency in Darius's voice. "Yes, my lord." He bowed and exited the hall.

Still seething, Darius stormed toward the sound plate mounted on the wall. He grabbed a nearby stick and struck it forcefully. The resounding clang summoned a guard, who quickly entered the hall and stood at attention.

"Call Mefford immediately," Darius ordered.

"Yes, my lord." The guard hurried away.

Minutes later, Mefford, Darius's son, entered the hall. "Father, you called for me?" he said with a mix of curiosity and concern.

"Yes, son," Darius said, gesturing for him to follow. They walked to a corner of the hall, where Darius leaned closer to his son and whispered something into his ear.

A wicked grin spread across Mefford's face. Without another word, he turned and left. He made his way to the stables, mounted his horse, and galloped out through the castle gates with his guard Merlon in tow, heading toward Glenwood Forest.

The ride was swift and purposeful, and as they reached the dense cover of trees, they slowed their pace. When they arrived at a massive oak, Mefford dismounted and handed his horse's reins to Merlon. Placing two fingers to his mouth, he let out a sharp whistle that pierced the stillness of the forest.

Moments later, a gaunt figure emerged from the underbrush, his head concealed beneath a hood. He approached Mefford cautiously before pulling back the fabric to reveal a sly grin.

"We have business," Mefford said quietly, his voice firm.

The man nodded, and the two exchanged hushed words. After a brief discussion, the hooded man disappeared back into the bushes. Mefford mounted his horse again and rode toward Bear Cave Castle with Merlon, his mind racing with plans.

When Mefford arrived at the castle gates, he noticed Lord Warhouse and his trusted guard Aldon approaching on horseback. They exchanged curt nods before entering together.

Inside the fortified walls, Mefford dismounted and greeted Lord Warhouse with a respectful bow. The lord, a towering figure with a stern demeanor, inclined his head in return.

"Welcome, Lord Warhouse," Mefford said. "My father awaits you inside."

They joined Darius in the castle, where he was sitting with Xinovia, Darius's wife, his confidante and advisor. She rose gracefully to greet Lord Warhouse, offering him a warm smile.

"Xinovia," Lord Warhouse said, his deep voice carrying a rare softness. He leaned forward and embraced her, pressing a kiss to each cheek. "It is always a pleasure to see you."

"And you, my lord," Xinovia replied, her tone smooth and polished.

Lord Warhouse turned to Darius, his expression shifting to one of focus. "You sent for me?"

Darius gestured for Mefford to approach. He spoke to his son, their voices low and urgent. After a brief exchange, Mefford nodded and departed the hall.

Darius turned back to Lord Warhouse, his expression dark with determination. "We have matters to discuss," he said, gesturing to a nearby table. As the two men settled in, Xinovia quietly observed, her calculating gaze taking in every detail.

The dying embers in Darius's study cast long, dancing shadows across the stone walls as the two men leaned closer. The scent of aged whiskey and burning oak filled the tense silence between them.

Darius's fingers drummed a slow rhythm on the armrest of his chair. "Thank you for coming, my friend," he said, his voice low but carrying the weight of command. The firelight reflected in his cold, calculating eyes.

Beyond the castle walls, Mefford's silhouette disappeared into the mist-shrouded Edgewood Forest, his horse's hooves muffled by the damp earth. The ancient trees seemed to lean in, swallowing him whole as he rode toward some unseen purpose.

Back in the study, Lord Warhouse accepted a crystal glass, the amber liquid within catching the fire's glow. "It is always an honor," he replied, his gaze never leaving Darius's face. "I trust there is much to discuss?"

Darius's lips curled into a smile that never reached his eyes as he murmured, "The time has come to restore this kingdom to its proper form." Darius leaned forward, his gaze intense. "Did you hear the news from the castle?"

"Yes, my lord." Warhouse nodded. "I received the announcement of the prince's upcoming wedding."

Darius's expression darkened. "This wedding provides the perfect opportunity to act. During the festivities, their attention will be divided, and their defenses will weaken. We must strike then, catching them by surprise."

Warhouse stroked his beard thoughtfully. "I agree, my lord. What would you have me do?"

Darius tapped the armrest of his chair, his mind already racing with plans. "Do you still send workers to the farm colony?" he asked.

"Yes. Twice a week, we send men there to collect food supplies for the city and the castle."

"Good," Darius said. "Can we substitute some of our own men for the usual workers? I need individuals loyal to us to infiltrate their city and the castle court."

Warhouse's lips curved into a sly smile. "Consider it done, my lord. Would you like this to begin next week?"

"Yes," Darius confirmed. "And what of the other lords? Are they still loyal to our cause?"

"They are. They await your command. They will act when the time comes."

"Excellent." Darius's voice was brimming with determination. "Invite them here next week for a private dinner. We will finalize the details of our plan then."

Warhouse nodded. "I will send the invitations immediately."

"One more thing," Darius added, leaning closer. "Do you have anyone within the castle court who can help us? Someone who can influence the rotation of the guards?"

Warhouse's face lit with recognition. "Indeed, my lord. One of the shift commanders, Irvin, is my wife's nephew. He is loyal to our family and would gladly assist us."

Darius grinned, a glimmer of satisfaction flickering in his eyes. "Perfect. Let him know we may require his services soon, and that I will reward him handsomely. He and his family will lack for nothing."

"I will speak to him discreetly," Warhouse said. "He will be ready when the time comes."

The two men exchanged a knowing look, and their pact was solidified. Several hours later, after further discussion of minor details, they concluded their meeting.

Lord Warhouse rose to his feet, his expression resolute. "I will take my leave now, my lord," he said, bowing slightly.

Darius stood and extended his hand once more. "Thank you, my friend. Your loyalty will not be forgotten."

Warhouse clasped it firmly. "We shall prevail, my lord."

Lord Warhouse departed the hall, his guard Aldon trailing behind him. He mounted his horse outside the gates and rode off into the gathering dusk, his mind already calculating the steps ahead. Back in the hall, Darius watched them leave, a small, cold smile playing on his lips.

Darius walked back into the main hall. He sank into his chair, the weight of ambition pressing heavily on his mind. His fingers tapped the armrest as he pondered the unfolding steps of his plan.

His eyelids grew heavy, and soon his head drooped as he slipped into a light doze.

But then a voice called his name. "Darius…"

His eyes snapped open. The voice had come from the dark corridor across from where he sat.

Rising quickly, he turned toward the sound.

"Who's there?" he demanded, his voice firm yet laced with unease. "Show yourself!"

A breath, close—right by his ear—answered him. "I am a Virgil."

Darius turned abruptly, but no one stood there. Only darkness and the stillness of stone columns flanked him.

"What is a Virgil? Reveal yourself!" he shouted again, drawing his dagger from his side.

"I have no body," the voice whispered calmly. "I am your ego. I am the voice of your desires."

His grip tightened on the handle of the dagger. "What do you want from me?"

"I've come to guide you," the voice replied, "to what you truly seek."

"And how do you know what that is?"

The air thickened as the voice answered, "You desire your brother's throne."

Darius stiffened. "Who sent you?"

"I told you," the voice said slowly, "I am the desire of your ego. I know you more intimately than you know yourself."

His brow furrowed. "How do I know you are real?"

"When the time comes," the voice replied, now sounding more distant, "I will come to you, or you may summon me."

"And what name do I call you by?"

A pause. Then the answer came.

"Call me Orb."

"Orb?" Darius repeated the name, tasting strange on his tongue.

"Yes. That is my name," the voice said with finality.

"Wait!" Darius called out, stepping forward. "Wait?"

But the voice receded further into the shadows. "Go to bed, Darius. I will return when you need me."

A second voice pierced the moment. "My lord… It is late."

Darius turned sharply.

Tapas, his trusted guard, stood at the edge of the hall, holding a torch. His expression was calm but concerned.

Darius said nothing. He looked around, half expecting the shadowy voice to return, then slowly sheathed his dagger.

Without a word, he walked past Tapas and disappeared into the corridor that led to his chambers, the torch in Tapas's hand flickering against the stone walls like the whisper of a secret never meant to be heard.

CHAPTER 7

Darius could not sleep as his mind was occupied with a strong desire to take his brother's throne. He called for his guards, Caine and Tapas, and all three men set out into the darkness, Darius riding closely behind his loyal guards. They navigated the familiar terrain of Bear Cave, then followed the winding path along the banks of River Ellyn North. The faint sound of rushing water accompanied them as they pressed onward toward the heart of Edgewood Forest. Their destination loomed ahead—a small, crooked hut nestled among the trees, where the enigmatic old gypsy known as Petra made her dwelling.

Darius pulled his reins as they approached, bringing his steed to a halt. He turned to Tapas and Caine, his expression firm. "Wait here. Do not follow me unless I call for you," he commanded.

"Yes, Your Grace." Tapas bowed slightly in acknowledgment.

Dismounting, Darius strode toward the hut with purpose. The wooden door creaked ominously as he pushed it open without knocking, stepping into the dim interior. The smell of herbs and burning incense filled the air, mingling with the faint crackle of a fire. At the center of the room stood Petra, her back to the door as she worked over a table laden with various peculiar items.

She turned at the sound of the door, her sharp eyes narrowing when she saw Darius. She set down the silver bowl she had been holding, placing the wooden ladle beside it before inclining her head in a respectful bow. "Your Grace," she greeted, her tone steady. "What brings you to my humble home at this late hour?"

Darius's gaze was unyielding as he stepped further into the room. "I need you to tell me what is to come," he demanded.

Petra regarded him thoughtfully before speaking, her voice low and foreboding. "The night speaks of treachery and death, Your Grace. The crows have gathered, their black wings ready to descend upon the land, feasting on the carcasses of those who will fall."

Darius's patience thinned, and he barked, "Speak plainly, woman! Enough of your riddles."

Petra met his gaze, her eyes gleaming with an unsettling intensity. "Your Grace, I see blood flowing like a river across the land. Beyond River Ellyn, the air will be thick with the cries of the grieving. The sword will clash against the sword, and only he ordained by destiny shall emerge victorious."

Darius stepped closer, his voice dropping to a dangerous growl. "Will anyone from my household fall in this chaos?"

Petra's expression softened slightly, though her tone remained solemn. "You and the young master will live, Your Grace. The threads of fate grant you more days yet."

Satisfied, though not entirely reassured, Darius reached for the pouch at his waist. He placed it in her outstretched hand, the sound of coins faintly jingling within. "See to it that I live through what is to come," he said. "Do this, and I will reward you further."

She nodded, her fingers closing around the pouch. "As you will, Your Grace."

Without another word, Darius turned and exited the hut, letting the door creak shut behind him. Outside, Tapas and Caine stood alert in the shadows.

Mounting his horse, Darius called out to his men. "Let's return to Bear Cave. We've lingered here long enough."

"Yes, Your Grace," Tapas responded, climbing onto his own horse.

The three riders moved swiftly, the forest enveloping them in darkness again. The rhythmic sound of hooves echoed against the trees as they retraced their path, Petra's ominous words lingering in Darius's mind like a shadow that refused to be shaken. As they approached Bear Cave, the first light of dawn began to creep over the horizon, casting long, eerie shadows across the landscape.

The morning sun bathed the royal chamber as Alaric summoned Prince Halsten. The king, dressed in his robes of deep purple and gold, exuded authority as he addressed his son.

"Halsten," he began, his tone both warm and firm. "It is customary and respectful to personally invite your immediate family—your aunts and uncles—to your wedding. You must travel to Castle Ridge and deliver the invitation to your Uncle Aiden in person."

Halsten inclined his head respectfully. "Yes, Father," he replied. "I will leave immediately."

Alaric nodded. "Take your trusted men with you and extend our love and greetings to him. Ensure the message is delivered properly."

"I will, Father," Halsten said, determination clear in his voice.

The king placed a hand on the prince's shoulder. "Safe travels, my son."

Gathering his closest companions, Halsten set out on the journey. Arthur, Leo, Frodio, Adikis, and Zoresh rode beside him, while his loyal guards, Asger and DeMarco, followed close behind. The morning was cool, and the golden light of the rising sun painted the plains of the River Ellyn North in hues of amber and green.

Their path took them through the serene EdenRock Forest, where the chirping of birds and the rustle of leaves created a symphony of nature. As they neared Castle Ridge, the distant sound of drums echoed through the air, signaling their approach.

From atop the castle walls, the watchmen spotted the prince and his entourage. They sounded a series of calls, and the gates swung open to reveal the majestic city of learning. Lord Aiden, clad in a deep blue robe trimmed with gold, descended the grand staircase to greet his nephew.

"Welcome to Castle Ridge," Lord Aiden said warmly, extending his arms as Halsten dismounted from his horse.

"Thank you, Uncle," Halsten replied, stepping forward to embrace him. "You remember my friends."

Lord Aiden smiled, nodding to each man. "Welcome, gentlemen. It is good to see you all." He gestured toward the castle. "Come in. You must be weary from your journey."

Inside the grand hall of Castle Ridge, shelves lined with ancient books reached up to the vaulted ceilings, and tapestries depicting the kingdom's history adorned the walls. Lord Aiden motioned for Halsten to take the seat of honor at the head of the table. His companions and guards took their places nearby, with Asger pausing to hand a rolled scroll to one of Lord Aiden's guards.

Once everyone was settled, Lord Aiden leaned forward. "What brings you to Castle Ridge this morning, Halsten?"

Halsten met the man's gaze. "Uncle, I have come to personally invite you to my wedding to Lady Freja and the upcoming Gladiator Games."

At Halsten's signal, Leif, one of Lord Aiden's guards, stepped forward with a scroll tied with a golden ribbon. He handed it to his master, who untied the ribbon and unrolled the parchment. His eyes scanned the elegant script, and a smile spread across his face.

"Thank you, my nephew," he said. "I would not miss this great occasion for anything."

Halsten's expression brightened. "Your presence will mean a great deal to me, Uncle."

Lord Aiden chuckled softly. "I remember your father's wedding to Isadora. It was a true celebration of unity and joy. I hope yours will bring that same spirit back to the kingdom."

After a moment's pause, Halsten asked cautiously, "Uncle, what of Darius and Mefford? Do you think they will attend?"

The mention of Darius brought a shadow to Lord Aiden's face. His gaze fell to the polished floor, and he drummed his fingers lightly on the table and avoided the question but proceeded to invite Halsten to the dining table.

"Come," he said, his tone shifting. "Let us dine. You must be hungry after your journey."

The banquet hall was a feast for the senses. The long table inside was adorned with an array of delicacies—succulent roasted beef, tender lamb seasoned with herbs, fragrant rice pilaf, and vibrant bowls of freshly picked fruits. Halsten and his men took their seats as servants moved swiftly, ensuring every plate was full and goblets were brimming with fine wine.

As they ate, the conversation turned to the history of Castle Ridge and the preparations for the wedding. Lord Aiden regaled the group with tales of the castle's ancient origins, his voice animated as he recounted its role in the kingdom's past.

When the meal concluded, he clapped his hands. "See to it that the prince's men are shown to their quarters," he instructed his aides. Then, turning to Halsten, he added, "Come with me, nephew. I have prepared a room for you."

Lord Aiden led Halsten down a quiet corridor to a room adjacent to his own. The space was bathed in soft candlelight, highlighting a luxurious bed draped with fine linens and surrounded by intricately carved furniture. A gilded desk sat in one corner, and a cozy sitting area was arranged near the fireplace.

"This room is reserved for the king whenever he visits," Lord Aiden explained. "It is yours for the duration of your stay. Your men are housed in quarters on the other side of the castle, and guards are patrolling the grounds to ensure your safety."

He pointed to another door within the room. "Through there, you will find stewards ready to serve you with anything you might need." Placing a hand on Halsten's shoulder, he offered a kind smile. "Rest well, nephew. Tomorrow, we can speak more of the matters at hand."

"Goodnight, Uncle," Halsten said, inclining his head.

As the door closed behind Lord Aiden, Halsten sat on the edge of the bed, reflecting on the day's events. The warmth of his uncle's hospitality and the grandeur of Castle Ridge filled him with a sense of pride for his family's legacy. Though questions about Darius lingered in his mind, he resolved to focus on the joyous occasion ahead.

The next morning, the grand hall of Castle Ridge was filled with the enticing aroma of freshly baked bread, roasted meats, and spiced tea. Halsten and his companions sat at the long dining table, their voices mingling in a soft hum of conversation. Sunlight streamed through the tall windows, casting a warm glow over the polished wooden floors and the tapestries on the walls.

Halsten took a sip of his tea, his gaze drifting toward his companions. "We'll stay for two more days, he said, addressing Arthur and Leo." Arthur nodded. Lord Aiden entered the hall with a calm but purposeful air. He approached, resting a hand on his nephew's shoulder.

"Halsten," he said, his voice steady yet tinged with significance, "there is something I wish to show you."

Halsten placed his goblet on the table and nodded to his friends. "I'll return shortly." He stood. "Lead the way, Uncle."

Lord Aiden gestured for him to follow, and the two made their way through the quiet halls. The sounds of the bustling morning gradually faded as they moved deeper into the castle. Finally, Lord Aiden stopped before a torch mounted on the wall. He removed it with practiced ease and looked at Halsten.

"This way," he said, pressing his palm against an unassuming section of the stone wall. A low rumble echoed through the corridor as the stone shifted, revealing a hidden passageway.

Halsten raised an eyebrow, his curiosity piqued. "A hidden door?" he murmured.

"Castle Ridge holds many secrets," Lord Aiden replied. "This one is perhaps the most important."

The air inside the corridor was cooler, carrying the faint scent of parchment and aged wood. The men walked in silence, their footsteps echoing off the narrow walls, until they reached an imposing set of double doors. Lord Aiden withdrew a heavy iron key from his robe and inserted it into the lock. With a turn and a soft click, the doors creaked open, revealing a magnificent library.

Halsten's eyes widened as he stepped inside. The room was breathtaking, its shelves filled with scrolls and leather-bound tomes that stretched three stories high. Ladders were positioned along the walls, granting access to the highest shelves.

Lord Aiden stepped inside and held the torch aloft. "This, Halsten," he began, his voice filled with reverence, "is the heart of our history. Every triumph, every secret, and every lesson learned is chronicled here. It is time you learn the truths that shaped our family."

Halsten's gaze swept over the room, the weight of his uncle's words sinking in. "Why now?" he asked.

"Because you are no longer a boy," Lord Aiden said firmly. "You will one day rule, and to do so wisely, you must understand the choices that brought us here—including why your father, Alaric, sits on the throne instead of your uncle Darius."

Halsten's brow furrowed. "Uncle Darius?"

Lord Aiden nodded, gesturing to one side of the library. "Everything you need to know is here. The scrolls are labeled by name and time. Read them at your own pace, and when you are ready, come to me with your questions."

Halsten stepped closer to the shelves, his fingers brushing against the smooth wood. "I will," he said quietly. "Thank you for trusting me with this."

Lord Aiden walked to another door within the library and opened it, revealing a small, elegant room with a luxurious bed and a writing desk.

Turning back to Halsten, his expression softened. "This will be yours one day. Castle Ridge is as much a part of your legacy as EdenRock."

Halsten nodded. "Thank you, Uncle."

Lord Aiden smiled faintly and placed a hand on his nephew's shoulder. "Take your time. The truths here will not only shape your understanding of the past but also guide your future."

With that, he turned and retraced his steps through the hidden corridor. As the stone door slid back into place, sealing seamlessly behind him, Halsten found himself alone in the library. He exhaled deeply, the quiet weight of the room pressing upon him.

He reached for three scrolls bearing the names of his father, his uncle Darius, and Lord Aiden. Settling in a nearby chair, he opened the one bearing his father's name and began to read.

CHAPTER 8

The life and reign of Alaric Verdant began amidst profound loss, yet it carried the promise of hope and renewal for EdenRock. Born into the noble lineage of the Verdant dynasty, Alaric had shown calm bravery even as a boy, remaining steadfast by his father's side. Under King Edward Verdant's tutelage, Alaric absorbed the lessons of leadership, the burdens of responsibility, and the delicate balance required to maintain peace. These early experiences shaped him into a poised and capable young man. But the sudden death of King Edward thrust eighteen-year-old Alaric into a role few his age could shoulder—that as the ruler of EdenRock.

The coronation, arranged with urgency to stabilize the realm, was both a political necessity and a moment steeped in tradition. In the courtyard of Aldrich Castle, a raised platform stood as the focal point of the ceremony. Draped in emerald-green and gold, the royal banners bore the crest of the Verdant dynasty—a majestic beast combining the features of a lion and a dragon. The symbol encapsulated strength, wisdom, and the legacy of EdenRock's rulers.

Alaric stood at the platform's center, his youthful figure framed by the flickering torchlight. Clad in royal attire, he emanated an aura of quiet confidence that belied his age. His golden hair caught the glow of the flames. Despite the weight of the occasion, his steady demeanor and composed expression reassured the gathered crowd that the kingdom's future was in capable hands.

To his right stood High Priest Evard, the custodian of EdenRock's ancient traditions. In his hands, he carried the Sword of EdenRock, a storied relic passed down through generations. The blade, polished to a gleaming brilliance, bore engravings of sigils representing wisdom, justice, and the line of kings before him. On Alaric's left stood Lord Matison, his late father's trusted viceroy. Matison's stoic presence underscored the continuity of EdenRock's leadership even in the face of change.

The coronation was preceded by Alaric's marriage to Lady Isadora Elferidge, a union that solidified alliances and strengthened the bond between noble houses. The ceremony was held moments before the crowning. Isadora, a vision of grace and elegance, stood at Alaric's side and assumed her role as queen.

As the coronation proceeded, the courtyard fell into a profound hush. High Priest Evard raised the Sword of EdenRock high above his head, the blade catching the firelight and casting shimmering reflections onto the faces of the gathered nobles and citizens. The weight of the moment was palpable, as though the spirit of EdenRock's forebearers lingered to bear witness.

Evard brought the sword down gently, resting its edge on Alaric's shoulder. The ancient rite invoked the responsibility now placed upon the young king—to uphold the laws of the land, protect its people, and rule with fairness and honor. Alaric knelt without hesitation, his head bowed in solemn acceptance. As he swore his oath, his voice carried the conviction of one ready to bear the mantle of kingship.

When the ceremony concluded, Alaric rose, the crown of his ancestors now resting on his brow. The crowd erupted into cheers, their voices reverberating through the castle walls. "Long live King Alaric!" they shouted. Standing beside Alaric, Isadora joined in the moment.

The high priest nodded solemnly, lifting the Sword of EdenRock with the reverence befitting its ancient legacy. As the blade passed into Alaric's hands, the young king gripped its hilt firmly, feeling the full weight of the realm settle into his grasp. The ceremonial act symbolized an unbroken chain of rulership stretching back through EdenRock's storied past.

Alaric, his royal cloak catching the cool evening breeze and trailing behind him, stepped to the edge of the raised platform, lifting the sword high above his head. A moment of profound silence hung in the air, as if the kingdom itself held its breath, absorbing the magnitude of the occasion.

Then, the silence gave way to a crescendo of jubilant cheers. The cry of "Long live King Alaric! Long live the king!" surged through the courtyard, echoing against the castle walls and spilling into the streets beyond. Nobles, knights, merchants, and commoners joined their voices in unison, the chant carrying a fervent sense of renewed hope.

In a display of loyalty and strength, soldiers clad in gleaming armor marched forward in disciplined formation. Their synchronized steps reverberated across the stone courtyard as they raised their swords in a salute to their new king. The clanging of steel against steel rang out like a solemn anthem, a tribute to the legacy of the Verdant dynasty and the future under its young ruler.

Alaric stepped forward to face the people. The firelight illuminated his features, revealing a determined expression. He stood tall, embodying the strength and composure of a leader ready to guide his realm. The cheers faded to an expectant hush as the crowd strained forward, their collective breath held. Alaric raised his hands, the golden circlet of EdenRock catching the afternoon sun.

"Citizens of EdenRock," his voice carried across the square, "your support humbles me. I stand before you not merely as your king but as your servant—as my father and grandfather stood before you in their time."

A murmur of approval rippled through the gathered people. The king's grip tightened on the podium as he continued.

"Our work is not yet done. The roads must be mended, the harvests protected, and justice made swift and fair. But I cannot do these things alone." He extended his hand toward the crowd. "With your strength beside mine, we shall honor our forefathers' legacy and build a kingdom worthy of our children's children."

The square fell utterly silent as he drew himself to his full height.

"This I swear upon my crown and my blood: I shall rule with integrity, defend with courage, and judge with mercy. So long as breath remains in me, EdenRock shall flourish!"

As the new king's words echoed off the stone buildings, the crowd erupted. Hundreds of voices united in the ancient chant: "To the Realm! To the Realm! To the Realm!" The rhythmic cry shook the very foundations of the square, a wave of loyalty rolling toward the golden throne.

The young king's presence resonated with a calm yet commanding authority. The weight of his words would set the tone for a reign filled with promise and challenges. His vision for EdenRock, though shaped by the legacy of his father, was also deeply rooted in his own ideals of justice and prosperity. The people sensed this, their faith in him unwavering.

As the coronation concluded, the skies above the castle came alive with the brilliance of fireworks. Explosions of red, green, and gold illuminated the night, the vibrant hues painting the heavens with a spectacle befitting the historic occasion.

Children in the crowd clapped their hands in awe, pointing at the dazzling colors that danced across the sky. Elders, their faces lined with wisdom and experience, watched with quiet satisfaction, their hope in the young king reaffirmed. The fireworks lit up the courtyard, casting fleeting but radiant light upon the faces of those gathered. The moment was both ephemeral and eternal, a memory that would linger in the hearts of the people for generations.

As the final trails of smoke dissipated into the night, his gaze was fixed firmly ahead. He descended the platform with steady steps, flanked by Isadora, High Priest Evard, and Lord Matison. Together, they moved through the parting crowd, the young king offering nods and brief smiles to those he passed. Each gesture carried the weight of gratitude and acknowledgment, strengthening the bond between the ruler and the subject.

The jubilant celebration had been but a fleeting prelude to the immense responsibilities that awaited Alaric. With the weight of the crown resting upon his brow and the echoes of his people's faith still resounding, he prepared to lead EdenRock into a new era shaped by the wisdom of his ancestors and the strength of his own convictions.

Under King Alaric's leadership, EdenRock entered a golden age marked by stability, innovation, and growth. Demonstrating profound wisdom and strategic foresight, he became renowned for his ability to preserve peace while advancing prosperity. He understood that the strength of a kingdom lay not only in its military might but also in the harmony of its people and the strength of its alliances. Through careful diplomacy, he forged strong ties with neighboring realms, ensuring that EdenRock held a position of respect and influence within the region. By striking a balance of power among the surrounding kingdoms, Alaric safeguarded the tranquility that his people cherished.

His governance was characterized by inclusivity and shared responsibility. He recognized that centralized power, though effective, might alienate the regional lords whose support was vital to the stability of the realm. Instead, he granted greater authority to the nobles of EdenRock's castles, fostering a sense of unity and collaboration. This network of governance allowed for efficient administration across the kingdom's vast territories while ensuring that the needs and voices of the people were fairly represented.

Economically, EdenRock flourished under Alaric. The kingdom's abundant natural resources, coupled with a robust trading network, created a thriving economy that brought prosperity to its citizens. The towns and cities grew in size and influence, their markets bustling with activity and innovation. EdenRock's quarries, fields, and lakes became symbols of its self-sufficiency, while its goods—renowned for their quality—became sought after in distant lands. The kingdom's cultural life blossomed alongside its economic strength, as artisans, scholars, and musicians contributed to a shared sense of pride in EdenRock's heritage.

The Verdant lineage thrived as well. Alaric and Isadora were blessed with three children, who would become the embodiment of their hopes and legacy. Each child, unique in their gifts and temperaments, played a vital role in the life of the realm.

Halsten Elliot Verdant, their eldest, was groomed from an early age to inherit the throne. Under Alaric's watchful guidance, he developed the qualities of a future king. Courage, fairness, and compassion were instilled in him through lessons, examples, and shared moments of reflection with his father. Alaric's unwavering focus on preparing Halsten ensured that the young prince will one day carry forward the Verdant name with honor.

Eleanor Verdant, the second child, distinguished herself with her intellect and natural charm. Her innate talent for diplomacy made her a valuable asset to the kingdom's relations with neighboring realms. Accompanying her parents during important meetings, Eleanor's keen insight and measured demeanor won the respect of dignitaries and the admiration of the court. She became a symbol of EdenRock's grace and intelligence, embodying the spirit of collaboration that defined her father's reign.

The youngest of the three, Vivienne Verdant, brought boundless energy and joy to the royal household. Her adventurous spirit and genuine curiosity endeared her to the people, from noble lords to ordinary villagers. Unburdened by the weight of succession, Vivienne explored the kingdom with an open heart, forging connections with its citizens and gaining an intimate understanding of their lives. Her presence was a constant reminder of the vibrancy and hope that underpinned EdenRock's prosperity.

The harmony within the Verdant family mirrored the unity of the realm, becoming a beacon of stability and inspiration. Children's laughter filled the castle halls, blending with the steady rhythm of royal duties performed with unwavering dedication. King Alaric's reign is a testament to the power of just leadership and the enduring values of the Verdant dynasty. His efforts ensure not only the prosperity of EdenRock but also the resilience of its legacy for generations to come.

Prince Halsten rolled up the scroll and placed it back on the shelf and walked out back to the hall. The young prince's heart was filled with pride at what his uncle had recorded about his parents.

After spending time with his friends and his uncle throughout the day, Halsten returned to his room and slept.

When the birds began to chip in the wee hours of the morning, Prince Halsten woke up, entered the study area, picked up the scroll with Darius's name on it, and seated himself in the same chair he had occupied the previous night. Unrolling the paper, he began to read.

Darius Verdant, Brother of
Alaric Verdant and Lord Aiden Verdant

The reading of the final testament of King Edward Verdant was a decisive moment that irrevocably altered the destiny of his family and the kingdom of EdenRock. In it, the king made clear his judgment: neither Darius nor his descendants would ever bear a noble title or be allowed entry into Verdant Castle. The reason was explicit and unforgivable—Darius had defiled his father's concubine, Xinovia, bringing disgrace upon the royal family. This decree cut deeply into Darius's pride, igniting a fire of resentment and ambition that would burn fiercely for years.

Darius's reaction to the testament was one of unrestrained fury. He openly threatened his younger brother, Alaric, vowing to reclaim the crown he believed was his birthright. The promises of loyalty he had once made to his father were forgotten, replaced by a simmering hatred for the family that had turned its back on him. Queen Edna, grief-stricken by her husband's death and unwilling to tolerate her son's hostility, ordered the castle guards to escort him out of Verdant Castle. Darius departed with his pride bruised and his heart hardened, leaving behind the family that no longer claimed him.

Even after the birth of his son, Mefford, Darius's bitterness consumed him. He refused to mend ties with his siblings and forbade Mefford from playing with Prince Halsten despite their early childhood friendship. His estrangement from the Verdant family became absolute, with the walls of Bear Cave Castle serving as both a physical and emotional barrier.

Following King Edward's death, EdenRock entered a period of solemn mourning. White flags adorned the realm's castles, fortresses, and towns, their stark simplicity symbolizing the kingdom's collective grief, a poignant reminder of the passing of a wise and just ruler. Across EdenRock, citizens paused their daily routines to reflect on the legacy of their king.

Thousands of citizens gathered in the courtyard, their faces etched with sadness and anticipation. Farmers, soldiers, merchants, and nobles alike united in their shared respect for the late king and their hope for the future.

The royal casket, crafted from the finest oak and adorned with gold and emerald inlays, was carried through the streets by the king's honor guard. The procession moved solemnly, the mournful sound of horns echoing through the capital. Behind the casket walked Queen Edna, her face veiled in black, accompanied by her two younger sons, Alaric and Aiden, their expressions stoic but heavy with emotion. The streets were lined with people, their heads bowed in silent reverence as they paid their final respects.

The procession went to the royal cemetery, a sacred ground reserved for those of the Verdant lineage. Nestled in the lush hills overlooking the kingdom, the cemetery was a serene and hallowed space. Ancient stone markers, each bearing the names of kings and queens long past, stood as silent sentinels to the legacy of EdenRock.

The burial ceremony was quiet, attended only by close family and trusted advisors. The high priest of EdenRock, clad in ceremonial robes, led the rites, invoking blessings for the departed king and strength for the kingdom in the days to come. As the casket was lowered into the earth, the assembled mourners placed their hands over their hearts, a final gesture of respect.

Far from the celebrations, Darius brooded in the dark halls of Bear Cave Castle. The king's testament and Alaric's coronation had solidified his place as an outcast, fueling his resentment. For him, the throne was no longer a symbol of duty or legacy—it was a prize to be seized, no matter the cost. He viewed Alaric's reign not as a continuation of their father's vision but as an affront to his perceived destiny.

As the years passed, Darius's isolation deepened. Bear Cave Castle became his fortress, a bastion of anger and ambition. He gathered followers, men and women who shared his thirst for power or who feared his wrath. These alliances were forged not through trust or loyalty but through intimidation and manipulation. Darius began to plot his return, convinced that the throne of EdenRock was rightfully his.

While Alaric's reign brought prosperity and unity to EdenRock, Darius lingered as a shadowy presence on the kingdom's borders. His estrangement from his family and his growing animosity toward his brother created a rift that threatened to disrupt the peace King Edward had worked so hard to establish. With each passing year, Darius's ambition festered, setting the stage for the eventual conflict that would test the strength and resilience of the Verdant lineage.

Darius bided his time in the quiet halls of Bear Cave Castle, his bitterness sharpening into a weapon. Though cast out from the family, he remained a force to be reckoned with—a storm gathering on the horizon of EdenRock's otherwise bright future.

Just as Prince Halsten placed the scroll with Darius's name back on the shelf, a knock sounded on the door. He walked over and opened it.

"Good morning, nephew," Lord Aiden said.

"Good morning, Uncle. Come in."

"Did you get some sleep?"

"I did," Halsten said. "Uncle, I would like to ask you a question."

"What is it, my prince?" Lord Aiden sat down.

"Father told me about you and Ava. How did you meet her?"

Lord Aiden bowed his head and cleared his throat before speaking. He leaned back in his chair, studying Halsten, who was sitting across from him. The young prince's posture was attentive, his palms resting lightly on his knees, his focus unwavering.

"You remind me of myself when I was younger," Aiden remarked with a small smile, folding his hands in his lap. "Curious, restless, always wanting to know more."

Halsten straightened, his interest piqued. "Is that why you spent so much time in EdenRock Forest? To study?"

"Exactly." Lord Aiden nodded. "The forest was my sanctuary. It offered peace, far from the demands of courtly life, but it also taught lessons that couldn't be learned within castle walls."

Halsten tilted his head, a furrow forming in his brow. "What kind of lessons?"

Aiden exhaled slowly. The memory came to him as vividly as if it had happened yesterday. "It began on an ordinary day. I had ventured deep into the forest, searching for a rare medicinal plant. My focus on the task was so intense that I overlooked the danger lurking nearby."

Halsten leaned forward. "What happened?"

"A tiger snake struck." Aiden's tone was steady but laced with the weight of the memory. "It was as quick as lightning. Its fangs sank into my leg, and the pain was immediate—a sharp, burning sensation that spread like wildfire. I collapsed, barely able to think as the venom coursed through me."

Halsten's eyes widened. "How did you survive?"

"I didn't save myself," Aiden admitted, shaking his head. "I thought it was the end. Lying there helpless as the forest darkened around me, I prepared for death. But then, out of nowhere, she appeared."

"She?" Halsten's curiosity sharpened.

"Ava Trucedale," Aiden said, her name lingering in the air. "She saved my life."

"Who was she?"

"A healer." Aiden's gaze grew distant as he recalled her face. "She emerged from the trees as if fate had sent her. Her voice was calm, steady, and reassuring. At first, I barely registered her presence, but then I felt her hands—quick and precise—working to save me."

Halsten was captivated. "What did she do?"

"She tore a strip from her dress to make a tourniquet and slowed the venom's spread," Aiden said. "Then, she crushed herbs she carried into a poultice and pressed it against the bite. Her hands never shook, and her focus never wavered. She stayed with me, talking softly, urging me to hold on."

Halsten's expression softened, awe creeping into his voice. "She must have been extraordinary."

"She was," Aiden said, a faint smile tugging at his lips. "When I woke hours later, I was in a clearing. The sunlight filtered through the trees, casting a golden glow over everything. There she was, sitting beside me. Her eyes held concern but also relief."

"What did she say?"

Aiden chuckled. "She said, 'You're awake. Good. I thought I'd have to carry you back myself.'"

Halsten laughed. "What did you say to that?"

"I told her I'd never met anyone so formidable. And I meant it. Ava wasn't just a healer—she was a force of nature. As I recovered, we spoke for hours. She used to collect herbs in the forest with her father to cure needy people."

"You loved her," Halsten observed, his tone quiet and reflective.

"Yes," Aiden admitted. "More than I've loved anyone else. Ava showed me a life I'd never imagined—one guided by compassion and purpose. She taught me what it truly means to serve others."

"What happened to her?"

The question struck deeply, but Aiden met his nephew's gaze. "Ava was taken too soon," he said heavily. "One day, while riding through the forest, her horse spooked. She was thrown, and…" He swallowed hard. "She hit her head on a rock. I held her in my arms, but I could do nothing."

Halsten lowered his eyes, his expression shadowed with grief. "I'm sorry, Uncle. That must have been devastating. How did you deal with her loss?"

"I still haven't to this day." Aiden's tone was heavy with sorrow. "For days, I wandered the forest aimlessly, haunted by her laughter and our shared dreams. EdenRock, once my sanctuary, became a place of unbearable grief."

"How did you end up at Castle Ridge?" Halsten asked.

Aiden's gaze lifted slightly. "Your grandfather saw my despair and offered me guidance. As we rode together one morning, he told me, 'Perhaps a new purpose can help you find peace.' He was right. I devoted myself to studying life, honoring Ava's memory in every way possible."

Halsten nodded, his expression thoughtful. "It seems you've carried her with you all this time."

"I have. Her memory is my guiding light. Everything I do—every decision I make—is shaped by her legacy. Ava taught me true strength lies in love, compassion, and the courage to serve others."

Halsten reached for his uncle's hand. "Thank you for sharing her story with me. It's something I'll carry with me always."

Aiden smiled faintly, his gaze steady on his nephew. "Remember this, Halsten—our greatest strength doesn't come from titles or swords. It comes from love and the resolve to honor those we've lost by living fully."

Halsten nodded, his expression firm with newfound understanding. In his eyes, Aiden saw not just a future king but a reflection of the hope and strength that would carry EdenRock forward.

CHAPTER 9

ON THE AFTERNOON FOLLOWING HIS meeting with Darius at Bear Cave Castle, Lord Warhouse summoned his personal guard to his study. His tone was sharp as he issued his orders.

"Send invitations to Lord Ian Bluevine, Lord Jed Burken, Lord Abe Luterodt, and Lord Lingard Kraft," he said, pacing the room with measured steps. "Inform them I am hosting a dinner tonight. Their presence is not optional."

The guard bowed deeply. "Yes, my lord. I will see it done immediately." He left the room swiftly to carry out the task.

The invited lords began arriving as the sun dipped below the horizon and darkness enveloped the realm. Each came accompanied by a retinue of personal guards, their banners fluttering faintly in the cool evening breeze. The castle, perched atop a gentle hill and glowing with the flickering light of torches, cut an imposing figure against the darkening sky.

The cooks at the Warhouse Estate had prepared an exquisite feast inside. The grand dining hall was adorned with tapestries and floral arrangements, the table set with silver goblets and intricately carved platters. The atmosphere was carefully crafted to reflect Lord Warhouse's attention to detail. While the lords were ushered into the hall, their guards were escorted to a separate chamber, where Molart Drone, Lord Warhouse's trusted commander, ensured they were fed and entertained.

Once all the lords were seated, the hum of quiet conversation filled the air. Goblets clinked as servants moved gracefully between the guests, refilling drinks and ensuring every detail was perfect.

Lord Warhouse rose from his seat, his stance drawing attention. Lifting his wine glass high, he declared, "To EdenRock."

The lords stood in unison and raised their own glasses. "To EdenRock, to the realm of Aldrich," they echoed, their voices resonating through the hall. With the toast complete, they resumed their seats.

Once the room had settled, Lord Warhouse fixed his gaze on his guests. "My lords," he began, his tone heavy, "I have called you here once more concerning what we discussed in our first meeting." A murmur rippled through the room. Lord Luterodt began speaking, his voice rising slightly. Lord Warhouse announced, "Darius is ready to meet with us before the king's council meeting next month. I will confirm the time and place with each of you soon."

The lords nodded in agreement. Lord Luterodt rose, lifting his goblet. "Tell Darius we stand ready to meet. We can't afford to sit and do nothing."

Lord Warhouse picked up a silver cup, raised it, and said, "To a good alliance."

The men did the same. "To a good alliance."

The room began to buzz with chatter and laughter as they drank and ate what was served before them. After a hearty night of feasting, the guests began to depart as Lord Warhouse and his wife stood at the entrance to bid them farewell.

Meanwhile, that same night, the air around EdenRock Forest grew still, except the rustling of leaves in the faint breeze. Mefford, accompanied by a gang of robbers led by Jason and his close allies, moved stealthily under darkness. Crude masks concealed their faces, and their weapons glinted faintly in the moonlight. Thanks to information provided by Darius's spies in the city, they knew exactly where to position themselves along the trading route.

Mefford crouched near a dense thicket. "Jason," he said, motioning toward the shadowed path ahead, "the traders will be here soon. Make sure your men are ready. No mistakes."

Jason nodded, gripping the hilt of his blade. "We're ready, Mefford. They won't see it coming."

The robbers settled into their hiding spots, their breathing barely audible as they waited. The moments stretched into an agonizing silence, but eventually the distant creak of wooden wheels and the rhythmic clatter of hooves broke the stillness. Traders riding alongside their carts were approaching, laden with goods and revenue from the traders' recent sales.

Mefford raised a hand, signaling the men to hold their positions. As the carts drew near, he gave a sharp whistle. The robbers emerged from the shadows, weapons drawn, their presence sudden and menacing.

"Stop where you are!" Mefford bellowed, stepping into the path. The traders, startled and outnumbered, barely had time to react before they were descended upon.

The attack was brutal and swift. Swords clashed, and shouts echoed, but the traders were no match for the organized assault. Within minutes, their goods had been seized, and the attackers had left but one survivor. A trembling young man, barely more than a boy, knelt on the ground, his hands raised in surrender.

Mefford approached him, his voice cold. "You will deliver a message to the king," he said, tossing a rolled parchment at the young man's feet. "Tell him he cannot stop me."

Jason leaned closer, his masked face inches from the kid's. "Run," he growled, "and don't look back."

The boy grabbed the message with shaking hands and stumbled to his feet. Without a word, he sprinted toward EdenRock, disappearing into the night.

Mefford turned to Jason and the others. "Gather everything. We leave nothing behind."

The robbers worked quickly to tie their horses to the wagons carrying the boxes of gold and goods, then vanished into the darkness as swiftly as they had appeared, leaving the scene eerily quiet once more.

News of the attack had already spread by the time the message reached EdenRock. The surviving young man handed the parchment to one of the king's guards, who delivered it to the throne room without delay.

Alaric read the message aloud, his voice taut with anger: "I am like a ghost and sometimes your shadow. I know you better than you know yourself. Keep making me rich."

The words echoed in the chamber, thick with disdain and mockery. The king slammed his fist onto the armrest of his throne. "How do these criminals always know where to strike?" he demanded, his voice reverberating through the hall. "How many more must die before we end this?"

Egron, standing beside him, shook his head grimly. "The precision of these attacks suggests they have informants, Your Majesty. Someone within our cities is feeding them information."

Alaric's eyes narrowed. "Then we must find these traitors. Double the patrols on all trade routes. Increase the guards at every post."

"Yes, Your Majesty," Aiden replied, bowing before hurrying to relay the orders.

The aftermath of the robbery sent shockwaves through the kingdom, inciting fear and anger among the citizens. The streets of EdenRock soon filled with protesters, their voices raised in outrage.

"Where is the king's protection?" a merchant shouted, his voice cutting through the din. "How many more of us must die before something is done?"

"We work, we pay taxes, and this is what we get?" another woman cried. "Our goods stolen, our lives endangered!"

The crowd swelled, their frustration boiling over as they marched toward the castle gates. Inside, Alaric stood at a window, watching the growing unrest with a heavy heart.

"We cannot ignore this any longer," Isadora said softly, joining him at his side. "The people are losing faith in us."

Alaric's jaw tightened. "I know. But until we root out the spies feeding these criminals, every move we make will be countered."

Isadora placed a hand on his arm. "Then we must act swiftly, my king. For the sake of the realm."

He nodded, resolute. "I will summon the council in the morning," he said. "This must end now."

Around three in the morning, Mefford returned from his latest raid to Bear Cave Castle, his satchel overflowing with valuables. He strode confidently through the dim corridors and descended into the dungeon, where they stored their loot. Setting down the heavy haul, he examined the glinting coins and ornate goods with satisfaction. Moments later, he sent a messenger to summon his father.

Darius appeared shortly after, his footsteps echoing on the stone steps as he descended into the cold, damp space. A broad smile spread across his face when his eyes fell on the bounty. He approached Mefford, placing both hands on his son's shoulders and pulling him into a rare embrace.

He pressed a kiss to Mefford's head. "You have done well, my son," Darius said, his voice filled with pride. "This belongs to us anyway. They've taken too much from us over the years. Now, we take it back."

Mefford smirked, a sense of accomplishment washing over him. "It's all here, Father. The finest spoils yet."

Darius inspected the goods briefly before motioning for his son to follow. "Come, let us leave this place." The two climbed out of the dungeon and into the castle's main hall.

On his way to his chambers, Mefford paused at a side table and grabbed a jar of wine. Pouring himself a generous goblet, he gulped down the strong drink in a few long swallows. Feeling heat spread through his chest, he wiped his mouth with the back of his hand and carried the jar to his room.

Once inside, the day's fatigue began to weigh him down. He collapsed onto his bed, the softness of the mattress pulling him into a deep, unrelenting slumber.

As Mefford drifted into unconsciousness, the lines between reality and dreams blurred. He found himself standing in the heart of a dense, shadowy forest. The air was thick and heavy, and a sense of foreboding clung to the atmosphere. Around him, his crew moved with stealth, their faces obscured by the dark hoods they always wore. Jason, his trusted ally, was standing at his side, leaning in to discuss their plan.

"The traders are just ahead," he whispered, his voice low but urgent. "Loaded with gold. They won't know what hit them."

Mefford nodded, gripping the hilt of his sword as they crept closer. Ahead, the faint outline of carts appeared on the horizon, illuminated by the moon's silvery glow. The traders were walking alongside them, their movements cautious, unaware of the danger lurking nearby.

With a sharp signal from Mefford, his crew sprang into action. They surged from the shadows, weapons drawn, ready to attack. But as they approached, the traders and their guards scattered, abandoning the carts and horses without a fight. The eerie silence that followed was unsettling.

Mefford turned to Jason, confusion etched across his face. "Why would they just leave?" he asked.

There was no response. Jason was gone. Turning quickly, Mefford scanned the area, but his men had vanished, leaving him alone. Unease gnawed at him as he stood frozen, caught between retreating or investigating the seemingly abandoned carts.

His curiosity won out, and he approached the nearest cart cautiously, his hand trembling as he reached for the latch. The air around him felt heavier with every step. When he opened the doors, his heart stopped.

Inside stood a massive beast, its hulking form barely contained by the cart's frame. It had the same glowing eyes as the beast that had tormented him since childhood, and they bored into his soul. Its chest heaved as it emitted a deep, guttural growl. The creature's jaws opened wide, revealing rows of razor-sharp teeth. With a deafening roar, it unleashed a torrent of fire straight toward him.

The ground beneath Mefford shook violently. He stumbled and fell backward, his breath catching in his throat. The heat of the flames seemed to sear his skin as he scrambled to escape, his limbs heavy with terror.

With a gasp, he jolted awake. His body was drenched in sweat, his breathing ragged as he sat upright in his bed. The room was dark, but the moonlight streaming through the window illuminated his pale, trembling hands. He wiped his forehead, his heart pounding so hard it felt like it would burst from his chest.

For a long moment, he sat motionless at the edge of his bed, sobbing, his mind struggling to separate the nightmare from reality. The terror of the dream lingered, gnawing at the edges of his thoughts. Somewhere deep within him, an unease took root—dreading that perhaps his actions would come to light one day and he would have to face the consequences of his deeds.

Darius entered his dim bedroom, humming a cheerful tune. The soft glow of candles filled the space, casting flickering shadows across the walls. On the edge of the grand bed sat Xinovia, her figure accentuated by a delicate white-gold gown that left little to the imagination. Her hair cascaded over her shoulders, and her gaze held an alluring invitation.

Without hesitation, Darius crossed the room. He leaned down and kissed her deeply, savoring the warmth of her lips. Pulling back slightly, he whispered, "You look divine tonight."

Xinovia smiled coyly but said nothing as she stood, her bare feet soundless on the plush rug. She turned to face him fully and, with a graceful motion, let her dress slip from her shoulders, the fabric pooling around her feet. The candlelight danced across her bare skin, highlighting every curve.

Darius's eyes lingered over her features. Xinovia met his eyes and smirked. Their lips found each other, and their kiss was fiery and consuming. They fell into their bed together, embraced in passion, oblivious of their surroundings as the night passed.

CHAPTER 10

ONCE THE SUN HAD REMOVED the chill from the early morning air, Prince Halsten and Lady Freja invited their friends to join them for a pre-wedding picnic at the picturesque Lake Tolki. The couple rode through the serene Blue Gate Forest, their horses' hooves echoing softly among the rustling leaves. DeMarco, Halsten's steadfast bodyguard, led a contingent of guards behind them. Lady Dhalia and Dora, Freja's closest confidant, rode beside them, the women sharing quiet laughter as they made their way to the lake.

Upon reaching the sparkling waters of the lake, they were greeted by the sight of their friends, who had gathered to celebrate with the newly engaged couple. The group exchanged warm greetings, their laughter ringing through the crisp air.

Halsten approached Frodio, Zoresh, and Adikis, his childhood friends from Aldrich City's lower class. They had spent their formative years at the military academy with Halsten and Freja's brother Albert. Despite their different stations in life, bonds of camaraderie and trust had been forged between them in the trials of youth.

With a playful grin, Halsten clapped Adikis on the shoulder. "Where do you all disappear to these days? You live such mysterious lives that keeping track of you is impossible."

Adikis gave a mock bow, his smile wide. "My prince, unlike the nobles, some of us still have to work for a living."

"And what is this work that keeps you so busy?" Albert asked, approaching from behind with a curious smirk.

Frodio crossed his arms, his tone teasing. "My prince, what we do isn't noble enough for royal ears."

Arthur raised his voice in a mock announcement, stepping forward dramatically. "Behold—the soon-to-be-married Prince Halsten Elliot Verdant and Lady Freja Marie Glenwood of Glenwood!"

Cheers and laughter erupted as the group surged forward, surrounding the couple with warm congratulations and friendly embraces.

Halsten took Freja's hand, his smile softening as he gazed at her. "You're the reason today feels so perfect," he murmured.

Freja blushed, her lips curving into a shy smile. "And you are the reason every day feels like a dream," she replied softly, her voice carrying only to him.

The group's energy filled the lakefront. Blankets were spread over the lush grass, baskets of food and wine unpacked, and the merry gathering settled in. Stories and laughter flowed freely as the friends shared humorous memories of Halsten and Freja, from childhood antics to recent adventures.

"Do you remember," Leo began, "when Halsten tried to impress Freja by climbing the old oak tree in the palace garden, only to get stuck halfway up?"

"Stuck?" Adikis exclaimed, chuckling. "I thought princes were supposed to be fearless!"

Halsten raised his hands in mock surrender. "In my defense, that tree was taller than it looked!"

Freja leaned into Halsten, her laughter soft and melodic. "It was the thought that counted. Besides," she teased, "you looked quite heroic up there before the guards had to rescue you."

The group howled in amusement, and even Halsten couldn't keep from smiling at the memory. He tightened his arm around Freja's waist, pulling her closer. "Anything to catch your attention," he whispered, causing her cheeks to flush.

As the sun climbed higher in the sky, the joyous atmosphere at Lake Tolki grew livelier. Jayden's lute provided a melodic backdrop, his gentle strumming harmonizing with laughter and conversation. The sweet scent of wildflowers mingled with the aroma of baked goods and ripe fruits from the picnic baskets, creating an air of carefree celebration.

The men, invigorated by the cheerful mood, formed a circle in the grassy clearing. With playful enthusiasm, they borrowed shields from the guards and, armed with swords, began the traditional sword-and-shield dance. The rhythmic clanging of metal filled the air as they moved in unison, their voices rising in spirited war songs. Their movements were precise yet playful, each shield beat echoing their camaraderie.

When the men concluded their performance, the young women, led by Lady Dhalia, stepped forward. Laughing and twirling, they performed the flower-dress dance, their light gowns spinning gracefully with each step. Their smiles were radiant as they turned toward the men, and the playful gazes exchanged added to the vibrant energy of the gathering. The men clapped and cheered.

Once they sat back down again, Arthur recounted a particularly embarrassing incident involving Halsten at military school, earning hearty laughter from everyone. Freja chuckled along, casting Halsten a teasing look.

"You'll never let me live that one down, will you?" he asked, his mock exasperation earning another round of laughter.

"Never," Freja replied with a mischievous smile, her eyes sparkling. She reached over to squeeze his hand, and he gave her a tender look that spoke volumes.

Throughout the gathering, Halsten and Freja's connection was undeniable. Their gazes met often, quiet smiles and subtle touches bridging the space between them. Their love seemed to radiate, drawing warmth from everyone around them.

Eventually, as the conversations and games carried on, Halsten rose and extended a hand to Freja. "Come with me," he said softly.

Without hesitation, she let him help her to her feet, and they strolled away from the group, their fingers entwined. They wandered to a secluded spot beneath a towering weeping willow at the lake's edge. The gentle rustling of its leaves and the soft lapping of water against the shore provided a serene backdrop, isolating them in their own private world.

Halsten sat down on the cool grass, the sunlight filtering through the branches overhead. He gestured for Freja to join him, and as she settled beside him, he took her hand in his, tracing slow, deliberate circles on her palm with his thumb. The intimacy of the gesture brought a soft blush to her cheeks.

His voice, low and thoughtful, broke the silence. "Do you ever think about the life we'll share?" he asked, his gaze fixed on her.

Freja turned to him, her expression open and sincere. "All the time. And every time I do, I feel excited…but also a little scared."

Halsten tilted his head slightly, his brows drawing together in concern. "Why are you scared, my love?"

After a moment of hesitation, Freja sighed and spoke. "It's the recent attacks on the traders," she admitted. "And the demonstrations. The anger of the people has put me on edge. I can't stop thinking about it."

Halsten's expression softened as he pulled her hand closer to his chest. "I know, my love," he said reassuringly. "These events have worried all of us. But my father is determined to find the robbers and bring them to justice. Once we've restored peace, we can continue our wedding preparations without fear."

"Oh, my prince," Freja said, her voice trembling with emotion, "I hope they are caught soon. I don't want these dark times to overshadow our wedding."

Halsten leaned forward, wrapping his arms around her and pulling her close. He gently lifted her chin, his eyes locking on to hers. "I will ensure you are always safe, Freja. You are my heart. Nothing and no one will ever separate us."

Her eyes glistened with unshed tears as she replied, her voice steady despite the emotion in her words, "I will always love you, Halsten Elliot Verdant, prince of EdenRock."

He kissed her forehead tenderly. "And I will always love you, Freja Marie Glenwood," he whispered. "You already make everything right."

A radiant smile spread across her face as she rested her head against his shoulder. They sat in peaceful silence, their friends' distant laughter floating across the lake like a melody. The world around them seemed to disappear at that moment. Their love felt unshakable, a bond strong enough to weather anything that lay ahead. Without speaking, they both understood this love would be the foundation of their future—a life built on trust, partnership, and unwavering devotion.

After a while, Halsten began to smile.

"What?" Freja asked.

"I saw you training the other day in the inner court of Glenwood," he said with a playful grin.

Freja blinked, surprise flashing across her features. "When was this?" she asked.

"When I visited Albert last."

She gasped, her hands flying to her cheeks. "I will break my brother's leg!"

Halsten laughed and shook his head. "Oh, no, don't blame Albert. He didn't bring me to the court."

"Then how did you see me?"

"I wandered away from the hall," Halsten admitted sheepishly. "I wanted to find you. When I saw you and Alfred through the drapes, I couldn't resist watching. I must say, you are incredibly skilled."

Freja's face reddened as she looked away. "I promised my father I wouldn't let anyone see me train," she explained. "It was the only condition under which he allowed me to learn."

Halsten tilted his head, his smile softening. "I like a strong lady— someone who is unsuspecting, beautiful, yet capable."

She chuckled, her confidence returning. "You should see Dhalia and Dora with a sword."

"Dhalia? Dora?" Halsten asked, his brows shooting up. "No way."

Freja nodded, her eyes twinkling with mischief. "Dhalia is the reason I decided to learn. Her father began training her when she was eight, and she taught Dora. When we started playing together, they would challenge the boys to duels. I begged my father for permission to train."

"And he allowed it?" Halsten leaned closer, intrigued.

"Eventually," Freja said with a laugh. "But only under strict conditions. I had to promise not to train in public and always to carry myself as a lady."

Halsten's grin widened. "Albert told me a little about it. But it was your father who mentioned it to mine."

Freja's eyes widened. "The king knows?"

"Yes." Halsten chuckled. "And he approves. He said a future queen should know how to protect herself."

"Really?" she asked with a smile.

"At this rate, you might be more skilled than me soon."

"You know, Halsten, excellence is what you always do, not when someone is watching," Freja said, placing her hands at her waist and lifting her chin in pride.

She bit her lower lip in amusement. "Oh, Halsten," she said, "you make me so happy."

He retook her hand, his thumb brushing lightly over her knuckles. "That's all I ever want to do, my love."

The pair stayed beneath the willow tree, wrapped in the quiet serenity of their love. The world beyond the lake seemed distant and insignificant compared to the promise of their shared future.

Halsten's expression turned calm and reflective as he gazed at the tranquil waters of Lake Tolki. Freja noticed the change and leaned closer, her brows furrowing with concern.

"What is it, my love?" she asked softly.

He turned to her, a wistful smile tugging at his lips. "This place," he began, gesturing around them, "it's where my ancestor, King Isolde, met his wife, Ida."

"Really?" Freja asked. "Tell me their love story."

Halsten's smile deepened as he adjusted himself on the grass beside her. "It's a tale passed down through the family," he began. "When Isolde turned eighteen, his parents, King Melkin Verdant and Queen Ingrid Cidel, arranged for young women from nearly every noble house to visit EdenRock, hoping he would choose a bride. But none of them captured his heart."

Freja tilted her head, listening intently. "How did he meet Ida, then?"

"One afternoon," Halsten continued, "Isolde was riding by this very lake when he saw a noble family crossing on the other side. He paused to observe them from behind a tree and was immediately struck by a young woman with silky black hair. She had her head out of the wagon, enjoying the breeze, and her smile…" Halsten trailed off, his voice softening. "He said her smile stole his heart in that moment."

Freja sighed, a dreamy look in her eyes. "It sounds like love at first sight."

"It was," Halsten agreed. "But before he could get a better look, someone called her back inside the wagon. Isolde couldn't let her go without knowing who she was, so he trailed their carriage to Shaw Hill. When they entered the city gates, he left his horse behind and followed on foot. He was so captivated that he lost himself in thought. A guard eventually stopped him and asked what he was doing."

Freja laughed lightly. "Oh, no, what did he say?"

Halsten chuckled. "He stammered something about admiring the city and quickly left to avoid suspicion. But from that day forward, he couldn't stay away. He returned to Shaw Hill, hiding in the bushes and hoping to see her again."

Freja smiled, her eyes alight with fascination. "Did he ever see her?"

Halsten nodded, his tone growing more reverent. "One day, on his way to Shaw through Tolki, he found her swimming in the lake with some other young women, surrounded by guards. When they noticed the Verdant emblem on his armor, the guards didn't stop him. Instead, they announced, 'The Prince of EdenRock has arrived.' The ladies quickly covered themselves, but Ida was among them."

Freja clasped her hands, leaning closer. "And what did he do?"

Halsten grinned. "He introduced himself, of course. 'Good day, ladies,' he said. 'I am Isolde of EdenRock.' The young lady, bold and unafraid, stepped forward. 'Good day, Your Highness,' she replied. 'I am Ida, from the house of Shaw, and this is my sister, Liv.'"

Freja's face softened, and she whispered, "How perfect."

"Isolde told her he had admired her from afar and hoped to meet her. Ida smiled and said, 'I know. I saw you at the lake, in the woods, and at Shaw Hill Castle.' She then walked up to Isolde, placing her mouth to his ear, and whispered, 'I was waiting for when you would be courageous enough to come for what you wanted.'"

Freja gasped. "She'd noticed him all along?"

Halsten nodded. "She had. Isolde was embarrassed but determined. He told her how her beauty and smile had enchanted him and how he'd spoken to the lake, vowing to cherish it forever if it helped him find his love."

Freja's cheeks flushed as she asked, "What did Ida say?"

"She walked closer to him again." Halsten's voice softened with the memory of the story. "'Ask me what you wanted to ask me,' she said, challenging him gently. Isolde, overcome, confessed his feelings.

"'Lady Ida,' he began, his voice steady but thick with emotion. 'For days, I have wandered these shores, speaking to the waters of you, the vision who has stolen my peace.'

"Ida tilted her head slightly, a soft smile playing on her lips. 'The waters have held your words, Your Highness?' she asked playfully.

"Isolde smiled, encouraged by her warmth. He took another step closer, his eyes locked on hers. 'Your smile ignited my heart the moment I saw you,' he confessed. 'Your eyes, as deep and endless as this lake, have haunted my dreams. My soul is yours—every beat of my heart now belongs to you.'

"Ida's cheeks flushed, but she held his gaze, her expression open and curious. 'You speak of dreams, my prince, but what of the waking world?'

"'The waking world is brighter because of you,' Isolde replied. 'The sight of your hair catching the sunlight, the way the breeze seems to carry your laughter, your voice has enchanted me. My lips can speak only your name, Ida of Shaw Hill. My hands ache to hold yours, not as a fleeting touch but as a promise of forever.'

"Ida's breath caught, her fingers instinctively brushing against her lips. 'You honor me with your words,' she said, trembling slightly. 'But words alone cannot bridge the distance between us.'

"Isolde stepped closer still, his voice lowering as he poured his heart into every syllable. 'Then let me close that distance. Let my arms shield you, my hands cherish you, and my soul be bound to yours. My eyes see only you, my ears long for your laughter, and my heart, Ida—it beats only for you. I beg you, unite the House of Shaw with the House of Verdant. Save me from this aching desire that burns brighter each day.'

"Ida's eyes shone with a mixture of joy and awe. 'You speak with such certainty, Your Highness. Are you not afraid your heart will lead you astray?'

"'Never,' Isolde replied. 'If I am led by love, I know my heart will guide me true. Ida, you are my guiding star, my light in the darkness.'

"For a moment, the world seemed to fall silent, the lake reflecting the brilliance of the sky as if mirroring the intensity of their connection. Ida stepped forward, her hand reaching up to rest gently on his chest. 'If your heart beats for me,' she said softly, 'then let mine answer in kind.'

"She leaned in, her lips brushing Isolde's in a tender kiss that sent a shiver through him. When they pulled apart, Ida smiled. 'You have my heart, Isolde of EdenRock.'

"His grin spread wide, his joy unrestrained as he turned to the lake. With arms raised, he shouted, 'Hear me, EdenRock! I have found love at Lake Tolki! Ida of Shaw Hill is the keeper of my heart!'

"Behind them, Ida's sister Liv placed her hands over her mouth, giggling with delight as their maidens clapped and the guards exchanged knowing smiles. Ida laughed softly, her hand slipping into Isolde's."

"Oh, my love, that was beautiful. What happened next?" Freja asked.

"My love," Prince Halsten said. "I am here because of their love, and it is their love that gives me hope for ours."

Reaching out, he wiped a tear from Freja's eye, and she embraced him. He kissed her on the forehead, and they sat there looking over the lake.

When the sun began to set, Prince Halsten, Freja, and their companions mounted their horses and began the journey back to Aldrich City. The group, still lighthearted from the day's festivities, rode in close formation as they passed through the dense Blue Gate Pass. The towering trees cast long shadows over the trail, their branches swaying gently in the evening breeze.

Suddenly, without warning, arrows rained down from the canopy. Their sharp whistling pierced the air, followed by startled cries as some struck the ground dangerously close to the party. Within moments, the group was surrounded by masked assailants who emerged from the forest, their faces obscured by scarves that revealed only their eyes.

Halsten's friends, ever vigilant, quickly dismounted and formed a protective circle around the prince, Freja, Dhalia, and Dora. Swords were drawn, and the air grew tense as both sides braced for a confrontation.

Halsten stepped forward. "Who are you?" he demanded, his voice cutting through the eerie silence. "Show yourselves!"

The assailants offered no reply, responding instead with raised swords and fighting stances. Without further warning, they lunged forward, and the forest erupted into chaos.

The clash of steel echoed through the trees as Halsten and his companions fought valiantly against their attackers. With the guards from Aldrich City by their side, they skillfully engaged the enemies in a fierce battle. Weapons flashed in the dim light, and the air filled with the sound of grunts, cries, and the occasional shout of orders.

Halsten's blade moved with precision, his every strike calculated and decisive. Freja, shielded by Dhalia and Dora, watched in tense silence, her heart racing.

Despite the party's skill and bravery, the number of attackers continued to grow. They seemed to be appearing out of the shadows. Some guards fell, their cries cutting through the chaos as they were struck down. One of the masked men, seizing the opportunity, broke through the defenses and grabbed Freja. His arm coiled around her neck, holding her tightly as he pressed a dagger to her throat.

"Stop," he bellowed, his voice cutting through the din, "or I will kill her!"

Halsten immediately raised his hand, signaling his companions to halt. The fighting ceased, and the forest grew eerily quiet once more, save for the ragged breathing of the combatants. Halsten stepped forward, his sword lowered.

"Let her go," he said, his voice steady despite the fury in his eyes. "I'll give you whatever you want. Just let her go."

The masked man tightened his grip on Freja, pulling her closer. His voice dripped with malice as he replied, "I will take her from you, so you'll know what it feels like to lose everything."

Halsten's jaw tightened, but his eyes remained fixed on Freja's. He could see her fear, but he also saw the fire of determination in her gaze. Before he could respond, Martin, positioned at the far left with Albert, charged at the group in a desperate attempt to free Freja. One of the attackers intercepted him, slashing him down with brutal efficiency. Martin collapsed to the ground, his lifeless body sprawled among the fallen leaves.

The masked man shouted, "Toss your swords over, or she dies!"

Halsten stepped forward slowly. "Wait," he said, his voice calm. He crouched and placed his sword on the ground but angled it slightly to the side as his eyes locked with Freja's. The unspoken plan passed between them in an instant.

In one swift motion, she drove her elbow into the attacker's ribs, forcing a grunt from him as his grip loosened. She darted toward Halsten's sword, her movements fluid and decisive. At that exact moment, Halsten pulled a knife from his boot and hurled it with deadly precision. The blade struck the assailant in the shoulder, forcing him to stumble backward. His eyes widened in shock as blood seeped through his clothing, staining it dark red.

Dhalia and Dora rushed to Freja's side, shielding her once again. With their leader down, the remaining attackers faltered. Halsten and his companions surged forward to drive them back. Some were slain in the ensuing skirmish, while others retreated into the forest's shadows, disappearing as quickly as they had appeared.

Despite his injury, the attacker managed to stay upright, supported by two of his comrades, who'd quickly moved to his side. In a swift, practiced motion, they hoisted him onto a horse. He clung to the saddle as the group retreated. Halsten's party, though momentarily outnumbered, continued to fight fiercely, their swords clashing against the remaining attackers.

As the skirmish dragged on, more of the masked men began to mount their horses and flee. However, one of them wasn't quick enough. Zoresh, with the reflexes of a seasoned warrior, pulled a knife from his belt and threw it with precision. The blade struck the fleeing man in the back of his right knee, and he collapsed to the ground with a howl of pain.

Two of Halsten's guards immediately grabbed the man and forced him up, holding him firmly in place. The sounds of battle faded as the remaining attackers disappeared into the forest, leaving Halsten and his companions to regroup. Breathing heavily, Halsten sheathed his sword and approached the captured man.

The assailant's face was partially obscured by a turban wrapped tightly around his head. Halsten reached forward and pulled it away, revealing a defiant expression. The man's eyes darted around the group, scanning their faces as if memorizing each one. His gaze finally locked onto Halsten, his mouth drawing into a faint, mocking grin.

"Who sent you?" Halsten demanded, his tone sharp and authoritative.

The man said nothing, his grin growing wider as he stared into Halsten's eyes.

"I won't ask again," Halsten warned, his voice low and menacing. "Who sent you?"

In response, the man spat defiantly on the prince's boots. A murmur of outrage rippled through the group, and Zoresh stepped forward, his expression dark.

"Let me deal with him," he growled.

Halsten gave a slight nod, and Zoresh moved swiftly. He looped a bowstring around the man's neck, pressing his knee into his back and pulling the string taut. The man gasped and clawed as his air supply was cut off. His face turned red and his struggles grew frantic, and he waved an arm in desperation.

Halsten raised a hand, signaling Zoresh to stop. Reluctantly, he released the tension, allowing the man to gasp for air. Halsten crouched down, leveling his gaze with the attacker's. "If you tell me who sent you, I'll let you go unharmed," he offered.

The man coughed, spitting blood onto the ground. Then, to everyone's surprise, he began to laugh—a hollow, eerie sound that sent a chill through the group. His bloodied lips twisted into a defiant smirk. "You will learn nothing from me," he rasped.

Zoresh moved to tighten the bowstring again, but before he could act, the man bit down hard. The sickening sound of tearing flesh was followed by a spurt of blood as his severed tongue fell from his mouth. Blood gushed uncontrollably, pouring down his chin and staining his clothes.

Freja and Dora turned away, their faces pale with horror, while Dhalia stood her ground, her expression grim but unflinching. The man's body convulsed violently as he choked on his blood. He fell to his side, his lifeless eyes staring blankly ahead.

Halsten stood up slowly, his expression a mix of frustration and disgust. "Search his body," he ordered. "See if anything can tell us who he was."

The guards obeyed, patting down the man's clothing and examining his belongings. They found nothing—no crest, markings, or documents—that could provide a clue to his identity.

Zoresh picked up the discarded turban and inspected it, shaking his head. "Nothing here either. These men were careful."

Halsten turned to his companions, his gaze somber. "Let's not waste any more time here. We've lost enough already."

Arthur and Frodio began digging a shallow grave for Martin, whose body lay nearby, and the rest of the fallen guards in their team. After they'd finished, Albert retrieved Martin's sword and placed it atop the grave, his expression heavy with sorrow. He bowed his head and murmured a quiet prayer, his voice barely audible over the whispering wind.

The group mounted their horses in silence, the weight of what had transpired hanging heavily over them. As they left the forest behind and rode toward Aldrich City, the unanswered questions lingered in their minds. The attack had shaken them, and the mysterious assailants' motives remained an ominous puzzle.

CHAPTER 11

THAT SAME NIGHT, THE LORDS who had previously dined at Lord
Warhouse's house began to file into Bear Cave Castle at the request
of Darius, conveyed through Lord Luterodt. Upon arrival at the castle
gates, each man was asked to leave his horse and weapons with his guard
before entering. The guards were taken to the Bear Cave guards' hall.

Darius, Xinovia, and Lord Warhouse stood inside the castle to greet
each lord and welcome them. Once all the guests had arrived, they led
them to the castle's grand dining hall, where they were seated around a
large mahogany table, and a mouthwatering meal was served.

Burning torches adorned the walls, and handmade banners displayed
the head of a bear. Near the back door were tables with firewood-baked
jars filled with wine and ale. The far corners of the room featured
decorated flowerpots with fresh-scented roses, tulips, and imported lotus
flowers. Underfoot, the polished floors showcased a carved head of a
bear in the shiny stone.

With a smile, Darius took his seat at the head, and Xinovia sat on his
right side. He picked up a golden cup, and stamped it on the table. Maids
entered the room, picked up the wine jars, and began to serve the guests.

Lord Luterodt, sitting to the left of Darius, noticed one of the maids,
a beautiful girl with silky black hair and brown eyes. With a grin, he
lifted his cup and said, "Hey, maid, can you serve me some wine?"

She brought her jar to his side and began to fill his glass. Lord
Luterodt lifted his left hand, placed it on her back, and slowly moved
it down to rub her buttocks. Startled, the maid jolted forward, spilling

the wine into his lap. "What a clumsy maid you are!" Lord Luterodt shouted, fuming.

She apologized, but Xinovia signaled with her eyes for her to leave the hall. The maid placed the jar on the side table and walked out, crying.

Darius and the other lords laughed loudly, but Xinovia covered her laugh with her hand.

Once they had quieted down, Darius stood up and said, "To EdenRock," lifting his cup high.

The lords and Xinovia followed suit. "To EdenRock, to the realm!"

Darius continued, "My friends, I have invited you all to an important discussion. But first, I want you to enjoy the drinks, the food, and the entertainment to lighten your hearts before we begin."

Xinovia announced, "My lord, the food is ready to be served." The lords smiled, and she clapped her hands.

Smiling, Xinovia said, "My lords, please eat and visit with my lord."

The men stood and responded in unison, "My lady."

Xinovia then headed to the door. Lord Brucken, cutting into his portion of roast, remarked, "This is a feast fit for kings, Darius. You've outdone yourself."

Lord Luterodt nodded in agreement. "Indeed, the hospitality here is exceptional. And to reference scripture, you have laid a table before me in the presence of my enemies, but they are not here to see me eat." Everyone in the room burst out laughing.

When Xinovia reached the door, the guards opened it for her. Mefford, entered, dressed in dark brown trousers and a jacket, black boots on his feet and a sword hanging at his waist. He stopped and embraced her.

"Mother," he said, kissing her cheeks.

"Son," she replied, pushing a strand of hair off his face before walking away.

Mefford removed his sword and placed it on a table near the door, then walked toward the dining table. "Father," he said, embracing Darius. The lords stood up, and Mefford turned to greet them. "My lords, welcome to Bear Cave."

The men bowed their heads and responded, "My prince."

Mefford sat down in the chair his mother had just vacated, took the cup before him, and beat it against the table. A maid entered, picked up a jar from the side table, and poured him some red wine. Mefford gulped it down in one tilt and asked for more. The maid poured another cup, placed the jar back, and left the room. Mefford picked up a plate and filled it with food, then began to eat.

After Darius, his son, and their guests had dined, Darius clapped his hands. A guard approached from a side door, and Darius whispered something in his ear, then sent him away. The back doors, through which the food had come, opened, and four young women entered. They wore white clothing—very little of it—with colorful beads around their waists. They were followed by three men, two with drums and one with a flute. Once inside, the musicians began to play while the women danced seductively around Darius's guests. The lords watched with varying levels of excitement.

Once the entertainment was over, the performers left the room. Lord Luterodt watched them go, dazed and licking his lips. Mefford noticed this, traced his eyes to the back of the young women, smiled, and shook his head. "Enjoying yourself, Lord Luterodt?" he asked with a chuckle.

Lord Luterodt snapped out of his daze. "Ah, yes, Prince Mefford. The entertainment was…quite captivating."

Darius stood up and began to speak. "My lords of the realm, thank you so much for coming to my home today. What we will discuss here is very important to the future of our kingdom. Our friend, Lord Warhouse, has informed me that you have taken the oath of blood, so anything we discuss here will be kept in your hearts until death. By taking the oath, you have sworn to face death if you show weakness or speak of our cause to anyone outside of this group, including your own family."

The lords responded in unison, "Yes, Your Grace, until death."

Darius continued, "The recent events—losing lives mysteriously and now our livelihood and fortunes—prove to all of us that our kingdom is weak and exposed." The room filled with murmurs and nods of agreement. "If we allow thieves to scare us, what else should we expect? Our neighboring kingdoms will take advantage of our weakness. If we can't stop robbers from terrorizing us, how can we stop an army? To have a weak king is like walking in a pasture and lighting it on fire at the same time—you choose to burn yourself to death."

The lords again murmured and nodded in response.

"You, as lords, are entrusted with the responsibility of leading and protecting our people, our land, and our properties," he said. "If we cannot do the simple things we are trusted with, how can we look into our people's eyes and ask them to sacrifice when needed? I know that some among you at the council are brave and would not stand for our kingdom being destroyed by some petty thieves. A weak king makes the work of brave people very difficult. I have called you here not only so you can listen to me babble but also to decide the future of our kingdom."

The lords continued to whisper as Darius sat down. The tension in the room was palpable, each man weighing the gravity of the situation and the decision they were about to make.

Lord Luterodt stood up. "My lords, our host is right. EdenRock has become a laughingstock. We have our citizens breathing down our necks for their losses. Very soon, the noble houses will be overrun by their anger. However, our king's weakness has brought us to this point, and there seems to be no end to this shame and embarrassment. Alaric is a coward—I believe things would have been better if our host, His Grace, who is the rightful heir, were on the throne instead."

The room fell silent as his words sank in. The gravity of the situation weighed heavily on the lords, each one contemplating their kingdom's future. Lord Warhouse stood up next. "Thank you, Your Grace, for bringing us to your home. You are brave, and what you have done with Bear Cave, along with the feeling of respect among your men, shows your strength and authority.

"I agree with you, my lords. The situation has brought panic to our kingdom, and traders are afraid to come to EdenRock because of the current unrest within our land. The disappearances, deaths, and robberies have affected everything. We are paying heavily to hire guards to secure farm supplies from the farm colony. Times have changed for us drastically in this short period, and we must act differently to survive. So, I support you, Your Grace, in whatever way you need from me."

Darius inclined his head appreciatively. "Thank you, Lord Warhouse. Your support means a great deal to me. The burden on our people is evident. Their fear, their frustration—it all points to one truth. We can no longer afford to let our kingdom suffer under weak leadership."

Lord Kraft, who had been sitting quietly until now, suddenly rose to his feet. His expression was contemplative, and his tone carried a note of hesitation. "My lords," he began, "I have heard all that you have said, and I agree that these are not the times we once enjoyed. The kingdom faces challenges that demand our attention." His gaze swept the room. "But perhaps…perhaps we should first speak with the king. Let us help him see the gravity of the situation and—"

The reaction was immediate. The room erupted into noise as the other lords voiced their disapproval. Some shook their heads, while others muttered angrily under their breath. The contrast between Lord Kraft's current suggestion and his more aggressive stance during their last meeting was glaring.

Darius's lips curled into a thin, humorless smile as he watched the scene unfold. He remained silent, letting the lords' dissent grow louder.

Lord Kraft, undeterred, raised his voice slightly to regain the room's attention. "As I said," he pressed on, "perhaps the king's plans have yielded some developments—updates that might benefit the kingdom's efforts. Before we take any drastic measures, we should consider whether the situation has changed."

Lord Luterodt scoffed, crossing his arms over his chest. "Changed? The only change is the number of lives lost and the goods stolen. How much longer must we wait for this so-called leadership to act?"

Lord Warhouse nodded. "The king's inaction has emboldened the criminals plaguing our lands. If there had been any progress, we would have seen it by now. Waiting for more updates while our people starve and our trade routes remain unsafe is no solution."

The murmurs of agreement around the room grew louder, and all eyes turned back to Lord Kraft. He hesitated, his confidence wavering under the combined weight of their disdain.

Darius finally spoke, his voice calm but cutting through the noise like a blade. "Lord Kraft, your sudden change of heart is curious. At Lord Warhouse's residence, you were among the most vocal about the king's failure, yet now you suggest we wait for his plans to bear fruit?"

Lord Kraft stiffened under Darius's gaze. "Your Grace," he said cautiously, "I am merely suggesting that we exhaust all avenues before taking action that could divide the realm. Unity is as crucial as decisive action."

Darius leaned forward, his hands clasped on the table. His expression hardened, and his tone carried a dangerous edge. "Unity is built on trust and strength, Lord Kraft. Tell me, do you truly believe the king has a plan? Or are you simply too afraid to act without his blessing?"

The room fell silent, the tension thick enough to cut. Lord Kraft shifted uncomfortably but did not immediately respond. Darius's piercing gaze never wavered, pinning him in place.

After a moment, Lord Luterodt broke the silence. "Enough of this hesitation," he declared, slamming his hand on the table. "The people are looking to us for answers, not excuses. If we wait any longer, nothing will be left to save."

The lords murmured their agreement again, their frustration replaced with grim resolve. Lord Kraft sank back into his chair, his earlier conviction visibly diminished.

Darius rose to his feet, commanding the attention of the room. Each word he spoke carried the weight of authority. "The time for waiting has passed," he said. "The kingdom needs leadership—real leadership. If the king cannot protect our people, it falls to us to do so."

The lords nodded solemnly. As the meeting continued, Darius outlined his vision for addressing the kingdom's growing instability. Though not everyone agreed on the methods, it was clear that the tide was turning, and the seeds of rebellion had begun to take root.

The air in the grand hall of Bear Cave Castle was tense, though the nobles attempted to maintain a veneer of civility. Darius's expression was composed, but his knuckles whitened as he gripped the armrests of his chair. Beneath his calm exterior, a storm was brewing. He leaned slightly to the side and whispered something into Mefford's ear. Mefford nodded, rose from his seat, and strode toward a side entrance. He retrieved his sword and exited without a word, the soft echo of his boots fading into the corridor.

The room fell silent. Lord Bracken's sentiments resonated with many in the hall, their frustrations mirrored in his bold declaration. Darius recognized the opportunity and rose to his feet again.

"My lords," he began, his voice steady but forceful, "we find ourselves at a crossroads. Patience has done nothing but diminish our standing and weaken our kingdom. We need a leader who will decisively restore EdenRock's honor and strength. I am ready to shoulder that responsibility, but I need your support."

The lords listened attentively, their loyalty to Darius growing more apparent with each passing moment.

"Thank you all for your visit and invaluable support," Darius continued. His eyes locked onto Lord Kraft, and a faint grin tugged at the corner of his lips. "Even you, Lord Kraft. But I urge you to show strength. Weakness does not endure, and courage will be required of all of us in the days ahead."

He straightened, his tone becoming more resolute. "I am grateful to have such steadfast allies as yourselves. At the right time, if the need arises, I trust I can count on each of you."

The lords responded in unison, "Yes, Your Grace." Only Lord Kraft hesitated, his eyes betraying a flicker of fear.

Darius's piercing gaze lingered on him briefly before sweeping across the room, and his expression hardened as he spoke again. "My brothers, remember this—our greatest strength lies in silence. I trust each of you to keep this close to your chest. The element of surprise will be our greatest weapon."

With that, he dismissed the gathering, though the lords remained in the hall, engaging in friendly conversations over wine and lingering in small groups.

Darius approached Lord Warhouse, who was nursing a goblet of wine near a corner of the room. He gestured for the man to step aside with him, away from the other nobles.

"How is our plan within the palace court progressing?" Darius asked, his voice low but sharp.

Lord Warhouse took a sip before responding. "We have several of our men already positioned," he said quietly. "Tomorrow morning, another trip is scheduled."

"Are you confident that no one has discovered the switches?" Darius pressed, his eyes narrowing.

"Yes, Your Grace. All precautions have been taken."

"Good." Darius nodded. "Keep me informed of every development."

Warhouse inclined his head respectfully, and Darius turned to walk away. However, before he could take another step, Lord Luterodt staggered toward him, swaying faintly as he approached. His flushed face and unsteady gait betrayed his overindulgence in wine.

"Your Grace!" he exclaimed, a broad smile spreading across his face. "Thank you for the delicious dinner and the hospitality. The food was exceptional, and the entertainment—well, it was good for the heart. If I weren't so respectful of your position, I might have joined those beautiful swans on the dance floor myself."

Darius allowed a faint grin to cross his lips. "Those who are not lords do not enjoy such privileges."

Lord Luterodt laughed loudly, but when he noticed Darius's cool expression, his laughter trailed off awkwardly. Darius leaned in slightly, his voice dropping to a sharp whisper. "Your advances toward my wife's maid, Lucile, were inappropriate."

Luterodt blinked, then grinned foolishly. "Lucile," he mused, "what a romantic name. Ah, Your Grace, those dove-like eyes of hers stir something in me I haven't felt in years."

Darius's smile turned cold. "Stay away from that one," he warned. "She's from Orin. Do you know what that means?"

Luterodt's face paled slightly. "Orin, you say?" he muttered nervously. "Oh, my lord," he then said, his sly grin returning, "perhaps I, too, should have an Orin woman for myself. I hear they are…skilled in the chambers."

Darius's expression darkened, though he maintained a controlled demeanor. Just then, a familiar voice whispered, "He does not respect you."

Darius's eyes turned cold as he leaned closer to Lord Luterodt, his tone calm but laced with menace. "You are lucky I like you, or I would have separated your head from your shoulders, fed it to my lions, sent your headless body to your family, and then attended your funeral to mourn you."

Lord Luterodt's smirk vanished, replaced by a mask of fear. He opened his mouth to respond but thought better of it. Without another word, Darius turned and walked away, leaving Lord Luterodt rooted in place, fear coursing through his veins.

Moments later, Mefford approached his father. He nodded silently, and Darius returned the gesture before joining the remaining guests, mingling briefly as they prepared to depart. One by one, the nobles filed into the courtyard, where their guards waited with ready horses. Mounting their steeds, they departed Bear Cave Castle, disappearing into the night.

As the last of the lords exited, Orb's voice returned, a whisper like a snake's hiss in Darius's ear. "Do not let him leave. He will betray you."

Darius's eyes narrowed, and he turned his gaze toward Tapas, his loyal commander, who was standing nearby with one remaining eye trained on him. Tapas nodded, understanding the unspoken command.

Darius called two guards to his side and gave them brief instructions in hushed tones. They bowed and left swiftly, mounting their horses and riding out of the compound. Three more guards, their faces obscured, followed shortly after. They veered off the main road into the forest, taking a hidden path to intercept their target.

The guards dismounted in the dense shadows, their horses blending into the trees. They waited silently, their swords drawn, the woods alive with the occasional rustle of leaves and the distant hoot of an owl. Within minutes, the sound of approaching hoofbeats grew louder.

Lord Kraft appeared, flanked by two of his guards. He slowed, peering cautiously into the darkness. "Who is there?" he called, his voice edged with suspicion.

No response came from the hidden figures. Lord Kraft scowled and gestured to his men. "Check it out," he ordered.

The two guards dismounted, their swords glinting faintly in the moonlight as they stepped toward the shadows. Suddenly, one of Darius's men lunged from the darkness, plunging a dagger into Lord Kraft's chest. He gasped, his eyes wide with shock as he toppled from his horse, clutching the wound.

His guards spun around, charging toward the attacker, but two more figures emerged from the bushes. In coordinated strikes, they slashed across the guards' abdomens, cutting them down with brutal efficiency. The men crumpled to the ground, blood pooling beneath them.

Lord Kraft lay on the ground, his breathing labored, his face contorted in pain. He sneered up at his assailants. "Darius's dogs," he rasped. "He is too much of a coward to kill me himself, so he sends you. Afraid I'd tell the king about his treachery."

Tapas stepped forward, pulling back his hood to reveal his scarred face. He smirked, looking down at the dying man. "You're right about one thing, Lord Kraft," he said coldly. "You won't live to deliver any message to the king. But it's not cowardice—it's strategy."

With a swift motion, he slashed Lord Kraft's throat, silencing him forever. Blood gushed from the wound, and the man's body fell limp.

Tapas spat on the corpse. "Let's see how the dead will carry tales." He turned to his men. "Dispose of the bodies. Throw them into the valley for the wolves."

They obeyed, dragging the lifeless bodies of Lord Kraft and his men to the edge of the hill. One by one, they shoved them over the precipice, the sound of them tumbling down lost in the night.

Just as they finished, Tapas's expression darkened. He turned and struck down both men with swift, precise blows without warning.

"Why, Commander?" one of them gasped.

Tapas sheathed his sword and grabbed the ankles of the fallen men. "Because only one person can hold a secret," he muttered. He dragged them to the edge and kicked them into the valley to join the others.

Tapas mounted his horse and rode, his hooves clattering against the stone, until he reached the Bear Cave Castle gates. Once inside the compound, he dismounted and went directly to the castle's hall, where Darius awaited him.

"My lord," Tapas said, bowing slightly. "It is done. Lord Kraft and his guards will not be able to speak to anyone, least of all the king."

Darius looked at him with satisfaction, a faint smile on his lips. "You have served me well," he said, clapping the commander on the shoulder. "Remember, you must carry this secret to your grave."

"Of course, my lord," Tapas replied solemnly. "No one will hear of this from me."

Darius turned away, his gaze fixed on the flickering flames of the hearth. The warm glow illuminated his sharp features, casting long shadows across the stone walls of his chamber. A grim sense of satisfaction settled over him as he whispered under his breath, "He who shows weakness shall die by the same flaw." He walked to his study, entered, and closed the door behind him.

A smooth yet sinister voice echoed through the chamber as the words left his lips. It was the unmistakable tone of Orb, the Virgil, his unseen tormentor. "He who lives by shedding blood shall one day see their blood on another's sword," the voice whispered, sending an icy chill through Darius.

His body stiffened, and his face twisted into a mask of rage. He spun around as if to confront the invisible speaker. "No one can kill me!" he bellowed, the sound reverberating off the stone walls. "I am a true descendant of Aldrich!"

His chest heaved with each breath, his fists clenched so tightly that his knuckles turned white. The silence that followed his outburst was deafening, broken only by the crackling of the fire. For a moment, it felt like the shadows were mocking him.

The door to the chamber burst open, and Xinovia hurried in, her emerald-green gown flowing behind her. Her face was a mixture of concern and alarm. "What upsets you, my love?" she asked.

Darius turned to her, his expression softening just slightly, though the tension in his body remained. "Nothing," he replied after a pause, his tone measured. "I was merely thinking aloud."

Xinovia stepped closer, her delicate hand resting gently on his arm. "Thinking aloud?" she repeated, her eyes searching his face. "Such thoughts bring you to shout at the walls?"

Darius forced a small smile, though it didn't reach his eyes. "The burdens of leadership weigh heavily, my dear. There is much to consider, much to plan. Sometimes, the mind needs release."

She studied him for a moment, her gaze sharp and intuitive. "The burdens of leadership do not include shouting into the night," she said softly. "Something else troubles you."

Darius's smile faltered, and he pulled away slightly, turning his back to her. He stared into the fire, the flames reflecting in his dark eyes. "It's nothing you need to concern yourself with."

Xinovia hesitated, sensing his growing agitation but knowing better than to press him further. "If you ever wish to share those burdens," she said, "I am here, my love. Always."

Darius gave a curt nod, his gaze never leaving the fire. "I know," he replied. "Now, go and rest. The night grows late."

Reluctantly, she retreated, casting one last look at him before leaving the room. As the door closed behind her, Darius clenched his jaw, the weight of words spoken by the invisible voice still pressing heavily on his mind.

In the silence, it returned, mocking and ominous. "You can dismiss her, but you cannot dismiss me, Darius. You cannot outrun what waits for you in the shadows."

Darius's face twisted with fury, and he grabbed a goblet from the table, hurling it into the hearth. The metal clanged loudly against the stone, scattering embers and sending smoke into the air. "Leave me be, you wretched specter!" His roar echoed in the empty hall.

The night fell silent once more, save for the crackling of the fire. But even in the quiet, the weight of Orb's prophecy lingered, gnawing at the edges of Darius's resolve. He stood alone in the flickering light, his shadow stretching long and dark across the chamber walls—a stark reminder of the forces he could not control.

CHAPTER 12

THE FOLLOWING DAY, THE KING called his council to brief them on the robbery update and discuss the attack on the prince and his friends. The noblemen arrived on horseback, while some women came in wagons, each accompanied by their guards. The king's guards announced each member of the council.

The Northern and Southern nobles gathered in the grand hall of Aldrich Castle. The atmosphere was tense, and the recent events hung heavily over the room.

As Alaric entered, the nobles rose in deference, bowing before their ruler. The king sat down at the head of the table, his expression grave. "My lords and ladies," he began, his voice steady and commanding, "we are gathered today to address two matters of great urgency. First, the increasing reports of robberies along our trade routes, and second, the recent attack on my son, Prince Halsten, and Lady Freja."

The room buzzed with murmurs of concern. Lord Ethan of Glenwood Castle was the first to speak. "Your Majesty, this escalation of violence endangers not only the crown but also the livelihoods of our people. Glenwood stands ready to assist in fortifying the trade routes and uncovering those responsible."

Lord Warhouse nodded in agreement. "Your Majesty, we must act swiftly. These attacks are not random. They are calculated, and the perpetrators are emboldened. Strengthening patrols along the main routes is imperative."

Lady Sarah Felton leaned forward, her voice calm but firm. "I propose a coordinated effort. Each noble house should contribute resources—soldiers, provisions, and intelligence—to ensure our kingdom's safety."

The king nodded at her suggestion. "A coordinated effort will indeed be required," he agreed. "Lord Murdoch, how many men can you spare for patrols?"

Lord Murdoch rose, his voice deep and unwavering. "Your Majesty, Murdoch Castle can send fifty of our finest guards to secure the trade routes. They can be dispatched immediately."

Alaric turned his attention to Lord Amos Bracken. "And from the South?"

"We can deploy an additional forty men from Bracken Castle. They are well-trained and experienced in forested terrain."

The king nodded. "Excellent. We will need every available resource to address this crisis."

Lady Elara of Glenwood Castle spoke next, her tone measured. "What of the attack on Prince Halsten and Lady Freja, Your Majesty? Is there any indication of who is behind it?"

King Alaric's expression darkened. "Not yet. Investigations are ongoing, but the attack was not a simple act of banditry. It was an orchestrated assault, and we suspect it may be connected to the trade route robberies. Until we know more, security around the royal family will be doubled."

The room fell silent as the gravity of the situation sank in. Lord Reginald broke the silence. "Your Majesty, the safety of the realm is paramount. Let us combine our strengths to root out this threat."

Dressed in the royal colors of EdenRock, Alaric reclined slightly in his seat at the head of the chamber. His piercing gaze swept over the gathered nobles before he gestured toward the floor. "My lords and ladies," he began, calm but commanding, "the floor is yours. Let us hear your thoughts on the way forward."

Lord George Salinas of Salinas Bay rose first, his weathered face etched with concern. "Your Majesty," he began, his voice steady, "this attack is not just an insult to the crown but to the entire realm. It strikes at our stability and safety. Your decision to deploy the army is sound. However, might I suggest bolstering these efforts with local militias? The people trust those they know, and local forces know the terrain."

Lord Edwin Cole nodded in agreement. "I support Lord Salinas's suggestion. Local militias could greatly enhance the search's efficiency. Speed is of the essence if we are to capture these criminals before they vanish."

From across the chamber, Lord Milton Shaw stood slowly. His tone was measured but carried an edge of skepticism. "Local militias may have their advantages," he said, "but this attack was no ordinary bandit raid. It was calculated and aimed at the royal family. Deploying the National Guard is necessary, but we must also prepare for the possibility that this was orchestrated by a force seeking to destabilize our kingdom."

Sitting nearby, Lady Sarah Felton shook her head dismissively. "Destabilization? I think you exaggerate, Lord Shaw. Inciting fears of conspiracy serves no purpose. Bandits, emboldened by the peace we've enjoyed, are the more likely culprits."

The Southern nobles, observing the exchange, began murmuring amongst themselves. Lord Amos Bracken rose abruptly, his voice resolute. "The king's actions are justified and timely. We must stand united behind him. This is no time for division or baseless speculation."

Lord Nicholas Bluevine, a Northern noble, responded sharply. "It is not division to demand that we understand the nature of this threat, Lord Bracken. The prince's safety is paramount, but we must ask why this attack happened now and whether it exposes vulnerabilities in our leadership."

Standing among the Northern lords, Lady Delena Longpatch nodded in agreement. "The king's orders are a good start," she said, "but they do not address the root cause of these attacks. Why now? Why target the prince? These questions demand answers."

From the Southern side, Lady Patricia Longrove rose gracefully. "My lords and ladies, while we debate these points, the perpetrators remain at large. We must support the king's immediate actions and allow the soldiers to apprehend the culprits. Speculation does not catch criminals."

Lord Obed Ramsgate stood next, his expression earnest. "We've been fortunate to enjoy peace under King Alaric's rule for years. This attack is not a reflection on his leadership but an anomaly. It must be dealt with swiftly and unitedly."

Lord Samuel Murdoch rose from the Northern side with a skeptical frown. "Unitedly, you say?" His voice was tinged with sarcasm. "It is easy to call for unity when you are far from the borders, untouched by raids and unrest. For some of us, the signs of weakness have been clear for years."

The chamber erupted, the Southern nobles voicing their disapproval of Lord Murdoch's remark. Alaric raised his hand, silencing the room. "Enough," he commanded. "This council is here to protect EdenRock, not to divide it."

Lord Ethan of Glenwood Castle rose and addressed the king directly. "Your Majesty, we must focus on immediate action while addressing the realm's long-term security. Deploy the National Guard, as you have ordered, but let this council investigate any potential conspiracies. Treachery within or beyond our borders cannot be ignored."

Lady Paulina Abbot, a strong-willed elderly woman, spoke next. "If treachery exists within our borders, it will not be easily uncovered. Let us support the king's immediate orders and reconvene when more evidence is gathered."

Suddenly, Lord Luterodt stood, his voice brimming with irritation. "This is no time to listen to an old lady who knows nothing of combat. We all know the Vendigores have always sought an opportunity to attack us. I say we gather our troops and march to their lands immediately."

Lady Paulina responded sharply, "My years on this council have greatly served this kingdom, Lord Luterodt. Unlike you, I think with my mind and not what lies between my thighs."

The nobles began to whisper, some stifling grins at her sharp retort. Alaric raised his hand once more, restoring order.

Lord Mark Green Hill stood next, his tone thoughtful. "My lords, let us not lose sight of our duty to the people. Panic serves no one. Swift action, paired with clear communication from the crown, will restore confidence across the realm."

Alaric rose from his seat, his expression resolute. "Your counsel is appreciated, and your loyalty to EdenRock is evident," he began. "The National Guard will proceed with their mission to search the kingdom and secure our borders. At the same time, I authorize this council to investigate any potential conspiracies with discretion. But above all, remember this: we are one kingdom. Our strength lies in our unity."

The chamber fell silent as the nobles absorbed the king's words. There were surely some of the council members who had aligned with Darius but were afraid to be found out. One by one, the lords and ladies left the council chamber, the weight of the kingdom's future heavy on their minds. Outside the castle, shadows lengthened as the sun began to set over EdenRock, its people looking to their leaders for guidance in uncertain times.

It was midnight after the council meeting, and the dungeon behind Bear Cave Castle was damp and cold, with flickering torches positioned along the stone walls. Mefford's guards entered silently, escorting a cloaked man whose face remained hidden beneath a heavy hood. Their boots echoed against the floor as they guided him into the storage room. Inside, Darius, Mefford, and Tapas waited, their expressions tense with anticipation.

Darius waved a dismissive hand toward the guards. "Leave us," he commanded. They bowed and departed, the heavy door creaking shut behind them.

Without a word, Darius approached the wall and pulled on a rusty torch bracket. A low rumble filled the air as a hidden door slid open, revealing a narrow passage. He gestured for the cloaked man to enter, followed closely by Mefford and Tapas. The secret chamber they entered was dim and confined, its air thick with the scent of old stone and secrecy.

Tapas stepped forward, gripping the man's cloak. With a swift motion, he pulled it away, revealing the man Mefford had met in the woods the night before. Tortoni stood tall despite the tension in the room, his face bearing the weariness of a hunted man.

"Tortoni, my friend," Mefford greeted him, though his voice was edged with frustration. "We need to keep you here until the king's search ends. It's not safe for you to be seen."

The man nodded silently, his face impassive.

Darius crossed his arms, his piercing gaze fixed on Tortoni. "How did this happen?" he demanded, his tone cold.

Tortoni took a steady breath before speaking. "My men and I followed the prince as instructed," he began. "We overheard their plans to ride to Lake Tolki. As you requested, we waited for the right moment." His eyes darted between Darius and Mefford. "We stayed hidden in the forest until they seemed comfortable. That's when we launched the attack."

Darius nodded slightly, urging him to go on.

"We outnumbered them," Tortoni said. "I did as you instructed—I seized Freja and intended to bring her to you. But the prince struck me with a dagger in the shoulder before I could escape with her. One of my men tried to intervene, but he was caught. I managed to flee with some of my men and stayed near the meeting point in the forest until your guards found me."

At this, Mefford's composure broke. "How could you lose Freja?" he shouted, his fists clenched. His voice echoed in the confined space.

Darius raised a hand, silencing his son. Mefford reluctantly stepped back, his jaw tight with frustration.

"And your men?" Darius pressed.

Tortoni straightened. "Most managed to cross back into our lands. I stayed behind to deliver the message personally. I thought it would be better coming from me."

Darius narrowed his eyes, his mind turning over the details. "Did anyone see your face?" he asked.

"No," Tortoni replied firmly. "I kept my disguise on the entire time. No one can identify me."

Darius's stern expression softened slightly, but his voice remained cold. "Good. That is critical."

Tortoni met his gaze. "You wanted chaos," he said bluntly. "We've delivered. The attack has thrown the royal court into disarray. The king is focused on the protests and will feel powerless under these circumstances."

Mefford, still simmering with anger, interjected, "But it wasn't enough. You were supposed to kill my cousin and bring Freja to me."

Darius turned his sharp gaze to his son. "Enough," he said, his voice like steel. "The chaos we've sown will weaken his resolve and prove more valuable than one captured noblewoman. Let the king scramble. Let him fear for his throne."

Tortoni shifted uncomfortably, glancing between the two men again. "What do you want me to do now?"

"For now, you stay hidden," Darius instructed. "Tapas will ensure you are taken care of. When the time is right, we will help you leave for the frozen lands. Until then, no one must know you are here."

Tortoni nodded, his expression resolute. "Understood."

Darius stepped closer, lowering his voice. "If you value your life, you will keep your men silent. Not a word of this reaches anyone outside our circle. Do I make myself clear?"

Tortoni held his gaze. "Crystal clear, My Lord."

Darius turned to Tapas, his expression cold and calculating. "Ensure he is well guarded," he commanded. "And keep me informed of the soldiers' movements. We cannot afford any mistakes."

Tapas inclined his head respectfully. "As you command, my lord."

Satisfied, Darius turned and strode toward the hidden door, his dark cloak billowing as he moved. Mefford hesitated momentarily, his frustration still evident, before following his father. Mefford cast a lingering glare at the man before disappearing into the corridor. The door slid shut behind them with a low rumble, the sound of stone grinding against stone filling the chamber.

Tapas remained for a moment, his gaze fixed on Tortoni. Then, with a curt nod, he left, the echo of his footsteps fading as he ascended the stairs. The dimly lit passage fell silent, the air thick with tension.

Upstairs in the castle, Tapas made his way to the kitchen. He moved efficiently, selecting a loaf of bread, a generous portion of roasted meat, and a wedge of aged cheese. He wrapped the food in a cloth and returned to the hidden chamber. He placed the food on a bench, picked up a torch off the wall and then pulled the concealed door.

Tortoni, sitting on the floor, rose when he entered. His face was drawn, his body tense with the weight of his predicament. Tapas approached and set the bundle on the rough wooden table in the corner.

"Eat," he said curtly, his tone leaving no room for debate. "You'll need your strength."

Tortoni nodded, his movements stiff. "Thank you," he said, though his voice lacked conviction. He tore off a piece of bread and began to chew, his mind elsewhere.

Tapas lingered for a moment, watching Tortoni closely. Then, without another word, he stepped back into the corridor. He reached for the handle, pulling it to shut the door. Tortoni sat alone in the dark hideout, the oppressive silence broken only by the faint crackle of the torchlight. He ate slowly, his thoughts a storm of regret and uncertainty. The past few days' events replayed in his mind—the ambush, the unsuccessful attempt to capture Lady Freja, and the prince's unexpected strength. His shoulder throbbed where Halsten's dagger had struck, a sharp reminder of his failure.

His gaze drifted to the door. Though he had followed Darius's orders without question, he now realized the danger of his position. He was both a tool and a liability—a pawn in a game he could barely comprehend.

He clenched his fists, the food on the table momentarily forgotten. "No one saw my face," he muttered, as if the repetition could erase the gnawing doubt in his mind. "No one knows who I am."

CHAPTER 13

A FEW DAYS AFTER THE MEETING with the council, Alaric and Prince Halsten strolled through the royal garden. The gentle rustling of leaves and the sweet fragrance of blooming flowers provided a tranquil backdrop to their walk. Behind them, Egron and DeMarco, their senior guards, followed at a respectful distance, granting the royals privacy.

After a while, the king gestured toward a stone bench beneath a grand oak tree. Its ancient branches stretched wide as if to shelter the weighty conversation about to take place. "Sit with me, my son," he said.

Prince Halsten complied, settling beside his father. He studied the king's expression, noticing the faint lines of thought etched into his features. "What is on your mind?" he asked, his tone a mix of curiosity and concern.

The king turned to his son, his gaze steady. "For years, our family has led this kingdom," he began. "From the days of Aldrich, the throne of EdenRock has been more than a seat of power—it is a destiny, a duty, and a legacy."

Halsten listened intently. His father's tone was grave, carrying the weight of centuries of tradition.

"When Aldrich established this kingdom, he created institutions to safeguard it and ensure its strength," Alaric continued. "These have been entrusted to every ruler who has ascended this throne. My father, King Edward, passed them to me, and I have spent my reign building upon them. I will pass them on to you one day, my son."

The prince frowned, his mind racing to keep pace with his father's words. "But why tell me this now?" he asked.

The king smiled faintly, placing a reassuring hand on his son's shoulder. "Because a wise ruler prepares his successor from the first day of his reign," he explained. "Halsten, you are of age now. Soon, you will marry Freja and begin building your own family. Life is unpredictable, and though I hope to guide this kingdom for many more years, I must ensure that you are ready for when the time comes."

Halsten nodded slowly, the king's words settling on him like the evening dew. "I understand. But what does this preparation entail?"

King Alaric's gaze grew distant, as if he were peering into the past. "There are things about this kingdom—secrets, resources, and alliances—that only the king and a select few trusted leaders know. These are the tools that have kept EdenRock strong through generations. Just as my father shared them with me, I will share them with you."

Halsten's brows furrowed. "What kind of secrets?"

The king leaned closer, lowering his voice. "Hidden fortresses, contingency plans for war, ancient pacts with other realms, and the true extent of our treasury and its defenses. Knowledge of our allies' strengths and, perhaps more importantly, their weaknesses. These things cannot be spoken of lightly, even within these walls."

The prince took a deep breath, feeling the immense responsibility that came with such knowledge. "I never realized the throne carried so much beyond what the people see."

Alaric nodded, his expression softening. "That is why we speak now, my son. A king's burden is great, but it is not carried alone. The institutions we inherit and improve are meant to ensure that no ruler stands alone in protecting the realm."

Halsten hesitated, his thoughts turning to his fiancée. "And what of Freja?" he asked. "Will she share in this knowledge?"

The king smiled warmly. "Freja will be your partner in all things. Her strength will support you, just as your mother's strength supports me. Some secrets, however, are known only to the ruler for the safety of all. You must learn what is shared and what must remain hidden."

Halsten nodded again, a new resolve forming within him. "I will not fail you, Father. I will honor our ancestors and protect this kingdom."

Alaric placed a firm hand on Halsten's shoulder, his voice filled with pride. "I know you will, my son. You have the heart of a ruler. Together, we will prepare for the future."

He reached into a velvet pouch hanging from his belt and produced a necklace with a pendant that gleamed faintly in the soft evening light. He held it up for the prince to see. "First of all, my son, I want to hand this over to you," he said. "This necklace has been passed down from Aldrich himself and is worn by all the true kings of EdenRock."

Halsten leaned forward, his eyes widening as he studied the intricate design. "Is this truly Aldrich's pendant?" he asked, his voice filled with awe.

The king nodded, turning it so the carvings caught the light. "Yes, it is. Look closely." He pointed to the image engraved on the pendant. "This is the image of the Ligons—the two mythical creatures said to have protected Aaron and his wife when they fled the Gols."

Halsten examined the pendant with reverence, his fingers brushing against its cool surface. "I've read of the Ligons in the histories, but to see their image like this… It's incredible."

Alaric smiled faintly. "Aaron crafted two identical pendants. One he placed around Aldrich's neck, and the other he gave to Uldrich, Aldrich's brother. This one," he said, holding the necklace higher, "was Aldrich's. It has remained with the true kings of EdenRock ever since."

Halsten's brow furrowed slightly, a question forming in his mind. "Father, what became of Aaron and Uldrich after they fell into the river?"

The king sighed, his gaze turning distant. "There are many stories, my son. Some say a man and a boy were found along a riverbank decades later, but no one has ever been able to verify the tale. Their fate remains a mystery."

Halsten nodded slowly. "And the prophecy?" he asked. "Is it true? The one about the king who rides a Ligon?"

King Alaric's lips pressed into a thin line. "The prophecy speaks of a king who will ride a Ligon, unite the kingdoms, and rule as the second coming of Aldrich. It is said that such a king would bring a new era of peace and prosperity to EdenRock."

"Do you believe in it, Father?" Halsten asked, his voice quiet.

The king hesitated for a moment. "Prophecies have a way of enduring, my son, regardless of whether they are fact or myth. But what is undeniable is the strength and wisdom Aldrich brought to our kingdom. If this prophecy inspires hope and unity among our people, it serves its purpose."

Halsten's curiosity deepened. "Do you think Aldrich truly died? Or could he have lived beyond the war?"

Alaric met his son's gaze. "History tells us that Aldrich went to war and never returned. But he entrusted his crown to his most loyal guard. That guard carried it back to EdenRock and placed it on Aldrich's son's head, crowning him in Aldrich's place. What became of Aldrich after that is lost to time."

Halsten held the pendant, his mind racing with the weight of its history and meaning. "It's incredible to think that something like this has survived all these years," he said, his voice filled with wonder.

Alaric placed a hand on his son's shoulder, his touch firm and reassuring. "This is more than a relic, Halsten. It is a symbol of the strength, resilience, and unity of our kingdom. And now, it is yours to carry forward."

Halsten looked resolute. "I will honor it, Father. I will honor Aldrich's legacy and our family's place in EdenRock's history."

The king smiled. "I know you will, my son. And when the time comes, you will lead this kingdom with the same wisdom and courage that Aldrich did." His expression grew serious. "Listen to me carefully, my son," he began, his tone commanding. "Every king has secret agents who serve as aides to the throne. They take a sacred oath, receive special training, and live in plain sight, their true purpose hidden from all but the king."

The prince tilted his head slightly, intrigued but confused. "Secret agents? Among the people?"

Alaric nodded. "Yes. They are the silent eyes and ears of the crown, crucial to maintaining the kingdom's stability. They operate without recognition or suspicion, and their loyalty is absolute." He leaned closer, his gaze sharp. "I will show you—but this information must never leave your lips. Not even Freja can know."

Halsten nodded. "I understand, Father."

"Walk with me to the palace guard tower." The king gestured for him to follow.

The two made their way toward the towering structure at the edge of the castle grounds. When they reached the base, Egron and DeMarco stood to attention.

"Clear the area," the king ordered. "I want privacy."

The guards bowed and moved to the outer walls. They remained at the tower's base while Alaric and Halsten ascended the narrow staircase.

At the top of the tower, the two paused, the vast expanse of Aldrich City stretching out before them. The soft glow of lanterns illuminated the streets below, casting flickering shadows on the walls.

Alaric turned to Halsten. "Do not point—simply look where I tell you to look," he instructed.

"Yes, Father."

The king gestured toward the city gates. "Look there. What do you see?"

Halsten squinted. "Soldiers guarding the entrance," he answered confidently.

Alaric smiled. "That is obvious. Look again. This time, find something that isn't immediately apparent."

Halsten frowned, scanning the area more intently. "I see the sculptures and the plants," he said after a moment.

The king shook his head gently. "Look deeper, my son. Find what has always been there but is often overlooked."

Halsten's brow furrowed as he focused. His gaze fell on a figure sitting near the gate. "A beggar is lying by the side of the wall," he said. "He's always there, asking for money or food."

Alaric nodded approvingly. "Yes. That man is part of the king's secret service. His role is to assess everyone who enters the city. He reports back through methods known only to him and a select few."

Halsten's eyes widened in astonishment. "A beggar? In the secret service? Are there others?" he asked, his voice brimming with curiosity.

The king gestured toward the chapel. "Now, look at the bell tower. Tell me what you see."

Halsten turned his gaze to the structure. "The bell ringer is lying beneath the bell," he said after a moment.

"Exactly," Alaric said. "He too is in service to the crown." The king then pointed toward the rooftops. "Look at the main buildings. What do you see?"

Halsten's eyes scanned the rooftops carefully. After a pause, he said, "People are lying on every corner."

A smile spread across King Alaric's face. "Good. You're beginning to see. These people are stationed there to observe, listen, and protect. Their work is invisible to most, but it is vital. They are known as the sky birds."

Halsten leaned on the stone ledge, shaking his head in amazement. "I've seen these people before but never thought to ask about them. I didn't even question their presence."

The king placed a hand on his son's shoulder. "That is their purpose—to be unnoticed and unremarkable. But know this, my son—many of them are around you and Freja daily, ensuring your safety. You will learn who they are in time, but it is not the right moment for that now."

"Mother and my sisters too?" Halsten asked.

"Yes, every royal has people around them for that purpose."

Halsten turned to the king, his expression serious. "This is the impressive, Father."

Alaric nodded, his expression proud. "Good. As a ruler, you must understand that strength lies in armies and those who work in the shadows. You will lead them one day, and they will serve you as they have served me."

The men stood silently for a moment, the vast city stretched out before them, but for the prince, it suddenly seemed filled with secrets waiting to be uncovered.

"Let us go back to the castle. Your mother and Freja will be worried about us," the king said.

CHAPTER 14

THE STUDY IN BEAR CAVE Castle was tense as Darius paced back and forth, his cloak billowing behind him with each determined stride. Across the room, Mefford sat at a large oak table, his brow furrowed as he watched his father's movements. The weight of the king's recent command to search every city for robbers and attackers hung heavily between them.

Darius finally stopped and turned to Mefford, his voice sharp. "The king has sent his soldiers into the land," he said. "This search will not stop until they have someone to blame. We must throw them off our trail before they look too closely at Bear Cave."

Mefford leaned forward, his elbows resting on the table. "How do we throw them off, Father?" he asked, his tone wary.

Darius's lips curled into a sly smile. "We create a distraction. We will find a new group of people and motivate them to carry out the robberies instead of you and your men."

Mefford's expression grew skeptical. "And where do we find these people?" he asked.

Darius's eyes gleamed. "We will select a few unknown individuals—those who live on the fringes of society. We will give them gold and let them flaunt it in the seedier parts of town. Word will spread that they are spending loot from the robberies. Those desperate enough will be drawn to the idea of easy wealth. Once we have their attention, we will arm them and send them to carry out new robberies."

Mefford leaned back in his chair, rubbing his chin. "That's risky," he said. "What if they are caught? They could identify me."

Darius waved a dismissive hand. "You won't be directly involved. I'll have Tapas arrange everything. He knows how to manage these matters discreetly. Your name will never come into question."

Mefford hesitated, his fingers drumming nervously on the edge of the table. "And what happens to these people after they've done the job? They could still talk if they're caught."

Darius's smirk deepened, his voice dropping to a cold and calculated whisper. "Once they've served their purpose, we will arrange a meeting to 'reward' them for their loyalty. But Tapas will ensure that none of them live to tell tales. Loose ends will be tied up—permanently."

Mefford nodded slowly, though his expression betrayed lingering unease. "If you're certain Tapas can handle it, then I'll trust your judgment."

Darius stepped closer, his imposing figure casting a shadow over his son. He placed a firm hand on Mefford's shoulder, his gaze intense. "Trust me," he said. "This plan will divert the king's attention and keep Bear Cave out of suspicion. The crown will waste resources chasing the wrong culprits, and we will remain untouchable."

Mefford sighed heavily, rising from his seat. "Very well, Father," he said. "I'll leave it in Tapas's hands."

Darius nodded, satisfied. "After this next attack, you and your men must stand down," he said. "The king will be preoccupied with planning the prince's wedding and the Gladiator Games. We must give the illusion of calm to avoid drawing unwanted attention."

Mefford's frown deepened, and he crossed his arms over his chest. "But I don't want Freja to marry the prince," he said bitterly. "She doesn't belong with him."

His father's expression hardened, though a sly smile tugged at the corners of his mouth. "Don't concern yourself with that," he said smoothly. "The marriage will not last. I will see to it."

Mefford's brows knitted together. "And how can you be so sure?"

Darius's voice dropped, filled with quiet confidence. "Because I have plans, my son, beyond this wedding. Freja may wed Prince Halsten, but she will never truly be his. This union is another pawn on the board, and I always control the game."

Mefford's frown eased slightly, though a flicker of uncertainty remained in his eyes. "I hope you're right, Father," he said. "Because I cannot stand the thought of Freja being by his side."

Darius gave his son's shoulder a firm pat. "Trust in me, Mefford. Everything is falling into place. Now, go and prepare. We must ensure the pieces are set before we make our next move."

"I disagree that we should halt our operation. Let's continue our plan and make the king very unpopular. That way, we can campaign and appeal to the citizens to remove the king and pave the way for you to take over."

Darius placed his hand on Mefford's shoulder again. "Son, we need to plan and be patient. Returning to what belongs to us will be easier if we take the time to get the citizens on our side. You may not understand it today, but you will when it comes. Remember, you will only see the organs of an ant if you take the time to dissect it."

Mefford inclined his head and left the room, his steps slow and thoughtful. Darius watched him go, the faint smile on his face fading into a calculating expression. He moved to the window, his hands clasped behind his back, and gazed out over the dark expanse of the forest. He turned and walked over to his chamber and lay next to Xinovia. He pulled her to himself, and Xinovia laid her head on Darius's chest as they slipped into deep sleep for the night.

The following morning, Darius summoned Tapas to his chambers. His voice was low and deliberate as he issued his instructions. "It is time to execute the plan," he said, leaning forward in his chair. "Find two of the lower guards and set things in motion."

Tapas nodded sharply. "It will be done, my lord."

He left the chamber and quickly sought out two guards from Bear Cave's ranks. Drawing them into a secluded corner of the castle, he spoke in hushed tones. "Listen to me carefully," he began, fixing them with a steely gaze. "Take these bags of gold and go to the lower west side of the town. Your task is to flaunt this wealth at the tavern."

The guards exchanged glances but said nothing, waiting for their commander to finish. Tapas continued, "When anyone asks where the gold came from, tell them you earned it through robberies. If someone shows interest in joining you, give them the weapons they need and suggest a target near River Ellyn South."

One of the guards frowned slightly. "And after that, Commander?"

"Report back to me as soon as the robbery begins," Tapas instructed. "Do not fail. The consequences will be severe."

The guards nodded, accepting the gold and their orders. "Yes, Commander," they said in unison before departing.

Two nights later, the guards entered a dark tavern on the lower west side. The air was thick with the smell of cheap ale and smoke, and laughter and music filled the room. The two men made a spectacle of their newfound wealth, ordering rounds of drinks for everyone and tossing coins to the prostitutes who descended from the upper floor.

Their largesse quickly attracted attention. A man approached their table, his eyes alight with curiosity. "Mind if I join you, gentlemen?" he asked, his tone casual.

The guards exchanged knowing looks. "Have a seat," one of them said, gesturing to the chair across from them.

As the man sat down, one of the guards, an older man with full beard, waved the women away and leaned in closer. "What's your name?" he asked.

"Rob Smoke," the man replied with a grin. "And I've got to ask—what's your business? I've never seen anyone spend gold like that around here."

One of the guards smirked and lowered his voice. "We got it from the trade robberies."

Rob's eyes widened slightly, but a wicked grin spread across his face. "Serves those nobles right. They make us work ourselves to the bone for scraps. It's about time someone took their share of the wealth."

The other guard leaned across the table; his conspiratorial tone. "Are you interested in joining us?"

Rob nodded eagerly. "Absolutely. Let me help you take from those who have more than their fair share."

"Good," the guard said. "You'll need to bring more men. Meet us here in two nights, and we'll give you the details."

Rob stretched out his hand and shook the guard's hand. "See you tomorrow," the guard said, and stood up before walking out the door.

Two days later, the guards reported back to Tapas. "The robbery is planned for tonight near River Ellyn South," one of them said.

"Good," Tapas replied. "Let me know as soon as it begins."

Meanwhile, Darius communicated the plan to Lord Warhouse, who discreetly informed the king. Alaric wasted no time. He summoned Prince Halsten, Adikis, Zoresh, Frodio, Leo, and several commanders to his chamber. "We have information on a planned robbery along the River Ellyn South," he said. "Go and intercept them. Ensure justice is done."

Halsten and his men hid along the trade route, their weapons ready, as night fell. The air was tense, and the only sounds were the rustling of leaves and the faint murmur of the river.

The prince told his men to stay alert when the traders appeared in the distance. Moments later, the robbers emerged from the forest, attacking the traders and tying them up. As they prepared to leave with the loot, Halsten and his team sprang into action.

A fierce battle erupted, swords clashing in the moonlight. Halsten and his companions fought skillfully, cutting down the robbers individually. Despite their bravery, the attackers were no match for the prince's forces. All sixteen were killed, leaving no one to capture.

After freeing the traders, Halsten ordered the robbers' bodies to be loaded onto a cart. The soldiers rode through the city streets with them in tow, the citizens cheering as they passed.

Back at Bear Cave Castle, the two guards responsible for orchestrating the attack entered the hall where Darius, Mefford, Caine, and Tapas awaited them. The guards bowed low, eager to deliver their report.

"The plan was executed successfully," one of them said. "The robbery occurred as planned, and the targets were distracted."

Darius smiled coldly. "Excellent work."

He reached for two heavy bags of gold and tossed them onto the floor. "Take your reward," he said, his tone gracious.

The guards bent to retrieve the gold, but as they did, Tapas and Caine drew their swords. Before the men could react, their bodies had collapsed to the ground, blood pooling around them.

Darius stepped forward, his expression unchanging. "Loyalty and silence," he said, "are the only guarantees of survival here."

Tapas wiped his blade clean as Caine signaled for the bodies to be removed. The hall fell silent again, the air thick with an unspoken warning.

Darius turned to Mefford and said with chilling finality, "Loose ends are never allowed to linger. Remember that."

When Mefford turned to leave, a commotion erupted near the compound gates. Both he and Darius turned toward the noise, their curiosity piqued. As they approached the yard, they spotted Jason at the entrance, his face red with fury as he shouted at the guards. His booming voice echoed, demanding passage into the compound.

Darius stopped in his tracks and folded his arms. "He's your friend. You deal with him," he said, turning on his heel and walking back into the castle.

Mefford sighed and raised a hand, signaling the men to let Jason through. They hesitated but eventually stepped aside, opening the gate to allow him entry. Jason stormed into the yard, his piercing glare fixed on Mefford. He sneered at the guards as he passed, his contempt evident.

"What is the meaning of this?" Jason demanded. "Did you go on an operation without us? Without informing me or my men?"

Mefford raised his hands in a calming gesture. "Jason, calm down," he said evenly. "It's not what you think."

Jason's fury did not abate. He stepped closer, his tone growing more heated. "Not what I think? You owe me and my men the courtesy of informing us! We brought you into this, and now you think you can act alone?"

Mefford's jaw tightened, and his patience was wearing thin. "What?" he said, his voice rising. "Ask you for permission? Who do you think you are? I am the son of the bravest man in this kingdom, and I owe you nothing—not on my land."

Jason's eyes narrowed, his voice dropping to a low growl. "Without me and my men, you wouldn't have the courage to step into the shadows, let alone claim this territory. And now you dare to act as though you're lord over me? You're pathetic, Mefford. If you had even an ounce of courage, you'd stop cowering here and take your father's throne."

Mefford lunged at Jason, his anger boiling over, but Jason was quicker. He slapped Mefford hard across the face, sending him sprawling to the ground. The yard fell silent, the guards stunned by the brazen act of violence.

Two of them rushed to Mefford's side and helped him to his feet. Mefford shoved their hands away and glared at Jason, his eyes burning with fury.

"You want a fight?" he said coldly. "Then you'll get one."

Jason drew his sword, his expression resolute and unflinching. Mefford grabbed a blade from a guard, and the two clashed in the center of the yard. The metal striking metal echoed through the compound as sparks flew from their weapons. Jason, the stronger and more experienced fighter, soon gained the upper hand, driving Mefford backward with a powerful blow that again sent him to the ground.

Mefford groaned but pushed himself back to his feet. "Guards!" he shouted. "Restrain him!"

The men surged forward, grabbing Jason and wrestling him into submission. Mefford picked up his dropped sword, his chest heaving with exertion and fury. He approached his former friend, now held tightly by the guards, and struck him across the head with the flat side of the sword's shaft. Jason cried out as blood trickled down his temple.

"Get this fool out of my compound!" Mefford bellowed, pointing toward the gate.

The guards disarmed Jason and dragged him out despite his struggles and curses. They shoved him beyond the gates and slammed them shut with finality. He stumbled but turned, his eyes blazing with rage.

"You'll regret this, Mefford!" he shouted. "Mark my words—you'll regret this."

Mefford stood his ground, gripping the sword tightly. "Stay away from here, Jason. If you come back, you won't leave alive."

The guards returned to their posts, and the compound became uneasy. Mefford handed back the sword he'd borrowed and turned toward the castle, his expression steely as he strode inside.

Jason mounted his horse, tied to a tree outside the compound, and rode off into the night. He stopped at a nearby tavern, his mood dark and brooding. He ordered several rounds of ale and wine inside, drinking heavily to drown his anger. After a while, he beckoned to two women from the brothel above the tavern, gesturing for them to follow him upstairs.

When they entered the room, Jason collapsed onto the bed, his exhaustion and intoxication evident. He slurred, "Take off your clothes. Make me happy."

The women exchanged a bemused look but obeyed, removing their garments. When they turned back to him, Jason was already snoring loudly, sprawled out in a drunken stupor. They sighed, collected their things, and left the room, leaving him alone to sleep off his anger and ale.

CHAPTER 15

THE MORNING SUNBATHED THE CASTLE'S main hall in a golden glow, illuminating the assembled nobles who had gathered at King Alaric's behest. The air was filled with anticipation as the king stepped forward, his commanding presence drawing every gaze. His robes of deep crimson and gold shimmered as he raised a hand to quiet the murmurs.

"Ladies and gentlemen," he began, his voice resonating with authority, "I stand before you today to announce the triumph of our kingdom. The band of robbers who dared to disrupt the peace of our lands has been defeated. Their efforts to sow fear and discord have failed. Justice has prevailed."

The hall erupted into applause and cheers. Lords and ladies exchanged smiles and words of relief, their faces beaming with joy.

Alaric allowed the celebration to crest before raising his hand again for silence. "I must commend the courage and loyalty of those who defended our lands. Their bravery ensures that the kingdom remains secure. However,"—his tone grew somber—"we must remain vigilant. Though this victory is worth celebrating, let us not become complacent. We will wait to see if further threats arise before setting the date for Prince Darius's wedding."

A hum of agreement swept through the room. Lord Ethan Glenwood, seated beside Lady Elara, rose to speak. "Your wisdom and leadership have guided us through these troubled times. The people of Glenwood stand ready to assist should the need arise."

Alaric inclined his head in gratitude. "Thank you, Lord Ethan. Your loyalty is noted and deeply appreciated."

Lady Sarah Felton rose gracefully from the opposite side of the hall. "Your Majesty," she said, her melodic voice carrying across the room, "we are heartened by this news. The nobles of Felton Court look forward to the joyous occasion of the prince's wedding. We trust that your patience will ensure the event's safety and grandeur."

The king nodded. "Indeed, Lady Sarah. It is a celebration that will unite our kingdom, and I will ensure it is a moment befitting its importance."

Lord Luterodt, a secret ally of Darius and also the king's council member, leaned forward. "Your Majesty, might I suggest you organize a big celebration for the citizens so the young men and our beautiful women can come out to celebrate? It would convey that a few greedy people cannot disrupt life in EdenRock."

"Lord Luterodt, I hope your suggestion to the king is meant for your desires. It seems your interest is in something else," Lady Paulina said.

All the nobles burst into laughter.

As the meeting concluded, they celebrated in the castle's grand banquet hall. Long tables laden with sumptuous feasts stretched across the room, and musicians played lively tunes as the wine flowed freely. The atmosphere was electric with joy and camaraderie.

Lady Delena Longpatch approached Lady Margaret Dansgrove with a goblet of wine. "Margaret, knowing the robbers have been dealt with is a relief. I feared for the safety of our caravans."

"Indeed," Lady Margaret replied, her lips curving into a mischievous smile. "Now we can finally turn our attention to the prince's wedding. Tell me, Delena, is it true that Lord Luterodt has asked for Olivia's hand in marriage for his eldest son, Clifford?"

Lady Delena raised an incredulous eyebrow, her expression a mixture of amusement and disdain. "Oh, Margaret," she began, her voice dripping with sarcasm, "if only you could have seen my face when the messenger delivered that proposal. I would rather Olivia remain single forever than marry her off to the son of that"—she paused, lowering her voice for effect—"hopeless goat."

The two ladies erupted into laughter, their merriment drawing the attention of nearby nobles. Lady Margaret, dabbing at the corner of her eye with a silk handkerchief, gestured subtly toward Lord Luterodt, who was standing across the hall regaling a small group of lords with an exaggerated tale.

"And can you imagine?" Delena continued, raising her voice conspiratorially for the benefit of their audience. "What would my daughter even be called? Lady Olivia Luterodt?" She shuddered theatrically. "God forbid! That name alone sounds like a curse, not a title. It doesn't even roll off the tongue like it belongs to a human being."

The ladies surrounding them dissolved into hysterical laughter, their mirth spilling into their conversations. Heads turned, including Lord Luterodt's, who paused midsentence, his brow furrowing in curiosity.

"Whatever could they find so amusing?" he remarked to Lord Warhouse, who was standing beside him.

Lord Warhouse chuckled softly, clapping him on the shoulder. "Women's humor, my friend. Best we don't ask."

Unfazed, Lord Luterodt returned to his storytelling while the ladies nearby continued their giggling. Lady Margaret leaned closer to Lady Delena, her voice still shaking with amusement. "Delena, you're going to have all the lords wondering what scandal we're plotting."

"Let them wonder," Lady Delena replied with a sly grin. "After all, they provide us with no shortage of entertainment."

The conversation dissolved into lighter banter as the celebration continued, the hall echoing with music and laughter from the nobles.

"Alaric is wise to hold off on setting the wedding date," Lord Nicholas remarked, swirling his goblet thoughtfully. "Rushing into such an event while threats loom would be unwise."

Lord Mark nodded. "True, though I imagine the people will be disappointed. They long for a celebration after these turbulent times."

At the head of the table, Alaric raised his goblet, drawing the room's attention once more. "To our kingdom!" he proclaimed. "To our unity, strength, and EdenRock."

The nobles raised their goblets in unison, voices ringing in a resounding cheer. "To the Realm! To the Realm! To the Realm!"

The celebration continued late into the night, filled with the relief of a hard-fought victory. The nobles and their king reveled in the day's triumph, united in purpose and hope for the future.

CHAPTER 16

A FTER THE GRAND CELEBRATION HAD ended, the castle fell into a peaceful stillness. Halsten and Freja walked through the dim corridors toward their separate quarters. They paused at the hallway's end, where Halsten gently took her hand.

"Goodnight, Freja," he said softly. He leaned down and kissed her, their moment lingering in the quiet of the night.

"Goodnight, Halsten," Freja replied radiantly before turning toward her chamber.

When she entered her room, she found Dhalia and Dora sitting and chatting by the fire. She closed the door behind her and began to sway gracefully, humming a cheerful tune and twirling as though she were dancing. Her smile was brighter than they had seen it in months.

Dhalia exchanged a knowing look with Dora before breaking into a wide grin. Rising from her seat, she curtsied playfully and said, "My lady, what has made you so blissful this evening? Is it the wine, or is there a secret we should know?"

Freja stopped twirling abruptly and approached the two women, her hands clasped to her chest. "Oh, Dhalia, Dora," she said, her voice brimming with excitement. "I can hardly believe it. The day is almost here—soon, I will be Halsten's bride. My heart is so full that I feel I might burst!"

Dora stood and clasped Freja's hands. "My lady, your happiness is contagious," she said gently. "But you have always known this day would come. Why the sudden emotion?"

Freja's expression softened as she looked between her two dearest friends. "Promise me," she said earnestly, her tone growing serious. "Promise me that you will not leave me when I become his wife. Do not let marriage or duty take you far from me. Swear it."

Dhalia rolled her eyes playfully. "Don't be ridiculous, my lady," she teased. "How could we ever cease to be your friends? We've been by your side since we were children. Nothing will change that."

Dora nodded in agreement, her tone reassuring. "Lady Freja, we will always stand by you, no matter where life takes us."

Still unconvinced, Freja looked at them. "Swear it," she demanded, her voice trembling with sincerity.

The two women exchanged amused glances before clasping Freja's hands tightly. "We swear it," they said. "We will always be by your side."

Freja pulled them into a tight embrace, "I'm afraid you will both marry and leave me to face this new chapter alone," she admitted with a smile on her face.

Dhalia leaned back and gently wiped the tears from Freja's cheeks. "Nonsense, my lady," she said with a mock-serious tone. "Any man I marry must agree to stay near you, or he can find himself an ugly duckling in another realm. I won't settle for less."

The three women burst into laughter, their shared joy filling the chamber. They moved to Freja's bed, flopping onto the plush covers like carefree girls. Freja lay with Dhalia on one side and Dora on the other.

In the quiet that followed, she smiled contentedly. "I don't know what I did to deserve friends like you."

Dhalia patted her hand. "You've always had us, Freja. And you always will. Glenwood girls don't break friendships."

With those words, the women settled into a peaceful camaraderie, their bond unshaken as they drifted into dreams of the coming days.

When Freja fell into a deep sleep, Dhalia and Dora pulled a blanket over their friend. Dora whispered, "Sleep well, my lady." Then, they tiptoed into the adjoining rooms. They sat down and spent several hours throughout the night sharing their memories of their friendship with Freja.

Meanwhile, Halsten lay in his bed, deep in sleep, while guards watched outside his chamber door. As the night wore on, he drifted into a vivid dream. In the dream, he found himself standing by the tranquil waters of River Ellyn North. The air was calm, but suddenly, the breeze shifted violently, and a fierce whirlwind approached him.

Halsten shielded his face with his hands, squinting against the storm. He tried to peer beyond the swirling chaos, but the force of the wind made it impossible to open his eyes fully. Just as abruptly as it had begun, the gale subsided, and a brilliant sun broke through, illuminating an approaching figure.

As it drew closer, the air became completely still. Halsten lowered his hands and gazed at the being before him, which was glowing faintly. It spoke in a deep, resonant voice. "Halsten, son of Alaric, what do you seek?"

Halsten stepped back, his brows furrowed. "Who are you?" he asked.

The figure ignored his question and repeated, "Halsten, son of Alaric, what do you seek?"

Halsten hesitated, his heart pounding in his chest. The figure repeated the question a third time.

Summoning his courage, Halsten replied, "I seek wisdom to follow my destiny."

As soon as the words left his lips, two men in black war armor appeared on either side of him. Dark cloth masks obscured their faces, and they grabbed Halsten by the arms, holding him firmly in place. His breath quickened as the glowing figure moved closer, its face now visible.

It was an older man with white hair and piercing blue eyes. He wore a flowing white robe trimmed in gold, radiating an aura of power and serenity. The man placed a hand firmly on Halsten's chest. Instantly, heat emanated from his palm, and steam rose from the contact. Halsten's knees buckled as he bowed his head, overwhelmed by the strange energy coursing through him.

Tears streamed down the prince's face as the older man spoke again, his voice commanding and comforting. "Peril knocks at your door, but follow your destiny. The path will reveal itself."

Halsten's heart thundered as the words echoed in his mind. Suddenly, a distant voice called his name, faint at first but growing louder.

With a gasp, he awoke, his body drenched in sweat. He sat up in bed, his breaths ragged as he looked around the room. His gaze fell on his mother, Isadora, who was seated by his bedside, her eyes filled with concern.

"Halsten," she said softly, touching his arm. "You were restless in your sleep. Are you unwell?"

He ran a hand through his disheveled hair, his mind still clouded by the vivid dream as he looked through the window to the morning rays piercing through. "I…I had a dream, Mother," he said, his voice trembling. "It felt so real. There was a whirlwind, a glowing figure, and men who held me. The figure spoke to me—called me 'son of Alaric.'"

Isadora 's brow furrowed, her concern deepening. "What did the figure say?"

Halsten hesitated, replaying the older man's words in his mind. "He said peril knocks at my door…but I must follow my destiny."

The queen regarded her son thoughtfully, her hand resting gently on his. "Dreams often carry messages, my son. Perhaps this one was a warning—or a guide. You must seek clarity and be vigilant in the days ahead."

Halsten nodded, though his mind swirled with questions. "It felt like more than a dream," he said, his voice barely audible. "It felt like a summons."

Isadora gave his fingers a reassuring squeeze. "Whatever it may be, you are strong. Your father and I believe in you. Trust yourself and the path that lies ahead."

Though his mother's words offered some comfort, Halsten couldn't shake the weight of the dream. He sat in silence, his hand tugging on the medallion around his neck, his thoughts consumed by the older man's cryptic warning and the shadow of peril that seemed to loom over his future.

CHAPTER 17

THE NEXT DAY, WHEN WORD of the robbery reached Jason's camp, it stirred unrest among the men. Many group members whispered among themselves, suspecting Jason had acted behind their backs, organizing the looting without their involvement. His absence from the camp only deepened their suspicions.

In the center of the encampment, Major, one of their most respected leaders, stood up, his voice cutting through the noise from the crowd. "This is a betrayal," he declared, his tone sharp with anger. "Jason, whom we trusted to lead us, has turned his back on us. Now that he's cozying up with his friend from the castle, he's trying to cut us out of the deal. What he seems to forget," Major continued, his voice rising, "is that we are the ones who made him who he is. Without us, he's nothing."

Another member, Boyd, nodded and stepped forward. "Major is right," he said, his voice laced with frustration. "What Jason is doing is reckless. He will expose us all by bringing outsiders into our circle and conducting operations without our knowledge. What if one of these friends of his talks? What if they betray us? He's putting every one of us in danger."

The men murmured in agreement, their anger mounting as the implications of Jason's actions sank in. Just then, the camp gates creaked open, and Jason rode in, his forehead bandaged and his expression tense. He dismounted, his eyes scanning the gathered men, all staring at him with suspicion and resentment.

"What are you all looking at?" he barked, waving his hand dismissively. "Find something to do and stop gawking."

The men didn't move, their anger simmering just below the surface. Major stepped forward, his arms crossed over his chest. "You've got some nerve showing your face here, Jason," he said coldly. "We trusted you, and you betrayed us."

Jason's face darkened. "Betrayed you?" he snapped. "What? You're all letting rumors cloud your judgment. I don't owe you any explanations."

Boyd stepped up beside Major. "Yes, you do. You're nobody without us."

Jason's hand went to the hilt of his sword, his voice rising. "I said, find something to do and stop this nonsense, I don't have to explain myself to anyone."

The crowd began to close in, their fury boiling over. Major's eyes narrowed as he spoke, his voice icy. "You forget, Jason. A leader is only a leader with loyal followers and now you have lost the loyalty of the men." Major said.

Jason stepped back, his gaze darting between the men advancing toward him. "Stop! I order you! what are you doing?" he shouted, his voice tinged with panic.

But his protests fell on deaf ears. The first man stepped forward and plunged a knife into his side. Jason screamed in pain, his knees buckling. Another man followed, then another, each stabbing him without mercy. Jason fell to the ground, blood spreading beneath him as their fury drove them to act in unison.

Once the final blow had been delivered, the men stepped back, their breathing ragged as they stared at Jason's lifeless body, sprawled in a pool of crimson. The air hung heavy with the weight of their actions, their once-dominant leader a forgotten figure on the cold ground.

Major stepped forward and regarded the corpse. He turned to face the men, his voice cutting through the tense silence. "This is what happens to traitors," he declared, his tone steady and resolute. "We are the Forest Knights. We do not spare those who betray us."

The men raised their bloodstained knives high, their voices ringing in unison. "Major! Major! Major!"

Major raised his hands above his head, crossing them into an X, symbolizing their unwavering unity and shared purpose. The men erupted in cheers, their adrenaline-fueled rage beginning to subside.

After a moment, Major lowered his arms and spoke again, his voice quieter but no less firm. "The Forest Knights stand together, and we hold no place for weakness or deceit. Let this be a lesson to any who think to betray us."

The men nodded. One by one, they dispersed into the shadows of the camp, their cheers fading into an uneasy silence. The once-lively camp grew still, the tension lingering in the air as Jason's body remained where it had fallen.

Major stood with Boyd by his side, staring down at the blood-soaked ground. His expression betrayed no regret, only the cold determination of a leader who had made a necessary choice. With a final look at Jason's remains, he turned and walked away, the heavy silence of the camp following him as the night deepened.

CHAPTER 18

MONTHS PASSED, AND THE KINGDOM entered a new summer season. The soldiers, after exhaustive searches, had found no further suspects for the robberies, and life gradually returned to its former peace. Once gripped by fear, the citizens now resumed their daily routines without concern. Traders returned to their journeys, and caravans traveled freely without incident. The markets thrived, the castles bustled with activity, and children played in the woods again. Young adults and youths often gathered at the lakefront for picnics and swimming, enjoying the freedom from fear.

King Alaric, observing the restoration of peace, summoned his council to the castle. When all were gathered in the grand hall, he rose from his seat, his expression firm yet pleased.

"My lords and ladies," the king began, his voice resonating through the chamber, "it has been months since the last attacks on our kingdom and trade routes. Our efforts, alongside the courage of our people, have restored peace and prosperity. It is time for the realm to celebrate our resolve and unity."

The nobles nodded in agreement.

"With that in mind," he continued, "I have asked Lord Matteson to send invitations to our neighboring kingdoms, inviting them to join us in celebrating two grand occasions—the Gladiator Games and the wedding of Prince Halsten and Lady Freja."

The hall erupted in cheers and applause, but the king raised his hand for silence. "Lord Warhouse," he said, "increase food shipments from the farm colonies. We must ensure that our city and guests are well-fed."

Lord Warhouse stood and bowed deeply. "It will be done, Your Majesty."

"Lord Murdoch," the king said, turning to another noble, "strengthen security along the kingdom's borders. We cannot afford disruptions as we welcome visitors from across the land."

"Consider it handled, Your Majesty."

The king's tone softened as he addressed the entire council. "In just a few months, Aldrich City will host nobles, traders, and commoners from all from our kingdom and beyond.."

The lords and ladies stood, their faces alight with pride and joy. They clapped and shouted in unison, "To the realm! To the Realm! To the Realm!" Their voices echoed through the grand hall before they dispersed through the castle's main entrance, energized by the king's proclamation.

As the council left, Alaric turned to his steward, Ofaro. "Send heralds to the city and surrounding villages," he commanded. "Let the people know that Aldrich City will soon host a celebration worthy of the realm."

The steward bowed low. "It will be done, Your Majesty."

With the king's orders set in motion, the castle buzzed with preparations. Invitations were dispatched, and the joyous news spread across the land. The kingdom braced itself for an event that would be remembered for generations.

Isadora and Lady Elara, Freja's mother, spent many afternoons with her, lovingly preparing for the upcoming wedding. Together, they selected the perfect wedding gown, debated the arrangement of flowers, and chose decorations for the grand celebration. Each moment was filled with warmth and anticipation, their bond growing stronger as they shared this special time.

"That gown," Isadora said, holding up an elegant silk creation embroidered with golden thread, "captures your grace and beauty perfectly, Freja. What do you think?"

Freja ran her fingers along the delicate fabric, her eyes shining with excitement. "It's exquisite, Your Majesty. But, Mother," she turned to Lady Elara, "what do you think?"

Lady Elara smiled warmly, her voice full of pride. "It's perfect, my dear. You'll look like a queen."

Freja blushed, her heart fluttering with joy. "Then this will be the one," she said.

Meanwhile, back at the estate, Dhalia, Dora, and Amelia—the young and devoted caretaker of Freja's quarters—worked tirelessly to ensure every detail was accounted for. They spent hours making lists, overseeing the packing of dresses and accessories, and coordinating with their helpers for the journey to EdenRock.

"I never thought planning a wedding would involve so many details," Dhalia said with a laugh as she folded a silk sash.

Dora nodded, setting a box of jewelry carefully aside. "It's worth every moment. This isn't just any wedding—it's Freja's."

After arranging a tray of delicate perfume bottles, Amelia said, "And we'll make sure it's perfect. Everything must reflect the love she shares with Prince Halsten."

Dhalia smirked playfully. "Careful, Amelia. Anyone listening might think you're the romantic among us, but you run away from any man who dares to speak to you."

The maid grinned but didn't deny it, focusing on her task. "If helping Freja feel as radiant as she deserves makes me a romantic, then so be it." The ladies giggled and then turned back to continue their task of transforming their friend into a beautiful bride.

The ladies used the rest of the days leading up to the festivities to finalize their preparations. Freja joined them one evening, her smile radiant as she watched her friends bustle about.

"Thank you, all of you," she said sincerely, her voice full of emotion. "I couldn't do this without your love and support."

Dhalia waved her hand dismissively, though her smile betrayed her affection. "Nonsense, Freja. We'd move mountains for you."

Dora added, "After this wedding, you'll have all the happiness you deserve."

Amelia stepped forward and took Freja's hand. "You've always been kind to everyone around you, my lady. It's an honor to be part of this."

Freja hugged them one by one, her heart full of gratitude. "I'm so blessed to have you all by my side."

With everything in place, the women of Glenwood prepared themselves and their helpers for the journey to EdenRock, ready to support Freja on the most important day of her life.

CHAPTER 19

As the day of the Gladiator Games approached, Freja, her brother, Albert, and their parents arrived in Aldrich City with their entourage. The group was escorted by Sir Alfred, the commander of Glenwood's army, and his men. Their arrival was joyous as Alaric and his family warmly welcomed them at the castle gates.

"It is an honor to host Glenwood's finest," the king said, firmly clasping Lord Ethan's hand. "Your presence graces this momentous occasion."

Lord Ethan inclined his head respectfully. "The honor is ours, Your Majesty. We look forward to witnessing the games and the unity they will bring to the realm."

Lady Elara exchanged pleasantries with Isadora while Freja curtsied before the royal family. Prince Halsten stepped forward, taking her hand with a warm smile. "Welcome, Lady Freja. Aldrich City shines brighter with your arrival."

Freja smiled faintly. "Thank you, Your Highness. It's a pleasure to be here."

As the week progressed, gladiators from across the kingdom and beyond, from Botan to Argos, began arriving in Aldrich City. They marched through the city streets in a grand procession. The citizens lined the roads to cheer and wave, marveling at the warriors dressed in ornate armor and carrying a dazzling array of weapons. Each gladiator walked with pride, adding to the spectacle.

Alaric and his family watched the parade with admiration from the royal balcony. Freja and Prince Halsten stood beside Dhalia, Dora, and Amelia, who waved enthusiastically at the passing gladiators.

When the delegation from Veran approached, Dhalia's attention was drawn to a young man among their ranks. He stood tall, his dark hair framing a face of quiet determination. His polished armor gleamed in the sunlight, and he carried a longsword with an air of confidence.

Dhalia leaned forward slightly, craning her neck over the balcony's edge to get a better look at the young man. Her heart skipped a beat as their eyes met. For a moment, it felt as though the noise of the crowd and the procession's grandeur faded. His gaze lingered on her, his expression curious yet steady.

Realizing she had been caught staring, Dhalia quickly pulled back, her cheeks flushing crimson. She looked around nervously to see if anyone had noticed, but her companions seemed engrossed in the parade—except for Amelia, who smirked knowingly.

"Dhalia," she whispered teasingly, "I saw that."

Dhalia turned to her friend, feigning innocence. "Saw what?"

"You were staring at that Veran gladiator as though he held the secrets of the universe." Amelia's eyes sparkled with mischief.

"I was not!" Dhalia protested, though the redness of her cheeks betrayed her.

Amelia leaned closer, her voice dropping to a playful whisper. "He was staring back, you know."

Dhalia bit her lip, her gaze returning briefly to the young man as he continued down the street with his comrades. She quickly turned away, hoping to avoid further scrutiny, but her heart fluttered at remembering their brief connection.

Unbeknownst to her, the young Veran gladiator stole one last look over his shoulder as he marched, a faint smile on his lips. The moment passed, but its significance lingered, hinting at possibilities yet to unfold.

Dora and Amelia broke out in laughter.

Dhalia turned to her friends, hit Dora on the shoulder, and asked, "What?"

The two women laughed hysterically. "I thought I heard anyone who wanted you would have to live next to Freja. Why are you looking at someone from Veran?" Dora asked.

Dhalia placed her hand on her lips and signaled them to keep quiet.

Mefford stood concealed within the brush with his guard, Marvin, watching the gladiators parade into Aldrich City. The citizens' cheers and the sight of the royal family waving from the castle balcony only fueled the storm brewing inside him. His hands clenched into fists, and he began pacing restlessly behind the bushes. His mind clouded with anger and the effects of alcohol, he stumbled and fell to the ground, cursing under his breath.

Frustrated and unable to bear the scene any longer, he mounted his horse and rode toward Edgewood Forest. The journey was wild and unsteady, branches scraping against him as he urged his horse through the dense woods.

When he arrived at a small hut on the outskirts of the city, he dismounted his horse. "Stay here," he said to Marvin, stumbling to the door. He pounded on it repeatedly, his knuckles slamming against the weathered wood.

Petra jolted awake inside. She wrapped a shawl tightly around her shoulders and moved cautiously to the door. Opening it, she was met with the sight of Mefford, his eyes wild, bloodshot, and brimming with fury.

Without waiting for an invitation, he pushed past her, stumbling into the small room and collapsing into a chair in the corner. Petra closed the door and turned to observe him, her expression wary but calm. She had seen him in volatile states before, but this time, the darkness in his demeanor unnerved her.

"Sir," she said softly, "what brings you here? What can I do for you?"

Mefford glared at her, his face twisted with rage. "Why is everything going wrong?" he demanded, his voice a growl.

Petra approached cautiously, her sharp eyes studying him. "Nothing in life comes easily, young sir," she said calmly. "Destiny and reality must align for fulfillment to come."

Mefford's lip curled into a sneer. "What good are you if you can't grant my wishes?" he spat.

She remained steady despite the tension that hung thick in the air. "Granting your desires is simple, sir. But beware—what you seek may lead to your destruction if it does not align with your destiny."

Her words seemed to enrage Mefford further. He surged to his feet, his voice rising to a scream. "Do what you're paid to do and stop trying to confuse me, or I'll spill your blood and burn this cursed hut to the ground!"

Petra flinched but held her composure. "What do you want me to do for you, sir?" she asked, her voice trembling slightly.

Mefford moved toward her with unrestrained fury, grabbing her by the shoulders. His face was mere inches from hers as he screamed, "I want them dead!"

Petra's eyes widened with fear. "Who do you want dead, my prince?"

Mefford released her abruptly and pulled on his hair in frustration. His voice cracked as he screamed, "The king, the queen, anyone—everyone! Just kill somebody! Just make me a prince!"

Petra backed away, her heart pounding as she observed the man before her, consumed by desperation and rage. She swallowed hard, her mind racing as she tried to weigh her response.

"Sir," she said carefully, her voice low, "I will do as you command, but know this—power gained without honor will bring ruin, not glory."

Mefford's face darkened, but before he could respond, she continued, her voice firmer now. "You must understand the cost. There is no turning back once blood is spilled."

Silence filled the hut for a moment, broken only by Mefford's labored breathing. His eyes bored into Petra, a storm of anger and uncertainty swirling within them.

"Do it," he finally snarled. "I don't care about the cost. Just make it happen."

As he glared at her, his face twisted in bitterness and confusion. Petra, her expression steady and calm, moved purposefully to a shelf where she kept her mystical tools. She pulled a small pouch from its resting place and retrieved a handful of crow feathers.

Without a word, she began circling them over Mefford's head, her eyes closing in concentration. Her movements were rhythmic, almost hypnotic, as she muttered a low chant under her breath. Mefford watched her intently, his fists clenching and unclenching as the tension in the room thickened.

After a moment, Petra opened her eyes. "You will surely be a prince at Verdant Castle," she intoned, her gaze piercing as it locked onto Mefford's.

With a flick of her wrist, she tossed the feathers into the hearth's flames. They sizzled and cracked, releasing a plume of dark smoke that filled the small room with a pungent, almost oppressive aroma. The air grew heavy, and an unnatural silence settled over the space.

Mefford's lips curled into a twisted grin before he erupted into a fit of hysterical laughter. The sound was jarring, echoing off the hut's walls as his body shook with uncontrollable mirth. He threw his head back, laughing louder and louder until he tipped the chair over.

Petra's eyes remained on him as he lay sprawled on the ground, his laughter slowly fading into ragged breaths. Exhaustion overtook him, and his body went limp as he slipped into a restless sleep.

She sighed, her shoulders slumping slightly as her tension eased. She fetched a woolen blanket from a nearby chest and carefully draped it over Mefford's body. Kneeling beside him, she placed a rolled cloth under his head as a makeshift pillow, her movements gentle despite his volatile behavior.

"Sleep, sir," she murmured. "For what awaits you is far more than you can imagine."

Rising to her feet, Petra returned to her work, her mind heavy with the consequences of Mefford's desperation and the ominous path he seemed determined to take. The flickering flames of the hearth cast shifting shadows across the room as the night deepened, marking the beginning of a dangerous chapter in Mefford's life.

Hours passed, and Mefford slept fitfully. His rest was haunted by a nightmare that gripped him with an unrelenting terror. In his dream, he was walking alone in the dense woods near Bear Cave Castle. The air turned icy, and an unnatural darkness enveloped him, blotting out the faintest trace of light.

Flames erupted from the surrounding trees, their crackling heat forcing him to stumble back. His eyes widened in fear as two massive beasts with the features of a lion and a dragon emerged from the darkness.

Smoke emanated from their nostrils. Their eyes burned with an other-worldly light, locking onto him with predatory intent.

Behind the beasts, two shadowy figures stepped forward, their faces hidden behind black cloths, leaving only their piercing eyes visible. They moved with cold precision, each carrying a bow, with swords hanging at their sides. Their silence was more unnerving than any sound they could have made.

The beasts lunged at Mefford, their mouths opening to unleash torrents of flame. He turned to run, but his legs felt heavy, as if the earth had conspired to trap him. The ground twisted and warped beneath his feet, making escape impossible. The creatures closed in, their fiery breath searing the air around him.

Mefford jolted awake with a gasp, his heart pounding violently. His body was sweaty, and his breath came in short, ragged bursts. He looked around the dimly lit hut, expecting to see the beasts ready to pounce, but there was nothing except Petra, sitting silently in her chair. Her calm gaze rested on him, her expression unreadable.

Without acknowledging her, Mefford struggled to his feet, his body trembling. "It was just a dream," he muttered, though the terror still gripped him. He stumbled toward the door, his hands fumbling with the latch as the first rays of dawn seeped into the room.

"Mefford," Petra said softly. "What did you see?"

He paused for a brief moment but then shook his head. "Nothing that matters," he replied hoarsely, refusing to meet her eyes.

Pushing the door open, he stepped outside. The bright light of the rising sun struck his face, forcing him to shield his eyes with one hand. He approached his horse, tied to a post nearby, and mounted it unsteadily. He spurred the animal into a gallop without speaking to Marvin, fleeing as if the nightmares still pursued him.

Petra remained in the doorway, her eyes narrowing with concern as she watched him disappear into the distance. The unease in her chest deepened, and she sighed, returning to her hut. The faint, acrid smell of burned feathers lingered in the air as she shut the door, her mind heavy with foreboding.

"Whatever path you've chosen, Mefford, he who seeks answers from the dead finds a ghost," she whispered under her breath.

CHAPTER 20

THE ATMOSPHERE WAS EXCITING IN the days following the gladiators' arrival in Aldrich City. Citizens from all walks of life flocked to the gladiator park, eager to watch the warriors train at their tent camps. It was a chance to familiarize themselves with the athletes and choose favorites to support during the games.

One late afternoon, Dhalia, Amelia, and Dora were escorted by six guards to the bustling training grounds. The air buzzed with energy as fighters from far and wide displayed their skills in preparation for the competition. The women strolled through the park, stopping briefly at several of the camps of gladiators. The variety of fighting styles and armaments on display was mesmerizing.

Eventually, they arrived at the Argos gladiators' training grounds. Dhalia's attention was immediately drawn to the young man she had noticed during the gladiators' march into the city. He had dark hair, striking brown eyes, and a commanding presence. A small silver ring glinted in his left ear, adding to his rugged appeal. His firm, confident stance and the quiet intensity of his expression captivated her.

Dhalia turned to Dora and Amelia, her voice steady but insistent. "Let's watch the Argos men for a while."

Dora raised an eyebrow, a teasing smile tugging at her lips, but nodded. "Of course. Lead the way."

She exchanged a knowing look with Amelia, who followed as the group moved closer to the fence surrounding the training area. From there, they had a clear view of the action.

In the center of the arena, the booming voice of the commander, Fentuo, rang out over the din of the camp. "Kudus!" he called, his tone both commanding and encouraging. "Step forward and show them the strength of Argos!"

At the summons, the young gladiator Dhalia had been watching stepped forward. He was tall, standing just over six feet, and moved with a controlled grace that drew the attention of everyone nearby. His sharp eyes briefly swept over the gathered spectators before focusing on the task.

"That's him," Dhalia murmured, her voice barely audible.

Amelia leaned closer, smirking. "The one you can't stop staring at?"

Dhalia straightened, feigning indifference. "He has potential, that's all."

Dora chuckled softly. "Potential? That's one way to put it. Maybe he can do other things."

"Other things like what exactly?" Amelia asked.

But Dhalia tapped Dora on the shoulder and said, "Watch."

Fentuo continued calling out gladiators one by one to step into the ring and challenge Kudus. One after another, each was swiftly defeated. Kudus sent his opponents crashing to the ground, many clutching bruised limbs or aching sides, unable to rise.

"Ogram!" Fentuo barked, his voice commanding attention as he summoned a larger gladiator from the sidelines.

The man stepped into the ring, towering at six feet four inches. His muscular frame and menacing grin made the crowd stir with anticipation. The other gladiators paused their training, their eyes fixed on the match unfolding before them. Tension hung thick in the air as calm and composed Kudus faced his hulking opponent.

The two men squared off, and Fentuo raised his hand. "Begin!"

Ogram wasted no time, charging at Kudus with astonishing speed for a man his size. His massive fist connected with Kudus's chest, sending him sprawling to the ground. The crowd gasped, stunned by the force of the blow. Kudus, however, didn't stay down. He rolled to his feet, a determined grin on his face.

"You're quick to get up," Ogram sneered, his voice laced with arrogance. "But I'll put you down for good."

He charged again, swinging a mighty arm. With impeccable agility, Kudus sidestepped the attack and leaped into the air, delivering a sharp kick to Ogram's back. The larger man staggered forward, releasing a grunt of pain as he tried to regain his footing. Kudus didn't wait—he seized Ogram's right arm and, using a sudden burst of strength, flipped the massive gladiator over his shoulder. Ogram landed hard on his back, the impact resonating across the training grounds.

A collective hush fell over the crowd as Kudus swiftly moved to pin his opponent, locking him in a chokehold. The man thrashed beneath him, his face contorted with effort as he tried to break free. Kudus's grip, however, was unyielding, his arms like bands of iron.

Realizing he couldn't escape, Ogram slapped the ground repeatedly in surrender, his body trembling with defeat.

"Enough! The fight is over!" Fentuo shouted, stepping forward to end the match.

Kudus immediately released Ogram and stood, his chest rising and falling as he caught his breath. The crowd erupted into cheers at his victory against such a formidable opponent.

Extending a hand, Kudus offered to help Ogram to his feet. For a moment, Ogram hesitated, his pride wounded. But after a brief pause, he accepted the gesture. Kudus hauled him up, their gazes locking. Ogram's expression was a mix of begrudging respect and frustration.

Fentuo stepped between them, clapping Kudus on the shoulder. "Well done," he said, his booming voice filled with approval. "You've earned your place among the best of Argos today."

Kudus nodded respectfully, stepping back as the crowd continued to roar. Among them, Dhalia watched from the fence, her heart racing as she exchanged a fleeting glance with the victorious gladiator. She quickly turned away, her cheeks flushing.

As Kudus left the training grounds, her gaze lingered on him. She barely noticed the world around her, lost in thought, until Dora's voice jolted her back to reality.

"Dhalia! Dhalia! Dhalia!" Dora's tone was teasing as she waved a hand in front of her friend's face.

Startled, Dhalia turned abruptly, blinking as she tried to refocus. "What? Were you saying something?" she asked, her voice flustered.

Amelia and Dora exchanged amused looks before breaking into a fit of giggles. Dora covered her mouth with her hand, her eyes sparkling with mischief. "Oh, someone is daydreaming. Why don't you just march right over to his tent and tell him what's on your mind?"

Dhalia's cheeks flushed again, and she swatted her friend's arm playfully. "Stop it! And for heaven's sake, no one should hear of this—not even Freja."

Dora grinned, pretending to zip her lips. "Your secret is safe with me," she said, breaking into laughter again.

Amelia smiled knowingly. "Don't worry, Dhalia. We'll keep this little moment to ourselves. But you should know, you're not very subtle."

Dhalia nervously looked at their guards. They had overheard the exchange, but they all maintained stoic expressions, their eyes fixed straight ahead.

"Thank you," Dhalia said. "I'd rather not have anyone, especially Freja, pestering me about this."

Dora smirked, her tone softening. "Fine, fine. We'll let it go—for now." The ladies stayed a little longer, watching the other gladiators' practice. Each gladiator displayed a unique skill, but it was the young gladiator who impressed them the most.

As the sun began to set, the ladies started their walk back to the castle. Dahlia's thoughts lingered on the young gladiator. She couldn't help but feel a strange mix of excitement and nervousness about the unexpected connection she had felt toward the man.

Not far from the training grounds, Prince Halsten and Freja rolled through the winding streets of Aldrich City, accompanied by DeMarco and Asger, two loyal guards. The energy of the upcoming games buzzed around them, and the streets were alive with the chatter and excitement of citizens preparing for the festivities. A cool evening breeze added to the pleasant atmosphere, and as the couple walked side by side, they had a playful energy.

"Are you that interested in the games?" Freja teased, her hand brushing lightly against Halsten's as they navigated the crowded streets. "Or is this just your way of pretending to be one of the common folks?"

He looked at her, a smile tugging at his lips. "Maybe I just enjoy spending time with you and needed an excuse to get you away from the castle."

Freja returned his smile. "I like that you think about these things. Your family has been wonderful, but time with just you? That's always special."

Halsten stopped for a moment, his tone growing more earnest. "I don't want to share your attention with anyone, my love. Not now, not ever."

She laughed softly, her eyes meeting his. "Is that so? I thought you were too busy with all the bureaucracy of princely duties to be concerned with stealing moments like this."

Halsten turned toward her. "Maybe I've learned to make time for the things that truly matter."

Her heart skipped a beat, a warmth spreading as his sincerity reached her. She held his gaze, her laughter softening into something more meaningful. "You've always been good with words, Halsten. But I wonder if you're as bold with showing affection when it's not just the two of us."

Halsten smiled, taking her hand gently but firmly. "Let me show you," he said, leading her toward a nearby garden.

The city's noise faded into the background as they entered the secluded space. It was peaceful, the flowers in full bloom, their vibrant colors glowing in the warm light of the setting sun. The air smelled faintly of roses and lavender, wrapping the moment in tranquility.

"I suppose I'll have to prove it, then," Halsten said softly, his voice barely audible over the gentle rustle of leaves.

Freja tilted her head, curiosity dancing in her eyes. "What exactly are you trying to prove, Halsten?" she asked playfully.

"That not everything in my life revolves around royal duties," he replied, his gaze unwavering. "Some things are about choice. About whom we let into our hearts."

For a moment, the world seemed to pause around them. The air between them crackled, their years of shared desires and moments culminating in this instant of vulnerability.

Freja's eyes glistened with emotion. "I think you're proving it right now," she whispered.

Without another word, Halsten leaned in, brushing his mouth softly against hers. Freja responded, her hand reaching up to rest lightly on his chest as their kiss deepened. Their lips parted slightly, and their tongues passionately embraced, expressing what words could not.

Nearby, DeMarco and Asger stood facing the other way, their stances alert as they ensured no one disturbed the moment of intimacy.

Halsten rested his forehead against Freja's as the kiss ended, his voice a soft murmur. "This is where I want to be, Freja. With you."

She smiled, her voice equally tender. "And I with you, Halsten."

They lingered in the quiet garden for a few more moments, savoring the peace before returning to the lively streets of Aldrich City.

As Halsten and Freja stepped back onto the road to continue their stroll, they noticed Dhalia, Amelia, and Dora approaching from the opposite direction. The three ladies greeted them respectfully with curtsies.

"Where have you been?" Freja asked, her tone warm but curious.

"We were watching the combat training of the various gladiator groups," Dhalia responded.

Halsten smiled. "Did you see any good fighters?"

"Yes," Dhalia said quickly, her tone betraying a touch of enthusiasm.

Dora and Amelia exchanged knowing giggles, their amusement evident.

Halsten raised an eyebrow. "Are we missing something?"

Dhalia shot a glance at Dora and Amelia, silently signaling them to remain quiet.

Freja, catching the exchange, turned to Dora. "What are you hiding from us?" she asked.

"Nothing, Lady Freja," Dora replied quickly, though her smile betrayed her.

Halsten chuckled. "Are you going to hide something from the prince of this land?"

"We are not hiding anything from you, my prince," Dhalia interjected, her voice steady.

Halsten tilted his head slightly, amused. "Dora, speak up, or I will see you're not invited to the wedding."

Dora laughed nervously, glancing at Dhalia for a moment before speaking. "Dhalia is in love with one of the gladiators," she confessed.

Freja gasped in mock surprise, laughter bubbling up as she turned to Dhalia. "Oh, I see! And who might this gladiator be?" she asked.

"There is a young, handsome gladiator from Argos," Dora replied, her grin widening.

"Dhalia!" Freja exclaimed. "Is this true?"

Dhalia blushed deeply, her composure faltering. "It's nothing," she muttered, glancing at the ground. "Dora exaggerates everything."

Halsten cleared his throat, a knowing smile on his face. "Let us visit the vendors before returning to the castle," he suggested, smoothly changing the subject.

"May we join you, Your Majesty?" Amelia asked.

"You may." Halsten gestured for the ladies to follow.

The group continued their walk, the earlier conversation leaving a cheerful energy in the air as they made their way toward the vendor stalls.

The vendors in the bustling market square greeted Prince Halsten and Lady Freja with excitement and respect. Their voices rose as the royal couple approached, and they bowed and curtsied while gesturing to their wares.

"Your Highness! My lady! Welcome to the market!" one vendor called out, her hands clasped in delight.

"Good day to you all," Prince Halsten replied warmly, nodding to the gathered citizens. He paused at a stall displaying an assortment of vibrant fruits, picking up a ripe apple and inspecting it. "Your produce looks exceptional this season."

"Thank you, Your Highness," the fruit seller proudly replied. "The recent peace has done wonders for our harvest."

Freja smiled as she examined a basket of fragrant herbs nearby. "These are lovely. I'm sure the castle cooks would appreciate such fresh ingredients."

Another vendor chimed in, holding up a jar of golden honey. "My Lady, this honey is from the finest hives in the region. It would make a perfect addition to your wedding feast."

Freja blushed lightly at the mention of her wedding but accepted the jar with a gracious smile. "Thank you. I'll be sure to mention it to the steward."

The group moved through the market square, and the prince and Freja frequently stopped to greet the citizens and admire the displayed goods. Halsten spoke with a butcher about the quality of his meats, while Freja shared kind words with a seamstress showcasing beautifully embroidered fabrics.

Freja's friends followed closely, enjoying the lively atmosphere. Dora leaned toward Dhalia and whispered, "You should have invited your gladiator friend to join us. He might've enjoyed this outing."

Dhalia shot her a pointed look, her cheeks warming, but said nothing, focusing instead on the colorful flowers at another stall.

After spending considerable time in the market, Halsten turned to the gathered citizens, his voice carrying over the bustling square. "Thank you for your hospitality and the care you put into your work. It reflects the strength and heart of our kingdom."

The citizens bowed and clapped as the royal entourage began their journey back to the castle. The camaraderie and warmth of the day left everyone in high spirits, and the excitement of the upcoming games and wedding added an extra spark to the lively atmosphere.

CHAPTER 21

That evening, Lord Warhouse arrived at Bear Cave Castle with his trusted guard, Aldon. As they passed through the gates, Aldon remained in the outer court with two of Darius's guards while Lord Warhouse proceeded inside.

Lord Warhouse turned to Darius. "I came as soon as I received your message."

"Thank you for coming, my friend," Darius said, his tone conspiratorial. "With the wedding and the Gladiator Games proceeding as planned, we must move quickly to capitalize on the chaos."

"Indeed, Your Grace. All preparations are in place, awaiting only your command."

"How many men can we position inside the city before the festivities begin?" Darius asked, leaning forward.

"With three trips a day for an entire month, we can move approximately 500," Lord Warhouse replied confidently.

Spreading a detailed map across the table, he pointed to strategic entry points and potential locations for the men to remain hidden. He and Darius spoke in hushed tones, punctuated by occasional nods and sharp gestures.

When their plans were finalized, Lord Warhouse rolled up the map and tucked it into the folds of his robe.

"I will send word when everything is in place," he said as he prepared to leave.

"Thank you, my friend." Darius clasped his arm. "We must ensure that no detail is overlooked."

Lord Warhouse nodded, bid Darius farewell, and departed the castle. He mounted his horse and rode off with his guard following behind him.

Early the following day, Lord Warhouse stood in the courtyard of his estate, observing as Aldon addressed a group of guards who had been carefully selected from the far Southern regions of the kingdom. These men had been offered double pay for their work and tasked with a critical assignment at the farm colony.

Aldon's voice was commanding. "Gentlemen, today you embark on a vital mission to the farm colony. Your task is to haul supplies of grapes, tomatoes, pumpkins, beans, wheat, corn, millet, rye, and barley back to Aldrich City. As thousands have already arrived, these provisions are crucial for sustaining the city during the games and festivities."

He paused, letting his words sink in. "The king has assured that your families will be cared for in your absence over the next month. If you have any messages, deliver them to me personally, and I will ensure they are sent."

His gaze swept over the men, his tone growing more serious. "You have been chosen for this mission because of your skills and loyalty to the king's court. Remember, secrecy and security are of the utmost importance during this assignment. Do not let your guard down for even a moment."

The men straightened, their faces solemn. "Yes, Sir," the men responded.

"Good," Aldon said. "Prepare yourselves and make the kingdom proud."

The guards saluted and began mounting their wagons, ready to embark on their mission. Lord Warhouse watched them depart with satisfaction, his mind already turning to the next step in the intricate plan he and Darius had devised.

He nodded to Aldon and departed without another word.

Aldon stepped in front of the assembled guards again, his tone firm. "Get moving before the sun rises. Stay alert and on task."

The group of twenty-one men with four sturdy carts mounted their horses and began their journey. They traveled northward through the thick woods, heading toward River Ellyn North, winding their way through dense trees and rugged terrain. The early hours were quiet, with each man scanning their surroundings, their focus sharp and deliberate. As the woods brightened with morning light, their spirits eased, and conversation began to flow freely among them.

When they reached the colony, the farmers welcomed them and promptly began loading the carts with fresh produce and grains, including grapes, tomatoes, pumpkins, beans, wheat, corn, millet, rye, and barley. While they did this, the guards rested, sharing a simple brunch of bread and dried meats. They prepared to return along the same path once the goods were all in place and securely strapped. The men mounted their horses and began the journey back to Aldrich City.

As they approached River Ellyn North on their return, the leader of the men raised his hand again to signal another halt. "Let's take a moment for a water break and water the horses," he said calmly.

The men dismounted, tying their horses to nearby trees. They stretched and drank from their flasks, enjoying the brief reprieve from the journey. The air around them was still save for the gentle rustling of leaves and the sound of the river flowing nearby.

Suddenly, dark figures emerged from the surrounding woods, their black robes blending into the shadows. The ambush was swift and ruthless. The attackers descended upon the unsuspecting guards with deadly efficiency, their weapons glinting in the filtered sunlight. The air erupted with the clash of steel, shouts of alarm, and cries of pain.

The guards fought valiantly but were overwhelmed by the assailants' precision and sheer numbers. Blood stained the ground as the attackers pressed their advantage, showing no mercy. One by one, the men fell, their bodies collapsing onto the forest floor.

Their leader stood apart from the chaos, his expression cold and detached. He watched as his comrades were slaughtered, his hand resting idly on the hilt of his sword. Realizing the betrayal, one guard broke free from the fray and sprinted toward the trees.

"Traitor!" the man shouted, his voice filled with fury and disbelief as he ran for his life.

The leader moved with chilling accuracy. He drew his bow, knocked an arrow, and released it without hesitation. It struck the fleeing man in the back. He let out a strangled cry before collapsing face-first, his body lying still among the fallen leaves.

As silence fell over the forest, the man turned to the attackers. "Dispose of the bodies," he ordered. "Burn the evidence and leave no trace."

The assailants nodded. They dragged the lifeless bodies toward the riverbank and began their grim task. Tapas stood silently, watching the scene without showing any compassion.

The attackers, now exposed in the daylight, removed their disguises to reveal uniforms identical to those of their slain victims. Moving swiftly, they covered the dead with branches and foliage to conceal the carnage. They then regrouped near the riverbank, awaiting further orders.

Two figures emerged from the shadows, their movements purposeful. As they approached, the attackers stood at attention. Darius and Tapas removed their disguises, revealing their identities.

The men immediately bowed, speaking in unison. "My lord."

Darius surveyed the scene with a satisfied expression. "Thank you for your service to the realm," he said, calm and commanding. "Now, assume your new roles and await further instructions. You will hear from me soon."

At his signal, Tapas stepped forward, pulling small pouches of gold from his saddlebag. He handed one to each of the attackers, the coins jingling softly as they exchanged hands. "A reward for your loyalty," he said curtly.

Darius nodded, his gaze sharp. "You know what to do," he said before mounting his horse alongside Tapas. The two men rode off, disappearing into the forest.

With the sinister mission completed, the leader of the group turned to the newly recruited men. "Load the weapons beneath the produce," he ordered.

The men obeyed without hesitation, carefully concealing the armaments beneath layers of fruits and grains. Once the task was complete, they saddled up and took control of the carts, ensuring everything appeared as before. Their procession continued toward Aldrich City with their seemingly harmless delivery.

This operation had only been the beginning. The same scheme was repeated over several weeks with chilling precision. A few groups of guards were sent along the farm colony route each time, only to meet a similar fate as the first, being replaced by impostors.

Once inside Aldrich City, the infiltrators seamlessly blended in with the population, unnoticed amid the bustling crowds preparing for the games and festivities. The sinister plan unfolded methodically, each step tightening the noose around the kingdom's unsuspecting defenses.

CHAPTER 22

Ｏne morning, a week before the Gladiator Games, Major and his men were stationed at their camp near Edgewood Forest. The afternoon's quiet was broken when a group of men on horseback appeared at the gate. The guards above the gate sounded the alarm, their calls echoing through the camp.

Hearing the commotion, Major stepped out of his tent. His men moved quickly toward the gate, drawing their swords and preparing for any potential threat.

As the group approached, one guard called, "What brings you here?"

One of the riders removed the cloth concealing his face, revealing himself to be Mefford. The guard looked up at Major for direction. Major met his gaze and gave a curt nod. The guard opened the gate, and the visitors rode into the compound.

Major descended from the balcony, his anger evident in every step. Reaching the gathered men, he grabbed a sword from one of his guards and pointed it at Mefford, his voice a low snarl. "You've got some nerve showing your face here after what you and Jason did."

Before Major could close the distance, one of the riders leaped from his horse with startling agility and delivered a powerful kick to his chest, sending him sprawling to the ground. The camp erupted into chaos as men reached for their weapons, but Caine removed his disguise, stepping forward with his sword drawn.

"Stand down!" he ordered as he pointed his blade at Major, who was struggling to rise. "What right do you have to attack Mefford?"

Major, his chest heaving, glared up at Caine. After a tense moment, he released his sword, signaling his men to lower their weapons. "What do you want here?" he demanded, his voice strained but steady.

"We have a proposal for you," Mefford replied evenly.

Major's eyes narrowed. He gestured toward the masked rider who remained on his horse. "Then let's hear it," he said, motioning for his men to allow the group passage.

The masked rider dismounted, joining Mefford, Caine, and Major as they moved into his tent. Boyd, one of Major's trusted guards, followed closely, his hand resting on the hilt of his sword. Meanwhile, some of Mefford's men and Major's men stood guard outside the tent of Major, ensuring there were no interruptions.

Inside, Major, with Boyd by his side, led Mefford, Caine, and the others to a dimly lit tent. He turned to Mefford, his tone laced with suspicion. "What is this proposal?"

The last man removed his mask, revealing a face that Major did not immediately recognize but that carried an undeniable air of authority. After scrutinizing it for a few seconds, Major's expression shifted to one of recognition. "Darius," he said with a sly grin.

Turning to Mefford, his tone sharp, he said, "Darius has no title; his name will not gain any favors here."

Before Mefford could respond, Caine stepped forward, his gaze sharp and unwavering. "You will address him as 'Your Grace,'" he said firmly.

Realizing his error, Major quickly composed himself and bowed deeply. "Your Grace, welcome to the home of the Forest Knights," he said.

Darius regarded Major with a cold, stern gaze but said nothing. Sensing the tension, Major gestured toward a chair. "Forgive my lack of decorum, Your Grace," he added apologetically.

Darius nodded slightly and took the offered seat. He turned his attention to his son and nodded for him to speak.

Mefford looked briefly at Tapas and then at Darius before addressing Major. "We need you and your men to help us take over the kingdom."

Major leaned back slightly, a chuckle escaping his lips. "You're out of your mind," he said, shaking his head. "All the soldiers from the kingdom are gathered here for the wedding and the games. How do you expect to take the throne with such numbers?"

Darius's voice cut through the room, calm and measured. "We will not attack during the wedding or the games."

Major's interest was piqued, and he leaned forward. "Then when?"

"We will strike the night after the prince departs for McKenzie Castle with his guards and retinue. Tradition dictates that the newly married prince sees off the visiting nobles and soldiers before traveling to his new home. By then, the kingdom's defenses will be significantly reduced."

Major nodded slowly, his curiosity growing. "And my role in this?"

"You and your men will ambush the prince and his guards on their journey to McKenzie Castle," Darius continued. "At the same time, we will launch an attack on the castle itself."

Major stroked his chin thoughtfully. "So, you're counting on tradition to thin their defenses and make them vulnerable. It's a bold plan. And the prince—what do you want done with him?"

Darius's voice turned cold. "Leave no one alive."

Mefford interjected, "Bring Lady Freja to me unharmed."

Darius nodded approvingly. "Freja belongs to Mefford. Ensure she is taken alive."

Major remained silent for a moment, calculating the risks and rewards. Finally, he leaned back and smirked. "It's a daring plan, Your Grace. But what's in it for me and my men?"

Darius didn't respond immediately. Instead, he gestured to Tapas, who stepped out of the room. Moments later, he returned with two guards carrying a large, ornate box. They placed it in front of Darius and opened it, revealing it was filled with glittering gold coins.

Major's eyes widened with greed, a grin spreading across his face. "Well, now you have my attention." His tone was light, but his intentions clear.

"There will be more," Darius said firmly, his voice laced with warning. "But remember—this arrangement must remain a secret. The day someone discovers our plan will be the last you draw breath."

Major's grin faltered slightly, but he nodded. "Understood, Your Grace. I'll make sure no one finds out."

Major extended his hand to seal the deal, but Darius stood, ignoring the gesture. Pulling his disguise back over his face, he turned toward the door. As he reached the threshold, he paused and spoke without turning. "Tapas will send word when the time comes."

Major rose and followed his guests outside, watching as Darius, Mefford, Caine, and their guards mounted their horses and disappeared in the distance.

CHAPTER 23

Late that afternoon in Aldrich City, Dhalia convinced Dora to accompany her to the market square, secretly hoping to glimpse the young Argos gladiator, Kudus. As they approached the Argos tent, they found the area surprisingly quiet compared to the previous day.

Dhalia spotted a man hanging clothes on a drying line and approached him. "Why is it so quiet here?" she asked. "Where are the gladiators?"

He paused in his work and turned to her respectfully. "My lady, the men are resting after the afternoon training session. They will resume practice this evening."

Dhalia hesitated briefly before asking, "Do you know where Kudus is?"

The young man nodded. "He went to the market center with Megateo, the master, and Ogram to get food for the tent."

"Thank you," Dhalia replied with a polite smile. Turning to Dora, she said, "Let's head to the market center."

The two women went to the lively square, where vendors called out their goods and citizens bustled about, trading and buying. They stopped at a fruit seller's stand, inspecting the colorful produce on display. The air was filled with the scents of ripe oranges, plums, and spices.

Dhalia picked up an orange and ran her fingers over its vibrant skin. "This one looks perfect," she remarked to her friend.

Dora chuckled softly. "I don't think you're paying attention to the fruit."

Dhalia smiled, though she didn't respond, moving to the next stand to inspect some plums. The market was crowded, and the noise of trade surrounded them.

Suddenly, shouts erupted from nearby. Chaos unfolded as a group of men began fighting amongst themselves. Weapons flashed as they clashed, their raised voices alarming the citizens—people scattered in all directions, seeking shelter from the sudden violence.

Dhalia and Dora froze as armed men moved toward them. The two guards accompanying them immediately stepped forward, drawing their swords to intercept the attackers.

"Stay behind us, my ladies!" one of the men barked.

The clash of steel rang through the air as the guards engaged the approaching men. The attackers moved with aggression, swinging their weapons fiercely. One of the guards parried a blow and countered with precision, forcing the man back. The other guard held his ground, expertly deflecting attacks from two opponents simultaneously.

Dora grabbed Dhalia's arm. "We need to move! This is no place to stand idle."

Dhalia nodded, her face pale, but she hesitated, scanning the chaos around them. Her eyes landed on a man and a woman standing inside a nearby shop, who motioned urgently for Dhalia and Dora to enter. "Quickly! You'll be safe in here!" the woman called out, her voice filled with concern.

Dhalia and Dora rushed into the shop. As soon as they stepped inside, the woman swiftly closed the door behind them. Before they could react, two men grabbed them forcefully from the shadows.

"What are you doing? Let us go!" Dora cried, struggling against their grip.

"Be quiet," one of the men snarled, his voice low and threatening.

Before they could resist further, the men struck them on the backs of their heads. The two women collapsed to the floor, unconscious. The men worked quickly, lifting their limp forms into two large baskets hidden at the back of the shop. They covered them with jute sacks, loaded them onto a waiting cart, and began riding away through the narrow alley behind the shop.

Meanwhile, the guards who had been with Dhalia and Dora searched for them, calling out their names as they moved through the market. Noticing the alley behind the shops, they went there to investigate.

They spotted two men riding a cart loaded with what appeared to be fruit baskets. The guards approached, their eyes narrowing with suspicion.

"Stop!" one of them commanded, raising a hand to signal the cart drivers.

The two men exchanged a quick, nervous look before whipping the reins and urging the horse to speed up. The cart jolted forward, bouncing over the uneven ground as they fled.

"After them!" the second guard shouted, breaking into a run.

As the guards pursued, armed men emerged from behind another shop, intercepting their path. The attackers brandished weapons and charged, forcing the guards to defend themselves.

One of the guards blocked a strike with his blade, gritting his teeth as he countered with a mighty swing. "Who sent you?" he demanded, though no answer came. His partner fought beside him, fending off two attackers at once. The attackers seemed intent on delaying them rather than delivering fatal blows.

Meanwhile, the cart carrying the unconscious Dhalia and Dora disappeared into the busy streets, heading toward the city gates. The guards, unable to break free from their attackers, realized with growing frustration that the captors were escaping with their charges. The ambush had been carefully planned, leaving the guards outnumbered and desperate to regroup.

The cart hit a rock along the road, causing one of the baskets to tumble off and spill its contents onto the ground. Dhalia rolled out, dazed, her head pounding as she tried to make sense of her surroundings. She opened her eyes just as one of the men jumped off the cart and approached her.

"Get back in!" he barked, grabbing her arm roughly.

"No! Let me go!" Dhalia screamed; her voice carried in the wind.

As the man tried to shove her back into the basket, a sudden blow to his side sent him stumbling. He turned sharply, pulling out his sword, and his companion leaped off the cart to join him. Before they could react further, two men—Kudus and Ogram—stepped forward, their swords already drawn.

"What do you think you're doing?" one of the kidnappers snarled, his stance defensive.

"I will advise you to run so I will not have to break your bones," Kudus replied coolly, his grip tightening on his sword.

One of the men smirked and turned to the other, "Who is this fool?"

The fight erupted fiercely. The man facing Kudus swung his sword in a wide arc, but Kudus moved with agility, dodging the strike and closing the distance between them. The kidnapper fought hard, his swings powerful, but Kudus's skill proved superior. As his opponent lunged, Kudus leaped into the air, using the man's shoulder as leverage to spring over him. Landing gracefully behind him, Kudus slashed the back of the man's knee, sending him crumpling to the ground.

At the same time, Ogram used his immense strength to overpower the second attacker, hoisting him in the air and slamming him down, causing his neck to break. Just then, two city guards arrived at the scene, swords drawn and ready. Kudus and Ogram stepped back, allowing them to restrain the attacker who had been slashed by Kudus in the knee, tying his hands securely in front of them.

Kudus turned to Dhalia, who was standing by Megateo, his and Ogram's master, trembling slightly but unharmed. He sheathed his sword and approached her, his expression softening.

"Are you all right, my lady?" he asked, his voice gentle.

Dhalia nodded. "I am well, thanks to you. I owe you my life."

Kudus smiled faintly, his eyes locking with hers. "It was my pleasure, always," he said, his tone sincere.

Dhalia blushed under his gaze but managed a small smile in return. "Thank you."

One of the guards turned to Dhalia and Dora. "Are you both unharmed?" he asked.

"My head hurts," Dora replied.

Amid the commotion, Kudus, Ogram, and Megateo slipped away quietly, disappearing into the forest before anyone could question them. Dhalia's eyes lingered on the spot where Kudus had stood, her thoughts swirling with gratitude and something more profound as the chaos around her subsided.

<hr>

When Dhalia and Dora arrived at the castle, Freja hurried to meet them, her face filled with concern. "How are you? Are you hurt?" she asked, her voice trembling with worry.

"We are fine, my lady," Dhalia reassured her, her tone steady but tired.

Freja embraced her friends tightly, her relief palpable. "Thank the heavens," she whispered.

Once they were seated, Freja brought water for them, her care unwavering as she ensured their comfort.

Halsten and Albert entered shortly after, their expressions solemn as they approached the women. Halsten spoke first. "We heard what happened. Are you certain you're unharmed?"

"We are fine," Dora replied firmly. "Some men intervened and rescued us."

Albert studied them closely, then nodded. "Good. I am glad you are well. We'll get to the bottom of this."

With that, Halsten and Albert left the room, accompanied by DeMarco and Anders. They headed toward the castle dungeons where the attacker was being prepared for interrogation.

The dungeon was dark and foreboding, the air thick with dampness and despair. As Halsten and Albert descended the intimidating corridor, they heard the screams of the attacker.

Upon entering the interrogation chamber, they found Axilla, the commander of Aldrich City prisons, waiting for them. He was a tall, imposing figure with a muscular frame and piercing eyes that instilled fear in prisoners and guards alike. Beside him stood Tomei, the king's alchemist, a man of small stature known for his unsettling methods and feared by many in the kingdom.

Halsten motioned for Axilla to join him. "Do we know anything about who is behind the attack?" he asked, his tone sharp with urgency.

"My prince, nothing yet," Axilla replied, his voice low. "The prisoner has refused to speak."

Albert folded his arms. "What are our options?"

"Tomei is here to use his concoctions." Axilla glanced at the alchemist.

Halsten turned to Tomei and gave a curt nod. "Do what you must. We need answers."

Tomei stepped forward, his small frame seemingly unthreatening, though the glint in his eyes suggested otherwise. He stood before the prisoner, his gaze locking onto the man's. "Do you even understand what you've gotten yourself into?" he asked, his voice soft but carrying a chilling edge.

The attacker looked at Tomei, confusion and fear flickering in his eyes. He remained silent.

Tomei smiled thinly. "He who rattles a bee's hive shall be the first to tell how painful its sting is."

Reaching into a pouch held by his assistant, he removed a red powder and poured it into a cup. He added water, and the mixture began to bubble and smoke, filling the room with a pungent aroma. The smoke swirled around the prisoner, whose eyes darted wildly, fear taking hold.

"What—what is that?" the prisoner stammered, his voice shaky.

Tomei leaned closer, his smile never faltering. "Fear lies in the bottom of the unknown. This, my friend, will loosen your tongue. Speak now, and you might spare yourself what comes next."

The prisoner hesitated, his resolve visibly crumbling as the smoke thickened. The room fell silent, save for the faint hiss of the concoction in Tomei's hands. Halsten and Albert watched closely, awaiting the prisoner's response.

Tomei nodded to the guards, who immediately pulled on the chains shackling the prisoner's wrists, tightening them against the wall. Another guard strapped a harness around the man's head, securing it firmly under his chin and fastening it to a metal bar behind him. This forced his head backward, his face tilted toward the ceiling of the dim cell.

Tomei handed the bubbling concoction to one of the guards, who grasped another strap beneath the prisoner's chin. Forcing his mouth open, he carefully poured the liquid down the man's throat. The prisoner choked and sputtered as the guards released the harness but kept a firm hold on the chains binding his arms.

Moments later, his veins began to bulge around his neck and arms, his face contorting in agony. He let out a piercing scream that echoed through the dungeon.

"I'll talk! Please, make it stop!" the prisoner cried, his voice desperate and broken.

Tomei raised a hand, signaling for the guards to lower the man's head. Stepping onto a nearby bench, he leaned in close, his ear tilted toward him. "Speak," Tomei commanded in a low voice. "Who sent you?"

The prisoner's mouth moved, his voice faint and strained. Tomei leaned closer, his patience wearing thin. "Who is it?" he demanded.

The prisoner attempted to speak again, but before he could form coherent words, his body convulsed violently. His head lolled forward, and his breathing stopped. One of the guards rushed to check his pulse, pressing his fingers to the man's neck. After a moment, he looked toward Prince Halsten and shook his head. "He's dead, my prince," he announced grimly.

Halsten's face darkened, frustration flashing in his eyes. "Search the body and his belongings for anything that might lead us to his employer."

"Yes, my prince," Axilla replied, stepping forward to examine the prisoner.

Without another word, Prince Halsten turned and strode out of the dungeon, his expression stern. Albert, DeMarco, and Anders followed closely behind, their footsteps echoing through the cold stone corridors as they left the building's grim confines.

CHAPTER 24

WHEN PRINCE HALSTEN AND ALBERT returned to the castle, they found King Alaric, Isadora, Lord Ethan, and Lady Elara gathered in the main hall. The tension in the room was palpable as the two young men entered and took their seats.

The king leaned forward, his expression grave. "Did you uncover anything about who is behind the attack?" he asked.

Prince Halsten shook his head, frustration evident in his tone. "Father, we were unable to obtain any useful information. The attacker died during the interrogation."

The king frowned deeply, his gaze darkening. "Do we know anything about the young man?"

"Axilla and his men are conducting an investigation. They are searching his belongings and questioning others to see if anything might point to who sent him."

Alaric sighed, rubbed his temple, and then turned to a nearby attendant. "Send for Commander Egron immediately."

Moments later, Egron entered the hall and bowed respectfully. The king turned his attention to him, pausing the conversation.

"Egron," he began, "I want all security measures strengthened immediately. This includes increased patrols at the city gates, our borders, and all public spaces. I will not risk another incident."

"Yes, Your Majesty," Egron said.

Alaric added, "Also, station guards at all the gladiator tents. If someone intends to cause further disruption, they may target the gladiators or their quarters."

Egron nodded firmly. "It will be done, sire," he said, bowing again before exiting the hall.

As the commander departed, Isadora turned her attention to Halsten. "Halsten, Dhalia and the guards mentioned a young gladiator named Kudus and his friends. They said these men saved their lives. Who is this young man?"

The prince sat back slightly, his expression thoughtful. "I believe Kudus is a gladiator from Argos. I've heard of him—he's been gaining attention for his skill at the training grounds."

"He sounds promising," Isadora remarked. "I hope we'll see him perform at the games."

Halsten nodded. "I look forward to watching him fight as well. From what I've heard, his technique and agility are impressive."

Lord Ethan joined the conversation, his voice carrying a note of intrigue. "A gladiator of such skill must have an interesting backstory. I am eager to see him in action."

Lady Elara, who had been quietly observing, added, "If this young man truly saved Dhalia and Dora, it is only right that we extend our gratitude. Perhaps he should be invited to the castle after the games."

Isadora nodded in agreement. "That would be a fine gesture."

The conversation shifted briefly to preparations for the upcoming Gladiator Games and wedding festivities, but the underlying tension from the attack lingered. As the meeting concluded, Alaric remained seated, deep in thought, determined to protect the kingdom from the shadowy threat that loomed over Aldrich City.

CHAPTER 25

The day of the Gladiator Games finally arrived, and cheers erupted in the coliseum as the citizens filed in, occupying every seat.

An announcer stepped forward, waved to signal for silence, and then began to call out the gladiators. The men marched through the stadium on their horses before the gladiators of EdenRock were introduced.

The teams were all dressed in armor bearing their kingdoms' emblems. Some dignitaries from the other kingdoms joined the royal family and the nobles on the podium to cheer on their teams. Dhalia, Dora, and Amelia sat behind Freja while DeMarco, Asger, and Ergon joined the other guards in vantage spots on the stage.

Before the first event, bets were collected from some citizens and gladiator handlers who wanted to earn coins in the competitions. Once everyone settled down, a platform was placed before the podium.

Tomei, the royal alchemist, stood up. He bowed to Alaric and the nobles before climbing onto the platform. Raising his arm, he commanded silence across the coliseum, his voice booming over the crowd. "Ladies and gentlemen, His Majesty Alaric and our noblemen and noblewomen welcome every one of you to this grand gladiator game! On this day, in the city of our forefathers, we celebrate to usher in the wedding of our prince, Halsten Elliot Verdant, and Lady Freja Marie Glenwood."

Halsten and Freja stood up, waved to the crowd, and then sat back down.

"As tradition dictates, the winner of these games will be granted his freedom and his bond paid to his master by the king." Cheers filled the coliseum as the crowd chanted free! Free! Free!

Tomei lifted his hand, and when quiet returned to the coliseum, he spoke again, "Some fight, and some of us just stand here and speak so we don't have to feel the pain of a blow,"

The crowd cheered at his playful jab, and he continued, "Enough of my rambling! People of EdenRock and our esteemed guests from near and far, enjoy the spectacle this coliseum has to offer!" He lifted a white handkerchief high into the air, and as it floated down, he declared, "Let the games begin!"

The crowd's chants reverberated through the massive coliseum. "To the Realm! To the Realm! To the Realm!" The atmosphere was electric as the anticipation for the first match peaked. The announcer stepped forward, his booming voice carrying over the excited spectators.

"Ladies and gentlemen, noble citizens of Aldrich City, welcome to the Gladiator Games!" he proclaimed, his enthusiasm igniting cheers and applause. "Today, warriors from across the realms will battle for glory, honor, and the pride of their kingdoms!"

The matches began, and the fighters were introduced one by one. Ogram, the towering warrior from the Kingdom of Argos, quickly became a crowd favorite. His sheer strength and commanding presence were matched only by his efficiency in dismissing his opponents. With every crushing blow he delivered, the cheers grew louder.

The crowd was also introduced to a nimble combatant from the city of Araba, whose agility and dual short swords contrasted sharply with the brute strength of his Skinot opponent, who wielded a massive broadsword. The diversity of fighting styles on display kept the audience on the edge of their seats.

When Kudus, Ogram's younger teammate, entered the arena, his quiet confidence captured everyone's attention. The announcer's voice rose again. "From the Kingdom of Argos, Kudus, the rising star!"

Kudus's first fight was against a warrior from Vegeet, a towering man who initially earned the crowd's favor due to his imposing size. They cheered enthusiastically as he raised his axe and roared. Kudus remained calm, his eyes focused on his opponent.

The fight began, and the Vegeet warrior charged, swinging his axe with immense power. Kudus dodged the strike effortlessly, his movements precise and calculated. The crowd gasped as he evaded another powerful swing and countered with a swift strike to the warrior's torso. The Vegeet fighter fell to his knees, clutching his side and begging for mercy.

The crowd's cheers quickly shifted. "Kudus! Kudus!" they shouted, recognizing the Argos fighter's extraordinary skill.

Dhalia, seated on the podium behind Freja, could barely remain still. Her eyes never left Kudus, and her heart raced with each clash. Whenever he emerged victorious, she exhaled in relief, but each new fight brought fresh anxiety.

Kudus proved himself formidable, moving through the competition with agility and precision. He dispatched warriors from Pegra, Rab, Saratini, Akelot, and Divan, each earning louder cheers and more tremendous admiration from the spectators. His strategy and skill were unmatched, and his every move was calculated to exploit his opponents' weaknesses.

One particularly intense match saw him face a skilled fighter from Botan. The Botan warrior, a seasoned gladiator, fought with relentless ferocity. The two combatants circled each other, trading blows and dodging strikes in a display of incredible speed and strength. The fight stretched longer than any of Kudus's previous matches, and the crowd watched with bated breath.

"You can do it, Kudus!" a voice from the stands rang out, though it was lost in the crowd's roar. Dhalia clenched her hands tightly, unable to take her eyes off the arena.

Finally, Kudus saw an opening. He feigned a strike to the Botan warrior's right, then pivoted, landing a clean blow to the man's shoulder. The Botan fighter staggered, and Kudus pressed his advantage, disarming him with a swift maneuver and forcing him to yield.

The coliseum erupted into thunderous applause. "Kudus! Kudus! Kudus!" the crowd chanted as he raised his sword in triumph.

As the games continued, the intensity in the coliseum grew. The gladiators showcased their strength, agility, and tactical brilliance in battles, leaving the audience in awe. Freja noticed her friend's reactions and leaned over with a teasing smile.

"You're more invested in this than the rest of us," Freja said quietly. "Should I be worried?"

Dhalia blushed but kept her eyes on the arena. "I'm just admiring skill," she said, though her voice wavered slightly.

Freja chuckled but said no more, her attention returning to the ongoing matches.

The games continued, each fight bringing new excitement and solidifying Kudus's place as one of the most skilled gladiators in the competition. The crowd's energy remained unrelenting as the day wore on, their chants echoing across Aldrich City.

After the final match concluded and the dust settled in the coliseum, Alaric rose from his seat, his regal presence commanding everyone's attention. The cheers and applause for the victorious gladiators filled the air, and he signaled for silence.

Tomei stepped forward, his small frame dwarfed by the grandeur of the arena. Holding a scroll in his hand, he addressed the audience, his voice amplified to carry across the expanse.

"Ladies and gentlemen," he began, his tone ceremonious, "this is the moment of truth. One gladiator stood above the rest among all the warriors who fought with bravery and skill. He has demonstrated unmatched prowess, resilience, and heart in every battle. Today, the king will bestow upon him the ultimate prize—his freedom."

The crowd erupted into cheers, their anticipation at its peak. Tomei raised his hand for quiet before continuing. "It is my honor to invite Kudus Volandes of Argos to step forward and receive the king's Medal of Freedom!"

The coliseum roared with approval as the audience rose to their feet, chanting, "Kudus! Kudus! Kudus!"

Kudus, his face calm but his eyes reflecting a mix of pride and gratitude, stepped forward from the lineup of gladiators. His footsteps were steady as he approached the platform where Alaric stood waiting. The king, adorned in his regal robes, held a gleaming medal.

"Kudus Volandes," he said, "you have earned your freedom through courage, skill, and honor. This medal symbolizes not only your liberation but also the respect of this kingdom."

He placed the medal around Kudus's neck as the crowd went wild. Kudus bowed deeply to the king, his heart swelling with gratitude, and acknowledged the roaring audience with a humble wave.

As he descended from the platform, Prince Halsten and Lady Freja approached him with welcoming smiles. Behind them followed Dhalia, Dora, and Amelia, who were watching the exchange intently.

"Kudus," Halsten began, extending his hand, "I am Prince Halsten. This is Lady Freja. Thank you for saving Dhalia and Dora."

Freja nodded, her smile kind. "Your actions were brave and selfless. You have our gratitude."

Kudus shook the prince's hand firmly and bowed his head to Freja. "It was the right thing to do, Your Highnesses. I only did what anyone should in such a situation."

Prince Halsten placed a hand on the gladiator's shoulder. "You are a man of honor, Kudus. I want to extend an invitation to our wedding as our guest."

Kudus's eyes widened slightly at the unexpected offer. He straightened and nodded respectfully. "It would be my honor, Your Highness."

Dhalia, standing slightly behind the prince and Freja, looked at him with a mixture of admiration and relief. She hesitated before saying softly, "Thank you again for what you did for us. I will never forget it."

Kudus met her gaze briefly and nodded. "It was my pleasure, my lady."

The prince and Freja excused themselves, rejoining King Alaric, Isadora, and the rest of their family as they returned to the castle, escorted by their guards. Kudus watched as they departed, his heart filled with a sense of accomplishment and a newfound hope for his future.

Behind him, chants of his name still echoed through the coliseum, a testament to his extraordinary journey and the freedom he had fought so hard to achieve.

When the group reached the castle, Prince Halsten, Lady Freja, and their friends gathered on the spacious balcony connected to the grand hall. The evening breeze was cool and carried the faint scent of blooming flowers, setting a relaxing atmosphere as they lounged and enjoyed each other's company.

"I see why Dhalia is so charmed by the young warrior Kudus," Freja teased, her eyes glinting with mischief.

Laughter erupted from everyone, and Dhalia's cheeks flushed a deep crimson. She looked down shyly. "My lady, please."

Eleanor leaned forward, her grin wide. "Aha! So that explains why she's been going out so often recently. The cat is out of the bag now."

"All those new dresses and elaborate hair styling—it was all for the gladiator, wasn't it?" Vivienne added, laughing.

Eleanor smirked. "So, what should we call you now? Mrs. Kudus, perhaps?"

Freja joined in with a playful nudge toward Dhalia. "I better hurry up with my wedding so you'll have my blessing to wed next. We don't want anyone stealing your gladiator!"

Dora chimed in. "Yes, Dhalia. Time is of the essence. He's quite a catch—we'd hate to see someone else swoop in." Her laughter was infectious.

Albert raised a hand, his tone mock-serious. "Give the lady a break. She has every right to find love without all this teasing."

Dhalia mouthed a silent "Thank you" to him, earning her a reassuring smile.

"He is very handsome," Amelia said, her voice light. "And skillful too."

"I wonder what else he's skilled at," Amelia added with a sly grin. "I suppose only Dhalia can tell us that."

Dhalia, mortified yet laughing, grabbed a pillow and tossed it at Amelia. The group dissolved into another round of laughter. The evening was filled with giggles and laughter as the friends sat to discuss the events of the day.

After a little while, everyone left the balcony, leaving Prince Halsten and Freja by themselves. Prince Halsten called for Anders, his trusted guard.

"Anders," he said, "go to the tailor and instruct him to visit Kudus's tent. Have him craft something elegant for Kudus to wear at the wedding ceremony tomorrow."

Anders bowed slightly. "Yes, Your Highness," he replied, departing to carry out the order.

The balcony was now quiet. Halsten and Freja remained seated, gazing out at the sprawling gardens illuminated by the soft glow of lanterns.

"Kudus is very skillful," Freja said.

Halsten nodded, "Indeed, he is a good fighter. He did very well in the games. However, you can tell he has had a tough life."

He turned to Freja, smiling. "Guess who else looks good?"

She tilted her head, playing along. "Who might that be?"

"A certain Freja," he said, his tone filled with warmth.

She laughed, the sound like a melody in the night air. "Really?"

Halsten's eyes softened as he reached for her hand, gently clasping it in his. "I will be happy to share the rest of my life with you. I have loved you since the first moment I saw you in the EdenRock garden," he said, his voice filled with sincerity. "You were standing among the roses, and I thought, 'How could someone look so perfect in a moment so simple?'"

Freja looked at him, her smile tender. "You've always had a way with words, Halsten. You've been so kind to me, so patient. I'm lucky to have you."

"No," he said firmly, his gaze unwavering. "I'm the lucky one, Freja. You are a light in my life, and I can't wait to spend the rest of my days with you."

They sat in comfortable silence, their hands intertwined as they savored the moment. Finally, Halsten leaned closer, his voice a gentle murmur. "I love you."

"And I love you," she whispered in return.

Their lips met in a soft, lingering kiss, a promise of the life they were about to share. When they finally parted, Freja stood reluctantly. "Goodnight, Halsten," she said, her voice tinged with sweetness.

"Goodnight, my love," he replied.

They exchanged one last look before departing to their separate quarters, their hearts full and their bond more potent than ever.

CHAPTER 26

THE MORNING SUNBATHED VERDANT CASTLE in a warm, golden glow, illuminating its ancient stones and giving the bustling palace a lively vibrance. The day after the Gladiator Games began with renewed energy as citizens of the realm and visitors from neighboring kingdoms filled the square. The air was buzzing with lively conversations, the rhythmic clatter of hooves, and the soft rustling of banners that danced gently in the breeze. The excitement from the weeklong celebrations lingered, creating an atmosphere of anticipation and joy.

Prince Halsten rode confidently through the square, drawing admiration and respect from all who looked on. Flanking him were his closest companions—Arthur, Leo, Adikis, Zoresh, and Frodio—each sitting tall on his horse, their camaraderie apparent in their subtle nods and shared looks. The prince was also guarded by his loyal protectors, DeMarco and Asger, whose polished armor gleamed like a sea of glittering steel in the morning light. The cadence of their horses' hooves echoed off the castle's grand stone walls.

The group approached the podium at the square's center, where the royal family awaited them with dignified composure. Alaric was seated, his regal bearing matching his attire—a rich purple robe embroidered with golden threads that exuded authority and wisdom. His sharp eyes scanned the gathering crowd, filled with pride and vigilance.

Beside him was Isadora, resplendent in a flowing white gown adorned with intricate purple stitching and delicate jewels that shimmered with every movement. Her serene elegance added to the grandeur of the occasion.

The ensemble of those present to witness the ceremony added to the grandeur of the occasion. The sound of the tower trumpet and the rhythmic beat of drums reverberated through the palace square, commanding the attention of all present. Alaric and Isadora rose gracefully from their seats, their movements signaling for everyone else to do the same. The crowd turned their gaze toward Prince Halsten, who approached with measured steps, exuding an unmistakable air of regal authority.

His appearance was striking. He was wearing white military-style trousers and a matching shirt layered beneath a pristine jacket of the same hue with cufflinks bearing the face of the kingdom's emblem—the Ligon. Gold trims adorned the sides and sleeves of his ensemble, and dark purple, blue, and gold military cords draped elegantly across his chest. His blond hair, reminiscent of molten gold, was neatly trimmed, and his clean-shaven face accentuated his piercing and sparkling blue eyes. His confident demeanor captivated the crowd, whose admiration was palpable.

Behind him, his loyal companions followed closely. Each wore a white jacket with gold trims similar to Halsten's, paired with black trousers that provided a striking contrast. Their polished boots and synchronized steps conveyed unity and pride, adding to the splendor of the procession.

The prince dismounted his horse with practiced ease. The rhythmic clatter of his boots on the cobblestone path was drowned out by the anticipation that filled the air. He began his walk down the grand aisle, which was lined on each side by ceremonial guards dressed in their finest military uniforms.

The guards stood at rigid attention, their polished swords held respectfully at their sides. Sunlight reflected off their armor, making the scene appear almost otherworldly. Beneath Halsten's feet stretched a luxurious red carpet, leading him toward the podium where the royal family and dignitaries awaited.

Amid the crowd, the young gladiator Kudus stood out. His polished black boots complemented his black trousers and jacket, under which he wore a white dress shirt. Though understated, his refined appearance and calm confidence drew admiration from the young females nearby. He watched the prince closely, his respect evident in his steady gaze.

Isadora smiled, her eyes never leaving her son. "He is every bit the prince we raised him to be," she said to the king.

As Prince Halsten reached the podium, he bowed deeply to his parents, and then to the assembled nobles. The crowd watched in reverent silence as he took his place on a thronelike groom's chair, the seat adorned with white, gold, and red ribbons, surrounded by vibrant flower arrangements displaying roses of various hues.

Seated on the podium, his eyes fell on a young boy staring at him intently as he scanned the crowd. Something about the child's gaze seemed strange. Halsten turned to Arthur next to him to make a quiet remark, but when he looked back toward the crowd, the young boy was gone.

Arthur leaned closer to his friend, his voice laced with playful teasing. "You look every bit the royal today, Halsten. I doubt Freja will ever let you leave the prince's chambers again."

The rest of Halsten's companions chuckled, adding a moment of levity to the otherwise formal atmosphere. Halsten smirked, brushing off Arthur's comment as he focused on the ceremony unfolding before him.

From their seats, Alaric and Isadora observed their son with proud smiles. Beside them, Princesses Eleanor and Vivienne exchanged looks, their admiration for their brother clear.

A sudden murmur rippled through the crowd as approaching hooves echoed across the square. All eyes turned to see a horse-drawn carriage, its polished surface gleaming under the sun. Freja had arrived. The carriage came to a smooth halt near the steps leading to the podium.

A guard swiftly stepped forward, opening the door. Freja emerged with poise, her every movement a display of elegance. She wore a breathtaking white gown that flowed like water, its intricate lace train held delicately by Dora and Amelia. Her golden hair, adorned with a gleaming gold pin, cascaded down her shoulders, while her emerald-green eyes sparkled with a brilliance that seemed to rival the lush hills of EdenRock.

The crowd collectively rose to their feet, and the soldiers snapped to attention, their swords raised in salute. Gasps of admiration filled the air as the bride, flanked by her friends, approached the podium.

Dhalia, walking closely behind Freja, stole a look at the crowd and immediately spotted Kudus. Her cheeks turned a vivid shade of red as their eyes met. She quickly turned her attention back to her friend, hoping no one had noticed her flustered reaction.

At the podium, Freja ascended the steps with effortless grace. She bowed deeply to Alaric and Isadora. Turning next, she bowed to her parents, who looked on with pride. Finally, she gave a respectful nod to the assembled nobles.

Standing beside High Priest Tover, Halsten watched her intently as she approached. His heart swelled with a mixture of admiration and gratitude. She was radiant, a vision of beauty and strength, and her presence felt like a calm yet powerful force anchoring him.

"You look stunning," he mouthed softly as she reached him.

Freja's lips curved into a gentle smile. "And you look every bit the prince you are meant to be," she mouthed back.

High Priest Tover stepped forward, his face solemn, his hands raised to quiet the crowd. The air grew still, charged with a sense of reverence and importance. Deep and resonant, his voice carried across the square as he began to speak.

"Today," Tover said, "we gather not only to witness the union of Prince Halsten Elliot Verdant and Lady Freja Marie Glenwood but to honor the strength and unity this bond represents. Their love and commitment reflect the kingdom's enduring spirit and a promise of hope for its future."

The crowd fell silent, their attention fully captured by his words. Halsten and Freja stood side by side, their hands brushing ever so slightly to reassure each other. The weight of centuries of tradition rested on this moment, and the kingdom held its breath in anticipation.

The wedding ceremony began with an air of reverence as High Priest Tover addressed the crowd.

"Ladies and gentlemen, esteemed guests, and noble families," he began. "We gather here today in the heart of Verdant Castle, surrounded by stones that have borne witness to centuries of history, to celebrate a momentous occasion—the union of two illustrious houses, the House of Verdant and the House of Glenwood."

The crowd listened intently, their faces reflecting admiration and respect. Tover's words flowed gracefully. "Today, we are here to unite

Prince Halsten Verdant and Lady Freja Glenwood in a bond of love and loyalty.

"This marriage is more than a union of two hearts. It is the fortification of an alliance between two great houses—a promise of strength and hope for our kingdom."

Halsten and Freja stood on the podium, their hands clasped. Alaric and Isadora, seated in regal splendor on their gilded chairs, exchanged proud looks.

The crowd's attention remained fixed on the podium. Halsten turned his gaze toward Freja, and their eyes met, a deep understanding passing between them in that quiet exchange. The intensity of the occasion weighed on them both, yet it bound them closer. Freja's heart fluttered, but she maintained her poise.

"To Prince Halsten and Lady Freja," Tover proclaimed, "your journey together begins here, in the presence of those who love and support you. May your union bring peace, strength, and prosperity to our lands."

The crowd erupted into applause, their cheers echoing in the air. Freja looked at Halsten, her voice soft but steady as she said, "Our moment has come."

Halsten smiled, his grip tightening on her hand. "Together, we'll honor this bond."

Tover raised his hands, signaling the crowd to settle as he turned toward Freja's father. His voice carried a note of reverence. "Who gives this beautiful lady to be joined in union with our prince?"

Lord Ethan rose from his seat. His voice, though steady, carried the weight of emotion. "We, her parents, give our beloved daughter, Freja Marie Glenwood, in marriage to Prince Halsten Elliot Verdant."

Freja stepped forward, her gaze filled with gratitude as she bowed to him. "Thank you, Father. Thank you, Mother."

Lord Ethan smiled gently.

A reverent hush fell over the crowd. Lord Ethan stepped forward, and he gently took his daughter's hand. With a smile, he placed her hand into Halsten's. Freja's heart raced, but the steady strength of her father's presence reassured her. As Halsten took her hand, their fingers intertwined, and they silently exchanged a vow of unity.

High Priest Tover stepped forward, his ceremonial robes swaying gently in the breeze. He turned toward Alaric and raised his hands. Sensing the moment's gravity, the crowd rose to their feet.

"Let us begin," Tover declared.

From the altar beside him, he took a white cotton cord adorned with small golden bells at each end. The sunlight danced off the bells, adding a touch of ethereal beauty. Holding it high for all to see, he began, "This cord has long symbolized love, unity, and purity. From the days of Aldrich the Conqueror to the time of King Isolde and now the present day, it has bound together those who vow to uphold the values of loyalty and harmony in their union."

Halsten and Freja extended their joined hands toward him. Tovar carefully draped the cord over them, bells jingling softly in the breeze. The sound, though faint, was melodious, blending seamlessly with the solemnity of the moment.

High Priest Tover continued, "The bells on this cord serve as a reminder to all who hear them. If love, kindness, and understanding reign in your home, the bells will remain silent, reflecting the peace within. But if anger, hatred, or discord should enter, the bells will sound—a warning to yourselves and the world."

The crowd listened intently, the depth of the symbolism resonating with all present. Freja looked at Halsten, their eyes meeting briefly.

High Priest Tover took a golden jar of rich grape wine and carefully poured it over Halsten's and Freja's clasped hands. The deep red liquid ran over their fingers, vivid and striking against their skin.

"Like the dark wine stains the mind, evil can stain the heart," he declared. "Let no hatred or evil ever enter your home, nor your hearts climb into a bed of ill desire."

The priest removed the stained cord from the couple's hands, the bells jingling softly as it was unbound. He gestured for an attendant to bring forth a bowl of pure water. With quiet reverence, Halsten and Freja washed their hands, the crimson of the wine dissolving in the clear liquid. The assistant handed each of them a clean white napkin, and they dried off before turning back to High Priest Tover.

The priest took another cord similar to the first and again fastened it around their clasped hands. "This cord is a symbol of your renewal," he intoned.

An assistant approached with a second golden jar, this one filled with water. Tover poured it over the couple's hands, the liquid sparkling as it caught the sunlight. "Just as fresh water does not stain, let your love be pure and true, unblemished by discord or deceit," he proclaimed.

The weight of the ritual settled over the crowd like a sacred shroud. The nobility and citizens of Verdant stood captivated. Halsten and Freja's expressions were serene but filled with the understanding of the profound vows they had made.

The high priest slowly removed the second cord, the bells chiming softly as they came undone. He clasped the couple's hands and raised them for all to see. His voice rang out over the square once again. "Behold the line of Aldrich! Behold the House of Verdant! Behold the future of EdenRock! Behold the future of the realm!"

The crowd erupted, their voices thunderous. "To the Realm! To the Realm! To the Realm!"

The air was thick with emotion, and the soft jingling of the bells was a lingering reminder of the sacred bond that had just been formed. Isadora discreetly wiped away a tear. King Alaric, standing tall, his gaze unwavering, wore an expression of deep pride as he looked out over his people.

As the applause began to quiet, the crowd started chanting, their voices filled with playful excitement. "Kiss! Kiss! Kiss!"

Halsten turned to his bride, a soft smile gracing his lips. He pulled her close, their hands still clasped. "My love," he whispered.

He pressed his lips to hers, a passionate and graceful kiss. The connection between them was palpable as the crowd watched with delight.

The square erupted once again. "To the Realm! To the Realm! To the Realm!"

As the cheers echoed through the square, Halsten and Freja remained locked in their kiss, their bond now sealed before their families, kingdom, and the realm they would one day lead.

Alaric stepped forward, quieting the square. He was handed a specially fashioned sword encased in a gilded sheath adorned with the crest of the Verdant family. Approaching Halsten, he held it out with both hands.

"I give you this Verdant sword," he declared. "It symbolizes the strength and protection of our realm. Use it to defend your home, your people, and all that is just. Never let it fall out of your hands, my son."

Halsten knelt briefly before his father, receiving the weapon with both hands. Rising, he nodded with solemn gratitude. "I will honor this gift, Father, and protect the realm with my life."

Isadora then stepped forward, holding a key forged from silver. Its handle was inlaid with emeralds, symbolizing the verdant lands of EdenRock. She approached Freja, her warm smile full of motherly affection.

"I give you this key, my daughter," she said. "It is the key to your home. Guard it well and let no other man share your bed."

Freja accepted the key with grace, bowing her head slightly. "Yes, Your Grace. I will honor my family name."

The king then turned to Halsten, "Let no other woman share your bed."

Halsten responded, "Yes, Your Grace, I will honor my family name."

The crowd once again chanted, "To the Realm! To the Realm! To the Realm!"

The festivities continued well into the evening. Lavish tables were set with sumptuous dishes, including roasted lamb, seasoned beef, bison, and chicken, alongside an abundance of vegetables and freshly baked bread. Ale and wine flowed freely, and guests' laughter filled the square. Food and drink were also provided for the citizens who had gathered to witness the wedding, ensuring no one was left out of the celebration.

Halsten and Freja thanked each noble and dignitary who'd attended the ceremony. They exchanged warm words with family and friends.

In the crowd, Halsten spotted Kudus and approached him with a smile. "Kudus," he began, extending his hand, "you have shown great courage and skill. I would be honored if you would stay in EdenRock and join my guard."

The Argos gladiator, though surprised, bowed respectfully. "It would be my honor, Your Highness. I pledge my loyalty to you and your family."

The prince placed a hand on Kudus's shoulder. "I would like to welcome you to formally join my team."

"Thank you, Your Grace. I am grateful for your kindness," Kudus said.

Halsten turned around and spoke to DeMarco, "Make sure he has all he needs."

The celebration continued late into the night. As the festivities wound down, the king and queen presented Halsten and Freja with their new home—McKenzie Castle. Located in the southern part of the kingdom, it would serve as their residence and the center of governance for that region. Halsten would hold the title of royal lord of the Southern territories, reporting only to the king.

Tomei stepped forward, his ceremonial robes swaying as the rhythmic beat of drums filled the square. He raised his hands, commanding the attention of the crowd. "Now it is time for the king to present the prince and Lady Freja with their advisors," he announced.

Alaric stepped forward. Halsten was standing by Lord Cameron, who stepped forward as well, along with Lady Emma.

"Lord Cameron," the king began, his tone authoritative yet warm, "will you accept the position of Magister to the Prince, offering counsel and guidance in the governance of his lands?"

Lord Cameron bowed deeply. "Yes, Your Majesty. I will serve with honor and dedication."

The king nodded approvingly and turned toward Isadora. She stepped forward, addressing Lady Emma with a gentle smile. "Lady Emma, will you accept the role of confidante and advisor to Lady Freja, serving as her ears and guiding her in her household?"

Lady Emma curtsied. "Yes, Your Majesty. I will carry out my duties faithfully."

The crowd applauded politely. Once more, Tomei raised his voice above the drumbeat. "Now the prince shall choose his house—those who will reside in his castle and provide protection to him."

Prince Halsten moved to the center of the podium, commanding the square's attention. He spoke clearly, his voice carrying over the crowd. "I call upon those who have proven their loyalty, courage, and strength to join my house."

He began to list the names, each one chosen with purpose. "Arthur, Leo, Frodio, Adikis, Zoresh, Asger, DeMarco, and Kudus Volandes, the gladiator from the Kingdom of Argos, now a free man by the king's decree."

As each name was called, the man came over to stand proudly beside the prince. The crowd murmured in admiration, many cheering for Kudus, whose journey from gladiator to honored member of the prince's house had captured their imaginations.

Tomei turned to Lady Freja, extending his hand toward her. "Lady Freja will name her house—those who will stand by her side in her new role."

She stepped forward, her voice filled with confidence. "I call upon Lady Dhalia, Lady Dora, Lady Amelia of Glenwood, Lady Olivia of the House of Brixton, Lady Dorcas of the House of Longrove, and Lady Stella of the House of Palm."

Each woman approached, curtsying before taking her place beside Freja. Their presence reflected the strength and unity of the alliances forged through this union.

Again, the crowd called, "To the Realm! To the Realm! To the Realm!"

Tomei raised his hands to calm them. "Behold the new houses of Prince Halsten and Lady Freja! May they serve with honor, wisdom, and strength."

The crowd responded with even louder cheers.

As the festivities began to wind down, the crowd chanted one final time, their voices echoing through the night. "To the Realm! To the Realm! To the Realm!"

It was a fitting conclusion to a day that offered new hope for EdenRock's future.

CHAPTER 27

As the vibrant celebrations of the wedding night drew to a close, the final guests departed the castle court under a canopy of stars. The royal family stood at the castle's grand entrance to bid everyone farewell. They exchanged words of gratitude and well-wishes with their departing guests, their expressions warm despite the long day.

"Thank you for coming, Lord Cameron," Alaric said, clasping the older man's hand. "Your presence made this day even more special."

"It was an honor to be here, Your Majesty," Lord Cameron replied. "The union of Prince Halsten and Lady Freja is truly a blessing to the realm."

Isadora smiled as she hugged Lady Emma. "Thank you for everything. Your guidance to Freja will be invaluable in the days to come."

Lady Emma curtsied. "It is my pleasure, Your Majesty. She is a remarkable young woman. She will make you proud."

Once everyone was gone, Alaric turned to his family. "It has been a long and joyous day," he said. "Let us rest—we must prepare for Halsten's departure to McKenzie Castle."

They entered the castle, their steps weary but their hearts full.

Halsten and Freja went to the prince's quarters, followed closely by their maids and guards. Amelia, ever vigilant, approached the couple with a gentle bow.

"My lord, my llady," she began, "I have instructed two maids to remain nearby tonight in case you need anything. Should you require assistance, they will notify me immediately."

Freja smiled. "Thank you, Amelia. You have done so much for us today."

"It is my honor, my lady." She bowed again before stepping back to allow the couple their privacy.

DeMarco approached Halsten, his expression resolute. "Your Highness, I have ensured that the perimeter of your quarters is secure. The night patrol is stationed, and all guards are on high alert."

Halsten nodded, placing a hand on the guard's shoulder. "Thank you for all the years of service. You have served me well, as always."

With a final bow, DeMarco and Anders departed to their rooms, leaving the prince and his bride to retire for the night.

Outside, the once-lively castle grounds were now cloaked in darkness. The remnants of the celebration—the grand tables, floral arrangements, and banners—cast long shadows in the moonlight. Only the steady footsteps of the guards patrolling the grounds broke the silence.

In the king and queen's chamber, Alaric and Isadora sat together on a plush sofa, the faint glow of candlelight illuminating their faces. Isadora rested her head on her husband's shoulder.

Halsten and Freja entered the prince's chamber and were greeted by the room's usual exquisite splendor. The room was designed with a pristine white theme, exuding elegance and serenity. A large, handcrafted bed took center stage, its four majestic posts draped with a sparkling white net that cascaded gracefully to the floor. Rose petals in shades of red, yellow, pink, and white were artfully scattered to form a romantic path that led to the bed.

Freja's eyes widened with delight as she took in the thoughtful details. "Halsten," she whispered, her voice filled with awe, "this is beautiful."

Halsten smiled, his gaze fixed on her. "Only the best for my bride."

In the corner of the room, two stunning accent chairs sat side by side, their white upholstery accented with gold. Beside them stood a matching table draped in a white-and-gold tablecloth, completing the harmonious design.

Freja moved toward the chairs, her hand lightly brushing the fabric. "The detail is incredible. It feels like a dream."

Halsten chuckled, stepping closer to her. "You deserve a place as perfect as you."

On the left side of the room, an open archway led to a cozy sitting area that opened onto a balcony overlooking the bustling city below. The evening lights of Aldrich City shimmered in the distance, casting a magical glow.

Freja turned toward the balcony, the cool evening breeze brushing her face. "This view," she said softly, "is breathtaking."

"To match the woman standing here," Halsten replied.

Freja turned to face him, her cheeks flushed with warmth.

On the right side of the room, another area had been prepared for Halsten. A study with sturdy, dark-wood furniture stood ready, exuding sophistication and utility. Beyond it was a private bath and sauna designed to meet the prince's needs. The polished fixtures and serene lighting added an air of luxury.

"I see they've spared no effort in making sure we both have our own spaces," he remarked.

"They've thought of everything," Freja agreed, her smile widening as she explored further.

On the left side of the room was a dedicated space for her. The room led to a private bath with a beautifully crafted tub gleaming under the chandeliers' soft light. Lit candles provided a calming and serene atmosphere. A second balcony extended from this area, offering a view of the city from another angle. The furniture in this section was delicate yet functional, adorned with intricate designs that reflected Freja's grace and poise.

After inspecting the room, Freja picked up a bell beside her dresser and rang it delicately. Two maids came in and filled the tub with warm water. Freja stood up from the dresser area, her hair let down, revealing her beautiful face and causing her green eyes to sparkle. She dropped her white gown, walked to the tub, and sat in it. The two maids took sponges, scrubbed her back and limbs, and washed her hair.

Halsten bathed and unwound in the nearby sauna with the help of some maids. Afterward, he changed into a white robe and entered the bedroom, where several candles had been lit. Halsten lay on the bed, waiting for his bride to come in. When Freja entered the bedroom, she was in a white gown, a female version of the one Halsten was wearing. She stopped in the middle of the room and dropped her dress, revealing her beautiful body, which seemed sculpted to perfection.

Halsten licked his lips as Freja bit down on her lower lip, smiling with a teasing expression. "You are beautiful," he mouthed to her.

"I love you," she whispered.

Halsten got up, walked over to Freja, took her hand, and led her to their bed. She looked into his eyes, and they sank into each other's arms in passion. A little while later, exhaustion overtook them, and they rested tangled together. Freja soon drifted to sleep.

As Halsten lay beside his new bride in their matrimonial bed, sleep pulled him into a vivid dream. It transported him to his childhood, when the world had felt simpler yet filled with challenges. He found himself in the heart of EdenRock Forest, the towering trees casting dappled sunlight on the forest floor. Halsten was with his cousin, Mefford, who carried a long rope coiled over his shoulder. Carefree and adventurous, the two boys made their way toward a steep hill they had decided to climb.

Mefford stopped and turned to Halsten, his youthful face breaking into a mischievous grin. The boys threw the rope several times until it caught on a tree stump, and Halsten pulled on it to ensure it was holding tightly. "I'll climb first," Mefford said.

Halsten nodded, trusting his cousin as he crouched slightly to give him a boost. Mefford climbed onto Halsten's back, his hands gripping his shoulders for support. "Hold still," he instructed, laughing as he scrambled up and reached for the ledge.

After several attempts and much effort, Mefford managed to pull himself to the top of the hill. He stood triumphantly, dusting off his hands, looking down at the prince and pulling the rope. "Climb up!" he shouted, his voice filled with excitement.

Halsten, still at the base of the hill, frowned in confusion. "Throw the rope down and help me!" he called back, craning his neck to see his cousin more clearly.

Mefford leaned over the edge, his grin widening. "Why should I?" he replied. "I climbed up here by myself. You should do the same."

Halsten's heart sank. "Please, Mefford. You said you'd help me. Don't leave me down here."

But Mefford only laughed, his voice echoing through the forest. "Figure it out," he teased.

At that moment, Darius appeared beside his son. His presence was commanding, even in the dream. He looked down at Halsten, his expression unreadable at first. Then, his face broke into a smirk. He and Mefford exchanged a look before both burst into laughter.

"Don't wait too long, Halsten," Darius said mockingly. "Or a monster might attack you in the dark."

Without another word, he and Mefford turned and walked away, disappearing from view. Halsten stood frozen at the base of the hill, his frustration and helplessness weighing on him like a stone.

Suddenly, a calm voice broke through the silence. "Halsten." He turned to see a man standing at the top of the hill, his white robes shimmering in the soft sunlight.

"High Priest Tover?" Halsten called out, his voice filled with surprise.

The priest didn't answer but threw down a rope, its end landing just a few feet from Halsten. The prince grabbed it and began to climb, his determination overriding his fatigue. He pulled himself up step by step, the priest's calm presence spurring him onward.

When he finally reached the top, he expected to see the high priest waiting for him, but to his shock, the hilltop was empty. Halsten turned in every direction, scanning the forest for any sign of him, Mefford, or Darius. The air was still, and the laughter and voices from moments earlier seemed to have evaporated.

"Where is everyone?" Halsten murmured, his voice tinged with unease.

He took a few hesitant steps forward, the silence around him heavy and oppressive. The hilltop felt different—otherworldly, as though it existed outside of time. A faint breeze rustled the leaves, carrying an unspoken message he couldn't decipher.

The dream faded as he stood there, alone and uncertain, leaving him with a lingering sense of mystery and unease. He awoke in his bed, Freja still peacefully asleep beside him. The echoes of the dream clung to him.

CHAPTER 28

A s the morning light seeped into the grand banquet hall of Verdant Castle, Prince Halsten and Lady Freja spent cherished moments with their families before their departure. The room was alive with laughter and farewells, though an undertone of bittersweet emotion lingered.

Lord Ethan, Lady Elara, Albert, and their entourage prepared for their journey back to Glenwood Castle. Lady Elara held her daughter's hands tightly. "You've grown into a fine young woman, my dear. You'll make a wonderful lady of McKenzie Castle."

Freja smiled warmly, her eyes glistening. "Thank you, Mother. I'll do my best to make you proud."

Albert stepped forward, offering his sister a protective embrace. "Remember, if Halsten troubles you, send for me."

Freja laughed lightly. "I'm sure it won't come to that."

Nearby, Lord Aiden stood with his guards. He approached Halsten, gripping his nephew's shoulder firmly. "Lead with the wisdom you've inherited from your father and mother. You'll do well."

"Thank you, Uncle," Halsten replied. "Your guidance has always been invaluable."

After heartfelt goodbyes, Lord Aiden mounted his horse and led his men out of the courtyard, leaving behind a trail of dust as they disappeared into the distance.

In a quieter corner of the castle grounds, Alaric took Halsten aside. "Son," he began, his tone filled with paternal pride, "you are ready for this responsibility. Remember, a good leader is both strong and compassionate. Earn the people's trust at McKenzie Castle—they will become your greatest allies."

Halsten nodded solemnly. "I will, Father. Thank you for your faith in me."

Meanwhile, Isadora spent time with Freja and her companions, creating a moment of levity amidst the farewells. "Freja," she said gently, "you will bring life to McKenzie Castle. Eleanore and Vivienne, don't stay at McKenzie for long. Come back as soon as your brother and his wife settle at their new home."

Vivienne laughed, her voice ringing out like a bell. "We will return as soon as they are settled, Mother."

Freja added, "I'm grateful for their support and yours, my queen. It makes this transition easier."

The courtyard became a flurry of activity as attendants loaded supplies and secured the wagons. Guards polished their armor, and horses were prepared for the long journey. Prince Halsten took one last look at Verdant Castle before mounting his steed. He turned to his father and mother, bowing slightly.

"Thank you for everything," he said.

Alaric gave a nod of approval. "May your path be guided by wisdom."

With that, the entourage set out. Freja, Dhalia, Dora, and Amelia climbed into an elegantly appointed wagon while Vivienne and Eleanor shared another. Forty-five guards flanked the party, their formation both protective and regal.

Crossing the stone bridge leading out of the castle, the group went through Abbot City. Townsfolk paused their daily routines to watch the procession, waving and cheering as they passed. Children ran to the roadside, their faces alight with excitement at the sight of the prince and his bride.

The forest pass soon enveloped them, the tall trees forming a canopy overhead. The sound of birdsong accompanied their journey, and sunlight filtered through the leaves. Freja gazed out, her thoughts a mix of excitement and apprehension.

Halsten rode alongside the wagons as they traveled, his gaze scanning the path ahead and occasionally drifting to the wagon holding his bride. "Freja," he called gently, "how are you holding up?"

She leaned out slightly, offering a small smile. "It's a lot to take in, but I'm ready. Thank you for asking."

"You'll love McKenzie Castle," he assured her. "It's not as grand as Verdant, but it has charm. The people there are loyal and kind."

From the other wagon, Vivienne chimed in playfully, "And don't forget, Freja, Eleanor and I will make sure Halsten doesn't become too serious."

Eleanor chuckled. "Consider it our mission."

Their laughter eased the tension. Even the guards exchanged smiles, their shoulders relaxing as they settled into the rhythm of the road.

After stopping to rest at inns each night for five days, McKenzie was now two days ahead.

CHAPTER 29

Fɪᴠᴇ ɴɪɢʜᴛs ᴀғᴛᴇʀ Hᴀʟsᴛᴇɴ ʜᴀᴅ departed, the Forest Knights, led under the veil of darkness by their grim leader, Major, moved with calculated precision through the dense woods along the banks of River Ellyn South. Their heads were cloaked in dark coverings, their identities masked by the shadows as they crept through the woods. The group's movements were silent and deliberate, like predators closing in on their prey. They crossed the river near the villages of Elderscroft and Longrove, the sound of their passage muted by the rushing water.

After traversing the terrain, they arrived strategically near the forested road leading to McKenzie Castle. The area, thick with towering trees and dense underbrush, offered the perfect cover for an ambush. Major raised his gloved hand, signaling his men to halt. The group instantly dispersed, melting into the surroundings with the ease of seasoned assassins.

Some of the Forest Knights climbed into the high branches, securing vantage points with their bows drawn and arrows notched. Others crouched in the underbrush, their swords glinting faintly in the moonlight. The air grew heavy with tension as they held their positions, waiting for the moment to strike.

Major stood near the base of a massive oak, his piercing eyes scanning the dark road ahead. His expression was one of steely determination. Turning to Boyd, his trusted lieutenant, he spoke in a low, commanding tone. "Are the archers in position?" he asked, his voice barely more than a whisper.

Boyd stepped closer, his movements equally measured. "Yes, Major," he replied. "The road is covered from every angle."

Major nodded curtly, his attention still fixed on the path. "And the swordsmen?" he asked, his voice sharp and direct.

"Orod and his men are in place," Boyd confirmed, gesturing to the shadows along the road's edge. "They're hidden on both sides. No one will pass through without facing us."

"Good." Major paused for a moment, his eyes narrowing. "We only have one chance to succeed. Please wait for my signal. No one moves until then."

Boyd nodded and retreated to his position, leaving Major alone by the large tree. Major clenched his fists, his resolve evident in the grim set of his jaw. He whispered to himself, "Tonight, we ensure the prince's reign ends."

The forest grew eerily quiet, the usual sounds of nocturnal creatures replaced by the tense stillness of men poised for battle. Their breaths were shallow as they waited for their target. The faint rustling of leaves and the distant murmurs of the river were all that could be heard.

From his vantage point, the Major could see the pale glow of the moonlight filtering through the canopy above. He knew the prince's entourage would pass through soon, and the stakes of their mission weighed heavily on him. Yet he remained unyielding, his confidence bolstered by the careful planning that had brought them to this moment.

Meanwhile, hidden in the surrounding darkness, the men exchanged silent glances, their nerves taut. Orod was crouched behind a cluster of bushes, his hand tightening around the hilt of his sword. "Let's hope the prince gives us a fight worth remembering," he muttered, a wicked grin on his lips.

Nearby, one of the archers whispered to his companion, "Do you think the prince will come this way? What if he's changed his route?"

"Quiet," the other man hissed. "This is the only way."

The soldiers held their positions, their focus unwavering. The forest seemed to hold its breath as they waited, every rustle of leaves or snap of a twig causing their muscles to tense. Major's eyes never left the road. The night stretched on, each moment fraught with anticipation.

Then, faintly at first, the sound of horses' hooves broke through the stillness. Major's ears pricked at the noise, his posture stiffening. He raised a hand, silently commanding his men to ready themselves. The rhythmic clatter grew louder, and shadows soon began forming against the soft moonlight.

Major squinted, trying to discern the riders and the wagons' contents following them. Though the figures were unclear, they moved with purpose, heading straight into the ambush. His jaw clenched as he signaled his men to prepare for an attack.

Far from the would-be ambushers, Prince Halsten stood in the warm glow of a campfire, a note clutched in his hand. The urgent message from his spies had arrived moments earlier, carried by a swift messenger pigeon.

"The road to McKenzie Castle is compromised," Halsten announced to his companions, his voice grave. He handed the note to Arthur, who scanned it.

Arthur looked up, his brow furrowed. "An ambush?"

Halsten nodded. "It appears so. Men were spotted leaving River Ellyn, heading toward the main road. We can't risk taking the direct route."

Zoresh stepped forward, his hand resting on the hilt of his sword. "Then what's the plan, Halsten?"

"We'll send Freja to rest for the night at Abbot's Castle with Lady Paulina," Halsten replied. "But we can't let them think they've succeeded. We need a decoy."

Arthur's eyes lit up with understanding. "You want them to believe they've ambushed the prince."

"Exactly," he confirmed. "We'll send a team of soldiers disguised as Lady Freja and me. They'll follow the planned route, drawing the ambushers out."

"And us?" Frodio asked, leaning closer.

Halsten's lips curled into a determined smile. "We'll take a detour. Asger, DeMarco, and I will lead a group across River Ellyn. We'll circle behind the Forest Knights and outflank them. Once the decoy draws them out, we'll strike."

Zoresh nodded approvingly. "Bold and effective."

"Asger," Halsten said, turning to his trusted guard, "choose a team for the decoy. They'll need to look convincing. Make sure the wagon looks like it's carrying Lady Freja."

Asger saluted. "Consider it done, my prince."

DeMarco stepped forward. "And the ambush team? Who will ride with you?"

"Arthur, Frodio, Zoresh, Kudus, and Adikis," Halsten said decisively. "We'll move swiftly and take them by surprise."

By nightfall, the plan was entirely in motion. A small group of soldiers, carefully selected for their physical resemblance to Prince Halsten and his entourage, prepared themselves for their dangerous roles. One soldier donned the prince's distinctive attire, confidently mounting a horse at the head of the group. A wagon followed closely behind, its occupants disguised as Lady Freja and her companions.

The decoy team departed Abbot's Castle, their movements deliberate and practiced to mimic a royal procession. The soldiers played their roles convincingly, maintaining a regal pace as they headed toward the ambush site.

Meanwhile, Halsten led the separate detachment across River Ellyn. The moonlight cast eerie shadows along the forest floor. Their movements were silent and calculated, a testament to their years of training and discipline.

As they approached the rear of the Forest Knights' position, Halsten raised a hand, signaling his men to halt. He crouched beside Kudus and DeMarco, his voice low and commanding. "We hold here. The decoy will draw them out. Once they're fully engaged, we strike."

Kudus tightened his grip on the hilt of his sword, his eyes glinting with anticipation. "They won't know what hit them."

DeMarco adjusted his armor, scanning the shadows where moonlight bled between the trees. "They are clever," he murmured, fingers tightening around his sword hilt, "but not clever enough. Tonight, we teach them the cost of betrayal." His soldiers shifted in the dark, blades glinting like bared teeth.

Ahead in the dark, perched in the gnarled branches of an ancient oak, Major watched the decoy team approach—their footsteps deliberate, their formation flawless. His predatory grin widened as he turned to

Boyd, his lieutenant. "There they are," he said, his voice a hushed growl. "Hold steady. Wait for my signal."

The decoy team advanced steadily, the clatter of hooves and wagon wheels echoing through the still forest. Major raised his hand, his archers silently drawing their bows. The tension was thick, the air heavy with the anticipation of violence.

When the decoy drew close enough, the Major's hand dropped, and chaos erupted. Arrows streaked through the night sky, slicing through the air toward their targets. The soldiers in the wagon dove for cover, their shouts echoing through the forest as they feigned surprise.

"Surround them!" Major barked. "Don't let anyone escape!"

The Forest Knights surged forward, weapons drawn, as they descended on the decoy team. But just as they were about to press their attack further, a commanding voice rang out from the shadows. "Now!"

Halsten and his men burst out from the woods, their swords gleaming in the moonlight. Their battle cries cut through the chaos, catching the attackers off guard. The sudden attack from the rear sent shockwaves through the ambushers, forcing them to regroup in disarray.

Leading the charge, Halsten engaged Major directly. Their swords clashed with a metallic ringing, sparks flying with each powerful strike. Major's skill was evident, but Halsten's relentless attacks forced him to retreat, his confidence visibly shaken.

Arthur and Frodio fought side by side, their movements precise as they cut down their foes. Nearby, Kudus wielded his blade with an unmatched combination of agility and strength, taking on multiple opponents at once and overwhelming them with calculated strikes.

The Forest Knights, now surrounded, began to falter. Realizing they had walked into a trap, Major shouted, "Fall back! Regroup at the rendezvous point!"

But their retreat was chaotic. Halsten's forces pressed their advantage, driving the ambushers further into the forest. The knights' formation crumbled as Halsten's men tightened their grip on the battlefield.

Major and Boyd, seeing no other option, fled toward the banks of River Ellyn. Halsten and DeMarco, mounted on their steeds, surged forward in pursuit. The dense underbrush clawed at their armor and horses, but they pushed on, determined not to let the men escape.

The sound of clashing swords and cries of battle grew fainter behind them as the pursuit carried them deeper into the woods. Halsten leaned forward in his saddle, his voice cutting through the night. "They're heading for the river! Don't let them cross!"

DeMarco nodded. "They know the terrain, but we'll outrun them!"

Major and Boyd reached the riverbank, their boots splashing in the shallow water as they hurried to cross. Just as they began to wade through the rushing current, Halsten and DeMarco closed in, their swords drawn.

Major turned briefly, his eyes meeting Halsten's. For a moment, there was no fear, only defiance. "You'll regret chasing me, prince!" he spat before disappearing into the river's shadows with Boyd at his side.

Halsten brought his horse to a stop at the water's edge, frustration etched across his face. DeMarco dismounted, scanning the opposite bank. "They're gone for now," he said grimly. "But we've weakened them."

DeMarco pulled his reins sharply, glancing at Halsten. "My prince, we need to return. Our men are still in the thick of the fight."

Halsten clenched his jaw, his frustration palpable. "You're right. Let's ensure they hold their ground."

The two charged into the melee, the battlefield illuminated by the first pale streaks of dawn. Asger, Arthur, Kudus, and the others fought fiercely against the remaining Forest Knights, their weapons flashing as they struck blow after blow.

Halsten dismounted, his boots hitting the ground as he drew his sword. Spotting Orod and Fada rallying their men for a counterattack, Halsten pointed it. "Take them down!" he commanded.

His charge brought him face-to-face with Orod. Their blades collided in a storm of sparks and steel. Orod was a seasoned fighter—his strikes were brutal and calculated. Halsten countered each blow with precision, his determination unwavering. Nearby, DeMarco squared off with Fada. Their duel was swift but deadly. DeMarco drove his blade into Fada's chest with a well-placed thrust, sending the Forest Knight collapsing to the ground.

After several deft maneuvers, Halsten disarmed Orod, forcing him to his knees. Around him, his companions subdued the remaining attackers. Adikis and Zoresh worked seamlessly, their blades cutting down any resistance. Arthur and Frodio captured several men, binding their hands behind their backs. Asger and Kudus secured the area, ensuring no enemies remained free.

Halsten scanned the battlefield as the dust settled, his relief short-lived when he noticed Leo breathing heavily, clutching his side. Blood seeped between his fingers, staining the ground. Arthur was the first to reach him, catching him as he fell to his knees.

"Leo!" he cried, his voice trembling.

Halsten rushed over, kneeling beside him. "Stay with me, Leo. Open your eyes!" he pleaded, his voice desperate.

Leo looked up, his face pale, his breathing shallow. "I'm sorry, my prince," he whispered, his voice barely audible. Then, with a faint smile, he added, "To the Realm…" before his eyes closed and he collapsed, lifeless.

Arthur let out a pained scream, grief overtaking him. In a blind rage, he unsheathed his sword and struck down one of the prisoners, his blade cutting through the man without hesitation.

"Arthur!" Halsten shouted, grabbing his arm before he could strike again. "Enough! We need them alive to find out who sent them."

Arthur trembled, his chest heaving with emotion. "He didn't deserve to die, Halsten," he choked out.

"No," the prince said, his voice steady but sorrowful. "And we'll make sure his death wasn't in vain."

The group solemnly buried Leo beneath a tree at the forest's edge. They marked his grave with his sword, its blade driven into the ground. Standing in silence, they bowed their heads, each mourning the loss of their loyal companion. They then gathered the rest of their fallen soldiers and buried them next to Leo.

When the burial was complete, Halsten turned to his men, his voice cutting through the heavy silence. "We move forward." The words were iron, unyielding. "We'll honor the ones we've lost by ensuring those responsible for the attack are brought to justice." His soldiers nodded, their faces filled with determination.

Back at the camp, Frodio and DeMarco had already begun interrogating the captured Forest Knights, starting with Orod. Yet despite their efforts—the threats, the demands—the captives remained defiant. Orod, in particular, exuded arrogance, his lips curling into a sinister grin as Halsten approached, as if he knew something they did not.

"You'll learn nothing from me," he sneered.

Halsten's gaze hardened. "We'll see about that."

Though the prisoners refused to divulge their secrets, Halsten resolved to take them to McKenzie Castle for further questioning. The captives were securely bound, and at first light, the group began their march toward the castle. The weight of Leo's death hung heavily on everyone's shoulders, but their resolve was stronger than ever.

The formidable towers of McKenzie Castle came into view as the sun rose. The guards atop the walls spotted the approaching group and sounded the drums to announce their arrival. The rhythmic beat echoed through the air as the gates swung open.

The guards formed two lines on either side of the gate, saluting as the prince and his entourage entered. Halsten dismounted, his movements sharp and purposeful. "Secure the prisoners in the dungeon cells," he ordered. "Double the watch and ensure no mistakes."

"Yes, my prince," a guard replied, saluting before leading the prisoners away.

Halsten turned to Frodio. "Send a message to Abbot Castle. Request Princess Freja's immediate escort to McKenzie Castle under strict protection."

Frodio nodded, quickly drafting a message. He tied the note to a pigeon and released it into the sky. The bird's wings cut through the morning air, carrying the urgent message above the trees toward Abbot Castle.

Several hours after the bird had been released, it landed at Abbot Castle. When the bird landed near the cages on the tower, a young bird attendant picked it up, untied the message from its feathers, and walked into the castle to deliver it to Lady Paulina, who read the message with a furrowed brow. Without hesitation, she summoned Sir Asgur. "Asgur," she said firmly, "assemble our best soldiers. You are to escort Lady Freja to McKenzie Castle without delay. Her safety is paramount."

"As you command, my lady," Sir Asgur replied, bowing deeply.

Within hours, the escort was ready. Lady Freja, accompanied by a heavily armed convoy, began the journey. Sir Asgur rode at the head of the formation, his gaze vigilant as they navigated the roads.

At McKenzie Castle, Halsten was standing atop the battlements, his gaze fixed on the horizon. The weight of responsibility pressed heavily upon him. Arthur approached, his grief still evident but his loyalty unwavering.

"She'll be safe, Halsten," Arthur said, touching his shoulder. "Sir Asgur won't fail."

CHAPTER 30

UNDER THE COVER OF NIGHT, while Halsten and his team were engaged in battle on the way to McKenzie Castle, a far more sinister plot unfolded within the walls of Aldrich City. Darius's men, who had infiltrated it in small groups over several days, moved covertly toward Verdant Castle. Disguised as regular townsfolk or guards, they blended in seamlessly.

Their mission was clear—gain control of Aldrich City and infiltrate the kingdom's heart, Verdant Castle. Their first objective was to eliminate guards posted at strategic vantage points. Operating in pairs or small groups, they executed their plan ruthlessly. Each targeted guard was subdued swiftly and silently, their bodies hidden in shadowy alcoves or abandoned buildings. The infiltrators then took their places, posing as the very guards they had killed.

As the city grew still and its residents slipped into a deep slumber, the second phase of the plan commenced. Soldiers from Bear Cave were led by Darius's lieutenant. The group moved cautiously along the shadowy perimeter of the city wall, staying out of sight of any remaining sentries. They converged beneath Aldrich City's gates, their numbers swelling as they silently regrouped.

The lieutenant glanced at the men around him, his eyes sharp and calculating. He raised a hand, signaling them to halt. With practiced ease, he placed two fingers to his lips and emitted a high-pitched bird call, the sound cutting through the stillness of the night. The signal was carried to the infiltrators stationed at the guard post and the towers overlooking the gate.

One of them, disguised in the king's livery, drew his dagger and approached his unsuspecting partner inside the guard post. Without hesitation, he plunged the blade into the guard's side, silencing him before he could utter a sound. Similar scenes played out in the other towers. Those loyal to the king were struck down by the infiltrators, who moved with grim determination.

A young guard stationed near the gate heard the commotion and turned to flee, intending to sound the alarm. However, one of the attackers—a burly soldier wielding a short sword—intercepted him, cutting him down before he could take more than a few steps.

With the defenders neutralized, Scrony stepped forward. "Open the gates," he commanded.

The infiltrators pushed the heavy gates open, their iron hinges groaning faintly. Outside, a column of soldiers from Bear Cave waited. They filed into the city, their faces grim with purpose.

Once inside, Scrony signaled one of his archers. "Send the signal to the castle," he ordered.

The man nodded, notching an arrow to his bow. He aimed it high, releasing it into the night. The arrow sailed through the air, its tip glowing faintly in the darkness. It landed near the castle, embedding itself deep in a wooden post.

Infiltrators already stationed around Verdant Castle sprang into action. They moved swiftly, targeting the king's men stationed at key points around the castle grounds. Each guard fell silently, their assailants vanishing into the shadows before any alarm could be raised.

Inside Verdant Castle, the atmosphere remained deceptively calm. Most inhabitants were fast asleep, unaware of the danger creeping ever closer. However, in the dim hallways, the king's remaining loyal guards began to sense something was amiss.

One of the senior guards, Captain Egron, was making his rounds when he noticed a trail of blood leading from the barracks to the outer wall. He stopped in his tracks, his hand instinctively reaching for the hilt of his sword. "Sound the alarm!" he shouted, his voice echoing through the corridor.

An infiltrator lunged at him from the shadows. Egron parried the attack with his blade, the clash of steel breaking the night's silence. The chaos alerted the rest of the guards on the city walls, sending waves of confusion and fear within the gates and the city.

The infiltrators multiplied quickly as reinforcement poured out of the woods to join their colleagues, overwhelming the guards at the gate and pushing the gates open. Tapas barked orders to his men. "Move in now! We take the city tonight or not at all!"

The attackers surged forward, killing everyone in their path as some followed Tapas towards the Verdant Castle's gates. Inside the castle, Egron and his remaining guards braced for the fight of their lives to defend the castle and the king's family.

One of the guards noticed movements near the castle gates and stretched his head to get a better view.

"Do you see that?" he whispered to his companion, his voice low and tense.

The other guard nodded. "Something's moving. It could be nothing."

"I will go and alert the commander," one of the men said and hurried away into the castle. They signaled their colleagues, and many more guards moved to their location, weapons ready. As they neared the edge of the wall to get a closer look, an arrow shot out of the darkness, striking one of them in the chest. He staggered backward, his eyes wide with shock, before tumbling over the side to the ground below.

"Archers!" one of the men shouted, panic surging through him. He stepped back quickly, threw down his sword, and ran away, leaving his colleagues behind.

Egron joined the men on the castle wall and took charge of the command.

"Guards! To arms!" he commanded.

Within minutes, the attackers emerged from the darkness and charged toward the castle gate with force as some engaged Egron and his men in shooting arrows at each other. Many of the guards on the castle wall fell to their death as the others overpowered the guards at the gates and entered.

Egron called out to his men, "To the castle!"

The soldiers followed Egron to enter the castle, and then they took their positions within the castle.

The attackers surged forward and spilled into the corridor, engaging Egron and his men in another fierce battle.

Alaric emerged from his chambers, his sword already in hand. Though still in his nightclothes, his bearing was regal and commanding.

"Who is behind this?" he demanded, his voice cutting through the chaos.

Egron saluted. "Your Majesty, we are not yet certain, but the city is under attack."

The king's expression hardened.

Egron shouted to the guards, "Get the king to safety," as he surged forward to face the attackers.

But the king shook his head firmly. "Go and protect the queen," the king said to the soldiers.

The selected guards saluted and rushed to Isadora 's chambers.

"My king, please be careful," one of the guards said.

Alaric moved forward to join Egron and the assembled soldiers in the main corridor. Clashing steel and battle cries echoed around them.

Tapas entered where the king stood with more men behind him. his voice cutting through the cacophony. "Surrender your position!" he shouted. "Lay down your weapons, and you will be spared."

Egron glared at him, his sword in hand. "We are not cowards like you!" he retorted fiercely.

Tapas smirked, unbothered. He turned to his men and spoke. "So be it! Soldiers, kill them all and leave the king for me."

The attackers redoubled their efforts and moved forward, fighting with renewed vigor.

The king's guards fought valiantly, meeting the invaders in a fierce clash. The attackers, however, were ruthless and relentless. Led by Tapas and his men, they cut through the defenders with brutal efficiency. Blood stained the cobblestones as they pushed deeper into the castle grounds.

Tapas, his sword dripping with blood, moved towards Egron with a smirk on his face. The attackers surrounded Egron and the king with their swords pointed at them. "Throw your sword down," he commanded.

Alaric spoke. "So, Darius sent you here."

Tapas gave a mock bow, his smirk widening into a grin. "Ah, so you've pieced it together at last. Surrender now, Your Majesty, and spare the lives of what remains of your loyal men."

Egron, standing steadfast at the king's side, interjected fiercely, "It is you who should surrender, Tapas! Lay down your arms, and perhaps we will show you mercy."

Tapas laughed, shaking his head. "Egron, Egron, Egron, always the loyal fool. The king isn't the one sitting on the throne. The king is the one who has the power to take the throne—and keep it." Without waiting for a reply, he turned to his men.

Tapas stepped forward, his sword raised as he addressed the king. "It's over, Alaric. Surrender, and perhaps I'll spare your life."

"Take their swords," Tapas commanded.

One of his men approached the king with a wicked grin, extending his hand toward his sword. "Hand it over," he growled.

Before anyone could react, Egron stepped forward with lightning speed, severing the man's hand at the wrist. The man screamed in agony as he fell to the ground, clutching the bleeding stump.

Tapas's face twisted with rage. "Seize them!"

The attackers swarmed forward, overwhelming the defenders with sheer numbers. King Alaric, his face grim, tossed his sword to the ground. "It is not over," he said quietly. "Do not throw your lives away needlessly."

Egron hesitated, his eyes blazing with defiance, but he followed the king's lead, lowering his weapon and then throwing it to the ground. The remaining guards, battered and bloodied, surrendered one by one. They were quickly bound with thick ropes and marched toward the main hall, their heads held high despite their defeat.

The captured defenders were led through the once-grand corridors of Verdant Castle, now filled with battle wreckage. Tapas strode ahead of the group. Behind him, Caine staggered, supported by two of his men. His face was pale from blood loss, but his expression was still twisted with fury.

Egron walked beside the king, his hands bound but his spirit unbroken. He leaned slightly toward Alaric and whispered, "This isn't over, Your Majesty. We'll find a way out of this."

Alaric nodded solemnly, his face unreadable. "Hold your strength, Egron. We may yet have a chance."

As they entered the main hall, Tapas turned to his captives with a cruel smile. "Welcome back to the throne room, Alaric," he said. "Enjoy it. It may be your last time here."

The castle grounds were tense as Tapas barked orders to his men. "Secure the palace and the towers," he commanded, "Send the message 'The lion has fallen.'" Turning to a soldier to his right, he added, "Find the queen. Leave no corner unchecked."

Moments later, one of the soldiers stepped into the courtyard, fitting an arrow with a strip of white cloth tied to its shaft. He aimed high and released it, and it arched gracefully into the sky before disappearing toward the eastern horizon.

Meanwhile, the attackers assumed strategic positions throughout the palace. Some stationed themselves at the lower hall entrances, while others climbed the towers, their weapons ready. Once a symbol of unity and strength, the castle stood under siege.

Inside the hall, two guards escorted Isadora through a secret door behind the king's study, through a tunnel toward the outer wall behind the castle.

But as soon as they emerged from the tunnel, swords were pointed at Isadora and her guards. The men killed the guards and then escorted Isadora back toward the palace.

The rhythmic pounding of drums reverberated from the towers, signaling the arrival of someone to the palace. A column of riders emerged from the wooded area east of Verdant Castle, their dark cloaks billowing in the night wind. Leading them were Darius and Mefford, both seated atop their horses with an air of triumph.

The sound of hooves striking the cobblestones grew louder as the group approached the gates. Darius and Mefford rode in with calculated majesty. Citizens who had dared to brave the night gathered cautiously in the shadows, their faces pale with fear and curiosity. Whispers rippled through the crowd as they watched the usurpers enter the castle grounds.

Darius's sharp gaze swept over the scene, lingering on the palace entrance, where his men stood at attention. His expression was cold and resolute, his look prideful.

Mefford dismounted first, his boots striking the ground with purpose. Darius followed, descending with measured steps. Side by side, they ascended the stairs leading to the castle hall. Darius stopped momentarily, took a deep breath, and continued walking.

Inside the castle, the air was thick with dread. Soldiers loyal to Darius lined the halls, their weapons ready as they saluted their leader. The subdued palace guards, bound and disarmed, knelt in rows, their heads bowed in defeat.

Darius paused at the entrance to the grand hall, his eyes scanning the opulent space. The flickering light of the chandeliers illuminated the faces of his captives, including King Alaric, who stood bound but unbroken in the center of the room. Egron, standing beside him, glared at Darius with defiance etched into every line of his face.

Darius took a step forward, his boots echoing against the marble floor. "So," he began, his voice cutting like a blade, "the lion has indeed fallen."

Alaric raised his head, meeting his brother's gaze with unwavering resolve. "It is you who have fallen, Darius," he said calmly. "You've abandoned honor for ambition. This kingdom will not bow to treachery."

Darius's lips curled into a mocking smile. "Spare me the lectures, Alaric. You always did enjoy the sound of your own righteousness. But tonight, the throne returns to its rightful heir."

Egron stepped forward, his voice filled with venom. "Rightful heir? You betrayed your blood and kingdom. You are no king, Darius."

Mefford, standing beside his father, drew his sword with a flourish. "Watch your tongue, dog, or I'll silence it myself."

Darius raised his hand, signaling Mefford to lower his weapon. "Patience, my son. Let them speak. It will make the defeat all the sweeter."

Just then, the doors to the throne room opened, and the men who had captured Isadora pushed her in.

"Well, well, well, see who we have here—the queen herself," Darius said.

He then commanded his men to take Isadora Alaric's side, and they obliged swiftly.

The tension in the hall was palpable. The castle, so recently filled with the echoes of celebration and unity, was now a chamber of betrayal and conquest. Darius strode confidently to the throne, his boots reverberating through the grand hall. He lowered himself onto the ornate seat, his posture exuding arrogance and satisfaction. Mefford stood nearby, his hands on the hilt of his sword, a smug grin playing on his lips as he watched his father relish the moment.

Darius looked into the eyes of his brother. "This is how you sit on a throne as a king."

"Anything ill-gotten never lasts. Your relish and hunger for power will not last," Alaric said. "You are a weak and miserable person with low self-esteem who is hoping to be relevant. Oh, brother, listen, is anyone cheering your name?"

Darius heard Orb's voice in his head.

"You are displaying weakness," the creature said.

Darius turned, fury in his eyes, and slapped the queen.

"You are mad, Darius!" Alaric said.

"My father did not deny me the throne. My mother and brothers took it from me by lying and deceiving him," Darius growled.

"It is your vices that got you here," Alaric said. "You slept with your father's concubine."

Orb spoke in Darius's mind. "Will you have them insult you in front of the people you rule?"

Darius pulled his sword and pointed it at his brother with anger in his eyes. After a while, he lowered it and said, "Look who now owns the throne, and look at you, brother."

Alaric looked up into Darius's eyes.

"You cannot cage a lion, thinking it might take a liking to you, for it might eat you up when it escapes the cage," Alaric said.

Isadora's eyes bore a piercing gaze into her captors, making the soldiers slightly uncomfortable.

Darius rose from the throne, descending the stairs slowly and deliberately. Each step was measured and calculated to exude dominance. His grin widened as he drew closer to the queen, his eyes gleaming with malice.

"What a waste," he sneered, his voice dripping with contempt. "You could have used your influence and intelligence to advise your husband to step aside. To hand the throne to its rightful owner. But no, you chose to cling to what doesn't belong to you."

Isadora 's eyes narrowed, her expression unwavering. Her silence was more cutting than any retort.

Darius's grin faltered for a moment before he leaned closer. "Do you think your defiance matters now? Look around you, Isadora. This castle, this throne—it's all mine."

Isadora held her ground, her voice calm but edged with disdain. "This throne will never be yours, Darius. You might sit on it, but you will never own it. The throne belongs to those who earn it, not those who steal it in the dead of night."

Darius straightened, his face darkening with anger. "You still cling to your arrogance. Do you think words can save you now?"

Isadora's lips curled into a faint, defiant smile. "No, Darius. Words won't save me. But they will outlive you. History will remember you for the traitor you are."

Observing the exchange from the side, Mefford stepped forward, his voice sharp. "Father, why waste your breath on her? She's nothing."

Darius turned to his son, forcing his anger into a cold, cruel smile. "You're right, Mefford. Words are wasted on the defeated. But I can let the queen warm my bed at my beck and call."

Without hesitation, Isadora spat directly at Darius's face. The grand hall fell into stunned silence. All eyes turned to her, her defiance as regal as her posture.

Darius froze mid-step, the smug grin vanishing from his face. He stood motionless, the spit gleaming on his cheek. His features twisted into a mask of rage as he slowly wiped his face with the back of his hand. "You will regret this insolence," he growled.

Orb's taunting and venomous voice echoed in his mind again. "Is that how low you have come? You let a woman disgrace you?" The words fueled his already burning anger.

Isadora remained steadfast. Her voice was calm, each word laced with cutting contempt. "You are a despicable pig, Darius. Nothing more."

His eyes darkened as he stepped closer and untied her hands. "I had a soft spot for you once. I even considered sparing you, perhaps making you my concubine. Allowing you to live in the shadow of my greatness. But now… Now, you've made me angry. You will suffer the same fate as your weak, foolish husband."

Isadora smirked faintly, unshaken. "Weak? Foolish?" she repeated. "You speak of my husband, but it is you, Darius, who is the disgrace. Your father gave the throne to Alaric because he saw you for what you truly are—a devious, adulterous coward unfit to rule. Your downfall is no one's fault but your own."

Darius's face was now inches from hers. His voice dropped to a venomous whisper. "You think you can stand here, powerless, and lecture me?"

Suddenly, in a flash of rage, he grabbed the queen's robe at her chest and ripped it, exposing her before the assembled court. Gasps of shock and murmurs of dismay rippled through the room. Isadora attempted to hit Darius, but his men held her back.

"Tie her up!" Darius commanded.

The men quickly bound her hands again.

Isadora stood tall despite the indignity. She held Darius's gaze. "This does not diminish who I am. I would rather die than stand anywhere near your vile, unworthy presence. Everyone look, this is what this traitor's whore of a wife cannot give him," she said.

King Alaric, bound but seething with fury, struggled against the men restraining him. "Darius, you will pay for this!" he roared.

Darius approached the king and hit the back of his head, rendering him unconscious. He grinned and turned back to Isadora. "Look at your husband, poor Alaric."

Orb spoke again, "This woman is gaining the affection of everyone here—look around you."

Darius's patience snapped, and he raised his hand as if to strike her. The room collectively held its breath, but he stopped himself, lowering his hand slowly as a wicked grin spread across his face. "Take them to the dungeons," he barked at the guards. "Let them sit in the darkness and see how much power she has left."

The guards hesitated, glancing at one another. Darius's sharp glare spurred them into motion, and they stepped forward to seize Isadora. Her regal defiance never faltered as she was led away next to the king, Egron, and the defeated guards. As they reached the hall's threshold, she turned to look back.

"Mark my words, Darius," Isadora said. "The seeds of treachery you have sown today, you will reap tomorrow. You may take the throne, but you will never truly rule this kingdom. It will rise against you."

Her words echoed off the stone walls. Darius watched as they disappeared into the shadows, his jaw clenched tightly. His fists curled at his sides, the warning lingering in the room like an unwelcome guest.

"Take them away," he muttered, though his voice betrayed the faintest trace of unease. He turned to Mefford, who stood stiffly beside him. "Strengthen the guard around the dungeons. I don't want her clever tongue poisoning anyone."

Mefford nodded but hesitated before speaking. "Father, the queen may be bound, but her words still carry weight. Perhaps we should consider…"

Darius shot him a warning glare. "Do not lecture me, boy. You are here to learn, not advise. Follow my orders and leave strategy to me."

He strode back to the throne and seated himself, gripping the arms tightly. The hall remained tense as his men stood in uneasy silence, unsure of what would come next.

CHAPTER 31

Darius rose from the throne, his voice cutting through the murmur in the hall. "Tapas, round up all the nobles and officials. Ensure no one enters or leaves the city until our reinforcements arrive. I want every group under control."

Tapas saluted sharply, his expression resolute. "At once, my lord."

He strode out to the courtyard, where the soldiers loyal to Darius stood in tight formation. Tapas raised his hand, commanding their attention. "Brave men of the kingdom! Lord Darius has claimed the throne as the rightful heir with your strength and loyalty. Today, history is written in our favor, and you will be rewarded for contributing to this victory."

The soldiers erupted into chants, their voices echoing through the courtyard. "Victory! Victory! Victory!"

Tapas lifted his hand again, signaling for silence. The chants faded, leaving only the crackle of torches in the cool night air.

"But our work is not yet finished," he continued. "Go to every noble house, every institution, and every stronghold loyal to the deposed king. Arrest anyone who swears allegiance to Alaric and bring them to the palace. If anyone resists, you have my command to kill them."

The soldiers roared their agreement, and their fervor reignited. Without hesitation, they dispersed into the city, their boots pounding against the cobblestones as they spread out in groups. They targeted the chapel, the prison offices, and the grand noble estates, leaving no corner untouched.

Meanwhile, outside the city, an old beggar named Otello approached, his tattered cloak billowing slightly in the wind. He shuffled toward the guards at the gate, holding out a battered tin bowl. "A coin for a poor soul," he pleaded, his voice hoarse.

One of the guards sneered at him and kicked him hard in the chest. Otello stumbled backward, falling into the dirt. The guard laughed cruelly and slammed the gate shut.

"Begone, old fool!" he shouted through the iron bars.

Otello gritted his teeth as he climbed to his feet, brushing the dirt from his ragged clothes. He cast one last glance at the gate before retreating into the shadows of the nearby trees. There, hidden from sight, he crouched behind a thick trunk and untied a horse tethered to a branch. The animal snorted softly as he mounted it with practiced ease.

Once seated, the beggar's demeanor shifted. Gone was the hunched, pitiable figure. In his place was a man with purpose and resolve. He urged the horse into a gallop, heading southward through the dense forest. The darkened trees swallowed him whole, his destination clear— the southern reaches of the kingdom, where word of Darius's treachery would soon spark resistance.

Within the city, chaos reigned as Darius's men tore through homes and institutions, dragging nobles and officials from their beds. Families pleaded for mercy as their patriarchs were hauled away in chains, while soldiers loyal to the deposed king were executed on the spot if they resisted.

In the chapel, priests prayed quietly for deliverance as soldiers stormed in, demanding allegiance to the new ruler. High Priest Tovar stood firm, refusing to bow to Darius's authority. A soldier drew his sword, silencing him with a single, brutal strike. Blood pooled on the stone floor, mingling with the flickering light of the sacred candles.

At the prison office, a warden's assistant who had served Alaric for decades worked feverishly to hide critical documents. The papers detailing loyalist operations and communication networks could mean death for many if discovered. His hands trembled as he pushed them into a hidden compartment behind a bookshelf, but the sound of approaching footsteps froze him in place.

The door burst open, and a group of Darius's men stormed in, weapons drawn. Their leader, a burly man with a jagged scar across his cheek, strode forward. "Search the place!" he barked.

The soldiers began tearing through the office, overturning furniture, and rifling through drawers. One of them pulled the hidden compartment open, revealing the stash of documents. He held them aloft. "Got something here!"

The leader snatched the papers, his eyes narrowing as he scanned the contents. He turned to the warden's assistant, who was now pale and trembling. "Where is the warden?" he demanded.

The assistant stammered, his voice barely above a whisper. "He—he isn't here. He's at his home."

The leader's eyes narrowed. "Take him to the palace," he ordered. Two soldiers grabbed the assistant, binding his wrists before dragging him away.

The leader turned to the rest of his men. "Mount up. We're going to the warden's house."

Meanwhile, Axilla, the warden, had already anticipated the danger. Alongside Tomei, he fled his home through the back gate of the city. The two rode under the cover of darkness, their horses galloping toward the southern part of the kingdom. The chilly night air bit at their faces, but neither dared to slow. They knew the fate that awaited them if they were caught.

At Axilla's home, his elderly parents sat in their modest parlor, determined to face whatever came their way after they had helped their son to escape. The peace was shattered when soldiers burst through the front door, their heavy boots echoing on the wooden floor.

The leader stepped forward. "Where is the warden?"

Axilla's father, a frail but resolute man, rose to his feet. "He's not here," he said firmly.

"Where did he go?" the leader pressed, his hand resting on the hilt of his sword.

The older man's gaze didn't waver. "I don't know."

The leader's expression darkened. "Tell me where he is, and I will spare your life."

The father's voice grew louder, laced with defiance. "Do your worst, soldier. What do I have to lose at this point?"

Without hesitation, the leader drew his sword and drove it into the older man's chest. Axilla's father crumpled to the floor, blood pooling beneath him. His wife let out a horrified cry and rushed toward her fallen husband, but a soldier grabbed her roughly.

"Where is your son?" he demanded, his grip tightening on her arm.

The woman's tear-filled eyes glared back at him. Her lips pressed together.

The commander, his patience gone, drove his blade into her abdomen. She gasped, her body collapsing beside her husband's. The soldiers watched as life drained from her eyes, and the leader wiped his blade on the edge of his cloak before sheathing it.

"Burn the house," the commander ordered, his voice devoid of emotion. "Let this be an example."

Several soldiers moved quickly, setting torches to the furniture and draperies. Flames licked at the walls, spreading rapidly. They exited, leaving the house to burn as they rode away into the night.

As the fire consumed the house, Axilla and Tomei rode further south, the distant glow of the blaze lighting the horizon behind them. Axilla's heart clenched, knowing his family had paid the ultimate price for his loyalty.

Tomei glanced at him, his voice heavy with urgency. "We can't stop now, Axilla. We must reach the Southern provinces. The resistance will need us."

Axilla nodded, his jaw set with determination. "They'll answer for this," he said. "Darius and his men will pay for every life they've taken."

The two rode into the darkness across the River Ellyn South.

While Axilla rode away from the city to escape persecution by Darius, the extent of the mutiny was unfolding.

At Lord Forest Eden's house, Tapas led a detachment of soldiers to capture him and his wife. They scoured every inch of the castle, their boots echoing through its stone halls as they searched. But, anticipating the attack, the couple had slipped out through a hidden passage leading to the castle's stables.

There, they hurriedly saddled their horses. The animals, sensing their urgency, shifted uneasily. As Lord Eden led them out of the stable, one of them neighed loudly.

Tapas, standing near the castle entrance, turned at the noise. His eyes narrowed, and he barked, "To the stables! Quickly!"

He and his men ran over, swords drawn. As they approached, Tapas spotted Lord Eden and his wife riding hard toward the forest. "Stop!" he shouted, his voice booming across the clearing.

Lord Eden looked back briefly but spurred his horse faster. His wife followed close behind, her face etched with determination.

Tapas growled in frustration, dismounted his horse, and stretched his arm toward one of his soldiers. "Give me a spear!" he ordered.

A soldier obeyed. Tapas adjusted his stance, raised the weapon above his head, and hurled it with practiced precision. It flew through the air, slicing the silence until a sickening thud echoed. Lord Eden's horse reared as its rider tumbled to the ground, the spear lodged deep in his back.

Lady Eden gasped, pulling her horse to a halt. She turned and saw her husband struggling on the ground. "Go! Get away!" he choked out, blood dribbling from the corner of his mouth. His voice was weak but insistent.

Ignoring his plea, Lady Eden dismounted and ran back to her husband. She knelt beside him, cradling his head. "I won't leave you," she whispered, tears streaming down her face.

Tapas approached, his boots crunching on the gravel as he closed the distance. Lady Eden rose to her feet, her fists clenched, and marched toward him, her eyes blazing with fury.

"You monster!" she shouted, voice trembling with rage. She swung her fists at him, but Tapas sidestepped her attack effortlessly. Without hesitation, he drew his sword and plunged it into her abdomen. Lady Eden's breath hitched, and her body fell limply to the ground beside her husband's.

Tapas sheathed his sword as soldiers moved swiftly and mounted their horses. Tapas stood silently for a moment, staring down at the fallen couple. "This is what happens to those who defy Lord Darius," he muttered before turning and walking away.

He then walked to his horse, mounted it, and ordered his men to ride back with him to the castle. The horrors of death filled the city as the smell of blood mingled with the crisp night air.

Back in the palace, several nobles from the Northern part of the kingdom were escorted into the dungeon, thrown into cells without any interrogation, and locked up near where the king was being held.

CHAPTER 32

THE FOLLOWING EVENING, AXILLA AND Tomei finally arrived at Abbot Castle, weary from their harrowing escape. Their horses trudged up the hill to the gates, and their riders slumped over from exhaustion. Drums echoed through the air, signaling their arrival. Guards on the walls peered down, recognizing the two figures approaching.

Lady Paulina and her half brother, Lord Stephen, the commander of the Abbot City Army, hurried to the castle's grand stairs to greet their unexpected visitors. Axilla dismounted his horse, his movements slow and labored. Tomei, however, collapsed onto the back of his horse, unable to muster the strength to get down.

"Axilla, Tomei, what brings you here in such a state?" Lady Paulina asked, her voice filled with concern.

Tomei raised a trembling hand, pointing to his dry, parched lips. His face was pale, and his eyes were sunken.

"Bring water for our guests!" Lady Paulina commanded, turning to a nearby guard.

Within moments, a servant appeared with pitchers of water. Axilla drank deeply, his hands shaking as he held the cup. Guards gently lifted Tomei from his horse, laying him on the stone steps, where he drank from a second cup, his breathing ragged but steadying.

Once the guests were filled with water, Lady Paulina welcomed the two men into her castle and ordered her maids to prepare dinner for their guests. Her brow furrowed with worry as she addressed them again. "What has happened? Why do you look so exhausted?"

Axilla wiped his mouth and straightened as best he could. "Darius attacked the palace and usurped the throne."

Lady Paulina's eyes widened in shock. She rose from her chair abruptly, her posture tense with disbelief. "When did this happen?" she demanded.

"Last night," the warden replied, his voice heavy.

"And what of the king and queen?" Lady Paulina asked urgently.

"We learned they are being held captive within the palace."

Lady Paulina turned to Lord Stephen, her face pale. "We must act swiftly. Summon the Council of Elders. This news cannot be ignored."

Stephen nodded, already signaling to a nearby guard. "I will ensure the elders convene immediately," he said.

Lady Paulina addressed a steward standing nearby. "Prepare rooms for our guests and ensure they are given food and rest. And summon the council." One of the servants was left to carry out Lady Paulina's first order while another was left to summon the council.

About two hours later, the council gathered in the grand hall of Abbot Castle. The room was filled with the murmur of voices as Axilla recounted the events at Verdant Castle, sparing no detail. At the same time, Tomei sat beside him, nodding occasionally to confirm the account.

After a lengthy discussion, the council turned to Lord Stephen. Elder Grauman, the eldest of the group, spoke with a firm voice. "Lord Stephen, as the commander of Abbot City's army, you must take immediate steps to secure the city and the castle. We cannot afford to be caught unprepared."

Stephen bowed his head in acknowledgment. "It will be done. I will double the watch on the gates and fortify the walls. The safety of Abbot Castle and its people will be my priority."

After the council had left, Lady Paulina turned to a steward by her side. She handed him a scroll. "This message must reach Prince Halsten at McKenzie Castle without delay."

The steward bowed deeply. "At once, my lady."

He climbed the castle tower with haste. In the light of the torches, he tied the scroll securely to a pigeon's leg and released it into the night. The bird flapped its wings and took flight, disappearing into the darkness toward McKenzie Castle.

Lady Paulina watched from the tower, her gaze fixed on the horizon. "Halsten must know," she murmured to herself. "The kingdom depends on him now."

Below her, the castle bustled with activity as Lord Stephen organized their defenses. Soldiers took their posts along the walls, archers were in place, and patrols were sent to secure the surrounding areas.

The rider approached McKenzie Castle's gate, his posture slumped with exhaustion but his eyes scanning his surroundings alertly. The drums sounded, the deep rhythm echoing across the grounds. On the balcony, Prince Halsten and Lady Freja stood side by side, their gazes fixed on the figure in the distance.

Freja leaned forward, and her brows furrowed in concern. "Do you recognize who is coming?" she asked.

Halsten shook his head, his eyes narrowing as he tried to discern the rider's identity. "No, I have no idea who it is."

As the rider reached the gate, the guards on duty hesitated until Captain Asger commanded, "Let him in." The heavy iron gates creaked open, and the rider urged his weary horse inside.

Asger stepped closer, his sharp eyes studying the man. He turned to DeMarco and gestured toward the rider. "Help him down."

Two guards moved quickly to assist the man, who nearly collapsed as he dismounted. His movements were slow and labored, his body betraying the strain of his journey.

Just as the guards steadied him, a group of riders arrived behind him. Adikis, Frodio, Zoresh, and Kudus dismounted and approached. Frodio's eyes widened with recognition as the man removed the covering from his head, revealing a weathered but familiar face.

"Otello!" Frodio exclaimed, stepping closer.

Kudus turned to Frodio, his tone questioning. "You know him?"

"Yes. He's from Verdant Castle."

DeMarco stepped forward, his hand resting on the hilt of his sword as he addressed the group. "Let's get him inside. He has important news."

The group escorted Otello toward the castle, and Prince Halsten met them at the grand doors. His gaze swept over the tired man, his expression curious and cautious.

"Bring him to the hall," he ordered. He turned and led the group inside.

Once they reached the hall, Halsten dismissed the guards with a wave. Only Freja and his closest companions—Frodio, Adikis, Zoresh, Kudus, Asger, and DeMarco—remained. The air was thick with anticipation as they gathered around Otello, who slumped into a chair.

Freja turned and ordered one of the castle maids to bring some water. The maid nodded and hurried out of the room. Moments later, she returned with a pitcher and a cup. Freja took the cup and handed it to Otello, who accepted it gratefully. He drank deeply, the color slowly returning to his face.

As he finished, Arthur entered the hall, his expression tense.

"Who are you?" Prince Halsten asked.

Otello glanced at Frodio, Adikis, and Zoresh before returning to the prince. "The prince doesn't know, does he?" he asked, his tone cryptic.

"Know what?" Halsten asked, his eyes narrowing.

Frodio hesitated before responding. "My prince, this is Otello. He is one of the king's secret operatives."

Halsten's brows furrowed as he studied the man. "Stationed where?"

"At the city gate," Otello replied, meeting the prince's gaze.

Halsten nodded slowly. "How do you all know each other?" he asked, his tone laced with curiosity.

Otello shifted uncomfortably before answering. "My prince, I bring urgent news from Verdant Castle."

The atmosphere in the room grew tense. "What has happened?" Halsten demanded.

"Darius has attacked the castle and taken control," Otello revealed, his voice heavy.

A wave of shock swept through the room. Freja gasped, placing her hand on Halsten's shoulder.

"When did this happen?" Halsten asked, his tone sharp and urgent.

"After midnight, on the day you departed for McKenzie Castle," Otello replied.

"And my parents? What of the king and queen?" Halsten pressed, his voice thick with concern.

"They are imprisoned in the dungeon by Darius," Otello said solemnly.

"What about Egron?" DeMarco asked, stepping forward.

"He is with the king, still fighting to protect him."

Freja excused herself quietly, leaving the hall through the side corridor. Her hand brushed the wall as she walked away.

Halsten stood abruptly, his determination evident. "Get my armor," he commanded.

Arthur stepped forward and placed a firm hand on his shoulder. "Your Grace, we need to plan carefully," he said. "Attacking without full intelligence would be reckless. We cannot risk losing more than we already have."

Halsten clenched his fists, breathing heavily as he considered this. "Then what do you suggest?" he asked, his voice edged with frustration.

"We need to gather more information," Arthur replied. "Otello, do you know the strength of Darius's forces and his plans?"

Otello nodded. "I overheard some discussions before I escaped. Darius has fortified the castle and sent his men to hunt down anyone loyal to King Alaric. His forces are well-coordinated and prepared for resistance."

Halsten's jaw tightened as he paced the room. "Then we must act swiftly but wisely. We will send scouts to gather intelligence on the castle's defenses. DeMarco, assemble the men and ensure they are battle ready."

DeMarco saluted and left the room to carry out the orders.

Freja returned, her expression resolute. "What can I do to help?" she asked.

Halsten turned to her, his voice softening for a moment. "We need the women mobilized to prepare supplies for war, if it comes to that."

A sharp knock echoed through the hall, drawing everyone's attention. A guard entered, holding a folded note in his hand. Arthur stepped forward and accepted the message.

Prince Halsten watched him intently. "What is it?" he asked.

Arthur scanned the note from Lady Paulina and then handed it to the prince. His nod was grave. "You'll want to see this."

Halsten took it, scanning the lines with his eyes. As he read, his face darkened, and he began pacing again.

"What's happened to Odus?" Zoresh demanded, breaking the tense silence.

Halsten frowned. "Who is Odus?" he asked, glancing at Frodio.

"He's the hunchback who rings the bell at the Verdant Chapel," Frodio explained.

Otello spoke up. "Odus is lying low. He will remain at the chapel as a contact if you need him, my prince."

Halsten paused mid-step, his mind racing. Arthur stepped forward, his tone measured. "Your Grace, we need to send messages to all the Southern castles, secure the Southern border immediately, and summon all the nobles to McKenzie Castle. We'll need their loyalty and support to move forward."

Halsten nodded decisively. "Send the invitations and issue orders to seal the border. No one enters or leaves without clearance."

Arthur bowed slightly before leaving the hall.

Moments later, Eleanor and Vivienne entered the room, their faces pale and filled with worry. "What's happened to Papa?" Vivienne asked, her voice trembling.

Halsten turned to his sisters. "Father and Mother are alive," he assured them. "We will rescue them, I promise you."

The two young women couldn't hold back their tears. Their distress filled the room, and Freja quickly moved to their side. She wrapped her arms around them, her voice soothing as she whispered reassurances. "Come with me," she said gently, guiding them out of the hall to give them comfort and privacy.

Halsten stood in the center of the room, his companions watching him closely. "We need to act swiftly," he said. "Every second we delay puts the kingdom and my parents in greater danger." He turned to his men, his gaze sharp and questioning. "Frodio, tell me, what was my father's assignment to you?"

Frodio's lips curled into a small smile. "Do you remember when we first met during military training?"

The prince nodded. "I do."

"At the time, we had just been selected from the orphanage to begin physical training. We didn't know your identity as the prince at the time, but we were given a clear directive—to watch over you and ensure no harm came your way. That was our mission."

Adikis interjected, "We had to keep our assignment hidden from you, which is why we worked to befriend you. It made protecting you much easier."

Halsten's brow furrowed as the memories resurfaced. "So that's why the three of you were always around during my most challenging moments?"

Frodio nodded. "Exactly. Our duty was to guard you, even when you didn't realize it. That's why we intervened that night. You were attacked by two of the other trainees."

Halsten's eyes narrowed. "I remember that. I'd already broken Gorm's nose when you arrived."

Zoresh smirked. "Do you think you could still recognize Gorm?"

"I believe I could," Halsten replied.

Zoresh's grin widened. "Gorm is Odus."

The revelation hit the prince like a jolt. "The hunchback bell ringer?"

"Yes," Zoresh confirmed. "In this network, operatives take on new identities whenever they're stationed in one place for an extended period."

Halsten's mind churned with questions. "And what of Tarto, Gorm's accomplice?"

Frodio answered, "Tarto now goes by the name Elvis. He's stationed in Walton City."

The prince nodded thoughtfully. "Who did you report to during all these years?"

Frodio stood tall. "We reported directly to the king. Now, Your Grace, we report to you."

Halsten met their loyal gazes and inclined his head in gratitude. "Thank you for everything you've done."

He turned to Otello, whose weary frame carried the weight of years of service. "Sir Otello, your duty has been invaluable. You may now retire here in McKenzie City as my security advisor. Arthur will arrange a place for you to rest and settle. Thank you for your unwavering service."

Otello bowed deeply. "It has been an honor, Your Grace."

Halsten's focus shifted to his companions as he began delegating tasks with precision. "Kudus and Adikis, I want you to oversee the training of the soldiers stationed here at McKenzie. Arthur, you'll assist me with planning and strategy. Zoresh, your role will be to mobilize additional troops from the surrounding cities. And Frodio, you will lead intelligence gathering. We need to stay ahead of every move Darius makes."

Each of them nodded solemnly.

Halsten straightened. "Now, let's prepare for the meeting with the nobles. We have much to discuss, and the fate of this kingdom depends on what we do next."

The men dispersed to their tasks, determined to restore the kingdom stronger than ever. As they moved with purpose, Prince Halsten stood in the hall for a moment longer, his mind already racing with the challenges ahead.

CHAPTER 33

A S THE FIRST RAYS OF the sun pierced the windows of his chamber, Darius stirred uneasily in his bed. The voice of the Orb, the Virgil, echoed in his mind, clear and commanding.

"To solidify your rule, you must annex other cities. Strengthen your reign through conquest," it declared.

Darius's brows furrowed in his sleep, his expression a mixture of irritation and intrigue. Though he didn't respond, the words lingered in the recesses of his mind, weaving themselves into his thoughts. The weight of the command pressed upon him, stirring an unease that refused to dissipate.

Finally, he opened his eyes, staring at the ornate ceiling. The lingering whispers of the Orb gnawed at him. He sat up slowly, running a hand over his face as the gravity of the suggestion began to take shape in his mind.

Annexing cities—spreading his rule beyond Verdant Castle—was a tantalizing prospect. It had struck at his ambition, igniting thoughts of an enormous empire that stretched across the entire realm.

Darius's eyes narrowed. "If I am to rule, I will do so on my terms," he said aloud, as though challenging the silent Orb. But the seeds of its suggestion had taken root, and he knew he could not easily dismiss them.

"Fetch Mefford," Darius commanded. "I require his counsel immediately."

The guard nodded and departed quickly. Darius paced the room, his mind racing. Though unwelcome, the Orb's voice had planted an idea he could not ignore. His rule over Verdant Castle was secure, but the question remained: What more could he achieve if he seized the cities surrounding his domain?

When Mefford arrived, his expression was one of curiosity, and Darius turned to him, his tone sharp. "Mefford, how strong are our forces?"

Mefford raised an eyebrow, sensing the urgency in his father's demeanor. "Our numbers are substantial, my lord. Strong enough to defend the castle and launch offensives if necessary. Why do you ask?"

Darius clasped his hands behind his back, his gaze distant. "Because I want to annex other cities to strengthen our rule."

Mefford's eyes flickered with interest, but he maintained a measured tone. "Annexation, father? That is no small feat. It would require careful planning, alliances, and the willingness to crush resistance."

Darius's lips curved into a faint, wicked smile. "I have never shied away from a challenge. Resistance only fuels my determination. I will begin with Abbot City, since it is close to the Northern border. I am sending Lord Warhouse and his army to annex it and kill that old witch Paulina."

Mefford smiled. "That will put fear in everyone since she is well-respected in the kingdom."

Before heading to the main hall, Darius summoned Lord Warhouse to the king's library. The room, filled with towering shelves of ancient texts and illuminated by the soft glow of a chandelier, provided a solemn backdrop for their meeting.

An hour later, Lord Warhouse entered, bowing deeply. "Your Grace, I came as soon as I received your message."

Darius stood near the large wooden table at the center, his hands resting on its surface. His expression was firm. "We must act swiftly to strengthen our position. Annexing nearby cities is essential to consolidating power. Please lead a force to Abbot City. Take it before the South has time to organize a defense under the prince."

Lord Warhouse's eyes gleamed with ambition. "I agree wholeheartedly, Your Grace. It would be an honor to carry out your order."

Darius nodded, his gaze steady. "I chose you for this mission because I trust your ability to execute it flawlessly. Bring Abbot City under our control, and I will make you Lord over the city. Godspeed."

"Thank you, Your Grace," Lord Warhouse said with a bow before leaving the library.

Once back at his residence, Lord Warhouse summoned his wife, Lou. She entered the room, her face etched with concern. "What is it, my lord? You look troubled."

He smiled faintly, placing a reassuring hand on her shoulder. "King Darius has given me a great honor. I am to lead an expedition to annex Abbot City. When it is done, Darius has promised to grant me the castle."

Lou's eyes widened with worry. "But, my lord, isn't this dangerous? Abbot City is no minor settlement. If the South retaliates—"

Lord Warhouse interrupted gently, "He who fears taking risks is destined to remain stagnant, or worse, lose everything. This is our opportunity, Lou. I will not let it slip through my fingers."

Understanding his determination, she nodded. "Then let me help you prepare."

She assisted him in donning his armor, carefully fastening each piece. When she finished, she removed a silver pin from her hair and pinned it to his chest. "Bring this back to me, my love, as a sign of your victory and safe return."

Lord Warhouse kissed her forehead. "I will. You have my word."

With his squire Aldon at his side, he descended the stairs, where a contingent of soldiers awaited him in formation. He addressed them with a commanding voice that echoed in the courtyard.

"Brave men of EdenRock," he began, "our new king, Darius, has entrusted us with a mission of great honor and importance. Today, we march to Abbot City to bring it under his rule. Think of the glory this will bring to your families and the elevation of your name in the annals of our history."

The soldiers raised their swords and spears, shouting in unison, "Victory! Victory!"

Aldon stepped forward, his voice steady. "Let's march!"

With that, the troops began their journey, their banners fluttering in the wind as they departed through the castle gates.

Meanwhile, in the palace, Darius prepared to further consolidate his rule. He sat on the throne, his posture commanding and his expression unreadable. Alaric and Isadora had been brought in under heavy guard and seated in chairs to his left as prisoners of the new regime. Despite the chains, Alaric remained defiant and would not bow to Darius. To Darius's right sat Xinovia, dressed in an elegant white and blue gown.

The nobles captured during the coup were marched into the grand hall one by one. They were forced to kneel before Darius, their faces a mixture of fear and defiance.

Darius's sharp gaze swept the room. His voice rang out with cold authority, reverberating against the stone walls. "Lords and ladies of EdenRock, you stand here today because you clung to a throne that no longer belongs to my brother Alaric. That era is over. It is time to swear your allegiance to the rightful king." He took a deliberate pause before continuing. "Those who support my rule, step to my right. Those who remain loyal to my weak brother move to the left."

A tense silence followed his command. The room seemed to hold its breath as the nobles exchanged uncertain glances. Slowly, a few began to move. Lord Nicholas of BlueVine Castle was the first to step to Darius's right, his expression grim. He was followed by Lord Edwin Cole of Cole Castle, Lady Margaret Dansgrove of Dansgrove Manor, Lord Stephen Emmitgrove of Emmitgrove Manor, and Lady Delena Longpatch of Longpatch Castle.

Lord Luterodt, who had not been arrested, joined the group by Darius's right side without hesitation. They exchanged smirks, their allegiance clear.

Darius turned his gaze toward the remaining nobles, his eyes narrowing with disdain. Lady Sarah Felton, Lord Martin BlueGate, Lord Milton Shaw, Lord George Salinas, Lord Walton, Lord Matteson, Lord Samuel Murdoch, and Lord Albert Cidel hesitated, their faces etched with defiance or uncertainty. Darius addressed them with a chilling smile.

"In one week," he announced, his tone laced with a venomous edge, "I will invite all of you to a grand banquet in the great hall. Use this time to consider where your allegiance lies. Will you stand with the rightful king or cling to the shadow of my pathetic brother? The choice is yours—strength over weakness, courage over cowardice. I suggest you choose wisely."

Darius turned to Tapas and gave a curt nod. Tapas immediately opened a side door, and a guard entered, carrying a silver tray holding the king's and queen's crowns. He stepped forward and knelt, presenting them to Darius.

Lord Luterodt, eager to prove his loyalty, stepped forward and lifted the king's crown from the tray. He approached Darius with reverence, bowing deeply as he held it aloft. But before Luterodt could place it on his head, Darius reached out and took it from him, fixing him with a sharp glare.

"I will crown myself," he declared. He placed the crown on his head with deliberate precision, adjusting it as he gazed out over the hall, a twisted grin spreading across his face.

Luterodt, flustered, quickly picked up the queen's crown and turned toward Xinovia. She rose gracefully from her seat and inclined her head slightly. He placed the crown atop her head with shaking hands, then stepped back into the shadows.

The guards in the hall erupted into a deafening chant, their fists raised high. "Long live the king!"

Darius raised a hand, and the room fell quiet immediately, the air thick with tension. His expression hardened when he looked toward the prisoners—King Alaric, Isadora, Egron, and the defiant nobles.

"Take them back to the dungeon," he commanded coldly. "Let them reflect on their choices."

The guards moved swiftly, binding the captives and ushering them out of the hall under heavy guard. Alaric and Isadora exchanged a glance, their faces stoic.

As they were led away, Darius turned back to the hall.

The room remained silent as he turned and ascended the steps to his throne. He sat down, adjusting his crown as he surveyed the hall, a picture of triumphant arrogance. At his side, Xinovia held her head high, her presence commanding.

Darius leaned back in his seat, his hand resting on the armrest. "This is just the beginning," he murmured, more to himself than anyone else. "EdenRock will kneel before me—or burn for its defiance."

CHAPTER 34

L ORD WARHOUSE, A STAUNCH ALLY of Darius's and a seasoned warrior renowned for his tactical brilliance, led a formidable force of soldiers on his mission to annex Abbott Castle. Alongside him were Aldon, his trusted lieutenant, and Lobo, a skilled scout. The group's confidence was evident as they crossed the bridge over the River Ellyn and entered the dense forest that bordered the river's terminus near the Kemit Sea.

On the first day of their journey, as the sun dipped below the horizon, the forest became bathed in twilight. Lord Warhouse reined in his horse and signaled for the company to halt. A soldier quickly dismounted and bowed before kneeling to offer his back, assisting Lord Warhouse as he stepped down from his steed with dignity.

Turning to Aldon, Lord Warhouse issued his orders. "Tell the men to set up camp here for the night. We'll need rest before continuing."

Aldon bowed slightly. "Yes, my lord." He turned to address the assembled soldiers. "Gentlemen, we stop here tonight. Prepare the camp."

The soldiers moved swiftly, their efficiency a testament to their discipline. Two men stepped forward as Aldon called them to set up a tent for Lord Warhouse. The sturdy canvas structure was erected with care, and soon after, two maids from the group entered to prepare a bath for their lord.

Inside the tent, the maids poured hot water into a wooden tub and added aromatic herbs to soothe Lord Warhouse's tired muscles. He entered the tent, removed his armor, and entered the bath. Steam rose around him as he settled into the warm water, his expression one of quiet satisfaction.

One of the maids approached with a soft sponge, bowing slightly before she began washing his shoulders. The other maid touched his hair, gently pouring water over his head. Warhouse remained silent, his mind preoccupied with thoughts of the campaign ahead.

Once he was clean, he stepped out and wrapped himself in a robe. A modest but hearty meal of roasted wild boar, freshly hunted by his soldiers earlier that evening, was set before him. He ate in silence, the crackle of the campfires outside providing a calming backdrop to his meal.

Once finished, Warhouse retired to his bed in the tent. Meanwhile, the soldiers gathered around their fires outside, sharing the boar meat. They exchanged quiet laughter and stories of past battles.

Despite the lighthearted atmosphere, the soldiers remained vigilant. A rotation of four-hour shifts was established for the night watch, ensuring the safety of the camp. Ever the reliable scout, Lobo took the first shift, his keen eyes scanning the area for any sign of movement.

As the camp settled into the night rhythms, the forest around them seemed to hold its breath. The flickering firelight danced on the trees, and the distant sound of the river mingled with the occasional rustle of leaves. Lord Warhouse slept soundly, his mind set on the mission that awaited him at Abbott Castle.

When morning broke, the lord summoned Aldon and Lobo into his tent. The air was thick with anticipation, the dawn light casting long shadows on the forest floor outside.

Seated at a small wooden table holding a map of Abbott City, Lord Warhouse leaned forward, his tone low. "Lobo," he began, ensuring his words would not carry beyond the tent walls, "our orders are precise. After we secure the soldiers loyal to Lady Paulina, we are to eliminate her and her family. This mission must be executed with precision and without witnesses."

Lobo's eyes narrowed. "What are your commands, my lord?" he asked.

"You and your men will remain concealed in the forest near Abbott City. Aldon and I will lead a smaller group to the castle, posing as guests.

Once inside, we will seize control of the castle and secure the gates. When the time comes, we will send a signal—an arrow fired high into the sky. That will be your cue to attack from the outside while we handle resistance from within."

Lobo nodded grimly. "Understood, my lord. We will ensure no one escapes to tell the tale."

Lord Warhouse's expression remained stony as he turned to Aldon. "Prepare the men for departure. Ensure the main force remains hidden until the signal is given. We cannot afford any mistakes."

"Yes, my lord," Aldon replied, bowing slightly before exiting the tent to relay the orders.

After a brief breakfast of bread and dried meat, the soldiers mounted their horses and set off again. The morning sun climbed higher as they traveled steadily toward Abbott City. The path wound through dense forest, the sound of their horse's hooves muffled by the soft earth.

By mid-afternoon, they reached the edge of Abbott Forest, the towering trees offering cover as they paused to review their plan. Lord Warhouse dismounted, spreading the map across a flat rock. Aldon and Lobo joined him, their expressions solemn.

"This is the layout of Abbott City," he said, pointing to key areas on the map. "Aldon and I will take a small contingent of soldiers to the castle. We will present ourselves as allies and guests of Lady Paulina. This will allow us to gain entry without raising suspicion."

He traced a route with his finger. "Once inside, we will secure the castle. I will send the signal when the gates are ours—an arrow fired into the sky. That will be your cue, Lobo. You and the remaining force will storm the city gates. By the time you enter, resistance will already be weakened."

Lobo studied the map carefully, nodding. "We'll remain hidden until the signal. My men are prepared."

Unbeknownst to Lord Warhouse and his men, two young boys hunting in the forest had stumbled upon the group. Abel and Alexander, hiding behind thick bushes, listened in shock as they overheard the conversation. Their faces paled as they realized the soldiers' plans.

As Abel shifted his weight nervously, his foot snapped a dry twig. The sharp sound shattered the silence, and Lord Warhouse immediately drew his sword. His men followed suit as they moved cautiously toward the source of the noise, their eyes scanning the dense underbrush.

Something suddenly darted out of the bushes, startling the men. They hesitated, then relaxed with nervous laughter. One soldier muttered, "Just a rabbit," shaking his head in relief.

Lord Warhouse sheathed his weapon, his expression still stern. Mounting once more, he dismissed the incident. "Let's move," he commanded, spurring his horse forward.

The group resumed their path toward Abbott Gate, leaving Lobo and his detachment concealed in the forest's shadows.

As soon as the soldiers were out of sight, the boys backed away slowly, their hearts pounding in their chests. Once safe, they turned and sprinted through the forest, navigating the familiar paths toward Abbott Castle. They reached the small servant's gate behind the castle kitchen, where their mother, Sarah, worked as Lady Paulina's chef.

Bursting inside, they were breathless but determined. Their mother turned to them, startled. "What on earth has gotten into you two?" she asked, wiping her hands on her apron.

"Mother, we saw soldiers in the forest!" Abel exclaimed, his voice frantic.

"They're planning to attack the castle!" Alexander added.

Sarah's face grew serious as she knelt in front of them. "Are you certain about this?" she asked, searching their eyes for any sign of doubt.

"Yes, Mother," Abel insisted. "We heard them talking. One of them called the leader Lord Warhouse."

Sarah's breath caught at the name. "Come with me," she instructed, taking each boy by the hand and leading them to the great hall where Lady Paulina, her brother Stephen, Axilla, and Tomeis were deeply discussing their plans to reach McKenzie Castle.

She paused at the threshold, bowing slightly. "My lady, forgive the interruption," she said, her voice steady despite her racing heart.

Lady Paulina turned to her with a warm smile. "What is it, Sarah? You look troubled."

"Abel and Alexander," she began. "They have something important to tell you."

Lady Paulina gestured for the children to step forward. "Speak, my boys," she encouraged.

Abel took a deep breath and said, "We were in the forest hunting when we saw soldiers. They were talking about attacking the city and the castle."

Lady Paulina's face grew serious. "Are you certain of this?"

Alexander nodded. "Yes, my lady. One of the men called the leader Lord Warhouse. He said they would kill you and open the gates for the rest of the soldiers."

A tense silence filled the room as everyone processed the information. Stephen was the first to speak. "If this is true, we need to act immediately."

Lady Paulina stood, her expression resolute. "You've done well to bring this to me," she told the boys. Reaching into her satchel, she handed each of them a gold coin. "Thank you for your bravery." She turned to Sarah and said, "See the boys safely out and return quickly."

Sarah nodded, ushering her sons from the hall. Once they were gone, Lady Paulina addressed the room. "If Lord Warhouse is involved, this is more than a raid. This is a coordinated effort to undermine the South. We must prepare."

Tomei, Axilla, and Stephen exchanged curious glances, their expressions marked by the gravity of the situation. Lady Paulina stood at the center of the great hall, her voice calm but firm as she addressed the gathering of castle servants, trusted guards, and commanders.

"We have received intelligence about Lord Warhouse and his men," she began, her gaze sweeping over the crowd. "They will arrive soon, but their intentions are far from honorable. They plan to kill us, annex our soldiers, and seize control of Abbott Castle. We must be prepared to defend ourselves and turn the tables on them."

The room grew tense as murmurs spread through the group. Lady Paulina raised a hand, silencing the whispers. She turned to Tomei, her expression resolute.

"Tomei, my friend, your presence here is fortuitous. Your knowledge will be invaluable. However, we must ensure they do not know you are here. Stay hidden until we need your expertise."

He bowed slightly. "As you command, my lady."

Stephen leaned closer to Tomei, who whispered instructions into his ear. Stephen nodded and turned to Lady Paulina, repeating the plan. She listened carefully, her expression growing thoughtful.

"We will welcome Lord Warhouse as planned," Lady Paulina said, her voice steady. "But we will be prepared for his treachery. Axilla," she continued, turning to the formidable commander, "have your guards ready to capture the men hiding in the forest. We cannot afford to be caught off guard."

Axilla stood tall and nodded. "He will regret ever stepping foot near Abbott City."

The preparations began in earnest. Guards were dispatched to the forest, hidden units were positioned near the castle walls, and the staff worked to maintain an air of normalcy. The castle buzzed with quiet activity, every household member acutely aware of the gravity of the situation.

The sun had long dipped below the horizon when the tower guards at Abbott Castle spotted Lord Warhouse and his men approaching. The faint flicker of torches bobbed in the distance, growing brighter as the group neared. The guards wasted no time sounding the tower drums, the rhythmic beats reverberating across the grounds, alerting everyone to the visitors' arrival.

Inside the castle, Lady Paulina prepared herself. She donned a regal gown of deep sapphire blue, the fabric shimmering under the torchlight as she descended the grand staircase with an air of calm authority. Her gaze was steady, her steps measured, and her presence exuded the confidence of a leader unshaken by the looming threat.

Lord Warhouse dismounted from his horse with practiced ease, his sharp eyes surveying the scene before him. Standing at the castle's entrance, Lady Paulina descended the steps gracefully to greet him. Her voice carried both authority and the warmth of a seasoned diplomat.

"Welcome to Abbot Castle, Lord Warhouse," she said, her tone cordial. "Please join us, we were about to have dinner before your arrival."

Lord Warhouse inclined his head slightly. "Thank you, Lady Paulina. Your hospitality is most appreciated."

The soldiers accompanying Lord Warhouse were similarly welcomed. Castle attendants escorted them to rest and refresh themselves before the feast. The air was thick with a pretense of camaraderie as the castle's staff worked to ensure every guest was comfortable.

Soon, the grand banquet hall buzzed with activity. The tables were laden with roasted meats, fresh bread, seasonal fruits, and fine wine. The warm glow of candlelight illuminated the intricate carvings on the walls, casting a regal ambiance over the gathering. Lord Warhouse sat at the head of the guest table opposite Lady Paulina, whose composure never wavered.

The room echoed with polite laughter and raised goblets as toasts were made to honor their "distinguished guest." Lord Warhouse, though outwardly gracious, maintained an air of suspicion. Lady Paulina, for her part, matched his caution with well-rehearsed diplomacy.

"My lady," Warhouse said, lifting his goblet, "Abbot Gate's wealth and generosity are unmatched. It is no wonder your city thrives."

Lady Paulina smiled faintly. "We believe in strength through unity, my lord. Prosperity is a shared effort, after all." Her words were measured, her tone neutral.

While the feast continued, Tomei, Axilla, and a group of loyal guards slipped out through the secret passage behind the castle. The narrow, shadowed corridor had been carefully maintained for centuries and was known only to those entrusted with its location. One of the boys who had overheard Lord Warhouse's plans guided them through the dense forest.

"Stay low and quiet," Axilla whispered, his voice barely audible above the rustling leaves.

The boy pointed toward a faint cluster of campfires flickering in the distance. "They're there, near the clearing."

Lord Warhouse's soldiers were gathered around a roaring fire in a clearing, their laughter echoing under the starlit sky. A freshly caught deer roasted over the flames, its aroma mingling with those from a pot of bean stew simmering nearby. Feeling secure in their secluded camp, the men had set their weapons aside, their guard lowered as they told jokes and shared hearty laughs.

Meanwhile, hidden in the shadows, Tomei, the cunning alchemist, crouched with Axilla and the loyal guards of Abbot Castle. He reached into his satchel, extracting a small bottle of clear liquid. Though resembling water, the substance was a potent poison he had carefully prepared for this moment. Handing his satchel to Axilla, he whispered, "Wait here," and began crawling silently toward the camp.

Every movement was calculated, his form blending seamlessly into the darkness. As he neared the pot of beans, Tomei's eyes glinted with determination. Whispering under his breath, he muttered a chilling incantation, "Death shall be the folly of those whose minds are clouded by hate, for out of their pot shall come the day of darkness."

He poured the poison into the stew, watching it disappear into the bubbling broth. He lingered momentarily, ensuring his actions had gone unnoticed, before retreating to his companions. Once he rejoined Axilla and the guards, they withdrew further into the tree cover, waiting for the toxin to take effect.

Meanwhile, in the grand banquet hall of Abbot Gate Castle, the mood remained cordial. Plates had been cleared, and goblets of fine wine were being refilled. Candles flickered, casting shadows across the stone walls, and the hum of subdued conversation filled the air.

Lord Warhouse rose from his seat, drawing the attention of everyone in the hall. He fixed his gaze on his hostess, his tone formal but laced with underlying menace. "Lady Paulina," he began, "I come as a representative of King Darius, ruler of the realm."

Lady Paulina's calm demeanor betrayed none of the alarm she felt. "And what does the king wish from me, Lord Warhouse?" she asked evenly.

He stepped forward, his heavy boots echoing across the floor. "The king requires your army to join him in the upcoming war," he declared.

Lady Paulina's brow furrowed slightly. "What war are you referring to, Lord Warhouse?"

Taking another step closer, he let a dangerous smile curl across his lips. "The king is preparing to march against his nephew. Prince Halsten has become a threat to his reign."

The atmosphere in the hall grew tense. Lady Paulina's gaze sharpened as she watched Warhouse walk boldly toward her throne. Without waiting for permission, he lowered himself into her seat, his audacity sending a ripple of unease through the room. The soldiers accompanying him moved into a menacing formation, their hands resting on the hilts of their swords as they loomed behind Lady Paulina and her attendants.

Warhouse's voice dropped, becoming more insistent. "The king has also commanded me to annex this castle and your soldiers if you refuse to comply willingly."

Lady Paulina remained silent for a moment, her expression unreadable. Then, rising gracefully from her chair, she approached Warhouse with slow, deliberate steps. "You come into my home, partake of my hospitality, and now you threaten me?" she said, her voice calm. "Have you forgotten the honor that is expected of a guest?"

Warhouse's grin widened. "Honor is a luxury, my lady, which the king cannot afford now. You will comply, or I will ensure that this castle and everything within it are taken by force."

Lady Paulina turned her back on him, her movements serene. She addressed her brother Stephen without turning around. "Stephen, what do you make of Lord Warhouse's demands?"

Stephen, who had remained silent until now, stepped forward, his hand resting on the pommel of his sword. "I think, dear sister, that threats made in someone else's home are the height of cowardice. And I think Lord Warhouse overestimates his position."

Warhouse's eyes narrowed, his grip tightening on the throne's armrests. "Careful, Stephen. You speak of treason."

Stephen smirked. "No, my lord. I speak of loyalty—to my family, city, and the true heir to the throne."

Lady Paulina turned back to Warhouse, her expression now cold and resolute. "You have made your intentions clear. Now allow me to make mine equally so. Abbot Gate stands with Prince Halsten. You and your men are not welcome here. The House of Abbot will not fight against someone who carries our blood in his veins," she declared firmly, her voice cutting through the tension like a blade. "Prince Halsten is the son of my niece, Isadora. How can you expect me to go to war against my flesh and blood?"

Lord Warhouse rose from the throne and approached her. His expression softened into a mask of false sympathy. "Lady Paulina," he began, feigning concern, "I want to help you. I do not wish to see any harm come to you or your people because of this decision."

But Lady Paulina did not waver. "No!" she declared. "I will not be responsible for the death of my nephew. His blood will not be on my hands. You may threaten me, Lord Warhouse, but my principles are not for sale."

The air in the hall grew colder. Lord Warhouse's sympathetic facade crumbled, replaced by a menacing glare. "Seize her!" he barked.

Before the guards could act, Stephen stepped forward, his hands raised in appeasement. "My lord," he said, voice calm but urgent, "please forgive my sister. She speaks from a place of emotion, not pragmatism. We will give you the soldiers you ask for."

Lord Warhouse paused, his icy gaze shifting to the man. Slowly, he nodded and returned to the throne, sitting back with a look of satisfaction. One of his men stepped forward and presented a scroll to Stephen. The commander handed it over solemnly, then stepped back.

Stephen unrolled the scroll and walked over to his sister, his steps heavy with the weight of what he was about to do. Reaching her, Lady Paulina's brother leaned in close in pretense, speaking softly. "Paulina, this is the only way to avoid bloodshed. If we resist, the city will suffer, and countless lives will be lost. Please, for the sake of our people, we must agree."

Lady Paulina's eyes bored into her brother's, searching for a glimmer of reassurance in his words. The weight of her responsibilities pressed down on her, and the room seemed to close around her. After a long, tense moment, she nodded slowly, her voice heavy with resignation. "Very well," she said, her tone marked by sorrow. "If it is the only way to protect Abbot and our people, I will comply."

Stephen placed a comforting hand on her shoulder, offering a faint, bittersweet smile. "You've made the right choice, sister," he said quietly. Then, turning back to Lord Warhouse, he announced, "Lady Paulina agrees to your terms. Abbot's soldiers will support your cause."

Lord Warhouse's smile returned, thin and calculating. "Wise decision," he said, his voice dripping with false magnanimity. "You have spared your people unnecessary suffering. I will ensure your cooperation is remembered."

Stephen carefully poured a small pot of hot wax onto the scroll, his hands steady. Lady Paulina pressed her ring into the wax, sealing the agreement with the House of Abbot's crest. The wax hardened quickly, solidifying the pact.

Lord Warhouse allowed a triumphant smile to cross his lips as he studied the seal.

The hall fell silent. Warhouse's smile faltered momentarily, his eyes narrowing as he processed her words. Then, with a sudden clap of his hands, he said, "Seize them," his voice echoing through the chamber.

The guards sprang into action, grabbing Lady Paulina and Stephen by their arms. Stephen glanced at his sister, silently urging her to remain calm. Without resistance, the siblings were escorted to their chambers. The heavy wooden doors closed behind them with a resounding thud, leaving a foreboding air in their wake.

Turning his attention back to the hall, Lord Warhouse barked at a nearby servant.

"Call the maids in here," Lord Warhouse commanded one of the guards.

The guard walked out and returned with five maids. Lord Warhouse pointed in front of where he was sitting and said, "Stand here." The guard urged the young women to move closer to where Lord Warhouse was seated.

Lord Warhouse stood up and walked in front of the ladies, scrutinizing them.

"What is your name?" he asked one of the maids, who had dark black hair and brown eyes.

"Lydia," the maid answered.

He pointed to the young woman and looked at the guard, "Prepare her and bring her to my chamber."

He turned to one of the other maids and said, "Show me the guest room."

The maid walked in front of him through the corridor to a door and pointed at it. One of his guards went to the room to inspect and then came back. "My lord, it is safe," the guard said.

Lord Warhouse waited for the maid to leave, and then he entered the room.

The room's opulence, with its rich tapestries and flickering candle-light, stood in stark contrast to the grim purpose in the air. He settled into a chair near the hearth, awaiting Lydia's arrival with an impatient scowl.

A few minutes after he had seated himself, a soft knock on the door broke the silence. One of his guards opened it, ushering Lydia, the maid, inside. She stepped into the room hesitantly, dressed in a plain white gown that emphasized her vulnerability. Warhouse dismissed the guard with a curt wave, and his gaze fixed on the girl as the door closed behind her.

"Turn around," he commanded, his voice cold and devoid of empathy.

Lydia froze, her fear palpable, but she complied, slowly turning her back to him. Warhouse's presence loomed behind her, his tone hardening. "Do as I say, and this will be easier for you."

"My lord…please," she stammered, clutching the edges of her gown. "I have done nothing to deserve this."

Warhouse's eyes narrowed, and he stepped closer, his voice a low growl. "I did not invite you here for your opinions, girl. Obey, or you will regret it."

Lydia's hands trembled as she struggled to hold back tears. She lowered her gaze, thoughts racing as she considered the futility of resistance. Warhouse moved to stand in front of her, his imposing figure blocking out the light of the fire.

A distant footstep echoed faintly down the hall. Lydia's heart quickened, hope flickering briefly before fading. Warhouse reached out, gripping her arm with an iron strength, his intent unmistakable.

Just then, there was another knock at the door—a loud, firm knock that startled both of them. Warhouse turned, his expression darkening as he barked, "What is it now?"

A muffled voice came from the other side. "My lord, urgent news. You are needed immediately."

Warhouse's grip on Lydia loosened, and he released her with an annoyed grunt. "Stay here," he ordered, his tone laced with irritation as he strode to the door.

The guard outside handed him a note. Warhouse scanned it, his brow furrowing. Without another word, he slammed the door shut and stormed down the hall, leaving Lydia alone. She stood there trembling, the weight of the moment crashing over her as tears streamed down her face.

With courage, she slipped out through a side door leading to the servants' quarters. She hurried down the narrow, dimly lit corridors, her breath coming in short gasps as she sought refuge among the other servants—unaware that fate, in the form of a single letter, had just bought her precious time.

That very moment, in the study above, Lord Warhouse sat at a desk, Lydia already forgotten. His attention was locked on the freshly delivered note in his hands—orders commanding him to ride for McKenzie after Abbott City. The parchment crinkled as his grip tightened, his mind already racing with strategy, oblivious to the servant girl who had just slipped through his grasp.

Meanwhile, in the forest, the soldiers under Lord Warhouse's command had finished their meal and were beginning to feel the effects of Tomei's poison. The warm atmosphere quickly turned to chaos as they clutched their stomachs in agony, vomiting and collapsing to the ground. Tomei, Axilla, and the Abbot guards emerged from the shadows, their swords drawn and ready. The soldiers, now weak and disoriented, were no match for the attackers, who slaughtered them with cold efficiency.

Tomei approached Lobo, who lay gasping for breath as the poison ravaged his body. Lifting the man's head with the tip of his sword, Tomei sneered. "I love it when tall men such as yourself fall under my feet. I will give your lord an even worse death so the two of you can meet in hell."

Lobo's eyes widened in terror as Tomei's sword came down, severing his head from his body with a swift, brutal stroke.

Back at the castle, Abbot's soldiers, disguised as Lord Warhouse's men, quietly infiltrated the sleeping quarters of Warhouse's forces. Sealing the entrances, they lit a mixture of Tomei's powders in banana leaves and threw them into the room. The soldiers inside awoke to choking smoke, coughing up blood as they bled from their eyes, their deaths swift and merciless, every single one of them.

Other disguised Abbot soldiers entered the castle to replace those on watch. As the soldiers returned to the quarters from the watch, they attacked, cutting them down without hesitation. By dawn, the castle had returned to the Abbott guards.

The household continued their duties without revealing what had transpired in the castle's halls.

When morning came, Lydia was trembling as she placed a plate of food before Lord Warhouse at the castle's hall: freshly squeezed juice, sausages, grapes, pineapple slices, flatbread, and a bowl of wild honey mixed with raisins. He waved for her to sit with him.

"Join me," he said, his tone laced with an unsettling edge.

When Lydia hesitated, he reached for the dagger at his belt, his eyes narrowing. The guard by his side moved closer, resting a hand on the hilt of his sword. Understanding the unspoken threat, Lydia took her seat at the table. Her hands shook as she reached for a piece of bread.

Warhouse smirked, savoring his meal as he watched her eat in silence. But as the minutes passed, he began to notice something amiss. The dining hall remained empty, save for a few of his guards. His senior commanders had not yet joined him.

He ordered Aldon, the guard he had dispatched, to return to the banquet hall. Instead, Lady Paulina stepped through a side door, followed by some of her guards and her brother Stephen by her side, her elegant form silhouetted by the sunlight streaming in from the corridor. Her lips curved into a cold, triumphant smile, and her brother, Stephen, followed closely behind.

Lord Warhouse glanced up from his meal, his brow furrowing with confusion. "Where is Aldon?" he demanded. "And my commanders?"

Lady Paulina's smile widened as she replied coolly, "He is not coming."

Warhouse set down his goblet, leaning forward in his chair. "What do you mean?"

Stepping closer, Lady Paulina clasped her hands before her. "Your commanders are dead, Lord Warhouse. All of them."

The words struck him like a hammer blow. His eyes narrowed, his confusion giving way to anger. "What is this treachery?" he barked, reaching for his sword. His movements were swift, his intent murderous.

Before he could draw the blade, his throat tightened painfully. He staggered, clutching at his neck as his breath grew labored. Panic flashed in his eyes as he fell to his knees, his fingers clawing uselessly at the invisible force constricting his airway.

"You poisoned me," he gasped. His gaze darted to Lydia, who was also gasping for air with her hands at her throat. Lady Paulina pulled a small bottle with clear liquid from inside her dress and handed it to one of the guards. "Give this antidote to Lydia," she ordered. The guard walked up to Lydia and helped her; he poured the contents of the bottle into Lydia's mouth. Instantly, she was able to breathe easily.

"You reap what you sow, Lord Warhouse," Lady Paulina said, her voice calm and cutting. "You came to my castle, violated my maid, ate my food, and sought to drag my family into treason against our blood. Did you think I would let you leave here alive?"

Warhouse's body convulsed violently as the venom coursed through his veins. Blood seeped from his nose and eyes, this once-formidable man reduced to a grotesque, pitiful figure on the cold stone floor. His vision blurred, and he saw Tomei and Axilla enter the room through the haze. Recognition flashed in his eyes, but it was too late.

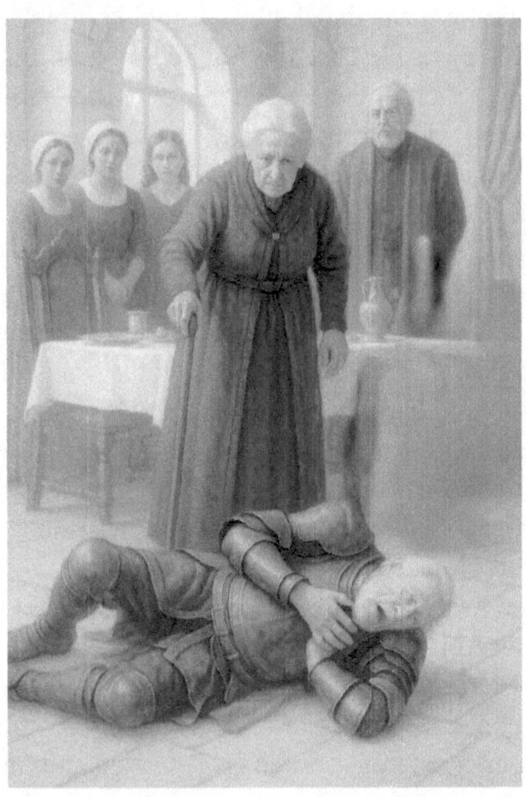

Lady Paulina approached him, pulling the letter she had previously given him from his waist belt. She unfolded it, then tore it in half. "You and your so-called king took over a throne that does not belong to you. You thought you could waltz into my castle and manipulate me? That I would betray my family? I felt underestimated, Warhouse. That was your final mistake."

She looked down at his bloated, lifeless body with disdain. "No one underestimates me and escapes retribution." Turning to her guards, she commanded, "Get this filth off my castle floor. He sullies even the stone he lies upon."

The guards moved swiftly, lifting the grotesque remains of Warhouse and carrying him out. Lady Paulina stepped into the castle yard, her walking stick tapping rhythmically against the floor. She greeted those she passed with a serene smile, as though the morning's events were no more than a minor inconvenience.

Behind the castle, near the stables, Tomei completed the final stage of Lady Paulina's plan. He carefully tucked a scroll into the saddlebag of Warhouse's horse and treated the harness with a subtle, undetectable poison using heated vapor from a kettle. The animal remained unharmed but would serve its purpose as the unwitting bearer of Lady Paulina's message. Tomei patted its flank, urging it toward the forest.

The horse galloped into the distance, carrying a grim warning and the beginning of Lady Paulina's calculated vengeance against Darius.

That spark reached its destination sooner than expected.

From a distance, the guards stationed on the walls of Verdant Castle spotted a lone horse charging toward the gates, its saddle empty. The absence of a rider sent a ripple of alarm through the watchmen. Within seconds, the watchtower drums boomed, their urgent rhythm echoing across the courtyard like a war cry. Two guards sprinted forward as the exhausted animal slowed near the gates, its breath ragged. With wary hands, one seized its reins and led it inside, and the other took the saddlebag and pulled a scroll from it.

Darius and Mefford emerged from the castle, their faces etched with confusion and concern. The state of the animal—without its rider but instead with a message in its saddlebag—puzzled and unsettled them.

As the guards secured the animal, something horrific occurred. Both men who had touched the reins suddenly collapsed, their bodies convulsing violently on the ground. Their stomachs swelled grotesquely, their faces contorting with agony as blood oozed from their eyes and mouths. Guttural cries echoed before their bodies fell still.

A hush overtook the courtyard. The gathered soldiers and servants stepped back, their faces pale with fear. The gruesome deaths left no doubt—the horse had been used to deliver a deadly message. Whispers of treachery rippled through the ranks, the atmosphere thick with dread.

"Pick up the scroll!" Darius commanded, his voice sharp and strained.

The rest of the men looked at each other, afraid to touch the bag.

Darius pulled a sword from one of the guards next to him and pointed it at another. "Fetch the scroll."

With hesitation, the guard picked up the scroll.

"Open it and read!" Darius commanded once more.

The guard opened and read the contents of the scroll: "If you want my men, come and get them yourself."

Immediately, the guard fell and began to convulse, blood oozing from his eyes.

Everyone stepped back from the dying man.

The muscles in Darius's jaw tightened, and he threw the sword, missing some of his men by inches. He turned furiously toward the castle entrance and entered with Mefford behind him. A surge of rage overtook him, and with a sweeping motion, he pulled the tablecloth from a nearby table, sending wine jars and goblets crashing to the ground.

"Everyone, leave the throne room!" he bellowed, his voice reverberating against the stone walls.

The room emptied quickly, the sound of the guards' hurried footsteps fading into silence. Darius paced furiously, his fists clenched. Mefford stood in the shadows, hesitant to speak. Suddenly, the familiar voice of Orb, the Virgil, slithered into Darius's mind, its tone laced with mockery.

"Do you see now?" it whispered. "You are weak. No one fears you. No one respects you. You are a king only in name."

Darius's fury ignited further. With a guttural growl, he grabbed a nearby sword and hurled it against the wall. It clanged loudly as it hit the ground, its impact leaving a faint scar on the stone.

CHAPTER 35

In the morning, the nobles from the Southern part of the kingdom began to arrive at McKenzie Castle. The courtyard bustled with activity as the lords and ladies dismounted their carriages and were escorted to the grand hall. Prince Halsten and Lady Freja stood at the entrance, graciously welcoming their esteemed guests as they filed inside.

As the nobles took their seats around the long, polished table, their conversations filled the room with tension and curiosity. Prince Halsten rose from his seat at the head, the soft hum of voices fading as all eyes turned to him.

"Noblemen and noblewomen of EdenRock," he began, his voice firm. "Thank you for coming on such short notice. Your presence here honors me and our shared commitment to the realm."

The nobles exchanged nods and murmurs of acknowledgment.

Halsten took a deep breath and continued, "By now, I trust you have all heard of the events at Verdant Castle. My uncle, Darius, has attacked and usurped the throne. He has placed the king and queen in the dungeon. Many of the nobles loyal to my father have been arrested and held captive under his tyrannical rule."

The room erupted into hushed whispers and gasps of disbelief. Lord Desmond Elderscroft furrowed his brow. "Your Highness, is there proof of this treachery?"

Halsten met his gaze squarely. "Yes. Reports from trusted sources, including those who narrowly escaped the attack, confirm these actions. My uncle has declared himself king, a title to which he has no rightful claim."

Lady Paulina Abbot added, "I have witnessed Darius's ruthlessness firsthand. His ambitions threaten not only the Verdant throne but the stability of the entire realm."

The room stirred with the sounds of both agreement and dissent. Lady Paulina stood, her cane firmly in hand, her voice steady and commanding. "Darius has no interest in peace. His ambitions have been evident since he was exiled from the palace. To engage him in person is to walk into his trap. I advise we communicate through a pigeon message, keeping our distance while gauging his response."

Lord Greenhill spoke, "Maybe we can send a delegation to reason with Darius."

Lady Paulina's sharp gaze fell upon him. "Reason with Darius? My lord, let me tell you of his ways. Before I arrived, Lord Warhouse—a man loyal to Darius—came to Abbot City under the guise of annexing it for the realm. He came with soldiers, prepared for treachery. Were it not for the courage of Axilla, Tomei, my brother Stephen, and the people of Abbot City, I would not stand here today. Lord Warhouse was defeated, sent to join his ancestors."

Lord Perkins rose from his seat, his expression grave. "My prince and noble lords and ladies gathered here, the situation before us is dire. Before King Edward's passing, he decreed that Darius and his lineage should never hold a noble title. Now, this man has taken our king and queen hostage, undermining the very foundation of our kingdom. We cannot sit idly by. I propose we engage Darius in pursuit of a peaceful resolution."

Lord Bracken rose, his brow furrowed. "Why do you say that, Lady Paulina? Perhaps if we meet with Darius in person, we can reason with him. Diplomacy might prevent unnecessary bloodshed."

The hall grew quiet as the gravity of the situation sank in. Lord Ethan of Glenwood Castle spoke up, his voice filled with concern. "Your Highness, what is it that you seek from us?"

Halsten straightened, his eyes scanning the room. "I seek your counsel and your support. Darius's actions are not just an affront to my family but to the very foundation of our kingdom. If left unchecked, his rule will bring chaos and ruin to EdenRock. Together, we must decide our next steps to restore the rightful king to the throne and ensure the safety of our people."

Lord Amos Bracken nodded thoughtfully. "I am finding it difficult to believe these reports. Let us find out what is happening in the palace."

Lady Ingrid of Brixton Castle interjected, "And what of his forces? Do we know the extent of his military power? Opposing him without a clear strategy would be folly."

Halsten turned to Arthur, who was standing nearby. Arthur stepped forward, addressing the room. "Darius's forces have taken over the armies of the various houses, but they are not invincible. Our scouts report that many of his men are spread thin across the north as he attempts to consolidate power."

The nobles exchanged glances, the tension in the room palpable. Lord Walton spoke, his voice filled with determination. "Your Highness, if we are to stand against Darius, we must unite our armies and act swiftly. The longer we wait, the stronger he becomes."

Halsten nodded. "Agreed, Lord Walton. But we cannot do this alone. We need the support of every noble house represented here. I ask you, will you stand with me to reclaim the throne and restore order to EdenRock?"

A murmur of agreement spread through the hall as the nobles began to rise, pledging their loyalty to Prince Halsten. Lady Paulina stood, her voice cutting through the din. "EdenRock has endured for generations because of our unity and resolve. Let us not falter now. Together, we will defeat Darius and restore the rightful king."

The room erupted in applause and shouts of affirmation. Halsten felt a surge of gratitude and resolve as he looked around the hall.

Prince Halsten stood, raising a hand to silence the room. "I have heard your thoughts and your counsel. Darius is my uncle, and I know his difficult nature well. Lady Paulina speaks the truth—his actions show no desire for peace. I agree that we must proceed with caution. We shall send a message and see how he responds. If it leads to an opportunity, I will go personally to Verdant Castle to assess the situation and ensure the safety of the king and queen."

Lord Aiden, who had remained quiet until now, rose to his feet. "I support the prince's decision. Let's send the message first and ask for a meeting. If he refuses, then we will prepare for the alternative."

The council voiced their agreement, and the meeting was adjourned. As the nobles began to leave the hall, Lady Paulina lingered, signaling for Tomei and Axilla to follow her into one of the castle chambers. There, she sat with them and Prince Halsten to discuss the details of their escape and the encounter with Lord Warhouse.

Axilla spoke first, his tone resolute. "Lady Paulina speaks no exaggeration. Lord Warhouse came to Abbot City with a false smile and a sword hidden behind his back. We barely had time to prepare, but with the loyalty of our people and the strategy of Tomei, we overcame him."

Tomei nodded, adding, "Darius's plans extend far beyond Verdant Castle. He seeks to dismantle the foundations of this realm, one city at a time. The south must be united under your banner, Prince Halsten, to stand a chance against him."

The prince met their eyes, grateful and determined. "I thank you both for your bravery and for standing with us. Your skills and counsel will be invaluable in the days to come. Will you remain at McKenzie Castle to assist us in this fight?"

Tomei and Axilla exchanged glances before Axilla responded, "We pledge our swords and our service to you, Your Grace. The South will stand strong under your leadership."

"Thank you, my friends," Prince Halsten said.

CHAPTER 36

Two days after the meeting at McKenzie Castle, Lord Aiden arrived at Verdant Castle. Standing at the top of the grand staircase, Darius descended to meet his brother. The tension between them was palpable as they exchanged formal nods before walking together into the castle.

Once inside the main hall, they sat silently, the weight of unspoken words filling the room. Finally, Darius spoke, his tone sharp but measured.

"What brings you here, Aiden?" he asked.

Lord Aiden leaned back slightly, his gaze steady. "Should you have to ask? You've taken our brother prisoner. Do the right thing and release him."

Darius's expression darkened. "I cannot let him go, Aiden. As long as he's free, the people will believe there are two kings in this realm. That would divide the kingdom."

Aiden leaned forward, his voice laced with urgency. "What are you planning to do with Alaric and Isadora?"

Darius exhaled slowly. "I haven't decided yet."

"Then send him into exile," Aiden suggested. "If you don't want him in the kingdom, let him leave and live out his days elsewhere."

Darius scoffed, shaking his head. "Exile? And what happens when he raises an army and returns? I already have Halsten to deal with, and you want me to add Alaric to the equation?"

Aiden straightened, his tone diplomatic. "Brother, this path will bring you nothing but ruin. If you're serious about strengthening the kingdom, release Alaric and focus on uniting the realm."

Darius gave a bitter smile. "You could join me, Aiden. Together, we could make this kingdom stronger—better."

Aiden shook his head. "You know I have no interest in politics or power struggles. I am content with my life as it is."

Darius studied him for a moment, then leaned back. "Fine. Visit Alaric, but hear me clearly—no tricks, Aiden. I won't tolerate betrayal."

Aiden rose from his seat, inclining his head slightly. "I only wish to see my brother."

Darius gestured toward the corridor leading to the dungeons. "You're permitted to visit him anytime. But know this—I am watching."

As Aiden walked toward the dungeon, flanked by two guards, Darius called out behind him, "I know you were at McKenzie Castle meeting with Halsten. What did you discuss?"

Aiden stopped momentarily but did not turn. "The Southern nobles seek a truce. They want to send representatives to meet with you."

Darius's eyes narrowed. "I'll think about it," he said curtly.

Without another word, Aiden continued down the dark corridor, turning the corner toward the dungeon. The clinking of the guards' armor echoed in the silence. His mind was weighed down by the thought of the deep fractures dividing the family and the kingdom.

Alaric and Isadora were sitting on a worn bench in the corner of the damp dungeon cell when Lord Aiden arrived. As soon he came into view on the other side of the door, both stood and approached the gate, their expressions a mix of relief and restrained hope. Lord Aiden stepped closer, his boots echoing on the cold stone floor.

"Open the gate," he ordered the guards.

The iron door creaked as it swung open. Lord Aiden entered and immediately embraced Alaric before turning to take Isadora's hands gently.

"How are you, brother?" he asked, his voice heavy with concern.

"As well as we can be, given the circumstances," Alaric replied.

Aiden turned to Isadora. "And you, your highness? How are you holding up?"

The queen gave a slight nod, her voice steady. "I am well, Aiden, as much as one can be in such a place." Her eyes filled with urgency as she asked, "How are my children? Have you seen them?"

Aiden offered a reassuring smile. "I have, recently. They are safe. Halsten stays strong, and Freja and Dhalia are keeping Eleanor and Vivienne company. They are well cared for."

Alaric placed a hand on the cell gate, his face etched with worry. "That is good to hear. But we must do more than hope. What news do you bring?"

Lowering his voice, Aiden glanced at the men stationed outside before bringing his head down and speaking discretely.

"Halsten is gathering support," Aiden began. "Axilla and Tomei managed to escape and are now at McKenzie Castle. They are aiding him, along with many loyal nobles. He convened a meeting to plan the next steps."

Alaric's eyes sharpened with resolve. "Then listen closely. Tell the Southern nobles to crown Halsten king of the South. Doing so will destabilize Darius's plans and divide his forces. It will buy time for a stronger resistance." Reaching for the shoulder of his brother, he whispered into his ear, "Tell Halsten that he is the true king of the kingdom and he should not let Darius steal it from him."

Before Aiden could respond, the guards returned, their footsteps signaling the end of the private conversation. Aiden straightened, his face composed.

"I will give him your message," he said firmly. He placed a reassuring hand on Alaric's shoulder and then turned to Isadora. "Stay strong. Help will come."

With a final nod, he stepped out of the cell, and the gate clanged shut behind him. As the guards locked it, he looked at his brother and sister-in-law before departing the dungeon. His steps echoed purposefully as he ascended, the small scroll hidden in his belt.

When Lord Aiden once again reached the grand hall of Verdant Castle, Darius was seated on the throne. He watched his brother approach, his posture exuding authority and self-assuredness.

Darius addressed Aiden in a tone that carried command and pretense. "Tell the Southern nobles I will meet with them. One week from today, I will receive them here in the castle to discuss the fate of the king and queen. If they agree to my proposal, I will consider yours." His tone hardened. "I will send Alaric into exile if he swears an oath to remain away from this realm. No tricks, Aiden."

Lord Aiden inclined his head slightly, his face unreadable. "I will convey your message to the nobles."

Without further discussion, he turned and strode out of the hall. Outside, his guards were already waiting with his horse. He mounted smoothly, glancing back toward the castle. Darius stood at the castle's entrance, his expression impassive as he watched his brother prepare to leave.

Aiden raised a hand in a curt farewell, then signaled to his men. With a sharp command, they began their journey back. The rhythmic pounding of hooves echoed as the group disappeared into the distance, leaving behind the tense weight of Darius's decree.

Lord Aiden rode toward McKenzie Castle as the evening sun dipped behind the hills, casting long shadows on the ground. The distant sound of drums echoed, signaling his arrival. From the castle's balcony, Prince Halsten emerged, the cool breeze brushing against his face as he looked down at the approaching procession.

"Welcome, Uncle," he called out, his voice warm.

Lord Aiden looked up and offered a tired smile. "How are you, nephew?"

"I am well. It's good to see you."

"Let us talk inside." Lord Aiden dismounted his horse and walked into the castle with Halsten.

As they entered the castle's grand hall, their boots sounded against the polished stone floor. Freja, Eleanor, and Vivienne appeared, their faces lighting up at the sight of Lord Aiden.

"How are Papa and Mother?" Vivienne asked eagerly, stepping forward.

Her uncle placed a reassuring hand on her shoulder. "The king and queen are well, and they send their love and blessings."

Eleanor's expression tightened. "Will Darius let them go?"

Lord Aiden sighed. "That is a matter your brother and I will discuss. But we must tread carefully."

"Thank you, Uncle. Please, tell them we love them," Vivienne said, her voice soft.

The three women excused themselves, leaving the hall. Prince Halsten gestured toward a chair at the head of the table. "Come, sit with me."

Lord Aiden settled in while Halsten took his place opposite him. DeMarco and Anders, who had been stationed at the entrance, bowed before exiting the room and closing the heavy doors behind them.

Once alone, Lord Aiden leaned forward. "I have a message from your father," he said.

Curious, Halsten watched Lord Aiden.

"The king said you are the true king, and do not let Darius take the throne from you," Lord Aiden said.

Halsten touched the pendant around his neck. "Father believes in me," he said softly, almost to himself. "Father and Mother want me to take the mantle of leadership. To be crowned king of the South."

Lord Aiden leaned forward, his voice steady and encouraging. "Your father sees your strength, Halsten. This is a call to action, symbolizing resistance against Darius and hope for the realm."

Halsten stood, pacing the room as the gravity of the situation settled over him. "How can I do that, Uncle, when my father is still alive?"

Lord Aiden rose to his feet, placing a firm hand on his nephew's shoulder. "The nobles need a leader they can rally behind. Darius's betrayal has already set the realm ablaze. You must be the light that guides them through this. I will gather the Southern nobles. I will share your father's words and rally their support. If you are to lead, you will need them."

Halsten nodded, his resolve hardening.

"Darius knew of our meeting here at McKenzie Castle," Lord Aiden said. "He asked with certainty, which leads me to believe something troubling."

Halsten's brows furrowed as he leaned back in his chair. "What are you implying, Uncle?"

Lord Aiden's gaze was steady. "I believe we have a traitor among us—someone feeding information to Darius."

Halsten's jaw tightened, his voice firm. "Who might that be?"

"I don't know yet," Lord Aiden admitted. "But we must find out before any more of our plans are exposed."

Halsten nodded, his mind racing. "I will speak with Arthur and Frodio. We will uncover the traitor, no matter how deeply they're hidden."

Lord Aiden stood, his expression resolute. "Nephew, if there's anything I've learned in my years, it's that betrayal often comes from those you least expect. Be cautious."

Halsten rose from his chair and extended his hand. "Thank you. Travel safely."

Lord Aiden clasped Halsten's hand firmly. "Take care of yourself and your sisters. And remember, the strength of EdenRock lies in its unity."

Halsten nodded. "Uncle, you must be tired from your journey. Get some rest. We will continue tomorrow," he said.

"DeMarco," he called, summoning his trusted commander.

DeMarco entered promptly, his expression serious. "Yes, my prince?"

"Call Arthur and Frodio to meet me here in the morning," Halsten ordered.

"As you command." DeMarco bowed slightly before leaving the hall.

Halsten stood in the quiet of the room, his thoughts heavy.

CHAPTER 37

ARLY THE NEXT MORNING, FRODIO and Arthur entered the grand hall, DeMarco following close behind. The tension in the room was palpable as they approached Prince Halsten, who sat at the head of the long oak table, his expression grave.

"Your Grace, I came as soon as I received your message," Frodio said, bowing respectfully.

"Sit down," Halsten said, gesturing toward the chairs. Frodio and Arthur took their seats while DeMarco stood at Halsten's side, his hand resting lightly on the hilt of his sword.

Halsten looked his men over, his gaze intense. "My uncle, Lord Aiden, has just departed after sharing troubling news. During his visit to Verdant Castle, he appealed to Darius for the release of the king and queen. However, he also informed me of something more alarming— Darius knew about my meeting with the Southern nobles."

Frodio's brow furrowed as he exchanged a concerned glance with Arthur.

"This means we have a traitor," Halsten continued. "Someone is relaying information to him. Frodio, I need you to use your network to identify who is visiting Darius from the South."

Frodio nodded decisively. "Consider it done, Your Grace. I'll begin investigating immediately."

Halsten turned his attention to Arthur, his tone more reflective. "My father sent me a message through Uncle Aiden. He advised that I take the crown as king of the South to consolidate the Southern nobles' support and resist Darius more effectively."

Arthur's face was thoughtful. "Your Grace, I believe that's a wise course of action. By uniting the Southern lords under your leadership, we can mobilize a larger army composed of soldiers from all the Southern castles. It will give us the strength to stand against Darius."

Halsten's resolve hardened. "Then it's decided. Before we do anything, let us see what the Southern leaders will say to Lord Aiden. Arthur, in the meantime, I need you to tell Adikis to work with the commanders of the Southern cities. The borders must be reinforced immediately. We can't risk Darius catching us unprepared."

Arthur stood, bowing slightly. "Yes, Your Grace. I will deliver your orders without delay."

As Arthur turned to leave, Halsten glanced at DeMarco. The room fell silent as the prince rose from his seat, studying faces of those present. "This is the moment that will define us. We stand not just for the South but for all of EdenRock. Darius may have taken Verdant Castle, but they will not take our freedom or legacy. We will prevail."

Frodio and DeMarco exchanged solemn nods before leaving to carry out their tasks, the heavy oak doors thudding shut behind them. The sound echoed through the empty hall, leaving Halsten alone with the weight of leadership. His fingers drummed against the armrest of his chair as his mind churned through the challenges ahead—each one more daunting than the last.

While Halsten wrestled with strategy, Frodio was already in motion.

The seasoned warrior moved swiftly through the dense woods, the undergrowth crunching softly beneath his boots. Soon, the outline of his secluded base emerged—a modest stone building nearly swallowed by the forest. Inside, the air was thick with the scent of ink and candle wax, the silence broken only by the occasional rustle of parchment or the scratching of quills from his small team of informants. Time was a luxury they didn't have, and Frodio intended to waste none of it.

He moved to a wooden desk in the corner, its surface cluttered with maps and coded messages. Sitting down, he took a deep breath, his fingers deftly selecting a small scroll and an inked quill. With practiced precision, he began to write a message, his hand steady despite the weight of his mission:

"Urgent. Investigate all recent movements and visits to Verdant Castle from the Southern region. Identify individuals meeting with Darius. Focus on those with access to our plans. Immediate response is required. Trust no one."

Once he was done, he folded the parchment neatly and sealed it with a wax emblem bearing his insignia—a subtle mark known only to his trusted contacts. He rose from his chair and went to the room's far end, where a line of coops housed messenger pigeons. Each one had been trained to deliver messages to specific operatives stationed across the Southern cities.

Selecting one of the birds, he tied the scroll securely to its leg, whispering as he worked, "Fly swiftly, my friend. The kingdom depends on you."

Frodio opened the small hatch at the top of the coop, releasing the pigeon into the night sky. It flapped its wings, disappearing into the darkness, carrying the critical message to his network. He watched it vanish before turning back to the room. "We need answers," he muttered, his voice low but resolute. "And we need them quickly."

In the quiet hall of McKenzie Castle, Prince Halsten sat alone, his thoughts weighed down by the gravity of his father's message.

Freja entered, her soft footsteps echoing in the silence. Seeing her husband deep in thought, she approached him gently. "Halsten, my love," she said, "what troubles you so deeply?"

He lifted his gaze to meet hers, his expression somber. "My uncle delivered a message from my father," he replied. "It felt more like a farewell than guidance."

Freja knelt beside him, her hand resting on his. "What did the message say?" she asked softly.

Halsten sighed. "The king believes it is time for me to be crowned king of the South. He wants me to unite the Southern cities and strengthen our position to resist Darius."

Freja's brow furrowed, but her determination soon replaced her concern. "How can I help, Halsten? I know my father would support your cause."

"We will need the support of all the noble houses," Halsten said.

"Perhaps I could visit the noblewomen to rally their support for your coronation."

Halsten considered her suggestion for a moment before nodding. "My uncle has already begun seeking the consent of the Southern lords, but your efforts would undoubtedly strengthen our cause. Speak to the women, Freja. They hold great influence over their families and their lands."

Freja smiled. "I will speak to my mother and enlist Dhalia to accompany me. Together, we will visit the noblewomen and garner their support."

Halsten reached for her hand, squeezing it gently. "I'll have Kudus and Anders accompany you with a contingent of men for protection. This journey could be dangerous."

Freja leaned in, pressing a kiss to his lips. "Your thoughtfulness gives me strength." Rising, she added, "Let me go and prepare. Dhalia and I will leave at first light."

Halsten summoned Kudos, who agreed to escort Lady Freja. They began preparing for the journey.

At first light, Kudus and Anders stood in the courtyard of McKenzie Castle, waiting with their men as the rising sun painted the sky in hues of orange and pink. The crisp morning air carried the scent of dew and the faint rustle of the trees. Freja and Dhalia emerged from the castle, their cloaks trailing softly behind them.

Kudus stepped forward, bowing slightly. "Your Highness," he greeted Freja. Then he turned to Dhalia. "My lady."

Anders followed Kudus's lead, bowing his head politely to the two women.

Kudus assisted Freja into the waiting wagon. "Allow me, Your Highness," he said, offering his hand. She took it gracefully, her smile brief but warm. Once she was settled, Kudus turned to Dhalia. He extended his hand, and she paused momentarily, her eyes meeting his. A quiet connection passed between them before she placed her hand in his and climbed into the wagon.

Kudus and Anders mounted their horses, and Kudus called to the group. "Let's march."

The small convoy set out, with the wagon carrying Freja and Dhalia trailing behind the mounted guards. It was pulled by four white horses, their movements smooth and steady under the guidance of the rider seated at the reins of the leading horse. The group traveled eastward along the river, the sound of hooves clattering softly against the earth mingling with the gentle flow of the water.

By evening, they reached Glenwood Castle. Freja's parents and her brother Albert were standing at the top of the grand stone stairs. Their expressions brightened as the entourage came to a halt in the courtyard.

Elara descended the steps first, enveloping Freja in a warm embrace as she stepped down from the wagon. "Welcome home, my dear," she said, her voice filled with affection.

Freja smiled, hugging her mother tightly before turning to her father. "Thank you, Mother. It is good to see you all."

Lord Ethan approached. "Welcome, daughter," he said with a kind smile.

Albert embraced his sister. "You look good," he said.

"And you as well, brother," Freja said.

"Thank you." Albert turned to Dhalia. "Welcome back to Glenwood,"

"Good to see you, Sir Albert," she said.

After brief greetings, the group moved inside the castle to the warmth of the sitting room. Once everyone was seated, Freja leaned forward, her expression serious.

"Mother, Father," Freja began, "I have come to ask for your help. Prince Halsten received a letter from the king. He has asked for Halsten to be crowned king of the South to unite the noble houses against Darius."

Lord Ethan nodded solemnly. "That seems both wise and necessary," he said. "Darius's claim to the throne is illegitimate. It is only right that we resist him."

Lady Elara placed a hand over her daughter's. "What can we do to support Halsten?" she asked.

Freja looked at her with a hopeful smile. "Mother, I was hoping you would accompany me to visit the noblewomen of the South. We need their support to consolidate the Southern houses. Your presence and influence would mean a great deal."

Lady Elara's eyes lit with determination. "Of course, my dear. It is time we acted. I will go with you and do all I can to rally their support."

Lord Ethan gave a nod of approval. "This is a noble cause. We stand behind Halsten and the South."

Lady Elara rose gracefully. "Let us prepare today and set out at first light tomorrow."

Freja embraced her mother. "Thank you. Your support means everything."

CHAPTER 38

A MONTH AFTER FREJA'S VISIT TO the noblewomen of the Southern part of the kingdom, the nobles gathered in the grand hall of McKenzie Castle. The atmosphere was tense, filled with whispered conversations and the occasional clinking of goblets. Lord Aiden stood at the head of the hall, his face solemn as he prepared to address the assembly. Beside him sat Prince Halsten, his expression thoughtful as he surveyed the crowd.

When they quieted, Lord Aiden addressed the room. "My lords and ladies," he began, his tone commanding, "we gather here to address the perilous state of our kingdom. The recent mutiny has torn apart our once-united realm at Verdant Castle. The king and queen are imprisoned, and the rightful order of EdenRock has been disrupted."

The whispers grew louder as the nobles exchanged uneasy glances. Lord Aiden raised a hand to silence them. "We cannot continue to live in uncertainty and division. The kingdom cannot thrive in its current state. We must take decisive action to restore order and find a path forward." He paused, allowing his words to sink in. "My brother, Darius, has expressed a willingness to meet and discuss the fate of the king and the future of this realm. I am prepared to lead a delegation to Verdant Castle to negotiate with him. This is a critical moment, and we must decide together how to proceed."

Lady Elara stood, her voice clear and unwavering. "Lord Aiden, how can we trust Darius's intentions? He has already betrayed the throne and imprisoned the king and queen. What assurance do we have that he will honor any agreement?"

A murmur of agreement rippled through the hall. Sitting beside his wife, Lord Ethan added, "We cannot afford to walk blindly into a trap. Darius has proven himself cunning and ruthless. This delegation must be prepared for any eventuality."

Prince Halsten rose. "You are right to be cautious, Lord Ethan, Lady Elara. Darius is not to be trusted, but we cannot ignore the opportunity to negotiate. However, we must not go unprepared. This delegation will include diplomats and those who can ensure its safety and integrity."

Lady Paulina Abbot stood, leaning slightly on her cane. "Prince Halsten is correct. This is not a time for recklessness. If Lord Aiden leads this delegation, it must be backed by the full support of the South. Darius must see that we are united and strong, not fragmented and weak."

Lord Amos Bracken stood next, his booming voice filling the hall. "I agree with Lady Paulina. Unity is our greatest weapon. Let this delegation carry our words and the weight of our collective resolve."

Prince Halsten nodded. "If this council agrees, we will select representatives from among you to join Lord Aiden in this mission. At the same time, we will continue fortifying our position here in the South. Should negotiations fail, we must be ready to act."

The nobles exchanged glances. Lord Aiden raised his voice once more. "The time for indecision has passed. Let us show Darius that the South stands as one, unyielding and resolute."

A wave of agreement swept through the hall. Plans were set in motion to form the delegation, and the meeting concluded with a renewed sense of purpose.

Prince Halsten and Lord Aiden decided to initiate Frodio's plan to find who among the nobles was revealing their plans to Darius. They lingered in the hall after the meeting as the nobles dispersed, saying specific, unique words to each one.

CHAPTER 39

WHEN THE SOUTHERN NOBLES ARRIVED at Verdant Castle, they were greeted with calculated hospitality. Standing proudly on the grand staircase with Queen Xinovia at his side, Darius extended his arms in mock welcome. Mefford stood just behind them, his ever-present smirk suggesting he was taking great delight in the unfolding spectacle. Tapas and Caine, the latter still nursing the stump of his severed hand, flanked the group.

As the nobles dismounted and approached, Lord Aiden led them forward. Darius descended a few steps, his smile strained but polite. "Welcome, lords and ladies of the South, to Verdant Castle. It is an honor to receive you," he said.

The nobles nodded in acknowledgment, exchanging measured pleasantries with their host before being ushered into the great hall. It had been restored to its former glory to project an image of strength and stability under Darius's reign. The imprisoned Northern leaders were seated at one end of the room, dressed in noble finery. Despite their outward composure, the tension in their faces betrayed their unease.

Moments later, the guards opened a side door, and Alaric and Isadora entered the hall. They were dressed impeccably, their regal bearing intact despite their captivity. The room fell silent as all eyes turned to them. Alaric held his head high, his gaze sweeping over the crowd, while Isadora walked beside him with quiet dignity.

Darius rose from his seat at the center of the dais. "My lords and ladies," he began, his voice resonating through the hall, "before we begin our deliberations, I must remind you of our sacred traditions."

The Southern nobles exchanged cautious glances. Darius continued, undeterred. "Our laws, as decreed by our ancestors, clearly state that the king's eldest son shall inherit the throne upon his passing. When my father, King Edward, departed this life—may his soul rest in peace—the throne should have been mine by right. But instead"—he paused, his eyes narrowing—"my brothers and our mother conspired to take what was rightfully mine. They bestowed the crown upon my youngest brother, Alaric."

Darius's gaze swept over the room, daring anyone to challenge his narrative. "To be fair to him," he said, his tone softening with feigned magnanimity, "I allowed him to rule for a time, even as I was unjustly banished to Bear Cave Castle. I endured exile, watching from afar as my rightful place was usurped."

He spread his arms theatrically. "But today, I have reclaimed what is mine. I have done nothing wrong—I have merely restored the natural order. After today's deliberations, I expect you to recognize and respect my rightful position as your king."

With that, he returned to his seat, his expression resolute as he scanned the room for signs of dissent. The Southern nobles sat in tense silence, their thoughts carefully concealed behind practiced expressions. King Alaric's jaw tightened, but he said nothing, his restraint a testament to his wisdom.

Lord Reginald stood. "Thank you for allowing us to meet with you here at Verdant Castle," he began, his voice steady and measured. He turned his gaze to Alaric and Isadora. "Your Majesties, it is good to see you both. Your strength and dignity remain an inspiration."

He then shifted his focus to Darius. "Your Grace, this kingdom has enjoyed peace and prosperity for many years under wise and capable rulers, most recently under King Alaric's stewardship. While we understand your sentiments regarding the throne, let us not forget that our late king, in his wisdom and sound judgment, chose to bestow the crown upon your youngest brother. His decision, made with the interests of the realm in mind, deserves our respect."

Before Darius could respond, Lady Longrove rose gracefully from her seat. "As leaders of this kingdom, we humbly request that you release the king and queen so they may be reunited with their children while we continue these discussions. We plead for their freedom regard-less of what the future holds for the throne. We will ensure their absence from Verdant Castle until these matters are resolved."

Orb whispered in Darius's mind, "That is disrespectful."

Darius stood up and said, "How dare you stand in my presence to tell me what is right and wrong?"

Lord Luterodt spoke next, stepping forward with his hands clasped in a gesture of mediation. "Lords and ladies, we have spent considerable time deliberating the issues. Let us break for a meal and grant His Grace, Darius, and Xinovia an opportunity to meet privately with his brothers, Aiden and Alaric, and Her Majesty, Isadora. Such a meeting may offer a clarity and understanding that our discussions alone cannot achieve."

Darius hesitated for a moment but ultimately agreed. "Very well," he said curtly, signaling the guards to escort the royal siblings and the queen to a private dining room. The remaining nobles filed into the grand dining hall, where an elaborate feast awaited.

Inside, tables groaned under the weight of roasted beef, lamb, and deer, accompanied by a colorful array of vegetables, fresh fruits, and wine. The nobles exchanged cautious glances as they took their seats, their wariness palpable.

Lord Luterodt addressed the assembly, smiling in an attempt to allay their fears. "To prove this meal is safe, I will gladly taste the food from any plate. If you wish for me to do so, raise your hand."

Four nobles lifted their hands, and he approached each table, care-fully sampling the food. Satisfied by his actions, the rest of the nobles began to eat, their initial tension giving way to muted conversations.

Meanwhile, Lord Reginald, sensing the weight of unspoken danger, slipped quietly from the hall. His instincts led him to the kitchen, where he paused in the shadows, overhearing a hushed conversation between two maids. His blood ran cold as he caught their words.

"The poison is in the wine. It will be sent in with the next round," one of them whispered.

Reginald's heart pounded as he turned to leave and warn the others. But before he could take more than a few steps, Tapas emerged from the shadows, casually spinning a carving knife in his hand. The tip hovered menacingly over one of his fingers as he smirked.

"Going somewhere, Lord Reginald?" he asked, his tone dripping with mockery.

Fear flashed in Reginald's eyes, and he bolted toward the hall, but two guards intercepted him, gripping his arms tightly. A third guard quickly gagged him, silencing his cries as they dragged him into a dark corner.

Tapas approached slowly. "You could have chosen to stand with King Darius and bask in the glory of his reign," he said, his voice almost conversational. "But no, you had to choose someone's past glory instead."

Reginald struggled against his captors, his muffled protests futile. Tapas leaned closer, his face a mask of cold disdain. "He who comes as a guest does not take the role of a hero," he muttered, pointing toward the hallway, where servants were carrying jars of poisoned wine toward the dining hall.

Reginald thrashed violently, but the guards held firm. Tapas's smirk faded, replaced by a chilling calm. "He who sees the nakedness of the devil," he whispered, "should not live to tell the tale."

With one swift motion, he drew the knife across Reginald's throat. Blood gushed from the wound, staining the floor as the man convulsed briefly before falling limp. Tapas wiped the blade on the edge of Reginald's cloak, ensuring it was spotless, before tucking it back into his belt.

Straightening his posture, he glanced down at the lifeless body. "A pity," he said, turning on his heel and disappearing into the shadows as if nothing had happened.

In the grand dining room, the nobles continued their conversations as servants poured them wine and water. The atmosphere carried a sense of unease. None of those gathered noticed the faint sediment at the bottom of their cups, nor did they suspect the lurking danger.

Lord Obed Ramsgate stood up to speak but suddenly began to sway on his feet. His face turned pale, and he collapsed to the floor with a loud thud, his cup spilling beside him. A murmur of concern rippled through the room. Lord Desmond Elderscroft, seated nearby, rose to assist but froze as dizziness overwhelmed him. Clutching the table's edge, he toppled forward, dragging the tablecloth and its contents to the floor.

Panic set in as more nobles began to feel the same effects. They staggered from their seats, clutching their heads or throats, their strength draining rapidly. Cries of alarm filled the hall, but it was already too late. One by one, they collapsed, leaving the air thick with dread and confusion.

At the head of the table, Lord Luterodt watched the chaos unfold with cold detachment. When the last noble fell, he stood, adjusted his robes, and signaled to the soldiers waiting outside. Lord Luterodt and Tapas left the room without a word as the soldiers stormed in, shutting the heavy doors behind them.

Inside, they began their gruesome work, blades flashing as they executed the incapacitated nobles. The thick stone walls of the castle muffled the screams of the fallen.

Meanwhile, Darius sat in a smaller dining chamber with Xinovia, Mefford, King Alaric, Isadora, and Lord Aiden. Tapas entered silently, expressionless, and gave him a slight nod. Without hesitation, Darius rose from his seat.

"Bring them," he ordered coldly.

Soldiers entered the room and seized the king, queen, and Lord Aiden, dragging them toward the grand dining hall. Despite their struggles, the captives were forced to witness the horrific scene. Blood pooled on the floor, mixing with spilled wine and shattered glass. The lifeless bodies of their allies lay scattered across the room.

Lord Aiden broke free from the soldier holding him and shouted, "What have you done, brother? This is madness! Your greed and wickedness know no bounds!"

But Orb's laughter was sounding in Darius's mind.

King Alaric's voice was steady despite the horror around him. "Mark my words, Darius—this insatiable greed will be your undoing."

Isadora could only sob, her tears falling silently as she turned her face away from the carnage. Darius, unmoved, motioned for the guards to escort them out.

"Take the king and queen back to the dungeon," he commanded. "As for Aiden, he has another purpose."

The guards dragged Alaric and Isadora out of the hall, leaving Lord Aiden at his brother's mercy. Darius turned and gestured to his soldiers and Mefford.

The guards roughly threw Lord Aiden to the ground at the castle gate. Darius loomed over him, his sneer etched with malice. Mefford stood there with a grin on his face.

Xinovia was at the entrance with a shocked look on her face.

"Go," Darius hissed. "Tell your precious nephew what you've seen here today. The next time you step foot in my palace, it will be your last. By the way, tell him I am the fulfillment of the prophecy."

Bruised and shaken, Lord Aiden struggled to his feet. He mounted his steed with difficulty and galloped away, his heart pounding with rage and sorrow. As he reached the edge of the forest, his horse reared at the sight of a figure slumped beside another horse. Aiden hesitated before dismounting. To his shock, he recognized the battered man on the ground.

"Egron!" Aiden exclaimed, crouching beside him. "What are you doing here?"

Egron's voice was weak but determined. "One of the guards who served under me helped me escape. Darius has no loyalty among his men."

Aiden handed the man his leather flask, the cool water reviving him slightly. "Can you ride?" Aiden asked.

Egron nodded, his strength returning as he pulled himself onto his horse. "Yes, I can."

Without another word, the two men rode southward, their resolve hardened by the atrocities they had witnessed.

CHAPTER 40

T HE SOUND OF DRUMS ECHOED across the plains as the figures of Lord Aiden and Egron appeared on the horizon, heading toward McKenzie Castle. The people inside gathered quickly, the tension palpable. Halsten, Freja, Eleanor, Vivienne, and Arthur made their way to the stairs, their eyes fixed on the approaching riders.

As the horses drew closer, Vivienne's face lit up with recognition. "It's Uncle Aiden!" she exclaimed.

Halsten stepped down, walking briskly to meet the riders. "Egron," he said with a mix of surprise and concern as he recognized the second figure.

Halsten waved to the guards, who rushed forward to help the former commander dismount. He was pale and visibly shaken, his body bearing signs of fatigue and distress. The guards supported him as they led him inside the castle hall.

"Bring water and prepare a place for him to rest," Halsten instructed them before turning to his uncle. "Come, let us go inside."

Freja, Eleanor, and Vivienne followed them closely. As they entered the castle, Freja immediately took charge. "Bring food and water for our guests," she directed the maids, who scurried to comply.

Inside the hall, Egron was seated at the table, a goblet of water pressed into his hands. Lord Aiden joined him, and the maids soon returned with food trays. Halsten and the others waited as the two men ate silently.

After they had eaten, Halsten called for Kudus, Arthur, Adikis, Zoresh, DeMarco, and Anders. The men gathered quickly, their expressions solemn as they took their places around the hall.

"What happened?" the prince asked.

Lord Aiden described the scene as they listened on in horror.

Gasps of shock filled the room as everyone processed the gravity of the betrayal.

"Why did he leave you alive?" Halsten asked, his voice steady but laced with anger.

"He wanted me to deliver a message," Aiden replied. "Darius threw me out of the palace, saying I should tell you, Halsten, what he had done. He warned me that it would be my last move if I ever set foot in the palace again. His words were clear—he intends to crush anyone who opposes him."

Vivienne's voice broke through the heavy silence, trembling with disbelief. "Why is Uncle Darius so evil?"

Aiden sighed deeply, his expression pained. "He is consumed by anger and resentment. He has never forgiven your grandfather for choosing your father as king instead of him."

The room grew tense, and Freja clenched her fists, her lips pressed into a thin line.

"Where are our parents now?" Halsten asked.

Aiden hesitated before responding. "I believe he has thrown them back into the dungeon. He's using them as bait, hoping to draw you to Verdant Castle. But I don't think he intends to release them, Halsten, even if you offer yourself in their place. Darius wants to eliminate every potential threat to his claim to the throne."

Freja's face darkened with resolve. "He's playing a dangerous game, using the king and the queen as pawns."

Aiden's voice dropped to a grim tone. "Before he let me go, he left me one more message for you, Halsten. He said, 'I am the fulfillment of the prophecy.'"

Halsten's eyes narrowed. "The prophecy…" His thoughts were racing. He turned to Frodio. "That's exactly what I told Lord Bracken."

Aiden frowned in confusion. "What do you mean?"

Halsten explained, "After we met with the nobles, Frodio advised me to tell each noble something unique. If Darius heard about it, we'd know who the traitor was."

"And you told Lord Bracken about the prophecy?" Realization dawned on Aiden's face.

Halsten nodded. "Yes. It was a test, and now we have our answer."

Freja's voice was sharp with anger. "Lord Bracken is the traitor!"

Adikis stepped forward, his expression hard. "What are your orders regarding him, Your Grace?"

Halsten shook his head. "Leave him for now. I have a plan." Turning to Egron, he asked, "How did you escape?"

Egron straightened slightly. "One of the guards I brought to the palace—a man still loyal to me—helped me. He used the chaos of the nobles' dinner as a distraction to lead me out through the back."

Halsten nodded. "You've been through much, Egron. Welcome to McKenzie Castle. Take your time to recover and regain your strength. You'll need it in the days to come."

Freja placed a reassuring hand on Egron's shoulder before turning to her husband. "We'll ensure he has everything he needs to recover."

"My prince, I am ready to serve you and help restore the kingdom," Egron said, his voice steady despite his exhaustion.

"Thank you, Egron," Halsten said. "My father trusted you, and I trust you as well. When you have recovered, we will put a plan into motion. Your experience will be invaluable."

Lord Aiden rose from his seat, his expression resolute. "We need to move forward with your coronation, my prince. The nobles must gather and swear their allegiance. It is the only way to unite the South."

Halsten nodded firmly. "You're right, Uncle. Let us proceed."

"I will send a message to the nobles to convene at McKenzie Castle," Lord Aiden said, already considering the logistics. "We must act swiftly."

Egron leaned forward, his voice urgent. "My prince, we also need to reinforce the Northern border immediately. Knowing Darius as I do, he will try something desperate to weaken us. He will not take your coronation lightly."

Halsten turned to Adikis and Zoresh, who stood near the hall's entrance. "I need you to ride to the Northern border," he told them. "Ensure we have enough men stationed there to protect against any incursion."

"Yes, my prince," Adikis replied, bowing slightly before leaving the hall with Zoresh.

"Kudus," Halsten continued, "Commander Egron will work with you to prepare our soldiers. He has spent years in battle and knows what we need for this time."

Egron extended a hand to Kudus, who clasped it firmly. "We will ensure they are ready, Commander," Kudus said.

Freja stepped closer to her husband, her expression resolute. "What can I do to help?"

Halsten turned to her, his tone gentle but firm. "My love, please prepare the women to make balms and ration food supplies. If this leads to war, we must sustain our people and the soldiers on the front lines."

"I will start immediately," Freja said. "The women of McKenzie Castle will do their part."

Lord Aiden straightened his cloak. "I will head out to Castle Ridge to personally invite the nobles. We cannot delay."

"Travel safely, Uncle," Halsten said. "Your efforts mean everything to the kingdom."

Lord Aiden bowed slightly and left the hall. As the door closed behind him, the room grew quiet momentarily. Halsten took a deep breath, meeting the eyes of those still gathered. "This will be a test of all of us, but together, we will stand against Darius and protect the legacy of our kingdom. Prepare yourselves—this is only the beginning."

The room emptied, and Halsten stood alone for a moment, gazing at the banners of EdenRock that hung along the walls.

CHAPTER 41

A FEW WEEKS AFTER EGRON HAD arrived at McKenzie Castle, Freja gathered the women in the town square. Standing at the center, surrounded by Eleanor, Vivienne, Dhalia, Amela, and Dora, she addressed the crowd.

"Women of McKenzie City," she began, her voice steady but firm, carrying over the murmurs of the gathered women. "We live in uncertain times. The stability of our kingdom is threatened, and we face challenges that will test our strength as a people."

She let her words sink in before continuing. "Our men are preparing for what may come, training to defend the honor and safety of this kingdom. But their strength alone will not ensure our survival. We, the women of McKenzie City, have an equally vital role to play."

The crowd grew quiet, their eyes fixed on Freja.

"We will manage the food supplies, ensuring there's enough to sustain our people and soldiers. We will make balms and remedies for the wounded should war come to our gates. And we will stand together, united in purpose, to protect our homes and families."

The women exchanged glances, some nodding in agreement. A voice from the crowd called out, "How can we help, Lady Freja?"

She smiled warmly, encouraged by their eagerness. "In the coming days, we will organize teams to gather herbs, prepare rations, and set up storage for supplies. Eleanor and Vivienne will oversee the food preparations, while Dhalia, Amela, and Dora will assist with the production of balms and remedies."

Eleanor stepped forward. "We will need every able hand to ensure we are prepared. There is much to do, but we can accomplish it."

Vivienne added, "The safety of McKenzie City depends on all of us working as one."

Freja nodded. "You are all daughters of this kingdom, and your contributions will be as vital as those of the men on the battlefield. In times of hardship, unity and resilience see us through. Tomorrow, we will begin. Meet us here at first light, and we will divide into groups to start our tasks. The days ahead will be difficult, but we will rise to the challenge. Together, we will protect all that we hold dear."

After the meeting, Freja received warm embraces from the women, each expressing gratitude for her humility and leadership. The women began to disperse, their expressions resolute as they spoke among themselves, preparing for the work ahead. Freja stood watching them, her heart swelling with pride.

Eleanor touched her arm gently. "You have won their trust," she said. "And with good reason."

Freja turned to her sister-in-law, her expression one of gratitude. "We'll need every ounce of that trust to get through this. But I believe in them, and I believe in us."

She smiled, reassured by their support, and before making their way back to the castle, she and her friends visited with several of them individually to offer words of encouragement. On the way, the group decided to stop to pick up some fresh fruits.

As they approached the bustling market, Dora glanced ahead and straightened her posture. "Look who's coming our way," she said, nodding toward a group of men approaching from the opposite direction.

The ladies followed her gaze and saw Halsten's trusted companions—Adikis, Zoresh, Kudus, Arthur, Frodio, and Commander Egron—walking toward them.

"Dora," Eleanor teased, "you're not even trying to be subtle."

"Ooh la la," Eleanor quipped, earning a laugh from the group.

"Oh, my! Look at Dhalia. She's turning as red as a ripe apple," Vivienne teased.

"Let's just keep walking," Dhalia muttered, her cheeks flushing a deeper shade as she avoided their playful glances.

The women straightened, each putting on their best impression of composure as they neared the men. A delicate handkerchief slipped from Dhalia's hand and fluttered to the ground. Unaware, she continued walking.

"Wait, Dhalia," Amelia said, bending slightly to pick it up.

Dora gently grabbed Amelia's arm, pulling her back. "Do you think you're the only one who noticed?" she whispered with a mischievous smile.

The other women exchanged knowing glances and giggles as they walked on. When the groups finally crossed paths, the men greeted them politely.

"Good afternoon, ladies," Arthur said, tipping his head.

"Good afternoon, gentlemen," Dora replied with a polite smile.

They passed each other, but a few steps later, Arthur stopped, noticing the handkerchief lying on the ground. He nudged Kudus. "Aren't you going to pick that up and return it?"

Kudus frowned. "Why me?"

"Why not you?" Frodio asked, grinning.

Arthur added with a smirk, "It belongs to Dhalia. It's only proper."

The men chuckled, watching Kudus hesitate, looking between them and the handkerchief. Before he could decide, a soft throat-clearing behind them caught their attention.

Kudus turned and saw Dhalia standing a short distance away, one arm crossed over her front while the other nervously twiddled with her fingernails. "Are you not going to get my handkerchief for me?" she asked, her gaze steady yet hopeful.

Kudus quickly bent down to pick up the delicate cloth. As he stood, he noticed Dhalia glance back at her friends, a faint smile playing on her lips.

When he reached her, he awkwardly extended the handkerchief, but before he could hand it over, she stepped closer. Her voice lowered, carrying an uncharacteristic boldness.

"Sir Kudus," she began, her eyes meeting his, "I have done everything I can to show you that I like you, but you seem completely blind to all my efforts."

Kudus stood frozen, the faint blush on his cheeks deepening. He tried to find words but failed, his mouth opening and closing without a sound.

Dhalia tilted her head slightly, her tone sharpening as she pressed on. "Even mice follow crumbs. If you didn't hear the rain last night, doesn't the wet ground tell you it rained?"

Kudus gaped at her, his hand still clutching the handkerchief.

Dhalia stepped even closer, her eyes locked on to his. "Look," she continued, her voice softening but her determination unwavering, "though it's not my role, I've given you every chance to see what's in front of you. I'm not your sister, Kudus, and I won't wait forever."

He opened his mouth to respond, but Dhalia snatched the handkerchief from him. As she turned to walk away, she glanced over her shoulder, her eyes sparkling with mischief. "If you don't hurry, someone else will. I won't wait my entire life," she said with a slight smirk. Turning back, she motioned to the oak behind the castle. "If you like what you see, meet me under the tree. I'll wait, but not for long."

With that, Dhalia spun on her heel and walked away, her head held high as she rejoined her friends.

Amelia leaned closer to her as they walked. "What did you say to him?" she whispered, curiosity glinting in her eyes.

Dora chuckled before Dhalia could respond. "Trust me, you don't want to know," she said with a knowing smile.

The women continued toward the market, their laughter trailing behind them, while Kudus remained rooted to the spot in stunned silence. His heart raced as he stared after Dhalia, her words echoing in his mind, leaving him torn between hesitation and an undeniable pull toward the tree.

When evening came, Kudus left the castle to meet Dhalia. The vast oak stood tall against the backdrop of the dimming sky. She awaited him there, her white dress adorned with a delicate blue floral print, the hem falling just above her knees. A barrette shaped like a blue flower pinned her dark, silky hair in place, framing her glowing face. She radiated elegance and charm.

Kudus approached her, dressed in a crisp military ensemble. His white shirt stood stark against the dusk, and his boots were polished to a gleaming shine.

He paused and bowed. "My lady," he greeted, his voice steady but warm.

Dhalia smiled, tilting her head slightly. "I thought you wouldn't come," she teased.

"I debated it," Kudus said with a soft chuckle. "After all, I was ambushed this morning."

Dhalia raised an eyebrow, feigning offense. "Ambushed? That wasn't an ambush. Trust me, Sir Kudus. You'll know when I truly attack—you'll carry the scars to prove it."

He laughed, the tension in his shoulders easing. "Thank you for inviting me," he said.

Extending his arm to her, he bowed again. Dhalia slipped her arm through his, and together they began to walk along the moonlit garden paths.

"I was surprised by what you did today," Kudus admitted.

Dhalia turned her head toward him, her gaze sharp yet playful. "I had to make myself clear. I couldn't risk your setting your eyes on someone else."

Kudus grinned. "Well, you succeeded."

She smiled before shifting the conversation. "Tell me about Argos."

Kudus's expression softened. "Argos lies far beyond the Southern desert. It's a land where the air is filled with children's laughter, the women are homemakers, and the men are traders of fine goods. It's a place of warmth and simplicity."

Dhalia's voice was gentle. "And your family? Are they still there?"

He nodded, a shadow crossing his face. "I have two brothers and a sister. They remain in Argos. My father, though, passed before I left."

"Do you miss them?" Dhalia asked.

Kudus hesitated, then shook his head slightly. "Let's talk about something else." Because of his discomfort, Kudus changed the subject. "How did you and Freja become so close?"

Dhalia glanced at him, grateful for the shift. "Freja and I grew up together in Glenwood. We became friends as children and have been inseparable since."

Kudus smiled wistfully. "She's lucky to have a friend like you."

They kept walking until Dhalia stopped abruptly and turned to face him. "Do you love me, Sir Kudus?" she asked, her voice steady.

Kudus froze, and Dhalia took a step closer, tilting her head slightly. "Well? Do you?"

When he remained silent, she leaned in, her voice lowering to a whisper. "You've never been in love before, have you?"

He shook his head, his cheeks warming.

Dhalia placed a hand on his chest, her touch light but firm. "What does your heart tell you when you see me?"

His lips parted, and he finally found his voice. "It tells me I'm happy," he admitted.

She smiled, her hand lingering on his chest. "I feel happy when I see you too," she said, her voice barely above a whisper.

When they reached the castle, they paused at the entrance. Standing on her toes, Dhalia leaned in and kissed Kudus gently on the lips. As she stepped back, she reached up to remove the barrette from her hair, letting her dark, silky locks cascade freely around her shoulders, the strands catching the soft glow of the lanterns. She stepped forward and tucked the barrette in Kudus's pocket.

She smiled one last time before turning and disappearing into the castle. Kudus remained where he stood, his fingers brushing his lips, the warmth of her kiss lingering as he gazed after her, his heart thundering in his chest.

CHAPTER 42

A FEW DAYS LATER, THE COURTYARD of McKenzie Castle buzzed with life. Southern nobles, citizens, guards, and loyal allies gathered under the morning sun, their faces displaying a mixture of anticipation and resolve. Lord Aiden stood at the center, his stately presence commanding the crowd's attention. Beside him stood Prince Halsten, the soon-to-be king, with Freja at his side. Eleanor, Vivienne, DeMarco, Anders, Adikis, Arthur, Zoresh, Dhalia, Dora, Amelia, and Frodio stood nearby, their expressions reflecting their unwavering loyalty.

Guards formed a protective ring around the gathering, their armor gleaming in the light. At the same time, the citizens of McKenzie City stood among the nobles, eager to witness this pivotal moment in the kingdom's history.

Lord Aiden raised his hand for silence. The crowd hushed, their eyes fixed on him. His voice, steady and authoritative, echoed through the courtyard.

"My dear lords, ladies, and loyal subjects of EdenRock," he began, "we find ourselves in uncertain times. Darius's treachery has shattered the peace and stability of our realm. He has unlawfully seized the throne, imprisoned our beloved Alaric and Isadora, and committed unspeakable atrocities against our nobles."

A wave of murmurs rippled through the crowd, a mixture of anger and sorrow.

"Before these heinous acts," Aiden continued, "I met with Alaric in captivity. With wisdom and foresight, he entrusted me with his final wish. He called for his son, the rightful heir to the throne, to be crowned king of the South. This coronation is not merely symbolic. It is a step toward unity, strength, and the resistance we must mount against the tyranny of Darius."

The crowd erupted into murmurs again, filled with excitement and hope. Among the nobles, Lord Cameron rose, his voice cutting through the noise.

"I agree with Lord Aiden," he declared. "The South needs a leader who carries the legacy of our kings and the strength to defend our people. I pledge my house and loyalty to Prince Halsten, our rightful king."

One by one, the other nobles stood, each stepping forward to place a gold coin engraved with the symbol of their houses onto a grand table at the center of the courtyard, a token of their unwavering support. The air buzzed with approval as house after house pledged their allegiance.

Finally, all eyes turned to Lord Bracken. He hesitated, his face betraying inner conflict. The buzzing of the crowd grew louder as they waited. He reluctantly stepped forward under the weight of their gazes, retrieving a coin from his pocket. Slowly, he placed it on the table.

"My house pledges to the South," he said, though his reluctance lingered in the air.

Lord Aiden nodded toward Halsten. He turned and lifted the crown, adorned with the intricate image of a Ligon, its golden surface catching the light.

Kneeling before Aiden, Halsten and Freja bowed their heads. Aiden spoke solemnly, his voice imbued with reverence: "Prince Halsten of EdenRock and Lady Freja of Glenwood, in the name of our people and the legacy of our ancestors, I crown you King and Queen of the South." May you rule with humility, compassion, and justice, and may the Lord guide your reign."

The crown was placed upon Halsten's head, and cheers erupted from the crowd, their voices rising in a unified chant. "To the Realm! To the Realm! To the Realm!"

McKenzie Castle's courtyard atmosphere was solemn yet charged with an undercurrent of hope and determination. King Halsten Elliot Verdant, newly crowned and wearing the regal cloak of the South, stood at the forefront, accompanied by Freja, his queen. The crown rested firmly upon his head, its weight a reminder of the responsibility he now bore.

His eyes scanned the gathering of nobles, commanders, and citizens. His gaze lingered momentarily on Freja, Eleanor, and Vivienne, who stood proudly in the front row. Freja's presence, steadfast and reassuring, bolstered his resolve.

With a deep breath, he began. His voice was steady but imbued with the gravity of the moment. "Nobles, commanders, loyal citizens of Southern EdenRock, today marks a turning point in the history of our great kingdom. I stand before you, not just as your king, but as a servant to the people of the South, bound by duty to protect our land and its honor."

The crowd rippled with approval.

Halsten's expression hardened as he continued. "My father, King Alaric, and my mother, Isadora, have been wrongfully imprisoned by my uncle, Darius. A man who was banished for his crimes now claims to be king. But he has not risen by the people's will—he has seized power through treachery and bloodshed. He rules not with justice but with fear."

His voice grew firmer, resonating through the hall. "We have endured his betrayal, cruelty, and unlawful claim to the throne. The time for endurance has passed. The South will not kneel to a usurper. We will not allow his darkness to spread further across our lands.

"I have been crowned king of the South not to divide this kingdom but to preserve its legacy. EdenRock belongs to its people. It belongs to those who seek justice, prosperity, and peace."

The hall erupted in cheers, and Halsten raised a hand, silencing the room. "But peace cannot be achieved while Darius sits on the throne in the North. He is a plague upon our kingdom, a shadow that must be cast away. And so, as your king, I declare today that the South shall rise. We will gather our strength, rally our forces, and march to reclaim what is rightfully ours."

A deafening roar of agreement swept through crowd. Nobles and soldiers alike thrust their swords into the air, and their voices united in a singular purpose.

"I decree that the South will go to war," Halsten proclaimed, his voice filled with conviction. "We will free my father and mother. We will restore the honor of EdenRock. And we will ensure that no tyrant, no matter how cunning, will ever defile our kingdom again." He placed a hand over his heart. "For justice. For our people. For EdenRock."

"Long live the king! Long live King Halsten!" chanted the crowd. The hall trembled with the fervor of their united resolve. Freja stepped forward, placing a supportive hand on her husband's arm. Her eyes shone with pride as she looked at him.

Halsten signaled for silence. "My lords, ladies, and trusted comrades, today marks the beginning of our resolve to restore EdenRock and establish those who will stand with me in shaping our future. I have chosen individuals whose loyalty, courage, and wisdom are beyond question to serve in key leadership positions."

His gaze swept across the room, meeting the eyes of those he was about to name.

"Sir Arthur," he began, gesturing to his friends standing at attention, "will serve as my viceroy, entrusted with overseeing the kingdom's affairs in my stead when necessary."

Arthur stepped forward, bowing deeply. "Your Grace, I am honored by your trust. I will serve you and the people of EdenRock with unwavering loyalty."

"Sir Frodio," Halsten continued, "will lead our secret operations. His skill in intelligence and strategy has proven invaluable, and I am confident he will ensure our plans remain ahead of our enemies."

"Thank you, Your Grace," Frodio said. "I will not let you down."

"Sir Adikis"—Halsten turned to the formidable warrior—"will take command of our defenses. He will oversee the protection of our borders and ensure our cities remain secure."

Adikis nodded firmly. "I will fortify the South, Your Grace. None shall breach our defenses."

"Sir Zoresh," Halsten declared, "will assume the commander of the interior role. His duty will be to maintain order and ensure the well-being of our citizens."

Zoresh stepped forward, his expression solemn. "It is an honor to serve, Your Grace. I will uphold justice and order within our lands."

"Sir Kudus," Halsten announced, his gaze resting on the soldier who had recently proven himself such a trusted ally, "will command the McKenzie army. He will prepare our forces for the battles to come."

Kudus saluted. "The McKenzie army stands ready, Your Grace."

"Sir Egron will command the Southern army. His experience in warfare will be vital in the days ahead."

Egron bowed his head. "Your Grace, I will lead our forces to victory."

"DeMarco," Halsten continued, "my trusted friend and protector, will lead the King's Guard. He will ensure the safety of our people."

DeMarco placed a hand over his heart. "Your Grace, I will guard the throne and all it stands for."

"Sir Otello will be my advisor on security affairs."

"Your Grace, I will serve well."

Turning to Anders, Halsten said, "You will serve as the castle commander, ensuring our home remains secure and well-managed."

Anders stepped forward, bowing respectfully. "Thank you, Your Grace. I will serve diligently."

Halsten turned to the assembled nobles. "Lord Cameron will lead the king's council, and my uncle Lord Aiden will be my trusted advisor. Their wisdom and guidance will help us navigate the challenges ahead.

"Finally," Halsten said, "Tomei and Axilla will oversee weaponry manufacturing."

The two men nodded in acceptance.

The room erupted in cheers and applause, the energy palpable as the people of Southern EdenRock stood unified under their new leadership. Swords were raised in solidarity, and the chant "To the King! To the Realm!" reverberated through the hall.

Halsten raised his hand once more, signaling for quiet. "Let this day mark the beginning of our resistance."

The crowd shook with collective determination. The people, united under their new king, prepared themselves for the battle ahead. EdenRock's destiny awaited them.

By nightfall, the news reached Darius in the Verdant Castle. Halsten had been crowned king of the South. Darius's face darkened as he paced the grand hall, his mind consumed with rage. Suddenly, the Orb spoke in his mind, its voice sharp and mocking.

"You've lost half your kingdom," it taunted. "Your nephew has taken the South. You hold a broken crown now, a king of fragments."

"Leave me alone!" Darius bellowed, his voice echoing through the vast space. In a fury, he overturned a heavy wooden table, sending goblets and plates crashing to the floor.

The commotion drew Caine, who rushed in, his single arm supporting him as he stood at a distance cautiously. "My lord, is there something I can do?"

Darius turned on him, his anger boiling over. With a powerful kick to the chest, he sent Caine sprawling to the floor. "Out of my sight!" he roared.

Caine staggered to his feet and quickly retreated.

Outside the hall, Darius yelled, "Tapas! Bring my horse!"

Tapas, ever loyal, hurried to comply. As Darius stormed into the courtyard, Xinovia and Mefford arrived, concern etched on their faces.

"Let him go," Mefford said, gripping his mother's arm as she moved to intervene. "He'll calm down. He always does."

By the time she hesitated, Darius was already in the saddle, his face a mask of fury. Tapas followed suit, mounting his steed. Together, they galloped eastward into the night, their horses' hooves pounding against the dirt road.

They rode through the darkness until they reached the small, decrepit hut tucked away in the woods. Darius dismounted abruptly and barked, "Stay here!" at Tapas before striding toward it.

Inside, Petra was arranging charms and trinkets on a dusty shelf. She turned in surprise as the door slammed open, revealing Darius, his face a storm of rage and desperation.

"Your Grace," she said, her voice trembling. "What brings you here?"

Darius sat in a chair and lifted his eyes to gaze at the woman.

"I'm going to war," Darius growled, his tone laced with impatience. "Tell me what you see!"

Petra nodded shakily, gathering two black feathers from a shelf. She held them briefly over the fire in the hearth, circling Darius before tossing them into the flames. Smoke filled the room, curling and twisting like spectral forms.

"What do you see?" Darius demanded again, his patience wearing thin.

Petra gazed into the smoke, her face pale. "Your Grace," she whispered. "I see blood. So much blood. It flows like a river. And a fox. A fox breaking free from its cage, running into the wild."

His hand gripped the hilt of his sword tightly. "What about my nephew? What do you see of him?" he barked, his voice rising.

She hesitated, her gaze fixed on the flickering fire. As she peered deeper, her face contorted in terror. From the flames, a creature emerged—part lion, part dragon, its fiery breath surging forward. It roared, the sound like thunder, and a burst of fire engulfed Petra.

Darius tumbled backward out of his chair, scrambling to his feet. He bolted out of the hut just as Tapas was approaching the door.

"What happened, my lord?" Tapas asked, startled by his master's panicked expression.

"Get back!" Darius yelled, pulling Tapas away.

The flames within the hut grew, consuming the walls with alarming speed. The two men went to stand at a safe distance, watching as the structure was reduced to an inferno.

Darius's chest heaved, his mind racing. "I've seen enough," he muttered, mounting his horse.

Tapas climbed onto his own horse without a word, glancing back uneasily at the burning remains of the hut. They rode back toward the palace under the cover of darkness, the haunting image of the fiery beast etched into Darius's mind.

CHAPTER 43

As THE DAY OF BATTLE drew near, the Southern part of the kingdom buzzed with fervent activity. Soldiers trained relentlessly in the open fields, their synchronized chants echoing through the crisp air. The rhythmic clanging of swords and shields blended with their determined cries. Women worked tirelessly in the courtyards and village squares, preparing provisions. Some stacked large sacks of grains, dried meats, and medicinal herbs while others stirred boiling balms or sewed bandages with precision and care.

At McKenzie Castle, King Halsten convened his trusted leaders in the grand strategy hall. The room was bathed in the warm light of torches and the flickering glow of a central hearth. Shadows danced on the walls, casting long shapes over a large map of EdenRock spread across the central table. Around it stood his most loyal commanders. Each man bore the resolute expression of one entrusted with the weight of the kingdom's future.

Halsten's voice broke the tense silence. "We will not cower before Darius, nor will we allow his tyranny to define the future of EdenRock. This kingdom belongs to its people, not to a usurper."

Arthur rested his hand on the table. "What are your orders, Your Grace?"

Halsten met his gaze with steely determination. "Fortify McKenzie Castle, in my absence. The Southern army will march at first light on Saturday. We will strike the Verdant Castle with such force that he will have no choice but to surrender. I do not want any surprises behind us."

The room was silent as the weight of Halsten's words settled over the assembled leaders.

Once the planning meeting was over, Halsten and Freja retreated to the quiet solitude of the castle balcony. They settled into a large bench, Freja leaning her head against Halsten's chest as the night air enveloped them in stillness.

She broke the silence, her voice soft but filled with concern. "My love, I wish this war could be avoided. But I understand how much this means to you. I pray for your victory and, more than anything, your safe return."

Halsten ran his fingers gently through her hair. "I know you are worried. Leadership is not without its burdens. If I do not lead by example, I risk losing the trust of my people. They need to see their king willing to stand beside them."

Freja lifted her head slightly to look into his eyes. "Do you think you will save your parents?"

"My father believes this war is necessary. He entrusted me with this task. The rest, my love, we must leave in the hands of God," Halsten said.

Freja sighed, resting her head back against his chest. They sat there for a long while, wrapped in each other's presence, taking solace in the fleeting peace of the moment.

Meanwhile, in the shadow of the tall shrubs at the back of the castle, Dhalia and Kudus sat together on a stone bench. The moonlight bathed the garden in a gentle glow, but Dahlia's expression was marked by worry.

She pulled a delicate comb from her hair, its intricate design catching the light, and handed it to Kudus. "I know we haven't known each other long," she began, her voice trembling slightly, "but keep this with you during the war. Bring it back to me—alive."

Kudus took it, his expression softening. "Are you afraid something will happen to me?"

Dhalia nodded, her hands clasping tightly in her lap. "Yes. But I know you're a skilled fighter. You'll survive if you fight like you did in the Gladiator Games."

Kudus chuckled lightly, though with a trace of sadness. "The battlefield is nothing like the games, Dhalia. There are no rules, and weapons come from every direction. But I promise you, I will return."

She looked at him, her eyes searching his face. "How did you become a gladiator?" she asked.

Kudus paused, lowering his gaze. When he finally spoke, his voice carried the weight of memories. "My father was a noble trader and councilman to the king of Argos," he began. "Our family had everything—wealth, status, security. One day, a nobleman of Argos entrusted my father with a large sum of gold to purchase several racehorses for his stables. But before my father could reach his destination, the caravan was attacked. The gold was stolen."

Dhalia's eyes widened, her hand clutching her chest. "What happened after that?"

"When the nobleman learned of it, he summoned my father before the king, demanding the return of his gold. But my father, having lost everything in the attack, could not repay him. The king ordered all of my father's properties confiscated, yet it wasn't enough to cover the debt. The nobleman then demanded me, his eldest son, as payment."

Dhalia gasped, tears welling in her eyes. "That's barbaric! What did he do to you?"

Kudus lowered his gaze. "He took me and sold me to Megateo's gladiator camp in Veran. That was the start of my life in the arena."

She reached for his hand. "And your father? What happened to him?"

Kudus hesitated, his voice thick with emotion. "He couldn't live with the shame. He took his own life the next day."

Dhalia pressed her hand to her mouth, her tears flowing freely. "Oh, Kudus. I'm so sorry. I can't imagine the pain you've endured."

His eyes softened at her genuine concern. "I've carried that pain for a long time. But meeting you has given me something I never thought I'd have—a reason to fight for more than survival."

She tightened her grip on his hand. "Please, promise me you'll come back alive. I cannot live without you."

He leaned closer, his voice resolute. "I promise, Dhalia, no war can take me away now—not when I have you to return to."

Her lip quivered as she whispered, "If it meant staying with you, I would follow you even to the land of death."

Kudus smiled faintly, reaching into his pocket to retrieve her comb. "I have to come back. After all, I still need to return this to you alive."

She laughed softly through her tears, lightly tapping his shoulder. "Don't tease me, soldier. My heart can't take it."

Their eyes met, and the world seemed to fade away. Slowly, Kudus leaned in, and Dhalia met him halfway. Their lips brushed in a kiss that spoke of hope, love, and the promises they silently vowed to keep.

As the stars above bore witness, the two held each other close, finding brief but powerful solace in this moment they shared before the trials ahead.

CHAPTER 44

THE SOUTHERN EDENROCK ARMY SOLDIERS gathered near McKenzie City a week before the impending battle. The sight was awe-inspiring—thousands of soldiers stood in formation, each castle represented by its finest warriors and, in many cases, their lords. Lords Cameron, Perkins, Lingard, Palm, Argus, and Ramsgate were among the nobles present, each accompanied by a retinue of loyal men.

At the forefront of the army, King Halsten sat astride a majestic white stallion. His dark brown, handcrafted leather armor bore the emblem of the Ligon on the left breast. He carried a matching shield, helmet, and sword. Behind him stood his trusted commanders.

The soldiers, clad in similar armor adorned with the Ligon emblem, stood in disciplined ranks. The air was thick with anticipation and the weight of what lay ahead. Halsten surveyed his army, his gaze steady and resolute.

"Men of EdenRock," he began, his voice carrying across the field, "today marks a pivotal moment in the history of our kingdom. The peace and honor of our realm have been stolen by tyranny and greed. But we stand here, united, ready to fight not just for our king and queen but for the very soul of EdenRock."

The soldiers stood silent, their attention unwavering as he continued. "This battle is not just ours—it is for those who came before us and for the generations yet to come. Let today's courage echo through the ages, proving that we are not a people who bow to injustice. We fight for freedom, honor, and this land's true spirit."

A wave of resolve swept through the ranks, agreement rippling among the soldiers.

Commander Egron rode forward. "You've heard the king's words!" he called. "We march with purpose, we march with honor, and we march for victory. Remember your training and fight with every fiber of your being. Move out!"

With that, the army began its march. Hoofbeats and boots reverberated against the earth as they set off.

They traveled for three days and nights, halting only when exhaustion forced them to rest. On the third day, they reached the windswept plains near Longrove, just beyond the River Ellyn South, and made camp as dusk settled over the land. Fires were lit, sentries posted—but Halsten's arrival was no longer a secret.

Word had already reached the enemy's ears.

The message found Darius as he finished his meal, the last drops of wine still staining his goblet. Before he could set it down, a guard burst into the hall, his chest heaving. "Halsten and his men are approaching the city," he gasped to the captain of the guard. The air in the room turned sharp, like the moment before a storm breaks.

That man, in turn, went to the grand hall and said, "Your Grace, Halsten and his army are advancing toward Aldrich City."

Darius got up. "Prepare the defenses!" he barked, and Tapas, Caine, and Mefford ran to the hall. "Get the soldiers ready. I want archers on every wall and loaded catapults. Bring Alaric and Isadora out to where Halsten can see them."

Tapas bowed quickly. "Yes, my lord," he said, retreating to relay the orders. Caine and Mefford followed suit, moving with urgency. Darius donned his black-and-silver armor, the polished steel catching the dim firelight of the grand hall. He secured his sword and ordered his guard to follow him.

Within the hour, the walls of Aldrich City bristled with armed men. Archers lined the battlements, arrows nocked, while below, ranks of soldiers formed a grim barricade against the coming storm. At the center of it all, Alaric and Isadora knelt in shackles, their pale faces lifted toward the horizon—a silent, brutal message meant for Halsten's eyes alone. Above them, Darius ascended the battlements, flanked by Tapas, Mefford, and Caine, their features carved into hard lines.

A message received. A challenge answered.

Halsten needed no herald. He stirred from his cot, the weight of the coming hours settling upon him. Without hesitation, he summoned his most trusted—DeMarco, Anders, Kudus, Adikis, and Frodio—who gathered in his command tent, their weariness sharpened into focus. The time for waiting was over.

The prince stood by the table, his voice low but firm. "Before we engage in battle, I need to rescue my parents. Darius will use them as shields or bargaining tools if we leave them in his hands. Their safety is paramount."

Anders frowned. "How do you propose we do this, Your Grace? The walls are heavily guarded, and Darius will have increased his defenses."

Halsten picked up a stick and crouched on the dirt floor of the tent, drawing a rough map. "We will enter through the underground passage that leads to the king's library. It's an old route my father showed me when I was a boy. Darius won't expect it, and most of the guards will be stationed on the walls, preparing for our frontal assault."

Kudus leaned in to study the map. "Once we're inside, how do we avoid detection? There will still be guards in the inner corridors."

Halsten's eyes flicked to Frodio, who nodded. "Odus, one of the bell ringers, will assist us. He's been waiting for this opportunity and has agreed to neutralize any immediate threats near the dungeon."

DeMarco adjusted his sword belt. "And if Darius catches wind of this plan?"

Halsten straightened, his hand gripping the hilt of his sword. "Then we fight our way out. But we will not leave my parents behind. We rescue them, or we die trying."

The group exchanged solemn looks.

Anders broke the silence. "We will follow your lead, Your Grace."

Halsten nodded. "Gather your weapons. We move now."

———⚬∕∕⚬———

"Let's move," Halsten commanded.

He and the selected group of men began approaching Aldrich City, the rhythmic clatter of hooves muffled by the grassy plain beneath them.

As they neared the city gates, the silence shattered. Flaming arrows streaked through the darkness, hissing as they flew toward them from the city walls.

"Ambush! We've been exposed!" DeMarco shouted, urging his horse into a defensive circle with the others.

Darius's voice boomed atop the city wall, cutting through the chaos. "Halsten—nephew! Surrender to me now, and I will let your parents live."

Halsten pulled his horse to a halt. His jaw clenched as he glared at the wall where Darius stood. "You are a cruel and disturbed man, unfit to call yourself a king," he shouted back. "By the end of tomorrow, I will serve your head to the crows!"

Darius's laughter echoed, cold and mocking. "Bold words, but I'll show you what happens to the bold in EdenRock."

Torches along the walls flared to life, illuminating a sight that made Halsten's blood run cold. Shackled and visibly weakened, Alaric and Isadora stood on the battlements, their heads on wooden blocks. Two executioners stood beside them, axes poised for the fatal swing.

"Look at them!" Darius jeered. "Your poor father and mother. If you think you can save them, come and try."

Halsten's heart pounded as he spurred his horse forward, galloping furiously toward the city wall. The fiery arrows continued to rain down, forcing his men to scatter and take cover, but Halsten pressed on, his determination blazing brighter than the flames in the sky.

Darius's dark eyes gleamed with sadistic satisfaction. He raised his hand high, signaling to the executioners.

"No!" Halsten bellowed, urging his horse to speed up.

But it was too late. Darius brought his hand down in a swift, merciless gesture. The executioners raised their axes and, without hesitation, brought them down. The sound of the blades cleaving flesh echoed in the wind.

Halsten skidded to a halt as he watched, horrified, the severed heads of Alaric and Isadora tumble from the wall. They rolled down the sloped ground, coming to rest near the edge of the plain, their lifeless eyes staring at each other.

Halsten dismounted, staggering toward them. His breath came in ragged gasps as he knelt, tears streaming down his face. "Father… Mother…" he whispered, his voice breaking.

From the wall, Darius sneered, savoring the sight of his nephew's despair. "There! Your precious king and queen. Come and get them, Halsten. And when you do, know their blood is on your hands!"

Halsten's hands clenched into fists, his grief transforming into a searing rage. He stood, his voice rising in a battle cry. "This ends now, Darius! Tomorrow, I will avenge my parents and bring justice to EdenRock!"

Behind him, his men gathered, their expressions grim as they rallied around their king.

⁓

Back at the camp, the air was thick with sorrow and determination. Halsten's commanders gathered around him in the central war tent. Lord Aiden stepped forward, placing a firm hand on his nephew's shoulder. His voice was steady, though his face betrayed the grief he carried. "Your Grace, I grieve with you. The sacrifice of Alaric and Isadora will not be in vain. This war will be their justice."

Halsten nodded silently, his jaw tight as he fought to contain the storm of emotions brewing within him. His eyes, fixed on the table before him, traced the edges of the map as though seeking solace in its orderly lines. Around him, his commanders remained quiet, sensing the moment's weight.

As the evening deepened, the camp grew still. The soft hum of night insects filled the air, broken only by the whispers of soldiers standing watch and the distant rustle of tents. Those not on guard sought rest, their minds heavy with the thought of the battle ahead.

Inside his tent, Halsten sat alone on his cot, his armor stacked neatly in the corner and his sword resting against the wall. He leaned back, exhaustion pulling him down until sleep finally claimed him.

⁓

In the dream, Halsten walked through a long corridor lined with figures. They stood silent and motionless, dressed in black war robes. Each figure carried a sheathed sword at its waist and gleaming knives at its sides. Their faces were obscured, and their presence both haunting and strangely reassuring. As Halsten moved forward, they parted for him, stepping back with an almost ceremonial precision.

At the end of the corridor sat an older man bathed in a radiant, otherworldly glow. The light from him obscured his face, yet his presence exuded wisdom and authority. On either side of him crouched two magnificent Ligons. The creatures were majestic, their golden-green scales glistening with an ethereal brilliance. Their lion-and-dragon-like faces were regal, their eyes intelligent and piercing.

"Come closer, my son," the old man said, his resonant voice carrying warmth into Halsten's core. "The time has come for you to be revealed to the world."

Halsten approached cautiously, his heart pounding. The man's glow intensified as he rose from his seat, moving toward the young king with deliberate grace. He held a sword unlike any Halsten had ever seen in his hands. The blade was adorned with intricate engravings that seemed alive with meaning and power—the same ones Halsten remembered from his father's blade.

"This is your destiny," the man said, presenting the sword. Halsten's hands were steady, but the moment's weight made his arms tremble as he accepted the weapon. "Take this and fight for the future of the kingdom."

Halsten looked up, squinting against the radiance. "Who are you?" he asked, his voice barely above a whisper.

The older man stepped back, a staircase of light materializing behind him. It ascended endlessly, vanishing into brilliance above. As he began to climb, he paused to look back. "You will know when the time is right," he said before disappearing into the light.

Halsten turned to look behind him, but the corridor, the figures, and the Ligons had all vanished. He stood alone, the weight of the sword in his hands the only tangible connection to the vision.

He woke abruptly, his breath coming in shallow gasps. The dim light of dawn seeped through the edges of the tent. He sat up, wiping sweat from his brow, and reached instinctively for the sword by his side. Lifting it, he examined the engravings on its blade.

For a long moment, the dream replayed in his mind. Though its whole meaning eluded him, he felt an unshakable certainty—it was no mere dream but a message, a calling. He rested the sword beside him and lay back down to rest.

The following day, Halsten woke before dawn, his mind resolute. He called for Anders, who quickly entered with the king's polished armor. Together, they fastened it piece by piece. The king stood tall, and Anders adjusted the final buckle.

As Halsten stepped out of his tent, the first rays of sunlight reflected off his armor. Before him, his army waited, a sea of mounted and ready soldiers, their expressions a mixture of anticipation and determination.

Halsten raised his voice, addressing them. "Brothers, there is a traitor among us," he declared, echoing across the encampment. "Someone has been revealing our plans to Darius, jeopardizing the lives of our people and our cause."

The soldiers glanced at one another, their tension palpable.

"Who is it, Your Grace?" Egron asked, turning to survey the crowd.

Before anyone could answer, Lord Bracken suddenly bolted on his horse, sprinting away from the assembly. A few guards made to pursue him, but Egron raised his hand. "Stop!" he ordered. "Give me a javelin."

A nearby soldier handed him the weapon. Egron stepped forward, his posture steady, his aim precise. He hurled it high into the air with a swift, practiced motion. It arced gracefully, piercing through the early morning wind before descending sharply.

A loud cry echoed in the distance. All eyes turned to see Lord Bracken kneeling on the ground, the javelin embedded in his back, pinning him to the earth. A hush fell over the soldiers.

Halsten mounted his horse. "We march!" he commanded.

The army began to move, their footsteps thunderous as they crossed River Ellyn South. They rode through the fields near Lake Toki, their banners flying high, the air heavy with the weight of what lay ahead.

When they reached the plains before Aldrich City, Halsten raised his hand, signaling the army to halt. He turned his horse to face his men.

"Men of EdenRock," he began, "Today, we march with heavy hearts. Today, we fight for justice and the memory of Alaric and Isadora, who were cruelly taken from us. This is not just a battle for vengeance but for our freedom, families, homes, and lives."

His gaze swept over the soldiers. "Remember, the evil we allow to fester today will find its way to our doorsteps tomorrow. We fight to ensure that no tyrant or oppressor can steal what is rightfully ours."

He raised his sword high, its blade gleaming in the sunlight. "Fight for your freedom! Fight for your family! Fight for EdenRock!"

The soldiers erupted in a deafening chant, their voices unified in resolve. "To the Realm! To the Realm! To the Realm!"

The ground trembled as the army resumed its march. They advanced toward the walls of Aldrich City, their swords drawn, their hearts ready for the battle that would determine the fate of EdenRock.

The Southern army emerged on the vast plains before Aldrich City. They advanced in disciplined formations, their shields and armor glinting in the sun. At their head, Halsten rode, the sword bearing the sigils of EdenRock strapped firmly to his side.

From the city walls, the drums began to thunder. The Northern army moved swiftly into position, forming tight ranks along the battlements. Darius was standing atop the wall, his black armor gleaming menacingly in the light. Mefford, Tapas, Caine, and Lord Luterodt flanked him, their expressions grim as they watched the Southern army close in.

Tapas raised his hand, his voice ringing out like a whip. "Archers! Ready your bows!"

On the field below, Egron spotted the movement from the wall and turned to his forces. "Prepare for cover!" he bellowed.

The soldiers moved steadily forward, their shields raised and locked in formation. At the center, protected by the shield wall, were men with battering rams and ladders, their faces set with determination as they approached the massive gate.

When the Southern forces drew closer, Tapas dropped his hand. "Archers! Fire!"

A volley of arrows rained down from the city walls, streaking through the sky like dark, deadly comets. The whistle of the projectiles filled the air before they struck. The Southern soldiers obeyed Egron's swift command: "Shields! Cover!"

The shields rose as one, forming a protective dome. The sound of arrows thudding against wood and metal reverberated across the field. Some pierced through gaps between the shields, striking soldiers. Cries of pain broke the marching rhythm, but the Southern army pressed on, undeterred by the losses.

Tapas paced the wall, his sharp eyes fixed on the advancing troops. "Reload! Prepare to fire again!" he barked.

From below, Halsten's voice cut through the chaos. "Do not falter! Keep moving forward!" His calm but commanding tone reignited the soldiers' resolve.

Another volley of arrows was unleashed from the wall, cutting down more of the Southern soldiers. Egron's voice roared over the din. "Shields up! Advance!"

The army moved closer, their pace steady despite the relentless assault. The soldiers bearing the battering rams shifted into position, their steps synchronized as they neared the gate. The ladder carriers stayed close, their eyes fixed on the looming walls above them.

Darius's lips twisted into a sneer on the battlements. "Let them come," he said to Mefford, his voice low and filled with venom. "Let them throw themselves against the walls of Aldrich City and see how futile their efforts truly are."

Mefford smirked, leaning over the edge of the wall. "They are determined, but determination will not save them."

Tapas raised his hand once more. "Archers! Fire at will!"

The relentless assault continued as the Southern forces reached the base of the wall. The battering ram pounding against the city gate reverberated like thunder. Ladders began to rise, pushed upward by the Southern soldiers, reaching toward the walls that had protected Aldrich City for generations.

Halsten and Albert rode along the ranks, shouting encouragement to their men. "For EdenRock! For freedom! For the fallen!"

The Southern soldiers roared in unison, their voices rising above the din of battle. Despite the arrows and casualties, they continued to fight. The siege of Aldrich City had begun.

From atop the walls, Darius's soldiers hurled massive boulders down toward Halsten's troops. The sound of them crashing into the shield formations echoed across the battlefield. Though some soldiers fell to their deaths under the crushing weight, the rest held steadfast.

"Hold the line!" Commander Egron bellowed from where he stood among the soldiers near the city gates. "Push forward!"

Despite the onslaught from above, Halsten's army moved with disciplined precision. Soldiers carrying ladders ran toward the walls, setting them firmly in place against the towering stone. Others stayed behind, forming protective formations to provide cover for their comrades. Archers, led by Kudus, Albert, and Tomei, fired arrows at the defenders on the wall, forcing Darius's men to duck for cover and giving the ladder climbers a crucial advantage.

"Keep those archers busy!" Kudus shouted, losing another arrow and watching as it struck a Northern soldier who had stepped too far into the open. "Do not let up!"

Meanwhile, Halsten, Adikis, DeMarco, and Zoresh each grabbed a ladder, rallying their men to climb alongside them. Halsten's face was a mask of determination as he ascended, his sword strapped to his back, his eyes fixed on the battlements above.

"Follow me!" he commanded.

Below, Egron and Axilla led the soldiers in pounding the battering ram against the gate. Its relentless force splintered the wooden barricades with each strike.

"Harder!" Egron urged, gripping the handle alongside the other soldiers. "Break it down!"

At the base of the wall, Frodio coordinated a group of archers who worked in tandem with the shield bearers. They fired in volleys, and as they reloaded, the shield bearers moved into position to protect them from the stones and arrows raining down.

"Shift left! Cover those climbers!" Frodio commanded, pointing to where a group of Southern soldiers struggled to ascend a ladder while Darius's men threw burning oil down its rungs.

Kudus and Albert stayed with their men, shooting arrows at the wall's top to distract the Northern soldiers as Halsten and his soldiers advanced.

From where they stood, Darius, Mefford, and Tapas scanned the chaos below. "Focus on the climbers!" Darius ordered, his voice carrying over the cacophony. "Do not let them breach the walls!"

Mefford waved to a group of soldiers behind him. "More stones! Prepare the boiling oil!"

Tapas leaned over the edge, hurling insults at the Southern forces. "You'll never take this city! We will bury you!"

But Halsten's army was relentless. As the archers provided covering fire, the ladder climbers pushed on, scaling the walls with determination. Halsten reached the top of his ladder and pulled himself onto the battlements, immediately drawing his sword and engaging a Northern soldier. Steel clashed as the two exchanged blows, but Halsten's training and resolve quickly overwhelmed his opponent. He pushed the soldier off the wall with a final, decisive strike.

DeMarco and Zoresh climbed up alongside Halsten, joining the fray. "Secure this section of the wall!" DeMarco shouted as he deflected an incoming strike with his shield. "Hold the high ground!"

Meanwhile, the battering ram broke through the gates with a resounding crash. The splintered wood gave way, and Egron led the charge through the opening, roaring, "For the South!"

As the Southern soldiers flooded the city, Darius's forces scrambled to regroup, but the tide was turning. Darius, still on the wall, clenched his fists in frustration. "Mefford! Rally the troops at the inner defenses! Do not let them reach the palace!"

Mefford nodded and ran toward the stairway leading into the city, shouting orders to the remaining Northern soldiers. Tapas stayed behind, furiously directing the archers to focus fire on Halsten and his men, who were now holding wall sections.

"Your Grace, the wall has been breached. We must get you out of here!" Tapas' tone was sharp and commanding as the chaos of battle raged around them.

Without hesitation, the guards flanking Darius and Mefford escorted them away from the wall. Caine stayed behind, rallying the remaining Northern soldiers to hold the line. "Hold them off!" Tapas barked, raising his sword. "Buy us time!"

Meanwhile, the Southern warriors, emboldened by their king's leadership, cut through Darius's forces with determination.

"Darius is escaping!" DeMarco shouted, his voice carrying over the clash of steel.

"Follow me!" Halsten dashed down the wall, his sword flashing as he struck down every soldier. Zoresh, DeMarco, and Anders trailed close behind, their blades clearing the way.

In their pursuit, the Southern warriors broke through wave after wave of Northern soldiers. Just as Darius and Mefford approached their horses, Halsten and his group closed the gap. The air grew heavy with the tension of impending confrontation.

Darius's guards tightened their formation around him, creating a protective barrier. Tapas stood at the forefront with other guards. "You won't reach him!" he growled, stepping forward with his sword raised.

The two sides clashed violently, and the fighting intensified around them. Amid the chaos, Tapas thrust his blade into Zoresh's chest, sending him to the ground with a cry of pain.

"Help Zoresh!" Axilla shouted to Tomei, who immediately rushed to the fallen warrior, pulling him to safety.

Halsten and his men fought valiantly, determined to prevent Darius from fleeing. Egron charged toward Tapas, engaging him in a fierce duel. Tapas pushed Egron back, causing him to stumble, but the seasoned commander quickly recovered, striking down two Northern soldiers as he closed in on his opponent.

Tapas lunged at Egron, aiming a deadly thrust at his back. Egron twisted just in time, dodging the strike and countering with a slash across Tapas's back. The man roared in pain but spun around, his blade meeting Egron's in a flurry of strikes. Their duel drew the attention of nearby soldiers, who paused briefly to witness the extraordinary display of skill.

Egron pressed the attack, delivering a series of precise strikes that forced Tapas to go on the defensive. With one final swing, Egron slashed across Tapas's sword hand, sending his weapon clattering to the ground. Tapas staggered back, clutching his injury.

Egron didn't hesitate. He drove his boot into Tapas's chest, knocking him to the ground. As the man struggled to rise, defiant even in defeat, Egron leveled his sword at his throat.

"Yield," he demanded coldly, his voice steady despite the chaos around him.

Tapas refused to kneel, his gaze filled with hatred. Egron, seeing no other option, twirled his blade before delivering a final, decisive slash. The strike severed Tapas's head cleanly, sending it tumbling to the ground.

On the other side of the battlefield, Lord Cameron wielded his sword with the grace of a seasoned warrior, cutting down one enemy after another as he pushed through the fray. His eyes scanned the battlefield, locking onto Mefford, Darius's ruthless son, who was slashing his way toward him.

Their blades met in a blinding clash. Cameron's strikes were calculated, each blow aimed to break through Mefford's defenses. But Mefford fought with brute savagery and precision, countering every move. The two warriors circled each other, their boots churning bloodied mud as they sought openings.

With a sudden, vicious twist, Mefford broke the lock and struck. His blade found its mark, piercing through Cameron's armor and into his chest. The nobleman staggered, his breath hitching as blood stained his tabard. He fell to his knees, his eyes fixed on Mefford in defiant silence before crumpling to the ground.

DeMarco, who had been fighting nearby, witnessed the fatal blow. "Lord Cameron!" he cried, his voice filled with anguish. But the battle raged on, leaving no time for mourning.

Kudus fought fiercely, expertly deflecting and countering each attack. One by one, his enemies fell before his relentless strikes. His movements were fluid and precise, honed by years of discipline and experience. He remained a pillar of strength on the battlefield.

Albert led the group ahead of Kudus, fighting their way towards Halsten while Kudus stayed at the back to ensure the Northern soldiers at the gate could not advance forward.

As the battle raged on, a Southern soldier, mortally wounded, stumbled backward and collapsed against Kudus. The weight momentarily threw him off balance. While trying to move the fallen comrade off his back, Kudus's sharp eyes caught a glint of metal—a Northern archer aiming an arrow directly at King Halsten.

Without hesitation, he sprang into action. He threw himself into the arrow's path with no time to raise his shield. The projectile struck him in the side, piercing through his armor. Kudus fell to the ground, his vision swimming as pain seared through his body. As he tried to rise, a rush of soldiers trampled over him, their boots leaving him bruised and battered.

"Kudus is down!" one of the Southern soldiers shouted amidst the cacophony.

Several of his comrades, noticing his plight, rushed to his aid. They formed a protective circle around him, fending off approaching enemies with shields and swords. One knelt beside Kudus, placing a hand on his shoulder to assess his condition. Kudus was unresponsive, his breaths shallow, and blood pooled around the arrow lodged in his side.

"We need to get him out of here!" one of the soldiers barked, his voice filled with urgency.

Another man nodded. "Clear a path! We have to move him to safety!"

The group worked together to carry Kudus away from the thick of the battle, shielding him from further harm as they retreated toward the rear lines.

As Kudus lay on a makeshift stretcher, his comrades worked quickly to stabilize him. The battle continued to rage, but their focus was on ensuring their fallen brother would survive to fight another day.

"Stay with us, Kudus," one soldier urged as he pressed a cloth against the bleeding wound. "The king still needs you." Though Kudus's eyes remained closed and his body limp, his comrades refused to let his bravery be in vain.

Amid the chaos, King Halsten pushed through the throng of soldiers. His eyes burned with singular purpose as he searched for Darius. Every swing of his sword was deadly, cutting down the Northern soldiers who dared to block his path. The Southern warriors rallied around their king, fighting fiercely to clear his way.

At the center of the battlefield, Darius stood on a raised platform, commanding his forces with an air of arrogance. His dark armor shimmered in the sunlight, and his piercing gaze scanned the battlefield until it locked with Halsten's. The two men stared at each other across the sea of carnage.

Halsten fought through the sea of soldiers, each step echoing his determination. Darius stepped out of his guards' protection, meeting his nephew halfway. The soldiers around them instinctively stepped back, forming an impromptu ring for the confrontation.

Darius smirked. "So, the boy comes to face the man. Are you ready to wield the sword against your uncle, Halsten? You're just a child playing king."

Halsten's jaw tightened, his voice steady and cold. "You are an evil and bloodthirsty man. Today, your tyranny ends. EdenRock will never bow to your madness."

With that, they charged at each other. Their swords met with a thunderous clang, sending sparks flying. Darius attacked with relentless ferocity, and Halsten countered with precision, parrying each blow and responding with calculated slashes.

"You've destroyed everything you've touched," Halsten said as their swords locked. "You've stolen our kingdom, murdered my parents, and betrayed your blood."

Darius snarled, pushing him back. "They were weak! Just like you. EdenRock needs strength to survive, and I am that strength!"

Halsten sidestepped a wild swing, delivering a deep cut across his uncle's thigh. Darius roared in pain and dropped to one knee, his blade falling a few feet away. "Fetch me the sword!" he commanded his soldiers, but Adikis, Frodio, Axilla, Anders, DeMarco, and their men pointed their swords at the Northern soldiers.

Those behind them began to part as the bell ringer Odus walked through and then bent to pick up Darius's sword.

"Give me my sword! I command you!" Darius said.

But Odus, the hunchback, stood up straight with no difficulty. To everyone's surprise, the lump on his back was gone. He held on to the sword, stepped back, and nodded to Frodio.

Darius snarled, "You will pay for this!"

Halsten looked at his uncle. "You've betrayed this kingdom and our family for nothing but your greed. Your reign of terror ends here."

Darius glared up at him, hatred burning in his eyes. "You'll fall just like the rest. You're nothing."

Halsten raised his sword high. "I am nothing like you."

With a swift, decisive motion, he brought his blade down. The sword struck true, severing Darius's head. It rolled to the blood-soaked ground, and his body crumpled lifelessly.

For a moment, the battlefield fell silent as the Southern soldiers and the remnants of the Northern forces turned their gazes toward them. Darius's head rested in the blood-soaked dirt, a symbol of the end of tyranny. Then, like the rumble of an approaching storm, a deafening cheer erupted from the Southern army.

"The tyrant is dead!" the soldiers shouted, their voices rising in unison. Their cries echoed across the plains, reverberating through the walls of Aldrich City.

Halsten turned to his men, his bloodied sword raised high above his head. His resolute voice carried over the noise. "EdenRock will be free once more!" he proclaimed.

The Southern forces, invigorated by their king's victory, surged forward with newfound strength and determination. Adikis, Frodio, Axilla, DeMarco, and Anders fervently led their battalions, cutting through the remaining Northern soldiers. Commander Egron, astride his warhorse, directed the cavalry with precision, encircling the enemy and severing their escape routes. There was no mercy for traitors—the Southern army fought with the fury of those defending their homeland and honor.

Mefford and Lord Luterodt, realizing the battle was lost, quickly mounted their horses. They urged their steeds toward the city gate, Caine and a handful of remaining Northern soldiers following close behind. Mefford's face was twisted with desperation as he shouted commands to his men, urging them to retreat.

But as the fleeing soldiers neared the gates of Aldrich City, a deafening roar pierced the air, unlike anything the men had heard before. It seemed to shake the very ground beneath their feet. Soldiers on both sides froze, their weapons falling limp in their hands as they turned their heads toward the sky.

From the direction of Luterodt City, near the coastline, two massive creatures emerged on the horizon, their silhouettes dark against the fading sunlight. As they drew closer, the details of their forms became unmistakable. Each was a majestic combination of lion and dragon, with their gold and green scales shimmering like molten metal. Their fiery eyes burned with a terrifying intensity, and their enormous wings beat against the air with the force of hurricanes.

"The Ligons," someone whispered, voice trembling with awe and fear.

The beasts soared toward the battlefield with an almost otherworldly grace, their roars echoing like thunder. Soldiers from both sides fell to their knees or fled in terror, unable to comprehend the sight before them. The Ligons descended toward the city gate, where Mefford, Lord Luterodt, and their remaining men desperately rode.

One of the creatures opened its massive jaws, and a torrent of fire spewed forth, engulfing the Northern soldiers in an inferno. Screams of agony filled the air as the flames consumed everything in their path. Luterodt and Caine were caught in the blaze, their cries silenced as the fire reduced them to ash.

Mefford froze in place, his eyes darting between the Ligons and the battlefield around him. His breath quickened as his mind wrestled with the surreal sight, struggling to reconcile it with the dreams that had haunted him for years. The beasts, the fire, and the prophecy all felt like a nightmare coming to life.

Unable to bear the weight of his confusion and fear, he dismounted his horse abruptly. His movements became erratic as he stripped off his armor, flinging his sword and shield to the ground. Everyone looked on in confusion and disbelief as Mefford, now naked, bolted into the forest on foot, vanishing into the shadows like a man fleeing his sanity.

Meanwhile, the Ligons circled high above the battlefield, their mighty wings sending gusts of wind that swept across the plains. The soldiers of both the Northern and Southern armies watched in stunned silence, their weapons momentarily forgotten. Then, one of the beasts broke away, descending in a graceful but formidable arc toward the ground.

The massive creature landed with a resonating thud in the heart of Aldrich City. Soldiers on both sides scattered, fear overcoming even the bravest among them. Only Halsten, DeMarco, Adikis, Anders, Frodio, and a few of their closest comrades stood their ground.

The Ligon, its glowing eyes fixed on Halsten, emitted a low, rumbling roar. Halsten, sensing no threat from the beast, raised his hand to halt his men. "Stand down," he commanded.

The soldiers hesitated, but seeing the confidence in their king's demeanor, they lowered their weapons. The Ligon stepped closer to Halsten, its massive paws crushing the bloodied ground beneath it. It stopped to tower before him, locking eyes with him. Halsten met the beast's gaze with quiet resolve.

The Ligon let out another low growl, softer this time—almost a hum. It then lowered its body to the ground, stretching its neck forward and motioning with its head, inviting Halsten to climb onto its back.

◆

Halsten glanced at his comrades, their faces a mixture of awe and concern. "This is destiny," he said, his voice filled with certainty. He sheathed his sword and approached the Ligon, placing a hand gently on its scaled neck. The beast remained still, its breathing steady and calm.

With a single fluid motion, Halsten climbed onto its back. It rose to its feet, its wings spreading wide, casting a shadow over the stunned onlookers. The soldiers of the South and even the remaining Northerners watched in silence, and their faces turned skyward.

The Ligon took a few powerful strides before leaping into the air. Its wings beat against the sky, lifting it effortlessly. Soaring upward, it joined its companion, the two Ligons now circling above the battlefield with Halsten astride one of them.

The sight was nothing short of miraculous. The soldiers below cheered wildly, their chants echoing across the battlefield. "Long live King Halsten, protector of EdenRock!"

Halsten's gaze was steady as he looked down at his people. The two beasts turned and flew toward the sea, their outlines growing smaller against the horizon. The soldiers and citizens of EdenRock stood in awe as their king disappeared into the sky, carried by the very creatures of prophecy.

A profound stillness settled over the battlefield. Bloodied but unbroken, DeMarco stood at the forefront of the Southern army. His voice, filled with quiet reverence, broke the silence.

"The prophecy has come to pass," he said.

The remaining Northern soldiers, their morale shattered, began to lower their swords. One by one, they dropped their weapons to the ground, signaling their surrender. The Southern soldiers, though weary, stood victorious, their gazes shifting to those who were surrendering.

The aftermath of the battle was grim. The bodies of fallen soldiers carpeted the land, stretching from the outskirts of Aldrich City to its gates. Among the dead lay noblemen from both the South and the North. Lords Cameron, Perkins, Lingard, Palm, Argus, and Ramsgate had perished, giving their lives for the Southern cause. Darius had fallen from the North, alongside Lords Bluevine, Cole, Emmitgrove, and Luterodt.

The Ligons returned, having carried King Halsten over the shimmering expanse of the Kemit Sea. They soared high into the sky, their forms framed against the setting sun before they descended again, heading directly toward Aldrich City. The majestic creatures landed with grace and authority before the palace gates, heralded by the gasps and cheers of the assembled citizens and soldiers.

The Ligon carrying Halsten lowered its massive head, allowing the king to dismount. He stepped down with poise, his armor marked by the day's battle. The crowd erupted into cheers, their voices a mix of relief, triumph, and adoration.

"Long live the king!" they chanted, their cries echoing through the streets.

Halsten stood tall between the two Ligons, their imposing forms flanking him like silent guardians. The creatures stayed by his side, their piercing eyes scanning the surroundings as if ensuring their charge's safety. The king's gaze swept over his people, feeling sorrow for the lives lost and determination for the future that awaited.

DeMarco approached, kneeling before his king. "The city is ours, Your Grace. The people await your command."

Halsten nodded solemnly. "This victory comes at a great cost, but EdenRock will rise again. We will honor the fallen and rebuild our kingdom stronger than ever."

As if understanding his resolve, the Ligons released a low, rumbling growl.

As Halsten made his way into the palace, it was clear to all that EdenRock had entered a new era—one shaped by sacrifice, courage, and the unwavering spirit of its people.

TO BE CONTINUED...

I hope you enjoyed this first installment of the
epic *When the Crown Bleeds* series!

Please write a review at your favorite online retailer—this
author would love to hear from you—and while you're
there, click to follow the author's profile so you'll be noti-
fied when the next book in the series is released.

FUN FACTS

Battle of Verdants was inspired by weekly short stories the author shared with his daughter, who had just left home for college. Over time, these stories formed the basis for the series, *When the Crown Bleeds*.

The character of Orb, the Virgil, was inspired by a dear friend named Virgil.

Most of the material is inspired by the author's research and interactions with people of different cultures and ethnicities.

About 80 percent of the book was written during the author's travels on airplane flights or in hotel rooms.

ABOUT THE AUTHOR

With a background steeped in theology, world history, political commentary, global economics, and global cultures, FK Menzz crafts richly imagined worlds that resonate with depth and realism. His writing merges the exhilaration of high fantasy with thought-provoking themes drawn from real-world struggles and intricate cultural traditions.

When he's not shaping empires or unraveling ancient prophecies, FK Menzz enjoys quiet moments with his family, wandering through factual and fictional historic towns and gathering information, often inspiring his stories' landscapes. Whether on the battlefield or in the throne room, he invites readers to walk in the footsteps of his characters, discovering what it truly means to love, lead, fight, and hope.

ACKNOWLEDGMENTS

This book, *Battle of Verdants*, the first in this series, is a tapestry of tales woven from the memories, adventures, and dreams shared with my beloved wife and cherished daughters. Each word and chapter is imbued with the laughter and love that define our lives, bridging the distances that sometimes separate us.

My wife's wisdom and warmth have illuminated my path, guiding me even through the darkest moments. This book reflects the enduring power of our love—a love that has nurtured not just our bond but also the incredible souls of our daughters.

My daughters are the heartbeat of every story. Though work may have taken me far, our shared stories have kept us connected, allowing us to explore new worlds together. Each tale was a whisper of my love, a testament that distance could never diminish our bond.

Salinas Valley, California, where I completed this book, has infused this narrative with a spirit of resilience and friendship. Its vibrant landscapes reflect the growth and blossoming of our story, from simple tales to a saga that will endure through the ages.

This series of books is dedicated to you—my inspiration, audience, and reason. May it always remind you of our shared adventures and a love so profound it knows no bounds.

With all my love,
FK Menzz